THE UNSEALING

ROBERT BRIGHTON

AN AVENGING ANGEL DETECTIVE AGENCY™ MYSTERY

COPPER
NICKEL
PRESS

Front Cover: The Electric Tower at the Pan-American Exposition, from an original by the Niagara Envelope Manufactory, Buffalo, New York, 1901. Author's Collection.
Cover Design: Mayfly Design

The Unsealing
An Avenging Angel Detective Agency™ Mystery
A Novel by Robert Brighton

Interior illustrations by Douglas Smith

ISBNs: 979-8-9865178-0-3 (hc); ISBN: 979-8-9865178-1-0 (pbk); 979-8-9865178-2-7 (ebk)
Library of Congress Control Number: 2022911925

For Laura

Inspired by True Events

A Word of Context

IN ANY BOOK SET IN A DIFFERENT ERA, THE VALUE OF A DOLLAR— prices of things—can be confusing. Today, it's tempting to marvel at entire houses that cost 'only' $5,000.

This book takes place mainly in 1901, and I've chosen to present prices as they were then and let readers adjust them, should they wish to do so. A useful if crude rule of thumb is to multiply 1901 dollars by 50. It's not perfect, but it will help. So a $100,000 insurance policy, for example, is probably equivalent to something like $5 million of coverage today.

Like starlight, the voices in this book have traveled 120 years to reach these pages. A lot has changed in American English since they began their journey. The language of 1901 can sound stilted to today's reader, but it contained and communicated nuances now lost to us. Therefore I have updated it as necessary to strike the right note in the modern ear. Also, many phrases that are in common use today across all strata of society (e.g., 'okay,' 'gonna') either did not exist in 1901 or would have been considered inappropriate. I have taken care to ensure that any idiomatic phrase found here is documented to 1901 or earlier.

Finally: While this work was inspired by actual events, it is most emphatically a work of fiction, not history.

Robert Brighton
October 2022

Contents

PART 1: CONQUEST

PART 2: RUMORS OF WAR

PART 3: RECKONING

PART 4: HARVEST

Overture

January 13, 1902
Monday

VOLKMANN, THE SALOONKEEPER, SET TWO TUMBLERS ON THE battered bar and filled them with Buffalo Club whiskey. A well-dressed man raised one, nodded to Volkmann, and drank it down. Glancing at the clock over the bar, he pulled a watch from his vest pocket.

"Is that the correct time?"

"It is, or very close," Volkmann said. "I set it twice a day by the factory whistle." He hooked his thumb in the direction of the Turner Bicycle factory down Kensington Avenue.

"Must be something wrong with my watch," the man muttered, twisting the stem. "I'm six minutes slow. We'd better get a move on. I'll take this one out and be right back," he said, picking up the other tumbler.

"Wouldn't you two be more comfortable inside?"

He shook his head and hurried out to a waiting automobile.

Through the ash-streaked front window, Volkmann saw the fellow hand the glass to his passenger, a woman in a white felt hat. The two shared a laugh about something as she took the glass from his hand. She grimaced as she gulped the liquor, then handed the glass to her companion. He tilted his head back to finish what was left, so far that he nearly lost his hat. He walked back into the saloon and set the empty on the bar.

"Thanks again," he said. He was about to leave when he stopped. "Oh, one other thing—a good cigar, if you please." He bought a Henry Clay, at fifteen cents the best one the shabby little saloon had to offer, and lit it at the gas jet. "Perfect," he said, sending a billow of smoke toward the ceiling.

Volkmann smiled and dropped the coins into his apron. "Drive carefully," he said. "It's starting to rain."

"That won't bother us," the man replied, smiling over his shoulder.

Volkmann watched him climb up into his automobile, say something to the woman, and settle his fedora. He found it strange that the man didn't take a minute to raise the canvas top. If not to keep the lady's clothing dry, at the very least protect the glossy leather upholstery. "First class machine, too," he thought. "I guess a fellow like that can afford to do as he pleases."

Volkmann watched the man's auto back up, a gold monogram prominent on the front footboard, and then turn left onto Kensington, toward Buffalo.

❦

Jimmy Landon and Bobby Nash liked to play mumblety-peg in an abandoned signalman's lean-to near the New York Central grade crossing, where Kensington Avenue humped up and over the tracks. From the shelter of their ramshackle clubhouse, the boys could watch the afternoon trains pass by, hurrying on their way to New York or Boston.

The boys were lured to the rickety structure, day after day, by their awe of the trains, the sublime fear the great machines inspired. The lean-to sat so close to the tracks that each passing train would first be felt through the soles of their feet. A distant throb, an electric reverberation of steel on steel, grew deeper and stronger as the thing neared and rose into their chests, making their hearts beat in time to the giant pistons. Then, two hundred yards before the crossing, a piercing steam whistle would erupt, rising in pitch from a warning wail to an intolerable scream. When almost atop them, the beast seemed to gather itself and then put on more speed, roaring by in a volcanic gale of sparks, cinders, and grit that threatened to tear their shanty off its foundation.

Then, as quickly as it had come, the great engine would rattle away into the distance, its clatter dwindling like the aftershock of an earthquake, its whistle dying away to a sonorous, echoing farewell as the locomotive began to stretch its legs in open country.

If the boys were especially lucky, an afternoon of waiting for trains would be punctuated by a passing automobile, a rarity in this desolate, industrial part of the city.

❦

Jimmy saw it first. An automobile, coming down Kensington, toward their hideout. And what an automobile! Wet, shiny, iridescent purple-black, a mechanical scarab scuttling along the wet boulevard, made a ribbon of gold by the setting sun—two thousand dollars' worth, at least, of gleaming wood, leather, and metal. Top-down in the pelting rain, running at full speed, probably trying to get home in a hurry.

A low tremor sounded the coming of the New York Central, gathering speed as it neared the outskirts of Buffalo. The 5:10 Express to New York City was a big one, too—eight passenger carriages, two baggage cars, one railroad mail car, and a caboose.

"Will you look at that beauty!" Jimmy said, pointing up the road at the approaching automobile.

"That is an awfully nice machine," Bobby breathed. "I've never seen one like it."

"Much too nice to be getting soaked like that."

"Yeah, and they'll be sitting in the rain for five more minutes, waiting for it to pass. He won't be able to cross now."

The boys watched the automobile creep toward the foot of the grade. The driver looked left, saw the train, and halted. He turned briefly to the woman beside him and then put on the power again, charging up the slope.

The boys froze in terror. What in the world was he doing?

"Hey!" Jimmy screamed involuntarily over the roar of the approaching train. "Look out!"

The little automobile surged forward, the hot breath of the locomotive almost on top of it, the engineer's face frozen in terror as he hung on the whistle chain. It was going to be close. Then, at the crest of the grade, astraddle the tracks, the vehicle seemed to falter and stall.

"Holy—" was all that Bobby managed to stammer out.

The moment of impact seemed so unreal that neither boy would remember anything about it, except for the sound. A sharp scream, they thought, which could as well have been the squeal of brakes as the engineer locked them down. In the next heartbeat, when they may have blinked or looked away, came the noise. A penetrating, screeching roar of crumpling metal and splintering wood, so loud they could feel it pass through their bodies as if they were themselves involved. Bobby later swore the sound had a *smell*, as though by sheer force it had smashed through one of his senses and into another.

The little electric automobile—or what was left of it—was tossed a good twenty yards from the tracks and had landed wheels up, with a pair of trousered legs protruding from underneath. The heavy storage batteries had broken loose from their mounts and, when the vehicle turned turtle, landed on the driver's head, crushing it as easily as a grape. The woman had been thrown clear of the vehicle and was lying crumpled in the rain, like a pile of bloody gauze in a battlefield hospital.

For thirty paces from the point of impact, the ground was littered with bits of man and machine, scattered by the hurtling train: shards of wood, shattered spokes, the lacquered handle of the control tiller. Near the upturned machine rested, prim and upright, the upholstered seat, torn and bloody and with bits of brain tissue oozing down the leather— and nearby, a man's hat and two ladies' shoes. The gruesome sight was too much even for the ghoulish curiosity of young boys, and they sprinted in horror to the nearest house with a telephone.

When the cops arrived, both boys would tell the same story—that they saw the man look, attempt the crossing, and then stop his machine at the apex of the grade. Set the handbrake, shut off the motor. And then *sit* there, looking straight ahead, doing nothing. The cops didn't buy it for a second. What did boys know about automobiles, which lever did this, what control did that? Besides, everyone knew that in the rain, these newfangled electric autos were jiggery things, prone to perverse faults and failures of wiring or switchgear. The damn electrical contraption had probably shut itself off on the tracks, its master incapable of coaxing it back to life. Until time ran out.

PART 1

CONQUEST

CHAPTER 1

Old Sparky

1889
Twelve Years Earlier

IT WAS THE ALPHABET THAT HAD BROUGHT THEM TOGETHER. AR-thur Pendle and Terence Penrose met when they were assigned to the same dormitory room at New Haven College. The pair occupied adjacent desks for four years, then for two more in the Law School. It was probably inevitable that after their graduation—in alphabetical order—they would take the same train to the booming city of Buffalo to establish themselves as Pendle & Penrose, Attorneys at Law.

For the next eight years, the two friends were an unstoppable legal team. A natural salesman, Terry Penrose rarely left a cocktail party or a club function without a new client in tow. Arthur, the more studious of the pair, was content feeding legal briefs into Penrose's oratorical machine.

Terry's aptitude for handshaking and back-slapping made him a magnet for the city's power brokers, always on the lookout for fresh political talent. When in 1897 the Erie County District Attorney announced that he wouldn't seek another term, everyone who was anyone thought that Penrose would make an excellent replacement. If things worked out, higher offices would follow: Governor, then Congress, then—time would tell.

So later that year, Terry Penrose was appointed the new Erie County District Attorney, the youngest man to hold the office. It was an undeniable triumph, albeit one made bittersweet by the need to say a professional goodbye to Arthur. Together they had grown into young men of consequence, but now the lonely shingle outside the Aston Building read simply: Arthur R. Pendle, Attorney at Law.

Without Terry Penrose's gift of gab, his quiet, intense former partner soon found himself struggling to find clients. Maybe I'm nothing without him, Arthur thought in his darker moments on the trolley ride home to his wife, Cassie.

❦

The paint in Terry's new office was still wet when the summer of 1898 brought with it a spasm of labor unrest that rippled up and down the East Coast. Coal miners, steelworkers, ditch-diggers, and railroaders alike stopped showing up at work and took to the streets to protest low wages and intolerable working conditions. Normally placid Buffalo was not immune to the contagion, either. The labor unions made sure of that.

Around dusk on August 24th, one of these marches got out of hand. Protestors and police clashed, fires were kindled in the streets, shop windows were shattered. The cops responded in force, rocks and bottles were hurled and then, as foul luck would have it, a hunk of brick brained a cop whose helmet had fallen off while scuffling with Bobby O'Shea, one of the ringleaders. Bobby was an amateur bare-knuckle boxer who didn't much care about causes; he just enjoyed a good scrap.

While no one ever knew who had chucked the deadly brick, it certainly wasn't O'Shea, who was busily trying to gnaw off one of the cop's ears when Fate descended. Wrong place, wrong time—and an epic stroke of bad luck for Bobby, even within the context of a life already chock-full of misfortune. The slain patrolman's brother officers fell on O'Shea like a thunderbolt, beat him half to death, and dragged the battered scrapper off to jail. Within a couple of days, he found himself charged with the capital murder of a police officer.

In August 1898, Old Sparky—New York State's electric chair—celebrated its eighth birthday, but its varnish had scarcely a fingernail scratch to show for it. The much-ballyhooed, decidedly modern device had dispatched only a handful of miscreants since its shakedown cruise.

After a couple of ugly mishaps—Sparky had taken a leisurely eight minutes to slow-cook its first occupant to death—people had begun to murmur that maybe electrocution wasn't quite so civilized a method as it had been billed. Tales of smoke wafting out of ears, exploding eyeballs, and the stench of searing human flesh threatened to turn public opinion against the Chair. Naturally, the politicians couldn't allow that. Someone had to get the jolt, and soon.

If everything went according to plan, that someone was Bobby O'Shea. Everyone wanted to see him fry, cops and citizens alike. And among the most strident among those baying for O'Shea's blood was Erie County's new District Attorney, Terence Penrose.

❦

Thus it didn't come as a surprise that the International Brotherhood of Wage Earners—the IBWE, or Ibbwee, as people said it—tracked Arthur down only a few hours after the announcement that Penrose would seek the death penalty. As the District Attorney's former law partner, Pendle would be the likeliest fellow to help O'Shea escape Old Sparky.

Arthur took the case. It was the right thing to do, and he needed the money. Going it alone hadn't gotten any easier. A victory in a capital case would establish himself as his own man and restore his wavering self-confidence.

By September, both the weather and the mood of the city had simmered down, but O'Shea's prosecution was heating up. To avoid the customary show trial and hammer out a deal, Arthur asked Terry to join him for nine holes at the Red Jacket Golf Club. Aggravated assault, maybe a few other minor charges thrown in to sweeten the deal, and O'Shea would do a couple years of hard time, tops.

"You know I need a conviction," Penrose said as they were walking between holes, bags slung over their shoulders.

"My client will consider a plea to lesser charges."

"Sorry. Has to be capital murder. The Chair." Penrose took a puff from his cigar.

"Come on, Terry, it's just us. No grandstanding."

Penrose stopped walking and turned toward his friend. "I'm not grandstanding. Look—the cops want his head. We have a brand-new Governor who wants to show he's tough on crime. I can't give up ground to a cop killer, or I'll look weak."

"I understand that people are hopped up about this thing. But you know as well as I do that O'Shea didn't kill that cop or any cop. If that brick had landed a few inches to the other side, it would have killed him instead."

"O'Shea put the cop into a position where he could be killed. That's enough."

"You can't send a man to the Chair for that. Manslaughter, at most."

At the next tee, they set their bags down, and Terry sucked on his cigar for a moment, thinking.

"Arthur, here's the way it is. I'm not even a year into my term. I get the death penalty on this, and I'm set. Two terms, easy. Plus, the police will do anything for me. I'll *own* them. And that makes the job of putting criminals away that much simpler. Isn't that a good thing?"

"Hold up a second," Arthur said. "This doesn't sound like you."

Penrose looked down and kicked at a loose piece of turf with the toe of his shoe.

"Sure, the man's guilty of battery," Arthur continued. "No question. And I could even see my way clear to something a little bigger. But capital murder? He's not to blame for that."

"I'm not saying he's to blame. I'm saying that we're blaming him. There's a big difference."

"That's not justice, Terry. It's revenge."

Penrose pulled on his cigar again and sent the smoke out of the corner of his mouth.

"Retribution, perhaps, not revenge," he said. "And retribution is the prerogative of the state. We can debate all day whether O'Shea's guilty or not guilty of this or that. And since you were the law school debate champ, you'd probably win. But in my world—the *real* world—he's guilty *enough*. Putting him in the Chair sends a message."

Arthur squinted into the sun. "I do understand the politics of the thing," he said. "But there has to be a way to please the police without lynching a man."

"Lynching? That's strong talk."

"What would *you* call it?"

"A metaphor. Symbolic."

"You'd electrocute a human being to make him into a symbol?"

Penrose chuckled. "Ah, now my debate champion shows up."

"Answer my question."

"Didn't God himself send his own son—entirely innocent, at that—to a grisly death in order to make him into a symbol?"

"You're not God, Terry."

"In this city, I'm what passes for him," Penrose said. "If you want your man to stay alive, there is only one way. I very much doubt you'll like it, though."

"How bad can it be? Try me."

Arthur felt a wave of relief as he waited for Terry's proposal. We can get this deal done, he thought. He wants to show me he won't play favorites as the DA. Fine, so be it.

"You know that the IBWE is flush with cash," Penrose said.

"Dues from thousands of members every month add up."

"Well, then . . . this could work if, say, you have the IBWE make a donation to the Governor's war chest, another to the Buffalo police benevolent league, and one to my reappointment fund. And this all goes away. He does two, three years, and life goes on. For O'Shea, I mean that literally."

Arthur looked at his friend, stunned. "Are you—"

"Now hold on," Terry said, holding up a finger. "You wouldn't be doing it for free. Did I fail to mention that you keep one-third off the top? The rest is distributed as I said. Your guy pleads down, does his time, and isn't too much the worse for wear. The cops are happy. The IBWE scores points with the rank-and-file. And you are very well compensated—and save your man's life."

Arthur looked out over the fairway and thought what a beautiful spot this was. He looked back at his friend and shook his head slowly.

"I can't do that, Terry. I'm surprised you'd even consider such a thing. What did we say when we joined Phi Delta Phi—that we would always be 'friends of justice and wisdom'?"

Penrose smiled. "That Phi Delta Phi horseshit was loads of fun when we were kids, but it's not the way things go. 'When I became a man, I put away childish things,' you know? I'm going to make a success out of my new post, whatever it takes. No more, no less. I'd like it if I could count on my best friend to help me do that."

"You know I'd do whatever I can to help you. But this is beyond the pale."

Penrose held up his palms. "No need to get all worked up. As they say, you have to—'play it as it lies.'" He put his ball down on the tee. "But I'm setting an early court date for this trial. If you have a change of heart, have it quickly."

"I'll have to beat you in court, I suppose."

"Yes, I suppose you will. But first, let's see if you can beat me in golf."

❦

Arthur studied for the trial as he hadn't done since law school. When the day came, he had constructed a masterly defense for his client and delivered an eloquent summation—not something he was usually good at.

It was a swift and speedy trial. Two weeks after the verdict was announced, Bobby O'Shea's short, shitty life fizzled out in the dingy cell in Auburn Prison where Old Sparky had sat so long unloved, stolidly bolted to the grey concrete.

❦

If Arthur had only a trickle of business coming in before, losing the O'Shea case stanched it entirely. He was beginning to worry about making his mortgage payment, his office rent, his club dues. Growing up poor had been one thing, but living poor as an adult was quite another.

Cassie commiserated with him after his loss, but whether she understood the larger potential implications, he wasn't sure. One thing was certain. There were more and more days when he had no work at all—not a will to draw up, not a property deed. Nevertheless, to keep up appearances, he left their spacious home on Columbus Avenue every morning at precisely the same time and took the trolley downtown.

In short order, however, it became too boring to sit in his office all day reading, so he began spending a great deal of time at lunch. Where once he'd snatched a 15-minute, 50-cent luncheon of cold cuts, a pickled egg, and a cup of coffee, now he lingered for two hours over a two-dollar lunch of three courses and an equal number of cocktails. Then he'd return to the office for a little nap and, in the afternoon, take long walks around the city to work it off until it was time to go home.

After one of these midday feasts, he was meandering back to his office to see if anything interesting had arrived in the mail. At the corner of Franklin and Eagle, he brushed by none other than District Attorney Terence Penrose, coming from the courthouse. Two months had passed since O'Shea's date with Old Sparky, but Arthur was still smarting and had not contacted his old friend to offer congratulations or accept condolence. He hadn't had the heart for either.

"Now, what have we here?" Penrose said cheerfully, as if nothing out of the ordinary had happened. "If it isn't the elusive Mr. Pendle."

"I'm sorry I haven't rung you," Arthur said. He'd missed his friend, but every time he'd picked up the telephone, it seemed to weigh a hundred pounds. "I—"

"Not a problem. That was a tough break. A fellow needs time to lick his wounds. It's good to see you."

"It's good to see you, too," Arthur said, his voice breaking. He looked down at his shoes and bit his lip hard.

Penrose clapped him soundly on the back. "Say, I'm on my way someplace now, but come by my office tomorrow, will you? I have a little something I want to run by you. Maybe the timing is better this time."

Arthur quickly wiped his eyes with the back of his hand. "Whew, the soot is terrible today," he said. "That was one good thing about the coal strike. The air was a lot cleaner."

"You aren't kidding."

"I'll be happy to come by. Say about 10?"

"That'll work," Penrose said. "See you then, old buddy."

❧

"I hope you know how much I admire you, Arthur," Terry said, in his huge chair, flanked by the state and national flags in the expansive office of the District Attorney. "You did the right thing, and there should be some comfort in that."

"Cold comfort," Arthur replied. "If I'd followed your lead, Bobby O'Shea would still be alive. I sometimes think it was my pride that killed him."

"I wouldn't take that on. O'Shea made his bed."

"I suppose."

"Look," Terry said, shifting in his chair, "that's why I wanted you to hear about an idea I had. How we could work together again on some of my smaller cases. Nuisance cases, which do nothing but clog up the system. I need someone I can trust, and you'd be a natural at it, too, with your negotiating skills and competitive instinct. Not to mention that we'd be partners again, of a sort."

Arthur wasn't sure that he'd expected a career dealing with small, 'nuisance' cases, but he needed the work, and the thought of being Terry's partner again was appealing.

"What would it entail?"

"On certain cases—inconsequential ones where someone makes a stupid mistake—the people involved are willing to do almost anything to make their legal woes go away."

"Not the donation thing again, I hope."

"Now, before you make a rash decision, listen to what I have to say. A little lubrication here and there to make the system work more efficiently is a positive good. And it's not as though guilty people in the smart set are getting off scot-free. It costs them something, like anyone else."

"Money," Arthur said, "but not their lives or their freedom."

"Exactly!" Terry said. "So how about this. I'll give you a case to look at. One case. If you don't like the smell of it, that's the end of it. Same terms as before—one-third for you, off the top. You don't even have to keep the money if it's not to your taste. Give it to the poor."

Arthur thought for a moment. "One case," he said. "But only one, and I'm not making any promises."

Penrose beamed. "None whatsoever! And if only for one case, I get my old partner back."

"Well," Arthur said, flattered, "we were a good team."

"The best. Now let me propose that on Friday, you and I have a lunch appointment. I'll tell you then what needs to be worked on. It's a real whale, too. After this one, if you like the work, there'll be as much as you can handle."

CHAPTER 2

Arthur Becomes a Fixer

OVER A SOMEWHAT BOOZY LUNCH ON FRIDAY, TERRY SPENT TWO hours and twice as many cocktails giving his friend the lowdown on Thomas Edward Histon. They shook hands on it, and Arthur said he'd arrange a meeting with their man.

At the appointed hour the next day, Arthur spied an expensively dressed, yet oddly shabby, fellow loafing outside the Iroquois Hotel in the heart of downtown Buffalo.

"Barbershop busy?" Arthur asked.

"Long wait," the shabby gentleman said. "Popular place on the weekend."

"Always a line."

Arthur turned and started walking away from the business district. The man followed him at a discreet distance.

When they left the crowds behind, Arthur slowed and fell into step with his companion. The man's cologne was overpowering, even three feet away and in the brisk air.

"You're Penrose's man?" the fellow said.

"I'm representing him."

"Can't be too careful. You know my situation?"

"I do."

Thomas Edward Histon was what every Buffalo businessman aspired to be: successful, rich—and anonymous. Not someone that people pointed out on the street or whom the press followed around, reporting on what brand of shoes he was wearing, where he was eating, whom he was sleeping with. Histon was as public a man as any cab driver and equally invisible. He could buy and sell half of the wealthiest men in the city, and yet precious few of them would have recognized his name.

That was because Histon's business was, quite literally, underground. For more than a decade, he'd been one of the leading contractors for Buffalo's expanding sewer system.

For most of the city's history, a flood of raw sewage gushed into Lake Erie. Recently, though, a number of families summering at Woodlawn Beach, nestled south of Buffalo in a little kink in the shoreline, began bitching to the city fathers about the smell and the unspeakable eddies of God-knew-what. The potentates could normally ignore such complaints from the hoi polloi—or blame it on Cleveland, as usual—until some of their own social set started dying from typhoid fever contracted at their vacation homes. Then something had to be done.

That something was sewers.

Thomas Histon had been making a decent living as a sewer-man in Columbus, Ohio, but the prizes were small in central Ohio. He had only to follow the Erie shoreline north to the nation's fastest-growing city. And in just a little more than a decade, Histon had made a fortune burrowing tunnels and trenches to carry away Buffalo's waste.

Sewers convey filth, but equally important, they move air around. Without proper airflow, liquid stops moving, and dangerous gases— poisonous and flammable—build up. And in industrial Buffalo, paper mills, chemical factories, refineries, even the municipal illuminating gas plant dumped everything they couldn't use or didn't want into the new sewers, which quickly became toxic, combustible underground rivers.

Histon had discovered that building his sewers just a wee bit smaller than the codes required, and with a handful fewer air vents, meant far more profit to him. Since even the best sewers stank, the lack of proper venting, ironically, created fewer neighborhood complaints.

There was no way of knowing what started the underground conflagration. It might have been a spark from the metal wheels of a streetcar, or an unlucky cigarette end falling into a manhole. By the time it burned itself out, the flames had immolated four firefighters sent down into the blazing poison soup in an attempt to quell the flames. And the heat that had built up underground caused almost a half-mile of Histon-built sewer line to collapse in upon itself, taking with it a trolley—fortunately empty except for its doomed motorman—and burying alive a couple of children curious about the smoke piping up like a teakettle from the manhole in front of their house.

Even considering his considerable financial resources, if found liable for the disaster, Histon was facing bankruptcy. And worse, prison time. His negligence of construction standards would be easy to prove. Terry told Arthur that Histon's little problem could be good for $5,000, a whale indeed for Arthur and everyone up the chain, if he could land it. Arthur was determined to show Terry that not only could he land it, but do so in style.

The two stopped when they arrived at a tiny, deserted square, too small to be called a park, but it had a couple benches in front of a statue of a somber-looking Civil War soldier. They brushed off a dusting of early snow and sat.

"To come to the point," Arthur said, "you can be cited for a variety of contract violations—not only of the failed sewer in question but for all of your sewers if they don't meet code. You'd bear the cost of rebuilding them. And the District Attorney will have to decide whether criminal charges are warranted—probably negligent homicide. Five to seven years in Auburn."

Histon gave a low chuckle, took off his hat, and ran his fingers through his oiled hair. Little wisps of steam were rising from his head in the damp cold. "You guys are as bad as the Black Hand," he said.

The Black Hand was an extortion racket run by Sicilian immigrants. Businesses that employed Italian labor usually considered paying protection money to the Black Hand as one of the costs of doing business. But it was penny-ante stuff, fifty bucks here, a hundred there.

"At least, you expect Italians to be crooks," Histon went on.

"If I'm wasting your time, please say so."

"I didn't say that," Histon said, jamming his hat back down on his head. "What have I got to do to make this go away?"

"A thousand to the family of the deceased children, five hundred to the trolley man's wife, two thousand to the fireman's fund, and another five thousand to the various other parties who can put all this aside for you."

"Eight and a half thousand bucks?" Histon said. "You must be joking. Did I add right?"

"For two dead children, a motorman, and four firefighters burned alive? I'd say you are getting a bargain."

"A few grand for the kids and the fireman, that's one thing. But five grand for the DA and the top dogs?"

"It might well be more, but Mr. Penrose appreciates your past support," Arthur replied. "Only you can decide whether it's worth it. It might take some of the sting out of it, though, that if you settle this, you'll likely be awarded the contract to repair the damaged sewers."

Histon didn't need time to think. "If that's the way it's got to be, then that's the way it's got to be," the sewer-man said, tipping his hat back on his head and letting out a little puff of steam. "Life goes on."

Not for seven other people, Arthur thought.

"Come by my law offices in the Aston Building Monday, noon—with your payment," Arthur said. "Small bills. Nothing bigger than twenty. Coins are fine too."

"And how am I supposed to get that much cash together in a day and a half? On a Sunday, at that?"

"I couldn't say. The timing is not ours. District Attorney Penrose has to decide whether to empanel a Grand Jury by the end of the day Monday."

Histon shook his head. "I'll be there at noon."

"I don't think you'll regret your decision."

"Are we through?" the contractor said, standing. "I gotta go and start getting things pulled together."

Arthur didn't stand. "All done, yes. I'll see you on Monday. Noon sharp, remember."

Histon grunted and ambled away, swinging his walking stick angrily. It took a full minute for the heavy scent of his cologne to dissipate.

I do seem to be rather good at this, Arthur thought. He supposed he should feel like celebrating, but didn't. In little more than a half-hour, he had earned almost $3,000—more than most anyone he knew made in a year. But the work stank as bad as Histon's sewers because he couldn't deny that his off the top one-third had a noisome origin—in this case, from the victims of greed and graft.

❧

After the Histon fix, Arthur quickly found reasons to justify his new trade. Helping the courts run more efficiently. Cutting through skeins of red tape. And after all, for almost a decade, he'd labored in Terence Penrose's shadow, helping his gregarious partner lay the foundations of a political career. Why shouldn't he benefit, too?

And, of course, the cozy blanket of cash deadened any whispers of conscience. Influence was a more reliable energy source than the electric current supplied by Niagara Falls itself. The DA's office was a giant magneto from which supply lines tentacled out to anyone the DA needed to cultivate or ensnare.

Week after week, Arthur showed Terry that he was no priggish, ivory-tower romantic but a hard-nosed, reliable fixer whose brilliant mind could conceive a dozen ways to get blood from a stone. Over the ensuing two years, Arthur became so adept that he stopped bothering to cultivate other clients and focused solely on doing Penrose's work. Any real legal business that came in over the transom was traded to other lawyers in exchange for future favors.

To the amazement of the bank, Arthur paid off their house in a single lump sum—with a bagful of crumpled notes and canvas sacks of coins. He bought his way into the best clubs and dressed Cassie in a style few women could match. And he spent huge sums on pleasures—anything a young man's heart could desire—whisky from Scotland, a fine German microscope, an automobile, cameras and darkroom equipment, and a top-of-the-line tandem bicycle for him and Cassie.

As the final days of 1900 dwindled away, in two short years Arthur Pendle had evolved from a target of secret snickering into one of the most-watched, and most-envied, young men in the city. And it might have gone on like that for many more years, had not a chance encounter ruined it all.

CHAPTER 3

The Woman in the Tunnel

January 1, 1901

IF NEW YEAR'S DAY WAS ANY INDICATION, THE NEW CENTURY promised to be a messy one. An unexpected warm front had moved through, turning the frozen slush into a sticky, grey ooze that adhered to Arthur's best overcoat. For Arthur, who prided himself on his immaculate appearance—from his carefully coiffed, chestnut hair and mustache to the soles of his gleaming shoes, this added insult to the usual injury of a Buffalo winter.

He'd had no choice but to endure it, since at the end of every month—weekends, holidays, and Sundays not excepted—he made the rounds for Terry down in The Hooks, the roughest part of town.

The do-gooders called the area 'the evilest square mile in the United States,' 'the Infested Zone,' 'the Diseased Quarter,' and worse. The sailors manning the lake steamers and the scruffy Canal people called it The Hooks, after the cargo hooks the stevedores used to move freight from boat to shore and back again. And at the end of a long, dry trip across the Great Lakes or along the Canal, it was the place a man could drink, gamble, and fuck away a month's wages in a single night and, if he survived, crawl back on board the next morning before the steam whistles blew.

Geography circumscribed these six blocks of Hell within a sagging trapezoid bounded by Commercial, Water, and Erie Streets, and pinned between the Erie Canal and the rail lines running through the Terrace Station. That containment was exactly what the temporal and spiritual lords of Buffalo wanted. It might have been Hell, but it had a fence around it. The tidy boundaries of The Hooks kept the bad elements where they belonged, and allowed politicians and preachers to campaign, raise money, and make a show of their virtue—from a safe distance.

They were all the same, these reformers. Some wore suits and others robes, but railing about the corruption and sin in The Hooks was for all a profitable endeavor. Churches were built and pockets lined with the ten percent skimmed off the top of all the cash sloshing around every month. This tithe kept the status quo in place, thirty days at a time.

Doing Terry's dirty work was a mixed bag. The fattest paydays— like the Histon sewer disaster—were infrequent, coming only after some unspeakable fuckup that rich people needed to dispense with. The bread-and-butter work, steady and lucrative, was the monthly collection from the dives down in The Hooks. Even with Lake Erie iced over and the Canal shut until the spring thaw, the take was considerable. In truth, the locals enjoyed the hijinks down in The Hooks all the more when the rough and tumble sorts were holed up for the winter back in Detroit, Cleveland, or in a hundred hamlets along the Canal.

Illegal gambling dens, saloons, and brothels knew they had to share the wealth with the cops and the ward bosses, the shysters who kept criminals out of jail, and everyone all the way up the chain to where it disappeared like Jacob's Ladder into the clouds. No one knew how high it went.

All they needed to know was that on the last day of every month, Arthur Pendle would be coming to collect. He'd begin his rounds around 5 or 6 p.m., maybe 7 or 8 in the summer, and walk the streets of The Hooks until the wee hours. It made for a long and wearing night. Even with a burly cop or two along for muscle, a well-dressed man with a satchel in hand was not a sure bet to make it home in one piece.

Arthur worked methodically from joint to joint, cops in tow, and unannounced would walk behind the bar or upstairs to have a chat with the man or woman in charge. The cops stayed near the door, so they could say that they never saw money changing hands. Arthur carried a whistle in case of any funny business he couldn't handle. And if the whistle wasn't strong enough medicine, in his overcoat he kept handy a Smith & Wesson revolver, which Terry had urged him to acquire. Arthur had gone straight to Walbridge's downtown and bought the nicest

THE WOMAN IN THE TUNNEL

one they had, a .32 caliber Safety Model, with no hammer to hang up on his clothing should he need to draw it in an emergency.

Arthur's typical transaction took less than ten minutes, if everything went smoothly. The money was handed over, usually in a wad of dirty bills. Arthur would count it, make a coded notation in a small notebook, and, if all checked out, drop the money into his satchel. And so on down the length of Canal, around State, Boiler, and Peacock, to return exhausted to the cab stand for the coach ride home. By the time he was done, his head was hazy from the noise and smoke, his clothes reeked of tobacco and stale beer, and usually it took him two full days of doing nothing at all to get his sea legs back.

By the time the sky began to glow on the first day of 1901, he'd already ruined a perfectly good pair of shoes. But another collection had ended with a full valise, although it had taken longer than usual. Everything was moving slowly in The Hooks on New Year's Day, when the normally bustling waterfront was nursing a colossal hangover under low winter clouds. On his way to the cab stand, the fog in Arthur's head was beginning to lift when the snow turned into sleet and then to freezing rain. Of course, he thought. He decided to duck into the Ferry Street pedestrian tunnel and avoid a drenching.

The Ferry Street Tunnel was dimly lit by small glass panels set in the sidewalk above and by what sunlight could sneak in from either end. The constant twilight made it a good place to get yourself rolled, if you weren't careful. Arthur kept one hand in his overcoat pocket, resting lightly on the Smith & Wesson.

The silhouette of a person was coming toward him from the other end of the tunnel. He curled his fingers around the grip of his revolver. As the figure grew nearer, he saw that it was a woman, well dressed, overcoat and skirts billowing out behind her in the cold blast of air rushing through the tunnel. She kept her eyes averted toward the wall and, in one gloved hand, held a small umbrella open in front of her like a shield. Arthur thought to stop her and ask if she cared for an escort, and then quickly reconsidered. She might mistake him for an assailant, and women often carried smaller but no less deadly firearms than his in their chatelaine bags. He relaxed his grip on the gun.

When they passed each other, the woman was moving swiftly, though smoothly and without haste, aiming for the daylight at the other end of the tunnel. As the distance between them closed, she glanced up to avoid knocking into him and, for the briefest moment, caught his eye. Then she turned away again and breezed past him, receding.

Arthur wheeled around and watched the woman's back, overtaken by a very strange feeling. He'd never seen this woman before, he was sure of that. But in that flashing glimpse, there had been something equally certain, a deep intimacy, as though they'd spent a hundred lifetimes together, or could. It was like the shock of recognition he'd had on occasion when catching sight of himself in a mirror, and only after a moment recognizing the face he'd lived behind all his life.

The woman's figure was briefly haloed in the tunnel's exit and then swayed gracefully up the stairs to Ferry Street. He wanted to shout after her, chase her down before she was gone for good. He wanted to tell her, as crazy as it would sound, that they were destined to be together.

He knew that if he didn't hurry, in a moment she'd leave him with a lifetime of regret. But his frozen feet wouldn't obey, and he couldn't hear his voice over the tidal rush of blood in his ears, louder even than the crashing surf along the Maine coast, where he'd left his boyhood—and so many other things—behind. A few heartbeats more, and the woman's silhouette had melted away.

CHAPTER 4

The Ashwood Social Club

THE WHISPERS ABOUT THE MEN AND WOMEN OF THE ASHWOOD neighborhood drifted through Buffalo like the factory smoke that blanketed the city. No one knew where the murmurs emanated, whose chimney had first belched them out, but they were impossible to ignore. 'The Ashwood Set'—up all night dancing, drinking, God knew what else. A little too modern for their own good, and it would catch up to them someday.

Not that any of the two dozen up-and-coming couples of the Ashwood Social Club gave a tinker's damn about gossip. Ashwood was the place for new ideas and new money, and the old fogies with their naughty chatter wouldn't understand any of that. They were just jealous.

The Ashwood Set knew they were the future of the city, the rising generation of Buffalo's elite. Let the stiffs keep their dowdy mansions on Delaware Avenue. Ashwood people would do as they pleased, indulge their modern tastes as the spirit moved. They were doing important work, remaking a once-provincial port town into a hub for industry and science, and if there were a few shenanigans along the way, what of it?

If Ashwood was the place to be in Buffalo, the Ashwood Social Club was the place to be in Ashwood. Most every Saturday evening, twenty or more of the most glittering of the *nouveaux riches* gathered to dance the night away in the gymnasium of the Ashwood High School. Most of the Ashwood Set could only fog the windows of the by-invitation-only Club dances, which—whether true or not—were reputed to be the navel of Ashwood's most dubious and louche doings.

The Club's best dancer was Alicia Miller, although for a year's worth of Saturdays, no one could remember her dancing with her husband, Edward.

Some thought that, after seventeen years of marriage and three children, perhaps the Miller marriage had cooled. Besides, Edward seemed to prefer spending Club nights chatting with Sarah Payne, the lovely young wife of a local dentist. Sarah wasn't much of a dancer, but she was certainly a head-turner, indisputably the most beautiful woman in Buffalo.

When he wasn't chatting up Mrs. Payne, Ed liked to flirt with Helen Warren, the wife of Dr. Frederick Warren, a surgeon. The year before, the Warrens had abruptly moved to Cleveland, despite Freddie's having what seemed a very successful practice in Buffalo. This raised more than a few eyebrows, since no one moved to Cleveland voluntarily without a damn good reason. True, a month or two before their abrupt departure from Buffalo, there had been a public and bitter argument between Freddie and Ed in the Red Jacket Golf Club's clubhouse. About what, though, was a mystery—and had become a topic of intense neighborhood speculation.

Still, no man would uproot his wife to another city over a meaningless quarrel with another gentleman. Whatever the reason for their removal to Ohio, nowadays only Helen returned, alone, to attend occasional Ashwood Club dances. Dr. Warren was conspicuously absent, probably sulking in Cleveland while his wife had fun back in civilization.

Yet it wasn't as though Edward didn't encourage Alicia to dance with the other men, and have some fun of her own. No one could accuse him of being old-fashioned, even if he was a little fussy in his dress and demeanor. Some said he was compensating for being undersized, small and slight. But however physically insignificant Ed Miller might appear, in what really counted—money—he was as tall as he needed to be. He owned an envelope manufacturing firm, a thriving one at that.

On the dance floor, Alicia Hall Miller's dainty feet and petite frame made her look like a ballerina, small and strong and lithe. She moved like a dancer off the floor, too—supple, sultry, commanding. No one would have called her a beauty, not in any classic sense. Her face lacked strong structure, and the voluptuous Cupid's bow of her lips tapered away too quickly toward the sides of her mouth, giving her a wry pout that could be mistaken for sarcasm. Some even said that she had a cruel mouth, but that was probably going too far. For whatever symmetry Alicia's face may have lacked, there was something in the way she carried herself, inclined her head, and rarely looked directly at the other person with her large, dark eyes that projected dominance and control. She spoke deliberately in an unexpected, husky contralto, sometimes pausing for so long to consider her next phrase that people conversing with her would jump in, thinking she was done talking. In such cases, she would wait patiently for them to finish and then pick right back up where she'd left off, as though the others had said nothing at all.

She and her husband had met when Edward was a boarder in her parents' house at the foot of Georgia Street, one short block up from the Erie Canal. Alicia's father was in the tack and harness trade, and being near the Canal and the lakefront gave him easy access to boatmen and teamsters always in need of equipment. The waterfront was famously filthy, the Canal practically an open sewer, a muddy trough of tea-colored, viscous fluid that spawned annual waves of typhoid and worse. By some stroke of divine favor, Alicia inherited her parents' unkillable constitutions. Despite the constant reek of manure and Georgia Street's year-round scab of oily grime, with each passing year, the three Halls seemed to grow ever more hale and hearty, while multiple sets of neighbors left home feet first.

Their diminutive lodger from the countryside, however, was not so inured to the hazards of city life. Edward had come to the city initially to try his hand unloading cargo from lake steamers, but that had been a preposterous idea. He had neither the strength nor stamina of a burly stevedore. After a shift, he'd drag himself home to the Halls' each night so fatigued that he was barely able to speak. It was Mr. Hall who told him that he was in the wrong line of work, that he might do better working with his mind instead of his muscle. Accordingly, Edward found a position as a clerk in a dry goods store, peddling hardware instead of unloading it, and he began to recover.

In July of 1885, though, Edward began to feel particularly poorly. Soaking sweats and chills soon turned into periods of delirium punctuated by bouts of severe diarrhea. Mr. Hall summoned the doctor, who opined that Ed was suffering from a particularly bad case of 'summer complaint,' a form of dysentery that flourished in the hot season. It was typically a disease of infancy, often fatal for tiny bodies, and Mr. Hall intimated that 'itty bitty Eddie' must have a baby's constitution to come down with such a malady. Old Mr. Hall also began to grumble about the cost of fronting food, shelter, and doctor's bills for a boarder who couldn't even earn the rent. After a week of Edward's constant sweating and shitting, Hall had had enough. At dinner one evening, he intoned that the next day he would have Edward removed to the Pesthouse on East Ferry Street.

That was too much for Alicia, who rightly protested that the Pesthouse was a quarantine hospital, mainly for cases of smallpox, and that moving the ailing Edward there would be tantamount to a death sentence. Let me tend to him, she said. I'll nurse him back to health, and then he can get back to earning his keep.

Mr. Hall could have sent Edward to his grave without losing a moment of sleep, but he could refuse his daughter Alicia nothing. For two more weeks, as Edward's life hung in the balance, Alicia spoon-fed him beef broth, helped him on and off the chamber pot, and changed his soiled bedclothes. Little by little, Ed rallied and, as Alicia had promised her father, was soon able to return to work and to earning his keep.

In time of need, concern and care are often taken, or mistaken, for love. During his long and perilous illness, Edward managed to fall head over heels in love with his nurse. And Alicia developed a sincere tenderness for her patient. Neither having yet known passion, compassion was close enough. Edward asked Alicia to become his wife, and six months after he had escaped a trip to the Pesthouse by only a few short hours, the two were married in the parlor of the Halls' home. After the brief ceremony and an overnight honeymoon to Niagara Falls, they set up housekeeping two doors up the hill from the in-laws.

CHAPTER 5

Valentine's Day

February 16, 1901
Saturday evening

IN ONLY THREE MORE MONTHS, BUFFALO WOULD HOST THE greatest festival the world had ever seen—the Pan-American Exposition, which would sprawl across the huge fairgrounds less than a mile from trendy Ashwood. It was only fitting in such an incomparable year that the Ashwood Social Club would go all-out with Valentine's Day decorations—even down to a weird, plaster Cupid dangling from the ceiling, outlined in flickering electric lights. Tonight's dance, a veneration of love, was a-rush with music, laughter, the whoosh of skirts, the clink of ice and crystal.

Between dances, Alicia sat down next to Cassandra Pendle and smiled. For an awkward minute, the pair sipped their champagne and brandy cocktails in silence, watching the other couples dance. Arthur was still on the floor, twirling one of the other women around to some unusually vigorous music. His hair was smoothly parted down the middle, in perfect symmetry with his lush mustache. Arthur was only a little taller than average, though his tailored clothes made him look long and lean, and his way of walking—athletic and erect—oozed self-assurance. Those who didn't like him might call Arthur's gait a swagger or a strut. But those were mostly men who said that.

Arthur's fitted frock coat led Alicia's eye upward to a set of broad shoulders and a high, tapered collar and cravat fastened with a large ruby, set into a circle of tiny diamonds. The collar accentuated his prominent jaw, which, despite his slightly dandy appearance, looked as though it could take a punch.

"You look radiant tonight, Mrs. Pendle," Alicia said, trying to break the ice.

She had been rightly hesitant to invite the Pendles. To add to the Club roster a couple who moved in such rarefied air would be quite a coup. To be rebuffed, on the other hand, would be a monstrous embarrassment and one not easily concealed from the other ladies of Ashwood. After much internal debate, she had decided to make the leap.

Cassie's dress was a magnificent flurry of green velvet and seed pearls, some dyed red to look like little hearts. Her light brown hair was curled in a tight halo above bright, blue eyes, set in a face that seemed a trifle too worn and white for a woman still in her middle thirties.

"You're too kind, Mrs. Miller. And please, call me Cassie."

"Very well, Cassie. I'm Allie to my friends."

Cassie smiled and took another sip of her drink, and returned to looking abstractedly at the dance floor.

"Mr. Pendle is a fine dancer," Alicia said, taking another tack.

"Arthur loves to dance. He was an athlete in college—at New Haven. He played lacrosse and was single scull champion his senior year."

"He has a rower's shoulders," Alicia said, immediately regretting the comment. Cassie didn't seem to notice. "Do you enjoy dancing, as well?"

Cassie shook her head. "I'm afraid I get so worked up with people watching that I develop two left feet. I prefer to sit and relax with one of these." She held up her cocktail glass and jingled the ice. "Or three."

Alicia laughed. "I'm sure you're a better dancer than you let on. Not that I disagree with you about the cocktails."

As the music died away, Arthur strode off the floor, dabbing his forehead with a handkerchief. As he approached the table where Cassie and Alicia were sitting, he inclined his head slightly, almost as if puzzled.

He made a courtly little bow toward Alicia. "Good evening, madam," he said. "Arthur Pendle, at your service. I see you're already acquainted with my better half, but I am at a disadvantage. Mrs.—?"

"Miller," she said. "Alicia Miller."

"Mrs. Miller," he said in a pleasing baritone, still wearing a slightly bemused aspect. Then he blinked, and his expression cleared as though he'd recovered a lost train of thought. "Enchanted. Happy Valentine's Day."

"And to you."

"Wonderful affair you get up here," he said, looking around. "Excellent music."

"Thank you," Alicia said. "You seem particularly to enjoy the fast dances, Mr. Pendle."

"Yes, I do, even if I'm now a bit overheated," he replied, pulling up a chair and folding his legs under it. "If your club plays ragtime music every week, you won't be able to keep us away."

"It's a little fast for me," Cassie said.

"Oh, not at all, dear," Alicia said. "It's a lot of fun to dance to. It has real energy."

Arthur leaned forward. "I agree with you, Mrs. Miller. It has a certain—I don't know exactly—*drive.*"

"Drive?" Alicia asked. "How do you mean?"

He looked at her for a long moment, considering.

"You might say I find it compelling in a visceral way." The two women waited for him to elaborate. Why not, he thought. "Let's put it this way. If Mozart appeals to the head, and Beethoven stirs the heart . . . I think ragtime speaks the language of . . ." He leaned over and whispered, " . . . *the loins.*"

"Arthur, for heaven's sake," Cassie said, reddening. "That's dreadful. We're guests here. Apologize to Mrs. Miller."

"It's all right. I think I know what he means," Alicia said to Cassie, without taking her eyes off Arthur's.

Arthur stood and extended his hand to Alicia. "May I have the honor of the next dance, Mrs. Miller?"

Alicia looked around. It wasn't really done, a man offering his hand first, but Ed was across the room, laughing with Sarah Payne.

"Is it a ragtime number?" Alicia asked him.

"Sorry to disappoint," Arthur said as the gramophone began to squawk. "A waltz." His hand stayed out.

"Just as well, I guess," she smiled, taking his hand and gliding out onto the dance floor.

He kept his torso fashionably arched away from her with the rise and fall of the waltz, and she abandoned herself to the music, letting him lead. They must have cut a dashing figure together because, at the end of the tune, there were smiles and scattered applause as Arthur handed Alicia off the floor and back to her chair. Edward was still with Mrs. Payne and was clapping and smiling too. Alicia was slightly surprised because Ed didn't smile very often—and even less so at her.

❦

"Ed, do you know anything about ragtime music?" Alicia asked as they were walking home that evening, spent.

"It's all the rage at the downtown music halls."

"Do you like it?"

"It's noise, if you ask me. Not what I think of as music."

"I like it."

"Of course you do."

"What does that mean?"

"You like to like the things I don't."

"Don't flatter yourself. I don't spend that much time thinking about what you like and don't like."

"Now, there's something we can both agree on."

They walked in silence the rest of the way to their home, an imposing, new house with a wraparound porch, bay windows, and a widow's walk. They tromped up the steps to the front door and into the large wainscoted foyer.

"I'm tuckered," Edward said, hanging up his overcoat.

"Me too. I'm going up."

"I think I'll read a little in my den first."

"Try not to fall asleep with the gas on again."

"That happened once. Three years ago."

"And you almost burned the place to the ground."

"But I didn't, did I?" He put his hand on the doorknob of his den, just off the foyer, to the left. "Good God, Allie, what did I do in some former life to deserve this?"

"I wonder that myself sometimes," she said, starting up the staircase. "When you do come up, remember to kiss the girls goodnight."

"I always do."

In her bedroom at the front of the house, Alicia threw herself down on the bed, still in her party dress. She looked at the ceiling, at nothing, and forgot about little Edward, stewing down there in his stupid little den. Instead, she found herself thinking about champagne, ragtime, Arthur Pendle, and his *loins*. She smiled, a flat and wry smile. Who says that sort of thing?

CHAPTER 6

Sunday Breakfast

ON SUNDAYS, ANNIE MURRAY, THE MILLERS' MAID, SERVED BREAKfast promptly at 8, so that the family could get to the Unitarian Church downtown in time for the service. Not a soul in the house—neither Ed, nor Alicia, nor their three daughters—enjoyed going to church. They did it solely for the benefit of Mrs. Hall, Alicia's mother, who lived with them on the third floor.

The Millers' breakfast parlor, in the rear of the house, was a place of relative calm, away from bustling Ashwood Street and the eyes of neighbors, who seemed always curious about the goings-on at Number 101.

"Girls, go on and start getting ready," Alicia said, noticing the time. The three girls—Mary Anne, Caroline, and Millicent—scampered up the stairs, chattering away.

Over the remains of breakfast, Edward was half-turned, looking out the back window, and Alicia leafing through a mail-order catalogue, one hand holding the book open and the other keeping her black, wavy hair out of her face. Mrs. Hall hadn't come down to breakfast, and it was getting late.

"Where in the world is your mother?" Ed said, blowing on his coffee.

"Not like you to care about that, Ed," Alicia murmured, not looking up from her catalogue.

"Well, what if she's lying dead upstairs or something?"

Alicia looked up. "Don't you wish."

"You know I would never wish ill on anyone, and especially your dear mother. But where is she? If she's going to eat anything before we go, she'd better get on with it."

"Her stomach bothers her. She's probably having an attack of dyspepsia."

"Dyspepsia," Edward said, emphasizing each syllable. "Dys-*pep*-si-a."

"That's what they call it."

"If you ask me, there's not a thing wrong with her stomach. It's all in her head."

"Can we change the subject?" Alicia said.

"Of course we can, dear. Merely showing concern."

She sat back in her chair and put the catalogue aside. "Do you think the Pendles had a good time last night?"

"Seemed like it."

"Do you think they'll want to join the Club?"

"If they'd want to join a little thing like ours. But they run in completely different circles."

"What circles?"

"Ivy Leaguers. Buffalo Club, Saturn Club. He's an attorney, supposedly a brilliant one."

"Perhaps you could ask him to do some work for your company," Alicia said.

"Rumor has it that he's too busy to take on new work."

"Have you seen that huge house of theirs up on Columbus?"

"I have indeed. Seems like a lot of house for two people."

"I wonder why they don't have children?"

"Why do you care so much about the Pendles?" he said. "Stars still in your eyes from dancing with Arthur?"

"We were having fun. I could say the same about your endless talks with Sarah Payne."

"Sarah's a friend, that's all," he said, sipping his coffee.

"You seem to have a lot of women friends. I wonder what you'd think if I acquired some male ones?"

"It'd be fine by me," he murmured, looking out the window again. "Say, there is one thing I've heard about those two. The Pendles. That house of theirs is the tip of the iceberg. A friend of mine told me that they run through $20,000 a year."

"Seriously? How is that possible?"

"You saw their clothes. They travel to New York all the time. I don't know what all. But my friend said that there's a bit of mystery where all their money comes from. Being an attorney is a good living, but not twenty thousand a year."

"Maybe they inherited?"

"Maybe," he said.

"They do seem to be the perfect couple, don't they?"

Edward rolled his eyes. "Every couple looks perfect from the outside," he said. "I'd wager people probably say the very same thing about us."

"Don't start, Ed. For once."

"Am I wrong? Every time someone we know splits up or has some other disturbance, it's the same story every time. 'My, and you two always looked so *happy!*' 'Oh my, no, we've wanted to murder each other for ten years!' That's how it always goes."

"And you say *I'm* cynical," Allie said.

❦

"DID YOU HAVE A GOOD TIME LAST EVENING, DEAR?" ARTHUR asked over a late brunch the morning after the dance.

"Yes, the people at the Club were very pleasant," Cassie said. "I had far too much to drink, though. Again."

"It's probably well to slow down a bit. But better alcohol than that other poison. If I have a vote."

Cassie shrugged. "It makes me feel better. Not so out of place all the time."

"Out of place? You're one of the most envied women in Buffalo. Look at this house," he said, gesturing around the opulent dining room. "And almost any door in the city—and in New York, too—is open to us."

"Because of *you,* Arthur. Only because of you. *Your* education, *your* profession. All those doors would slam in my face if I weren't on your arm."

"Nonsense. Yours is one of the finest families in all New England."

"No one knows that here but you."

"And you know what my *profession* amounts to. Not exactly what I envisioned back at the old *alma mater.*"

They ate quietly, and Arthur picked up the morning *Courier.*

"I'm sorry I'm not a dancer, Arthur. I know how much you love dancing."

"Cassie," he said, looking over his paper, "you don't need to be a dancer. We don't even have many opportunities to dance, so I'm not missing anything."

"I feel always that I'm disappointing you."

"Will you stop? You always get so morose after we are with other people. I wish we'd never gone to that damn dance." The paper went up again.

"Perhaps it would be a good idea to join the Ashwood Club, and you could dance every week?"

"We can join if you like, but only if you promise not to be such a Gloomy Gus afterward. You don't like social events, so why throw yourself into more of them?"

"To make you happy," she said. "And I do like watching you dance. You and Alicia Miller made quite a couple."

"She is a fine dancer," Arthur said into his newspaper.

"You liked holding her. I could tell."

Arthur folded the newspaper carefully and set it next to his plate. "You're not going to let me read this, are you?"

"I'm only being honest," she said. "You liked holding her. And who could blame you? Look at that body of hers. Do you know she's 42?"

"I did not," Arthur said.

"She's six years older than I am, and look at how much better she looks than I do. That tiny waist—and her breasts. What woman looks like that after three children?"

"Corsets are magical things."

"I beg to differ. I've seen enough women in the nude to know that what's inside Alicia Miller's corset looks every bit as good as what's outside."

"I don't have your experience, I suppose," he said. "I had fun dancing with her, and that was the extent of it."

"Then I think we should join. I'll telephone Alicia today. But be careful, Arthur, a woman like that could turn your head."

"No one's going to turn my head, dear," he said, and went back to his paper.

CHAPTER 7

The Brass Monkey

THE GIRLS WERE STILL AT SCHOOL, AND MRS. HALL WAS AT THE market, when Edward got home. He hung up his coat and stood in the foyer, flipping through the stack of afternoon mail on the entrance table.

"You're home early," Alicia said, coming down the hallway from the rear parlor, where she'd been reading a book.

"Tomorrow's going to be a long day," he said, looking up. "A big order going out, so I'll be late. I figured I'd rest up." He went back to leafing through the mail.

"Guess what?" Allie said.

"What's that?" he grunted, opening a piece of mail with his thumb. "Why don't we have a letter opener on this table? I keep putting one here, and it always vanishes. It's nothing short of vandalism to do this kind of damage to a perfectly good envelope." He held up the letter to show the jagged tear along the upper edge.

"Cassie Pendle telephoned me today. The Pendles want to join the Club!" she said.

"That's nice. Say, do you know that today Gaines solved the Mystery of the Missing Nickels?"

"The what?"

"That's what he and I have been calling it. We advertised in last month's issue of *Modern Stationer*—a nickel promotion. Stationers send in a nickel, and we send them a dozen sample envelopes in all different sizes and types. We had a huge response, but quite a few of the letters were coming in without nickels in them, only the little response coupons. We couldn't figure it out for weeks. And today, Gaines watched from a little peephole we put in the mailroom and caught one of the girls red-handed, opening the letters and pocketing the nickels! Can you imagine? We pay those girls a dollar a day, and they still can't keep their hands to themselves."

"A dollar a day? That's starvation wages, and you know it."

"They're just *girls,* Alicia. Either married or living at home. They don't need more than a dollar a day."

"What did you do about the one who was taking the nickels? Did you reprimand her?"

"We turned her over to the cops," he said.

"The police? For a few missing nickels? God, Ed, if she took two of them, it was a ten percent raise."

"It's not a matter of the money. It's the principle of the thing. So they came and hauled her off. Not my problem anymore. And believe me, those other girls won't dare touch a single nickel now."

Allie rolled her eyes. "You do what you like," she said. "Did you hear what I said a minute ago?"

"Hear you what?"

"About the Pendles."

"What about them?"

"Ed, you could try the patience of Job sometimes."

"I don't have the Pendles on the brain like you do. What about them?"

She scowled. "Like I said already, Cassie Pendle telephoned me today. They want to join the Club! That'll really put the Ashwood Social Club on the map."

"Ha," he said. "Some map. Map of what, a ten-block area?"

"I would like to know why—a simple answer is sufficient—why you have to diminish the things that are important to me? I show rapt interest over your lousy nickels. I listen as though they were my nickels going missing."

"The way you go through money, they are."

"Wonderful. Say the word, King Midas, and we'll pull the girls out of private school. And I'll dress like a washerwoman. You don't seem to mind when Helen Warren wears a dress that costs $100, if it cost—a nickel."

"Very funny. Helen's pleasant to me, at least."

Allie put her hands on her hips. "Naturally, every other woman's a princess, while Allie's a harpy who only wants to dance and spend money."

"Do *not* put words in my mouth," he said, pointing.

"And do *not* point your finger at me."

He retracted the offending finger. "I never said you were a harpy."

"But you think it, and don't deny it. And as for Sarah Payne and Helen Warren—why don't you fuck them and get it over with? I'm sick and tired of being strung along. Not that you'd have enough sap to keep up with either of them."

"Don't tempt me," Ed said with a smirk. "I'm sick and tired of sleeping by myself."

"That was your decision, mister. Don't you blame that one on me!"

"Allie, keep your voice down, will you? Annie's back in the kitchen. You want her to hear about our sleeping arrangements?"

"I don't give a good goddamn what the fucking maid hears!" Allie roared. "You've got a lot of nerve bringing up our sleeping arrangements."

"Well, who wants to sleep next to a cold fish?"

Alicia's face was bright red, and she backed up a step to the telephone table in the hall, and her hand fumbled across a paperweight, a brass effigy of a monkey, which was sitting on a few message blanks next to the telephone. It was the 'See No Evil' monkey from a little set she'd bought the girls some time before. She hefted it in her hand.

"I ought to brain you for that, you little asshole," she said.

"I dare you!" Ed sneered. "Go ahead and try. You couldn't hit a cow's ass with a banjo, let alone—"

Allie had already launched the paperweight. Ed was too stunned to duck, and the flying monkey hit him squarely on the forehead.

"God damn you!" he yelled, clutching at his forehead. "That fucking *hurt!*"

A trickle of blood started from between his fingers, and when he removed his hand from his forehead, the wound began gushing like an oil well. He yanked a handkerchief from his breast pocket and pressed it against his head. In moments the white linen was saturated with an astonishing quantity of blood. He felt suddenly queasy and sat down on the staircase, pressing the seeping cloth hard against his forehead.

Alicia's fury had turned into horror at the sight of the blood streaming out of his scalp. "I'm calling Dr. Massey!" she yelled, picking up the earpiece of the phone. She was asking the operator to connect her when the doorbell rang.

"Annie!" she shouted over her shoulder to the kitchen, "will you answer the goddamn door?"

The frightened maid scurried to the door and passed Ed sitting on the stairs, a trickle of blood running down his face.

"Mr. Miller!" she said in alarm. "Oh my God. Can I help?"

"Just help me get out of sight before you open the door," Ed said and stumbled back to the kitchen, blinded by blood and almost bowling Allie over as he careened down the corridor, leaving bloody handprints on the wallpaper as he went.

"Annie!" Allie howled, putting her hand over the mouthpiece of the telephone. "Are you fucking deaf? Answer the goddamn door, will you? Can't you see I'm on the phone?"

Annie opened the door. It was the neighbor lady, Mrs. Stoddard, from across the street. She peered around Annie and saw Allie standing in the hall, near the telephone table, the earpiece to her ear.

"Is everything all right? I happened to be passing and heard some— commotion—and wondered . . ."

Allie hung up just as Dr. Massey picked up and rushed to the door, shoving Annie out of the way. "Oh yes, everything's fine, Catherine," she purred, smiling warmly.

Mrs. Stoddard looked down the long hall past Allie and saw Ed sitting in the kitchen, holding a crimson rag to his head.

"Are you sure?"

"Yes, I'm sure, but I do thank you for your concern," Allie said, maneuvering in front of Mrs. Stoddard, who was still trying to look around her. "I'm sure we'll be seeing you soon. Have a wonderful evening." She shut the door, knowing that within a quarter-hour, Mrs. Stoddard would alert every other woman within four blocks that she had come up on the Millers' front porch and had heard Alicia cursing up a blue streak while poor Mr. Miller was bleeding profusely.

Allie picked up the phone again and, this time, connected with Dr. Massey. She told him that there'd been an accident and that he should come straightaway.

Back in the kitchen, Edward had swapped his handkerchief for a large dinner napkin, soaked it, and was working on a fresh one.

"You stay away from me," he muttered when Alicia came in.

"Massey's on his way. I didn't mean to—how badly are you cut?"

"What does it look like? I'm bleeding like a stuck pig. I can't lift the damn cloth off my head long enough to see. What do you care, anyway?"

"I said I was sorry. It was an accident."

He glared back at her. "Uh-huh. Just send the fucking doctor back when he gets here, will you? If I'm still alive by then."

When Dr. Massey arrived, the bleeding had slowed, but the inch-long wound from the brass monkey needed almost a dozen sutures to close it up, which hurt like mad.

"Are you two going to be all right?" he asked Edward quietly as he was packing up to go.

"Who knows?" Edward said. "I guess so. If I survive her."

❧

The following morning, Ed's forehead was throbbing and sore. He couldn't fit his stiff derby hat over the thick bandage, so he rode downtown bareheaded in a trolley full of curious commuters. It was drizzling by the time he reached his office, and he had to wipe away a trickle of watery blood sneaking under the bandage and oozing down his temple. He'd have to put on a dry bandage in the office, but then he could go next door to the factory and let his machines drown out the memory of yesterday. He found it meditative, the rhythmic envelope machines tirelessly cutting, folding, gluing, and complaining only when they needed a little oil here or there.

"Look what the cat dragged in," his business partner Howard Gaines said when Edward stepped into their office, shaking off raindrops. "Hey—what happened to you?"

"Don't start," Edward said. "Not in the mood."

"Mum's the word, chum."

"I'm sorry, Gaines. I don't mean to snarl at you."

"Don't mention it. I'm sure you've got a lot on your mind. Oh gee," he said, "I didn't mean it like that. Though that was kind of funny."

"Allie beaned me with a monkey."

"She what? A monkey?"

"A brass paperweight. A little monkey thing. We had a squabble, and she threw it at me. Hit me square on the noggin. Twelve stitches."

"That's bad, Ed. I'm sorry."

Edward went down the hall to the washroom to clean up. When he got back, he sat down in his chair with a deep sigh.

"I'll tell you one thing. I'd be happier living alone. Probably safer, too."

His friend took a bite from a half-eaten pastry sitting on his blotter. "Sticky bun?" he asked, gesturing to the box on his desk. "They always make me feel better."

"I don't see how you can eat those things. Like a sponge soaked in glue."

Gaines smacked his lips loudly. "More for me. Ed, you've been saying how rough it is at home since we became partners."

"I know. I need to stop bitching about it and do something." He touched his bandage.

"You could find another woman, you know," Gaines said. "You're a catch."

"Not as long as Allie's in the picture. She'd kill me for sure if I took up with someone else. She doesn't even like it that I'm friendly with Sarah Payne or Helen Warren."

"I don't know Mrs. Warren," Gaines said, "but God sakes, I've seen Mrs. Payne around the city. She is a knockout."

"No doubt about that," Ed said. "But we're only friends. She's not the type to do anything improper."

"More's the pity," Gaines said, laughing. "I might consider coming off the bench for that one. But seriously—this just-friends stuff with women is dangerous. If Allie even *thinks* you're up to something, she could sue you for divorce. You don't want that."

"On what grounds? You're not a married man—"

"Nor ever will be."

Edward ignored him and went on. "—but you know as well as I do, in New York State, the only acceptable grounds for divorce is adultery. And that's a difficult thing to prove."

"Maybe, but I read about this all the time in the *Police Gazette*. Here's how it goes. Allie hires a private eye. A New York City agency, not the local dummies, so that no one around here will recognize them. They follow you around for a while and make up whatever they want. Then you're done for."

Ed frowned and winced. "I could beat her to the punch, I suppose, and hire one of my own."

"That is not a half-bad idea, old man," Gaines said.

CHAPTER 8

Sweet Teeth

SARAH AND SETH PAYNE HAD BEEN MARRIED FOR A LITTLE MORE than nine years and had an eight-year-old daughter, Margaret, whom they called Maggie.

After their wedding, Seth had opened a dental office in Ashwood. Yet after only five successful years, he'd surprised everyone by moving his practice to Batavia, a hamlet east of Buffalo, which long ago had been bypassed by the Erie Canal, and just about everything else since. Batavia was, as people liked to say, 50 miles east and 50 years behind Buffalo.

Sarah and Maggie stayed in Ashwood, in their modest home on Norwood Street. Every Saturday morning, they dutifully took the train to Batavia and returned on Sunday evening. Sarah was content enough with the arrangement, partly because Seth seemed better on his own and partly because it gave her an excuse to miss church on Sunday. Her father was a retired Presbyterian minister, but Sarah had never enjoyed the droning solemnity of services and sermons, all of which bored her to tears. She much preferred to sleep late, luxuriate over coffee in her dressing gown, and read the newspapers.

Two homes and two weekly train fares consumed every penny, and then some, of Seth's income, but Sarah was rarely seen in anything but the latest fashions. How she could afford a fashion-plate wardrobe on a small-town dentist's living, however, was less a mystery than people liked to believe. It was simply that Sarah was so entrancing that several of Buffalo's best dressmakers and milliners treated her clothing as an advertising expense. If Sarah Payne was wearing something, she wore it well, and it brought in business. Her slim, graceful figure showed every inch of fabric to advantage, and somehow she could navigate Buffalo's cobblestones without putting so much as a peacock feather out of place on the enormous millinery confections balanced atop her head.

Sarah had never seriously considered Seth Payne as a potential match and, at 18 years of age, hadn't been thinking of settling down. But the minister's daughter had let the handsome but dull dental student get a little too close a couple of times, and a hasty wedding was arranged, with her father officiating. As luck would have it, Sarah soon found out that it had been a false alarm. There had been no pregnancy, but now she was stuck with Seth. She'd made the best of it, and when Maggie came along, life brightened up again. The little girl was a delight, pretty and sassy and outspoken like her mother, and with the same penetrating, grey-blue, almost violet eyes, strawberry blonde hair, and fine features. The dressmakers had started making clothes for them both, and on the streets of the city, the pair looked like mismatched but equally fetching twins.

Other than Maggie, clothes, and hats, Sarah had two other notable weaknesses—ice cream and Edward Miller. There was a certain something about the tidy little businessman that appealed to her. And his careworn and wounded expression offered her a challenge that she took seriously: to make 'little Eddie' smile. She was good at it, too.

❧

The wound on Edward's head had begun itching like mad under the bandage, so much so that he called Dr. Massey. The doctor told him that itching was a sign of healing and, for God's sake, leave it alone until the stitches came out, or he'd risk opening it up again. Between the constant itching and the cold silence at home—as much from him as from Allie—by the time Thursday rolled around, it had been a very long week.

He had worked himself into a profoundly surly mood by lunchtime, and spurned Gaines' cheery invitation to take their midday meal together. "No thanks, I'm going to grab a root beer or something," he said. "I'm not very good company today anyway."

He'd purchased a soft felt hat a full two sizes too big for him so that he could have some decent headwear when out and about. He placed it over his itchy bandage and walked downtown to find something to eat. Edward was known for his sweet tooth, and when his mood was low, he'd often forgo a proper lunch for some candy and a float at the huge Lang's Candy Store, 444 Main Street.

Two blocks from Lang's, he was mulling what flavor ice cream he might like. He wasn't minding his steps when a lady passing him on the sidewalk suddenly held out her umbrella directly in front of him, like a gate. He stopped abruptly, irritated.

"I beg your pardon, madam. You very nearly speared me with that thing," he muttered.

"That's what you get for trying to knock me down and wearing a silly disguise, too," the lady said.

He looked up and saw that it was Sarah Payne, dressed in her usual splendor. She had the offending umbrella in one hand and a small hand-bag in the other. She was clearly enjoying his discomfiture.

"Oh, my, Sarah," he said, lifting his floppy hat and grimacing as it tugged on the bandage. "I'm so sorry. I wasn't paying attention. I didn't know it was you."

"I certainly hope not," she said, "considering that evil scowl you had on when I stopped you."

He replaced his hat delicately. "Of course not," he said. "I always smile when I see you."

"Though it looks as though smiling might hurt a little," she said, nodding the plumes of her hat in the direction of his forehead. "Fisti-cuffs at your age, Eddie? Really?"

"I banged it on a beam going down the basement stairs."

"You poor dear!" Sarah said. "It must hurt terribly."

"Not too bad. I've got a hard head, I guess."

They stood there on the sidewalk for an uncomfortable moment. It was the first time they'd ever spoken more than two words outside of one of the Ashwood Club events.

Sarah cleared her throat, putting one small, gloved hand in front of her mouth. "Are you going to Lang's?" she said.

"I thought I'd have ice cream for lunch today."

"Maybe order an extra scoop to put against your forehead."

He caught himself with a little start. "Where are my manners?" he said. "Won't you join me?"

She smiled. "At last. I was afraid for a moment I'd have to invite myself."

They went into Lang's together, which was always bustling with conversation and the tinkling music of glassware. "I'll go get us something," he said.

"Here," she said, opening her tiny purse.

"No, no," he said. "Nothing doing. What would you like?"

"Surprise me," she said, sitting down at one of the gleaming marble-topped tables. Several of the other guests craned around to have a look at her as she carefully arranged herself.

He brought over two dishes of chocolate ice cream, and they dived in.

"This is so fun," Sarah said. "I like the way you approach lunch."

"If I could, I'd eat like this every day. But I don't want to have to buy all new clothes."

They ate in silence for a little while, to the clink of spoons.

At last, Sarah had had enough. "Excuse me, sir," she said, "may I ask what you've done with Eddie Miller? From the Ashwood Social Club?"

"What?"

"What what? What's become of the little chatterbox I know from the Club? You haven't said ten words to me this whole time."

"I'm sorry," Edward said. "I ought to be in a more talkative mood."

"How about you start, then, by telling me the truth about how you got that lump on your noggin?"

"I told you already."

"Eddie. Don't lie to me. If you don't want to tell me the truth, then say, 'Sarah, I refuse to tell you.' Don't make up some cock-and-bull story about cracking your head on a beam. Of all things! You're not tall enough to hit your head on anything."

Edward blushed. "I know."

"Now, don't mope. I like you just the height you are, and not a half-inch taller. You could even be a little shorter, and you would still be perfect. Come on now. Why don't you tell Sarah what happened to your poor little head?"

"It was Allie." He looked ruefully down at his ice cream.

"Allie? Did she hit you with a baseball bat or something?"

"It was a paperweight. A monkey."

"A monkey?"

"That doesn't matter," he said. "It's a brass thing. Must weigh a full pound. She and I were quarrelling, and she threw it at me."

"Then she does have a future in baseball," Sarah laughed. "Come on now, don't be cross. It was a little joke."

"I know. I'm not cross. It hurts to smile. You'll never guess why she threw it at me."

"That's a fair assumption."

"She was angry about *you.*"

"About me? What did I do to her?"

"Nothing," he said. "She's jealous that I like to talk with you. And she thinks you make goo-goo eyes at me at the Club."

"Well?"

"Well what?"

"I do make goo-goo eyes at you."

"You *agree* with her?"

"How could I disagree? But she's got only herself to blame for my goo-goo eyes." She batted her long lashes at him.

"I thought you'd be outraged."

Sarah licked the final spoonful of chocolate ice cream off her spoon. "Let me tell you a little story, Eddie boy," she said.

"All right."

"It's about me and Seth."

"Are you sure you want to tell me?"

She cocked her head at him, her plumes fanning a whiff of her perfume in his direction.

"Sure, I'm sure. You know Seth drinks."

"I've seen him have a cocktail at our parties. You mean more than that?"

"Oh yes. *Considerably* more."

"I am sorry to hear that. It's a hard habit for a lot of men."

"Women, too," she said. "You would be surprised how many women drink like fishes. Lots of things I could tell you, Eddie. In any event, Seth drinks."

"I don't know what to say."

"Have you ever wondered why I don't live with him in Batavia?"

"No," Ed lied. "Never crossed my mind."

"Are you trying to hurt my feelings?"

"Not in the least! Tell me if you would like. I'm all ears."

"When we lived together, I'd drop by his office at the end of the day, and we would walk home together. But then I started finding him sitting like a statue in his dental chair. He'd fallen asleep sniffing ether."

Ed shook his head. "That stuff is awfully dangerous."

Sarah raised her eyebrows. "No kidding. And on top of the drinking. I wasn't about to have our little daughter wander over someday and find her daddy dead as a doornail. Or he could blow us all to kingdom come if he lit a cigar with all that flammable gas in the air. I told him I was coming to Buffalo, and Maggie and I would visit on weekends."

"Did he object?"

"He put on a little show, as men do, but that's all it was. The truth is, he'd prefer to be with his medicine cabinet than me. If we'd stayed in Batavia, he'd drag us under with him. I wasn't about to let that happen. I want to have some fun in life while I'm still young, Eddie, not watch my husband kill himself."

"Perhaps there's something I can do to help? I could talk to Seth, if you like."

"While that's very gallant, and I'm grateful, it wouldn't help. The whole reason I brought this complex mess up was to explain why I agree with Allie—oh, and I suppose, to let you know a little bit more about me. What makes me tick."

"That's the most interesting bit," he said without thinking.

She looked at him with a slight smile. "Then here is the moral of the story. It'd be very tempting to blame all my troubles on Seth. And I'll bet you a dish of ice cream that it's easy for Allie to blame you for hers. Yet it's never that way. For all I know, Seth started drinking himself stupid because when he married me, I was an eighteen-year-old girl who didn't want to be married at all. What man wouldn't be disappointed by that? It's never only one person's fault when things go wrong—however much we'd like to think so.

"So—if I were Allie, and you were my husband, and some strange and beautiful woman—if you don't mind my saying—started making eyes at you, you can bet your bottom dollar I'd be miffed. With Miss Goo-Goo Eyes, sure, and with you. But,"—she raised her index finger—"this is where Allie and I must part company. Because I'd blame myself, too. I'd have to admit having had a hand in letting things get to the point where my husband was susceptible to another woman's charms."

Edward took it all in, watching her face. "I understand your point," he said, "and I confess I feel a little ashamed. Allie and I have been strangers for longer than I'd like to admit. We blame each other for it. It's like a whirlpool we can't get free of."

"We have a lot more in common than ice cream, Eddie."

"You're wiser than I am," Edward said. "You could go by Solomon instead of Sarah. Still Biblical, too."

"Nah. Nothing more than common sense. Besides, my father was a minister, and I never liked Solomon. He shouldn't have threatened to cut a baby in half, even as a joke."

He laughed, and even though it smarted, it felt good to smile.

"Sarah," he said, "I must admit I was at a complete loss for what to say to you when we sat down."

"You were being a little shy. I found it rather charming."

"It's refreshing to have someone to talk with," Edward said. "A woman, too. My men friends only want to talk about business or golf. Or who's got a bigger house."

"It's the same with women," she said. "Women are just as competitive. Talking with women is like a sparring match. Most of them are trying to find something rotten to say about me to someone else." She paused. "Not that I haven't been guilty of that myself—on very rare occasions, naturally."

He shifted a bit in his chair. "I am afraid of what Allie's reaction will be," he said, "if at the next Club affair I sit and talk with you."

"With good reason," she said, pointing with her plumes again. "She'd probably kill us both."

"Do you think—there's any way we could find, you know, another place to meet?"

"You naughty little man!"

Edward reddened. "I didn't mean anything improper."

"I'm making fun, silly. And I don't mind naughty. Why, look at you, blushing!"

"I'm not blushing. It's my damaged head throbbing."

"If you say so. Sure, we can sit and gab. Why don't we come here? It's so busy, no one pays us any mind. If we see anyone who knows us, we can say we bumped into each other on the sidewalk. It's true, since we did that very thing today."

"When you almost impaled me?"

"I remember it a little differently. A rude man in an oversized hat was about to bowl me over, and I had to defend myself."

"All right, I'll agree to your version of the story, if we can agree on a date for our next pow-wow."

CHAPTER 9

A Good Cigar

WILLIAM ROSCOE, ASSISTANT ERIE COUNTY DISTRICT ATTORNEY, couldn't have been older than 35, maybe 40, but he was paunchy and pallid and had thin, straight hair, which he kept plastered to his head with too much pomade, giving him a persistent odor of almonds. Terry had laughed at him more than once, saying that he should submit his recipe to Madame d'Arcy's *Beauty Talk* column in the Sunday papers, which the lovely Madame would use as an example of what *not* to do.

He may not have liked them, but Roscoe put up with Penrose's jokes, and laughed along. He had had his eye on the District Attorney's office ever since Penrose had appointed him his deputy, plucking him from an obscure position as a rather indifferent prosecutor. What Terry liked about Bill Roscoe was not the man's legal skill but his willingness to bend the rules a little here, a little there, when it made sense. Roscoe's winning percentage was much higher when he 'improved his lie a little,' as the fellows at the golf club euphemistically called cheating.

Roscoe was thus well-suited as a go-between for the DA's more unsavory activities. Terry was smart enough to keep a prudent distance between his person and those who carried out his darkest commands. 'If it worked for Henry II, it'll work for me,' he would say. He did make a single exception—for his friend Arthur Pendle, who it seemed was the only human being that Terry Penrose trusted implicitly. Accordingly, when Arthur Pendle appeared in the courthouse, he was never fobbed off on Bill Roscoe, but instead was ushered graciously into the presence of the District Attorney himself.

Penrose reckoned that Roscoe, should he succeed him as District Attorney, would be a compliant and useful adjunct—especially if Penrose were in higher office. The trick was to teach his protégé enough about the foul machine of politics, maintain a safe distance, and ensure that Roscoe could be implicated for any charges of wrongdoing that might inconveniently fall on the DA's head.

Penrose had his feet up on his desk late one afternoon when Roscoe rapped on his closed door. "Mr. Penrose?"

Terry blew out a lungful of smoke and had almost got both feet on the floor when Roscoe cautiously opened the door a crack and peeked his head in. "Mr. Penrose?"

"Yes, yes, Roscoe, come in. What is it?"

"May I close the door, sir? It's a sensitive matter."

Penrose nodded and put his cigar down into a gigantic crystal ashtray. Roscoe sat opposite him.

"We have a little problem in the McClure case," Roscoe said.

Chet McClure was a drummer—a traveling salesman. On any given day, a small army of drummers tramped around Buffalo, lugging with them cases of sample merchandise and headfuls of old jokes. Toys, hats, nostrums, cooking gear, musical instruments—whatever one could desire, some commercial traveler had it to show. After spending a day, or a week, in the city, they'd all be off again to peddle their wares at the next whistle-stop.

Chet was an itinerant representative of an Indiana concern that made sprays and powders formulated to kill fleas and bedbugs. These products were sold door-to-door to housewives, who not infrequently welcomed the arrival of a traveling man from out-of-town as much as they longed to banish domestic vermin. But the drummer's happy round of lonely homemakers was not without occupational risk, as McClure learned. A few weeks before, Mrs. Alfred Mitchell, a housewife in the Ninth Ward, had lodged a serious complaint about him. She claimed that during his sales pitch, he had asked to inspect the Mitchell beds for traces of bedbugs, and she'd complied. For her trouble, Chet McClure had taken criminal advantage of her, right there in her marital bed, at precisely 2 o'clock on a Thursday afternoon. Mrs. Mitchell told the law there could be no doubt about the time—being penetrated in broad daylight was certainly something she'd remember.

McClure was scooped up by the cops that evening as soon as he returned to his hotel. He was indicted the following day, and even by Penrose standards, the ensuing trial was brutally efficient. Without a familiar soul in the city to vouch for him—and a fractious posse of outraged citizens eager to defend the honor of the violated housewife—McClure was quickly convicted. He was handed a five-year term from the jury and a long-distance divorce from his wife, and told to be thankful he was getting off so easy. True enough, during the trial, the Buffalo *Enquirer*—notable mainly for printing the best gossip—had written that Mrs. Mitchell was rumored by some to be having an affair with a local man, and might be looking for a scapegoat in Chet McClure. That dubious scuttlebutt was promptly squelched by the DA's office, and the trial concluded as expected.

"Problem?" Terry replied. "He's going away for five years. Where's the problem?"

"Well," the ADA said, drawing out the word, "you know he's been cooling his heels in the stir since we picked him up a couple weeks ago."

"How's prison life treating him?"

"Same as it treats anyone like him," Roscoe said. "But here's the thing. Yesterday when we got the conviction, the boys were boxing up his personal effects in storage—and in the pocket of his trousers found this." He held up a small, brightly colored piece of paper. Terry squinted at it over his desk.

"A ticket stub?"

"Yes. From the Teck Theater."

"Will you come to the point, Bill? Sometimes, I must say, you're tedious."

"The stub is from a vaudeville matinee, the day of the assault. And that matinee went from noon until three."

"You're saying that McClure was watching *vaudeville* when he was said to be banging Mrs. Mitchell?"

"It appears so, yes. I wanted to bring it to you immediately."

"Let me see that stub." Terry reached across his desk and took the item from Roscoe's hand. He put on his reading glasses and examined the paper carefully. Then he set it down gently on his blotter, opened the top of a cedar humidor on his desk, and took out a long, oil-black cigar.

He clipped the end and handed it over to the Assistant DA, who gazed at it with something like reverence. "An *Alvarez?*" Roscoe murmured. "This is a fifty-cent cigar, Mr. Penrose."

"And you've earned it, Roscoe, by bringing that ticket stub to me. You did the right thing."

"I thought you'd be upset," he said. "I mean, the fellow's innocent, and it's going to be embarrassing—"

"A special cigar demands a special lighter, don't you think?" Terry interrupted.

"I suppose so, yes."

"Well, then, here you go." He handed the ticket stub back to Roscoe, who looked puzzled. "You need a good flame to light that beauty."

Penrose took a match from his match-safe, struck it, and held it out across the desk. Roscoe stuck the Alvarez in his mouth and leaned forward, steadying the cigar.

"No, your other hand," Penrose said. "You need a bigger flame."

Roscoe held up the ticket stub, and Penrose put the match under it. "There you go. Now light away, and let's have a smoke." He slid the giant crystal ashtray across the desk.

The Assistant DA held the flaming ticket stub under the Alvarez. It burned just long enough to get a good ember going, and then Roscoe dropped the remains into Terry's ashtray, where it smoldered into nonexistence.

"Now, isn't that an excellent cigar?" Terry mumbled, puffing on his stogie. "There'll be more where that came from, too, if you stay as sharp as you have been today."

CHAPTER 10

California Jack's Chop Suey

CHARLIE HONG AND HIS TWO BROTHERS OPERATED A CHOP SUEY house at 452 Michigan Street, ten minutes' walk but a world away from cheerful Lang's Candy. The three Hongs had been at that address since 1890, when they had been smuggled into the United States by a local ne'er-do-well, Ed Young. For reasons unknown, Young went by the name of California Jack, despite having never been closer to California than Cleveland. As most Chinese were assumed to originate in California, and Ed made a good buck ferrying illegals a few at a time across the Niagara River from Canada, it seemed a likely enough moniker.

The Chinese Exclusion Act, enacted years before, prohibited any Chinese immigration into the United States. The law and the border were sufficiently porous, however, that a hundred or so a year turned up in the Buffalo region, mostly in Niagara Falls, where chop suey and other Chinese dishes were popular among tourists seeking out the exotic. There wasn't as much call for it in Buffalo, so most of the 'Celestials' ran laundries. Charlie Hong and his brothers were the exceptions, mainly because California Jack had set them up in business, and they owed him.

Not too many white people who visited Charlie Hong's restaurant, though, had ever tasted the chop suey. It was an open secret that the Hongs ran a 'hop joint'—a downscale opium den frequented mainly by Chinese, but also by locals who enjoyed the pipe. There was a small lunch counter on the ground floor of the building, and Charlie did whip up the occasional batch of stir-fry to keep the cops looking the other way. The opium was smoked on the upper floor, where the acrid fumes could escape into the heavens instead of seeping up through the floorboards and giving everyone away.

Every few months, California Jack would row his old boat across the river to Fort Erie, collect 200 pounds of smoking opium—five wooden chests, each containing 40 pounds of rubbery balls about the size of a lemon, wrapped in paper—and hurry back to Buffalo. The trade itself would have been legal, but for Jack's evasion of the 37.5% tax on opium and for his being an unlicensed seller of the drug. Druggists, dentists, and even soda fountains were all permitted to peddle opiates, but only with a license. That was easy enough to obtain, but acquiring one would put California Jack under the Government's scrutiny, best avoided. If one had a narcotics license, Uncle Sam knew where to look for his cut, and if the powers that be didn't like your look, they could find plenty of other things that could make a fellow's life miserable.

A full bowl of chop suey—when the Hongs made it—cost a dime. A single pipe of opium, enough to send a novice smoker to dreamland, went for $1.50. Since the sour smoke burned the throat, at least two beers, 25 cents per, were required to keep from coughing up the holy fumes. If the smoker didn't know how or was too lazy to prepare the opium and the pipe, Charlie got another dollar for helping. Thus even the casual one-time user would bring in at least a couple of bucks and, after the first experience, there weren't a lot of casual, one-time users. And at $16 a pound, raw opium smuggled directly from Canada cost only a little more than the pork and vegetables, oil, fuel, and equipment that went into cheap chop suey.

Not that running a hop joint was all fun and profit. Users did occasionally die, and their bodies would have to be lugged down the narrow stairs and quietly disposed of. Cops and other officials had to be paid off. And since most Americans didn't much like Chinese, there was always the risk that Charlie or his brothers might be run into Police Headquarters as useful stooges for crimes that they had not committed.

The joint was closed the last day of every month. Addicts could cry and whine as piteously as they liked, but California Jack's hired muscle kept them at least two blocks away. It was important not to give the collections man any cause to complain. If he saw nothing amiss, he'd take his cash and be on his way. If he witnessed criminal activity with his own eyes, though, then chances were the place would either be shut down posthaste or, worse, the monthly juice would go up substantially. Thus the end of the month was as sacred as the Sabbath.

On the 28th of February, Charlie Hong followed the usual procedure. He hung the 'CLOSED' sign on the front door and shooed away the habitués, promising them a little something extra if they came back tomorrow. He stationed himself behind the counter, looking as respectable as it was possible for him to look. Around 5 o'clock in the afternoon, a cop rapped his nightstick on the front door glass. Charlie opened the roller shade to see who it was, then unfastened the bolt and opened the door for the cop and his companion, a rakish young man in a derby. He then fastened the door again and pulled the shade.

The cop and the young swell walked up to the lunch counter. The cop kept an eye on the door while the one in the derby plopped a leather grip on the counter, unfastening the top. Charlie, who knew the drill, slid a thick envelope over the counter. The man in the derby gave him a small smile, expertly examined the contents of the envelope, and dropped it into the bag. The two waited there for a minute, the gentleman eyeing Charlie. "And?" the young man said. "Yes, yes, so sorry," Charlie said, reaching into a pocket. He placed his hand flat on the lunch counter, then quickly withdrew it. The man put his hand over the thing and slid it toward him, off the edge of the counter, and into his trouser pocket. It happened so fast that it might as well have been a shell game. He nodded at Charlie and said to the cop, "all done here." The cop adjusted his nightstick, for no other reason than to remind Charlie that he had one and would love an excuse to put it to work.

Charlie then accompanied the two men to the front door and let them out into the cool, late afternoon sun.

On the sidewalk, the cop glanced at the man in the derby, who was jotting something in a pocket notebook with a small, gold mechanical pencil. "Where to next, Mr. Pendle?" he said.

❦

Cassie was waiting up for Arthur when he arrived home a little after midnight.

"You're home," she said, giving him a kiss on the cheek. "I'm always relieved when you get back."

"Me too," Arthur said. He set his leather case down in the parlor. "I hate the end of the month."

"Were you able to get everything done?"

"Yes. A clean sweep. No monkey business."

She shifted her weight from one foot to the other, blocking him, like a bellhop expecting a tip but not wanting to be impolite.

"Oh, yes," Arthur said. He reached into his trouser pocket and took out a small, flat paper package, about the size of a silver dollar. "I have your stuff." She took it from him with both hands and tucked it into her robe. "Thank you, honey," she said, and kissed his cheek again. She stood out of the way and let him hang up his hat and coat.

"Can we sit for a few minutes?" He gestured to the parlor off the hall. "I wanted to talk with you."

"Of course." She sat down next to him on the davenport. "What's on your mind?"

"I see people all the time who are perfect slaves to that stuff," he said, pointing to the pocket of her robe. "There's not the slightest good that comes of it."

"I beg to differ," she said merrily. "It takes away pain, doesn't it?"

"For a while," he said. "But you're not in pain."

"Pain comes in many disguises. After a hard day, don't you enjoy a cocktail to help you relax? How am I so different?"

"You know why it's different."

"More people die each year from alcohol than from this," she said, holding up her little envelope. "You can't open the paper on any given day without reading about someone drinking himself to death."

"It's well-known that alcoholism afflicts only those who are already weak in body or mind. Drugs turn healthy people into wrecks."

"Oh, I don't know. They make me feel like Joan of Arc."

"Cassie," he said, taking her hand in his, "I don't understand why you need it. Not too long ago, it was every once in a great while, but recently it's almost every day."

"It's not every day. You're not here most of the time."

"I am here a lot of the time."

"Maybe, but your mind is usually off someplace else. I don't know where, but somewhere. How about we let each other have our little escapes?"

"Do you find our life so confining?"

Cassie laid her hand on his thigh. "Not in the slightest. Our life isn't like everyone else's, and that's difficult sometimes. To be different."

He shook his head. "I do sometimes wonder what kind of life we've built."

"What kind of life does anyone build?"

"Sometimes I want to knock it all over and start again."

"Wouldn't we all? If only to escape judgment."

"Judgment?" Arthur smirked. "That's a fairy tale. There's no justice in this life, and there certainly won't be in the next. If there is a next."

"I'm not so sure about that," she said.

"You've not done anything to be judged for, anyway. If either of us should worry about that, it's me."

"I never gave you a child—that's a woman's duty. Worse, I never wanted to."

"I never cared for children either. And I'm sure I've let you down in other ways."

"You've never let me down. And maybe we would have been happier if we had had children."

"We're happy enough."

"We're not like everyone else, Arthur."

"I've told you that's of no consequence. I love you."

"And I'm grateful. But I predict that the love we have won't be enough for you, eventually."

"That's simply not so."

Cassie tried to smile. "Dear Arthur. You're very kind to me," she said. "You always have been."

"I'm no saint, Cassie."

"Saints are dull as dishwater," she said. "Now, then, I think I'll go upstairs. It's been a long day."

"Maybe try to sleep without taking anything?"

"Don't you worry about me."

Her footsteps faded away up the staircase. He got up, went to the sideboard, and poured himself a stiff drink. He sat down heavily in his armchair and unbuttoned his pants, which were feeling tighter after so many fine lunches and cocktails. It bothered him, the little roll of flesh developing around his waist. In college, he'd been lean and hard, and now when he looked at himself in the mirror, naked, he could still make out the musculature of his youth, but less and less distinctly. He stared into the eye of the dead fireplace, the accusing black grate and porcelain sclera set deep in the walnut paneling they'd imported from Europe. They'd been so proud of it.

❧

'Five Fours,' as they called it, became a standing date. Four o'clock in the afternoon on Thursday—the fourth day of the week—at Lang's, 444 Main Street. Sarah would arrive a little early to claim a table, and Edward arrived precisely at 4. He would get them an ice cream float and a few of whatever special candies Lang's had that day. Sarah always offered to pay, and Edward always declined. It was a joyful little ritual.

A shared love of sweets in a busy candy shop was something in which a man and a woman could safely indulge without spawning too much gossip. And it avoided the scrutiny that their conversations at the Ashwood Club had attracted. Anything more intimate, away from the chaperoning eyes of the public, would have been taboo.

Vanilla Cocoa Creams were on sale that day at only sixty cents a pound. Edward bought a box for each of them to take home, and a few to sample while they enjoyed their float.

"Be careful," Sarah said when he brought the boxes to their table. "I might eat all of those right here and now." Her slim form, accentuated by a fur-trimmed brocade jacket, made it seem like she'd never eaten a bonbon in her life.

"Not if I get them first."

When their ice cream floats were delivered, they clinked glasses. "Five Fours!" they said in unison, as usual.

"Now tell me—what's on your mind this week, Eddie?"

"Mostly work," he said. "We had a huge order to get out for the Pan-

American. I had to ask the girls to work extra shifts."

"That's wonderful!"

"'Wonderful?' Allie thinks that envelopes are boring."

"They're nothing of the sort," she said. "Every one of them contains a little secret. Something that might change the course of someone's life. I'd like to read all of them."

"You should work for the postal inspector."

"I may inquire. I would so love to see your factory one of these days."

"You would?"

"Why wouldn't I? I've used probably a million envelopes and never seen how a single one of them was made. And since you have women making them, I'd like to see whether you're treating them nicely or if you're a mean, horrible man when you're not eating ice cream."

"I hope I'm not a mean, horrible man anytime." He put his finger to his lips. "But don't ask Mrs. Hall."

"She's a hideous old shrew, is she not?"

"You don't know the half of it!"

"Why have you told me only half?"

"I'll tell you a story, then, if it'll satisfy your curiosity."

"I don't know if it will, but you can try," she said, settling back in her chair and taking a big sip of ice cream float.

"Once I overheard Allie and her mother talking—"

"Eavesdropping! It's almost as good as being a postal inspector."

"You know, you're right—I *was* eavesdropping," he said. "I'm a bit ashamed of myself. And I shouldn't tell you things like this. Hanging out the dirty laundry."

"Ed-die," she said, drawing out the syllables in a plea. "Out with it! You can't tease me like this and then hide behind your—laundry. And anyway, it can't be nearly so bad as getting attacked by a monkey."

He laughed. "No, I suppose not. So what did I hear but Mrs. Hall going on and on about something I had or hadn't done, and Allie was agreeing with her—"

"She was *agreeing* with her? Why, she should have been defending you like a lioness!"

"Allie usually agrees with her mother. Especially when it comes to my shortcomings."

"You poor dear!" Sarah said. "You deserve better."

"I don't know about that." He looked away, flustered. "Heavens, now I've lost the thread."

"It doesn't matter. I understand the important point. You've got the two of them needling away at you."

"It does feel sometimes like I'm living behind enemy lines. But I've gotten used to it."

She delicately picked a vanilla cream out of the box and examined it, then popped it into her mouth. "I don't like to hear you talk that way."

"What way?"

"Resigned. Defeated. As though you're plodding on, day after day. Until you die."

"That's rather grim."

"It's also rather honest. Every day wasted is one we're not getting back. Dying is the only thing we must be resigned to. Everything else in the meantime, we can change."

"Allie never changes."

"Everyone changes. All the time."

"I should have said, I can't change Allie."

"You're probably going about it the wrong way."

"How so?"

"Oh, Eddie. You're a big businessman, and yet little Sarah has to teach you these things? What I mean is that you can't change someone else. It's impossible. They can only change themselves."

"Then you agree it's hopeless."

"Not a bit. What I mean is you change *yourself,* and others will adjust without even thinking about it. Try this as an experiment—change something about the way you relate to Allie, and see what happens."

"I wonder what I'd change?"

"For one, you can stop feeling so sorry for yourself."

"I don't feel sorry for myself."

"See how it works?" she said. "I told you something you should change about yourself, and what did you do? Refused to do it. And that's what anyone would do. But let's say every time I thought you were feeling sorry for yourself or being resigned—what if every time you did that, I got up and left? Walked right out and left you staring at my delicious chocolates and float. You'd change then, wouldn't you?"

"Yes, that would do the trick. I see your point."

"Then you understand. When you go home, try it yourself. You'll find out pretty quickly how Allie feels."

"All right, I will, but I don't want to go home just yet."

"Nor do I want you to."

CHAPTER 11

Small Talk

AT THE NEXT MEETING OF THE ASHWOOD SOCIAL CLUB, ARTHUR wasted no time seeking out Alicia for another dance, and then another. As the night wore down, the exhausted pair were relaxing with yet another cocktail and getting better acquainted. Alicia's lips had gone pleasantly numb, and Arthur's long legs were stretched out and crossed at the ankles, as though he were in his overstuffed chair on Columbus Avenue.

"And your parents?" Arthur asked. "I'm familiar with your mother, Mrs. Hall, but I'm not acquainted with your father."

"He passed away a little more than a year ago."

"My condolences. I didn't know."

"How could you?"

"Had he been unwell?" Arthur asked.

"No, the man was strong as a bull. It was an accident. He and mother were coming over to our house for Christmas dinner. It was icy, and he slipped on our front steps. He went down and broke his hip. Ten days later, he contracted pneumonia, and that was that."

"That's dreadful."

"It was. And I had asked Edward time and again to clean the ice off our front porch steps. As usual, he was too busy."

"An avoidable tragedy, if you don't mind my saying."

"Finally!" she said. "Someone willing to state the obvious. My father would be alive today if Edward had cleaned away that ice. Not that Edward would ever admit it."

"I'm sure he was a good man to have raised such a fine daughter."

She smiled. "I was an only child, so he doted on me."

"I'm sure he loved you very much."

"He's probably the only man I've ever truly loved."

"That's a provocative statement," he said.

She took the last sip of her cocktail and didn't reply.

"May I get you a refresher?" he said, nodding toward her empty glass.

She knew she'd already had plenty, but it felt so good to sail away slowly, one sip at a time, the music and the dancers swirling around her, caressed by Arthur's baritone. Like death must be, she thought, drifting away to some other, better place.

"Mrs. Miller?"

She started. "I *am* sorry," she said. "I was enjoying the moment and must have been daydreaming."

"They're the best dreams of all. Because we can direct them."

"On that poetic note," she said, "I would very much like another cocktail." He smiled, stood up, and stretched, like a cat, slowly and languorously.

"Be right back. Keep my seat warm."

Allie smiled to herself. I'd love to, she thought.

"Tell me more about your father," he said after she'd had a little of her fresh drink.

"I don't want to bore you."

"You could never bore me. I will freely admit that I find you fascinating. If you'll take no offense."

She flushed. "Please. My father—he was kind, a good businessman, and very upright. A man of a different era, you might say. He was never comfortable with modern life."

"In what respect?"

"For most of his life, he managed a harness and saddle operation. Loved it. And then when a family friend asked him to leave the saddlery business and join a new company—which made cast iron toys—he laughed."

"That's quite a change."

"He thought it was absurd. I remember him coming home one evening and telling mother and me about it, thinking we would have a good laugh too. But we didn't. We encouraged him to give it a try. He was used to working with metal. And the owner planned to make electric toys, too. The wave of the future."

"Did he take your advice?"

"I feel rather badly about it. I've never told anyone—"

"Mrs. Miller," he said, looking at her until she looked back. "You don't need to say another word. But I do want you to know that whatever you choose to say goes no further."

She studied his face for a moment, found something in it that intrigued her.

"Mother and I—no, in truth, it was mostly my doing—said that he never would get another chance like that. He thought we'd lost our minds, the harness trade had been good to him, and so on. But at a certain moment, I think he concluded that if he didn't do it, he'd disappoint us or look like a relic. No man wants to think of himself as old. So he made the leap in 1893."

"I don't like the sound of 1893."

"Exactly. The Panic. It was a complete disaster. Who had money then to buy expensive toys? The company failed in less than a year."

"Those were hard times. I think most of my work for two years after that was refereeing bankruptcies."

"My father was too proud to declare bankruptcy, so he and his partner were sued by more than twenty shareholders, who said—publicly— that he'd inveigled them into investing in a scheme. It crushed him. My father's reputation was everything to him."

"A man after my own heart. The one thing a man can't live with is shame."

"That's what he thought, too. It took most everything he had to settle all those lawsuits. His former employer had replaced him, so he couldn't go back to his old business. After the dust settled, all he had left were a couple pieces of real estate that provided him and my mother a small income. If he hadn't kept those, I don't know what might have happened."

"It's a very sad story."

"He—withered, after that. He never fully recovered."

"That must have been difficult to bear."

Alicia looked away. "When I think of my father, I feel guilty. He was the man I loved most, and yet between my bad advice and then Edward's laziness about the ice . . . I killed him."

"Try not to think that way, if you can," he said. "I don't mind saying that I believe you gave him good advice. To leave the harness trade, that is. That industry will be a distant memory in ten years. He would have had to find other work soon enough."

"You're saying that to make me feel better."

"Not at all. It's being swept away by the electric motor and the internal combustion engine. Cleaner, quieter, faster than horses—and soon, stronger, too."

"It's awfully kind of you to say."

"It's an unfortunate fact of life that a lot of times doing the *right* thing isn't the *best* thing."

She took another long drink. She tilted her head back to feel the liquid burn her throat, and let him to examine her long, smooth neck. She knew he was watching, could sense that his breaths were shallower, coming more quickly. Another couple of these, she thought, and God only knows what I might do.

"By the way," she said, knowing that she needed a new train of thought, "if you don't mind my asking—"

"Ask away."

"Wherever did you acquire that accent of yours?"

He laughed. "You've got that the wrong way around. You're the one with the accent."

"I am not! I'm from right here in Buffalo."

"I grew up in Maine. Little place called Brunswick. And so to me—everyone who's not from there has an accent."

"Is that where you were born?"

"Oh no," he said. "You wouldn't know the place."

"I was an ace geography student in high school, I'll have you know."

"All right. Nineteen degrees, forty-seven minutes south latitude, eighty-six degrees west longitude," he said.

"Smarty-pants. I'll bite. Where's that?"

"In the South Pacific Ocean, west of Peru. I was born on shipboard. My father was a ship's master."

"How fascinating!"

"It was. I spent much of my boyhood—my younger brother, too—on board. Everywhere from China to Cape Horn. My father captained a guano ship."

"Guano?"

He leaned toward her. "*Bird shit,*" he whispered into her ear, a bit boozily. "They mine it in the tropics. For fertilizer."

"There's a lot I can learn from you, Mr. Pendle," she said.

"I'm a veritable expert in avian excrement."

"And is your father still in the excrement business?"

"No, he died when I was thirteen. My brother, mother, and I were aboard when he died. He had a brain hemorrhage. After that, we came back to Maine. I've not been to sea since."

"My condolences," Allie said. "How awful."

"It was especially difficult for my mother. Two young boys, no means of support. She took in boarders to put me and John—that's my brother—through prep school and then college."

"And where are they now?"

"New York City. My brother is five years my junior, and he and my mother live on the Upper East Side."

"Do you miss Maine?"

"Not even a little," he said. "The Maine I knew—shipbuilding and seafaring—is all gone now. Textile mills and lobstering, that's all there is these days. I wanted to be an attorney, and Buffalo is a good place to be one."

He folded his hands. "Ah well, that's more than enough about me. Tell me something that you're just mad about."

"Hmm, that's a good question," she said. "I love reading. Music. Dancing. Interesting conversation. Maybe that's why we get along."

"You think we get along?"

"I think we could, so long as you behave yourself."

"As Oscar Wilde said, 'I can resist anything except temptation.'" He chuckled and finished his drink.

"I'll keep that in mind. Now tell me something you're mad about."

He looked at her steadily. "Present company excluded?"

"Oh my," she murmured.

"I'm sorry, that was too forward. My apology."

"No, no, I was simply taken by surprise."

"Then, to answer your question seriously—"

"Were you not being serious?" Allie said, having some difficulty with the word 'serious,' her lips having gone completely numb.

"What would you say if I was being serious?"

"Ask me after one more cocktail," she said.

"Before I go and get you a refill, I will tell you that I'm mad about anything electrical. In fact—I just purchased a little electric automobile." He got up and made for the bar.

I'm in trouble now, Allie thought, watching him chatting with another gentleman at the bar. She thought of the sound of his whisper, the feel of his warm breath against the nape of her neck. I haven't been this soaked since—never, she thought. I wonder if I have enough time to visit the ladies' room and take the edge off. And where the hell is Ed? I don't need him spying on me.

She was looking around for her husband when Arthur returned with two fresh glasses.

"Thank you, Mr. Electric," she slurred, taking the glass. "Or maybe you'd prefer General?" She giggled. "You know, I'd like to learn how to drive an automobile. Ed has one, but he won't let me drive it."

"Come out with me for a ride sometime. I'll teach you."

She wanted to jump up and get on with the lesson but, through the haze of alcohol, somehow kept herself in check. "Oh, I don't know about that."

"My, I am forgetting myself tonight. How about this instead? Let's all of us go out in our machines together when the weather breaks."

"That sounds delightful," Alicia said. "And in the meantime, it would be a lot of fun to continue our discussions. You're an easy person to talk with, Mr. Pendle."

"As are you, Mrs. Miller. And if you wish, you may call me Arthur." He pronounced it 'Aah-thaa.'

"Then I must be Allie. Or Alicia, of course, whichever. I'll come when you call, either way."

He looked up at the ceiling and then turned back to her.

"I wonder when I should call you Allie, and when I should call you Alicia?" he said. "They're different. Night and day."

"I don't know of a good rule," she said, giggling again.

"I think I have one," he said, leaning toward her, "but I'm not going to tell you. Not just yet."

"You don't seem like a man who cares for rules."

"I'm an attorney," he said. "How would it be if I went around breaking all the rules?"

"I don't know. It might be interesting."

"Then let me propose one to govern our further conversations. Let's call it our *pas de deux*," he said with a trace of a wink. "To use a dancing term."

"And that is?"

"That there will be no rules at all. No rules, no limits. We can think or say anything we want, anything at all. Whatever comes to mind." He stuck out his hand. "Deal?"

"Deal," she said, taking his hand, which felt hard, not at all as she'd imagined the hand of a bookworm lawyer. "You have strong hands," she said.

"A lot of rowing for a lot of years will do that."

They shook on it. No one noticed except Sarah Payne, who was standing off to the side, eating a small piece of chocolate cake. Ed was still nowhere to be seen. Nor was Helen Warren.

CHAPTER 12

Cassie's Scheme

"HOW ARE YOU FEELING THIS MORNING?" CASSIE ASKED ARTHUR over breakfast.

"Well enough. The last of the month is always trying."

"I don't like that this work is taking such a toll on you."

"It pays the bills."

"It won't forever."

"Terry will certainly be reappointed. So probably another five, six years."

"What then?"

"Start up my law practice again, I suppose."

She turned in her seat to face him. "Listen. I have another idea."

He picked up his coffee cup and made a mock toast. "Let fly, madam," he said.

"Real estate."

He took a bite of his toast. "Real estate?"

"Think about all these new housing divisions being built here in outer Buffalo. Tonawanda, Kenmore, Amherst."

He nodded. "It's a mad market for real estate, no doubt."

"And fortunes to be made. Why, look at what our house is worth today, only six years after we bought it."

"I think I know where you're going with this—"

"Now, don't you pooh-pooh me, Arthur."

"I'm not! You always think I'm such a Doubting Thomas," he said. "What I was going to say was—it's a good idea. I've thought about it myself from time to time. Buy up some land and build houses on it."

"Think about it. More freedom for us. To go to New York or Shelter

Island. Europe. We don't have children, but we're as trapped here every day as if we did. Remember how we used to say that if we didn't have children, we didn't want to live like people who do?"

"All too well. We should be free as birds."

"Then what's stopping us?"

"One little word," he said. "Capital. Or rather, lack of it. We don't have enough to invest on the scale we'd need to. And in view of my, shall we say, unusual way of earning a living, we'd never get a loan. I could never tell a bank what I do."

"Ah," she said, "but that's where you're wrong. We do have capital, or access to it. From my family. And possibly from yours."

"Borrow from them?"

"No. Invest it for them. My parents have money that they could invest, and I'm sure they'd like to. But they don't know anyone who can find them good properties. And there are so many swindlers out there, they wouldn't trust anyone. But their only daughter lives in Buffalo, the fastest growing city in the nation. And their son-in-law is an attorney."

"I'm listening," Arthur said.

"And they're not going to ask for collateral or financial statements from us like a bank would. We invest the money, improve the property, sell it, and pay them their money back with interest. And we keep the profit."

"A couple of my uncles might be interested in that type of deal," Arthur said.

"Who wouldn't be? You and I know lots of people with money to invest. We find the properties, you do the legal paperwork, and the rest is easy."

Arthur took a deep sniff and closed his eyes. No more Terry Penrose, except at the club or on the golf course. The respect that money could bring. Why shouldn't he be a tycoon, even? He'd been a champion before, at New Haven. *Magna cum laude,* winner of the Cleveland Cup in single scull. Since then, he'd almost forgotten what real victory felt like.

"I would love to get out from under Terry Penrose," he said.

Cassie bobbed in her seat like a little bird. "I just knew you'd love my idea! Why don't I write to my father and ask him?"

Arthur smiled, making the little crows-feet at the side of his eyes that she loved.

❦

They had to take the train to New Haven to pitch the idea to Cassie's father. He wasn't the type to write a check without, as he put it, 'looking the other fellow in the eye,' even if that fellow happened to be married to his beloved only daughter. Whatever he saw in Arthur's must have been enough, however, because on the train back to Buffalo, they huddled together in their sleeping compartment, looking at Mr. Lane's check.

"See how easy that was?" Cassie said.

"Like falling off a log," he replied. "I can hardly believe it. Let's do ask some of my relatives, too, and get them in on it."

And with a few letters and a few train trips here and there, which felt more like little holidays than they did work, in two months, they had amassed the staggering sum of $100,000 from almost a dozen relatives from Connecticut to Maine.

Capital had turned out to be the easiest problem to solve. With money now in hand, the challenge facing Cassie and Arthur was how to invest the money, in what properties, and how to structure the investments. Arthur soon found that although there were lucrative real estate deals happening all the time, they seemed to be already in the hands of more seasoned brokers or developers. And those people wanted such a large cut that there wouldn't be a lot of profit left over. This was a wrinkle they hadn't considered.

CHAPTER 13

Automobiling

May 18, 1901
Saturday

IN BUFFALO, A RARE DAY OF BLUE SKIES, LIGHT BREEZE, AND CLO-
ver and dandelion in fragrant bloom was not a day to be spent indoors.
Thankfully, Mrs. Hall had decided to remain at home, which left seven
of them to enjoy an afternoon of automobiling in the orchard country
northeast of Buffalo, toward Lockport.

Edward had insisted that the ladies should try riding in a different
machine than their own. He, Cassie, and the three girls squeezed into
the Millers' automobile and fell behind fast, as their small machine
struggled with so many passengers. Arthur and Alicia were sailing along
the road in his Babcock Electric runabout, Arthur manning the tiller.
The Babcock didn't have a steering wheel, but instead a long control
handle that rose up between the driver's legs.

"Would you like to steer?" Arthur said. "To see how it feels?"

"I don't know—"

"Put your hand over mine. I'll steer, and you can get the feel of it."

She put her hand on top of his and felt how responsive the little
machine was to the slightest movement of the tiller. He took his hand
away, and she soloed for a few hundred yards.

"Lesson One complete," Arthur said, taking back the control.
"You're a straight-A student so far."

"That is so exciting! It's like I imagine flying would be. Nothing at
all like driving a horse."

"That's why they call them 'horseless carriages.'"

Alicia laughed. "Yes. That was a bit of a stupid comment."

"It's not stupid. I was having fun with you."

"I'm having fun too."

"I know this sounds trite, Allie, but I feel I've known you forever."

"It's been only three months. Since Valentine's Day."

"Doesn't feel like it. Actually, I think enough time has passed to let you in on a little secret."

"You know how I love secrets. What is it?"

"Let's stop here for the others to catch up, and I'll tell you." He stopped the car and turned off the power. The country was silent but for the hum of bees and the rustle of new leaves.

He took a breath. "All right then. Here it is. And the best part of the secret is that it's actually both our secret."

"Now I'm intrigued."

"This happened on New Year's Day, this year, in the morning. As I was walking back to my office from the waterfront, it started to rain, and so I ducked into the tunnel under Ferry Street."

"Yes," she said. "I know it well. Not far from where I grew up."

"I got inside just as the rain and sleet started really picking up. As soon as my eyes adjusted, I saw that there was only one other person in the tunnel. A woman, walking toward me. I'll never forget the way she moved, so graceful, so sure of herself, even in that dismal place. I couldn't make out her face until she was almost next to me because of the light behind her, and also—she kept her umbrella half up in front of her face. And here's what stopped me dead in my tracks. Merely from the way she walked and a glimpse of her face—in the blink of an eye, I thought—I felt, I *knew*—something instantly about her."

"This is something out of Mary Shelley! Who was she?"

"It wasn't *who* she was, it was *what* she was."

"Come on now! Stop keeping me in suspense. And the others will be along any second."

"You need to learn patience, Allie. In any case, what I felt was very strange, nothing like I'd ever felt before. It was a feeling—that this woman was the *one*. My other half. My *soulmate*. It was a dead certainty, if I'd only known this person years earlier, she would have been mine. Forever."

"Now that's intriguing. And very mysterious."

"To say the least. And when I close my eyes, I can see it as clearly as though it were happening now." He studied her face for a moment. "Now that you know *what* she was—can you guess *who* she was?"

She thought for a second. "I'm going to say it was Cassie. I'll bet this mystery woman was your wife, and your head didn't recognize her at first. But your *heart* had. That would be so romantic. Something out of a novel."

"It would be. But you'd be wrong. Guess again."

"I don't have another guess."

"All right, I'll have to tell you quickly before the others get here. It was *you*."

Alicia's eyes went wide. *"Me?"*

"Yes, you. The first time I saw you at the Club, I knew it immediately. I'd barely been able to get that face out of my mind—when I saw it again. *You* were the woman in the tunnel. I swear it." He sat back in the leather seat, looking at her.

She looked away. "I'm not sure what to say."

"Now, don't get cross. Remember—'no rules.'"

"No, I mean yes. I don't mind that you said it. I only wonder what you *mean* by saying it. You don't seem like a man given to unplanned utterances."

"A fair point. It's very clear to me what it means. In that moment, I looked into the face of the person that I was meant to be with. The woman who was my destiny."

"Arthur, do be careful what you say now."

"Didn't you just observe that I'm not one for unplanned utterances? You're right, I'm not. In my line of work, I've learned to be very careful about what I say, and especially what I write. But I have decided that I shall always tell you the truth. And the truth is that I knew it then—and I know it now—that the woman in the tunnel and I were put into the world to be soulmates. *You* are that woman, and there is not the slightest question about it in my mind. It's the reason I can't stop looking at your face—"

"That's very strong language." She looked out over the orchard fields again, blinking.

"You could slap my face if you like."

"Don't tempt me." What a farcical statement, she thought. You could put your hands on me, climb on top of me, and I wouldn't dream of stopping you. I could almost beg you for it right now. It hurts, thinking about how much I—

Arthur interrupted her musings. "Allie?"

"Yes?" she said, trying to catch her breath.

He bent over and whispered in her ear, heedless of whether Ed and the others would drive up. "I'd like you to answer one question for me. If you will, then I promise I'll never speak of this again."

She could feel his breath against her neck and pulled away. "You're torturing me, Arthur."

"Then answer me quickly, and our torments will end. Were you in the Ferry Street Tunnel on New Year's Day?"

She glanced at him, brushing away a wisp of hair taken by the breeze. "I was walking home," she said softly. "I'd stayed the night at my parents' old house."

"Then you *are* the woman in the tunnel."

"So it would seem."

He looked over his shoulder, up the road behind them. Still no sign of Edward and the others. "Why were you alone? What was passing through your mind, the thought I read on your face? I do have to know, and desperately, Alicia."

"You called me Alicia," she said with a start. "You said you had a rule about that but wouldn't tell me what it was. Why did you use my full name just now?"

He looked back up the road and then leaned close to her.

"I wanted to reserve it until you had let me inside you."

"Inside me? How am I supposed to take that?"

"You can take it any way you like, but I meant—inside your heart. Inside your soul. Sharing them with me, and *only* me. 'Alicia' is a deep name and must be reserved for deep things. Now—quickly! Tell me, *Alicia*. Why were you in the Ferry Street Tunnel that morning?"

She looked him full in the face. "I chose to spend New Year's Eve alone. I had a—I don't know what it was, a superstition, I suppose—that if I didn't see Edward at midnight—or my girls, or my mother, 1901 would truly be a new year."

"How so?"

"No more now. Another time."

He nodded, and they sat in silence, listening to the breeze.

"What now?" he said.

"What do you mean?"

"Are you going to tell Ed? About this conversation?"

"Should I?"

"It's all right if you do. It's your secret now, too. I gave it to you. You can do with it as you please."

"No, I don't think I'll tell him."

"Why is that? A man you barely know tells you that he caught a glimpse of you walking in a gloomy tunnel and determines you were intended as his soulmate. Don't you think your husband ought to know that?"

"He wouldn't understand."

"Most men wouldn't."

"That's not what I mean. Edward doesn't believe in things like soulmates."

"He doesn't? How could that be?"

"Edward . . ."

"—is a fine gentleman. I don't mean to imply anything to the contrary."

"I was about to say, 'doesn't have a romantic bone in his body.' He's an envelope maker. He doesn't write the letters, you know, the sentiments. He only makes the things to wrap them in."

"That's a fascinating perspective."

"I've had seventeen years to think about it."

Arthur turned around in the seat again to look for the others. "I still don't see them. Could Edward's machine have given up the ghost?"

"Doubt it. It's slow. Let's just sit here awhile. I need to think."

"It's a beautiful spot. Growing up, it was all seashore, huge rocks, and pine trees. This is much calmer scenery."

"Isn't Cassie your soulmate, too?"

Arthur looked at Alicia with a puzzled expression. "How could she be? Every person has but one soulmate."

"Out of all of the people in the entire world?"

"Without a doubt. Cassie is probably more my conscience than anything. She tells me what to do. And I all too often ignore her, to my detriment."

Alicia laughed. "Cassandra's Curse. They say we all have the devil on one shoulder and an angel on the other."

"Which one are you?"

"You really do want me to slap you, don't you?"

Behind them, there was the clang-clang of an automobile bell.

"We'll have to wait and see about that," Arthur said. "Here come our better halves."

"I want to talk more, Arthur."

"We will. And soon," he said. "Very, very soon."

CHAPTER 14

Playing the Market

CASSIE AND ARTHUR WERE STILL PUZZLING OVER WHAT TO DO with $100,000 in cash when Arthur had an epiphany. When it came, he was at the Saturn Club. He'd been having a drink with Edwin Baker, a principal in one of Buffalo's leading brokerage firms.

Arthur was out of breath after sprinting nearly the whole way from the trolley stop to his house. Time was, he thought, I could have run five times that distance without getting winded. That's going to change, too.

"Cassie," Arthur called from the foyer. "Are you here? We need to talk."

Cassie came gliding downstairs and looked at her panting husband with concern.

"What's wrong?"

"Nothing's wrong. I have a solution to our real estate problem!"

"Supper will be on the table in a half-hour," Cassie said. "Can we discuss it then?"

He could hardly contain himself but knew Cassie would be much more receptive once she'd had a few glasses of wine.

"Listen to what I learned this afternoon at the Club," he began when the maid left them to their meal. "I was talking with Ed Baker—"

"The stock and bond man?"

"Yes, from Bartlett & Frazier."

Cassie nodded.

"He said that if we have money lying about, it'd be smart to put some in the stock market now."

"Isn't that a rather risky proposition?"

"There's risk in anything. Even if we stuffed the money in our mattress, we'd have to worry about the house burning down. Ed said the risk is very low now—that the market is 'money drunk.'"

"Never heard of that."

"It means that Morgan and the other big financiers are flooding the markets with money, buying up whatever they can. There's so much demand that share prices have nowhere to go but up."

"You know what they say about things that go up."

"I know, but old sayings aren't good investment principles. I read the quotes every day. Things do go up and down, but the trend for years has been all up. We've missed out because we've been putting our money in the bank, where it's gathering dust."

"I don't disagree with you," Cassie said, sipping her wine. "And I'm not opposed to investing if you think it wise. But not too much. Let's start off slowly until we know what we're doing."

"But see, that's the problem. If we put only a little in, we only get a little out. If we invest what we have in the bank, it's never going to amount to enough to give us *freedom*."

"That's why we're doing this real estate business. That will bring us freedom, in due course."

"That might take years. It's already taken longer than either of us thought to break into this real estate game. Instead, consider this. We're sitting on $100,000 in cash. All that money, not earning anything for our families, and it's certainly not paying us anything."

"It's earning two percent," Cassie said feebly.

"Two measly percent? That's pathetic. Ed tells me we could make two hundred percent!"

"And he may be right. But it doesn't change that we don't have a lot of money to invest."

"We have a hundred thousand dollars."

"Which is not our money."

"Our families entrusted it to us to invest it, not to hoard it."

She put down her fork. "For real estate. We never said a thing to anyone about stocks."

"Well, we ought to have. Ed Baker said he's got every dime of his own invested right now. He's even borrowed money to invest more."

"Why wouldn't he? He's got the inside track. He knows when to buy and sell. We don't."

Arthur tossed his napkin onto the table. "Honestly. You were all excited about real estate, and we didn't know anything about that either. But you aren't excited at all about stocks. Maybe because it was my idea and not yours."

"That's silly."

"If I can graduate *magna cum laude* from New Haven Law and pass the Bar exam on the first go, I can certainly manage something as simple as stocks and bonds. Ed Baker is no genius, I can tell you that. But he's made a king's ransom in the market."

"We wouldn't even know which shares to buy."

"I do," Arthur said with an air of triumph.

"You do?"

"I do. Copper."

"Copper?"

"Name the biggest new industry in the entire world. The thing that's completely going to change everyone's life. An industry that needs copper, mountains of it."

"I don't know. Cooking equipment? For restaurants or hotels?"

"No, not cooking equipment." He pointed to the flickering gas jet above their table. "Electricity."

"You told me to think of something that uses copper."

"In a year, this gaslight will be replaced with electric lamps. And every one of the generators that make the electricity has copper windings inside. The lines that carry the electricity from the generating stations to our house are copper. The electric motor in my automobile—more copper. Imagine—one day, everyone in the United States may have an electric car! Imagine how much copper that would require."

"That seems a bit far-fetched, but I take your point."

"Oh, also—what's happening at this very moment, right here in Buffalo?"

"The Pan-American Exposition?"

"Exactly. And you know that the whole of the Exposition grounds is illuminated with electric light. It's the theme of the whole fair. People are starting to call Buffalo 'the Electric City' now, not 'Queen of the Lakes' anymore. Times have changed, Cassie. If we invest now, while it's early, by next year we'll probably have doubled our money. At least."

"I don't know enough to argue about it. Still, we can't very well invest someone else's money in something that might go down. How could we ever tell our families that we lost their money? At the very least, we'll have to go back to every one of them and get their permission before we change course."

"We don't have the time," he said. "And I talked with Ed about how we can protect everyone. The thing to do, he said, is to borrow on top of what we invest, so that if share prices do go down, we have money enough on hand to wait it out until it goes up again. He said that some investors are borrowing up to 100 times their investment. If they have a single dollar to invest, they borrow $100 and make 100 times as much on their investment."

"That's madness. Absolutely not."

"I agree with you," he said. "I'm not suggesting that scale of borrowing. But say we take our $100,000 and borrow only one times what we have. Now we have $200,000. If we invest that, and it goes down a little, we're still way over the original hundred thousand. Then we can wait for it to go back up.

"Meanwhile, these copper stocks pay dividends, and we use that as income so that I don't have to keep working with Penrose. Or pay it all out to our investors, I don't care. Besides, in a year—if copper stocks keep rising—the $200,000 should be worth a million. Then, we sell. We pay off the $100,000 loan, and we're left with $900,000. We pay our investors their $100,000—and let's say we give them a 50% return. That's $150,000 to them. After all that—we're left with *$750,000* in profit, Cassie. All of it ours, free and clear." He paused. "And how much did it cost us to make $750,000?"

"A hundred thousand?"

"No," he said. "It cost us nothing. The $100,000 was our investors' money. The other hundred was a loan. Oh, there's a bit of interest, but that's not much. That's the beauty of this plan, Cassie. Other people put up the money, and we keep the profits. In this case, three-quarters of a million dollars. In a single year."

"It's almost inconceivable," she said. "One has almost to be a mathematician to understand it. Are you sure?"

"Of course I'm sure."

"It sounds enticing, but I don't know. It still seems risky."

"What if our investors knew that we'd had a chance to make them a 50% return in practically no time at all but let it pass by? They'd not be pleased, I'll wager."

Cassie sipped her wine. "This real estate business has been more difficult to break into than I'd imagined. I've even thought it might be the better part of valor to return the money."

"And if we did, we'd forever be laughingstocks in all of New England."

"Neither of us wants that. If you are confident we can do this without losing any principal, then I'll trust you."

"You won't be sorry," he said, raising his glass and throwing ruby sparkles on the tablecloth.

❦

"All done," he said the following afternoon when he got home. "Mrs. Arthur Pendle, we are now the proud owners of 5,000 shares of Montana Copper stock, at $40 a share."

"Two hundred thousand dollars," she whispered. "I hope we're doing the right thing."

"You'll know it was when we sell it at $200 a share . . . which it will be next year, Ed thinks."

"That would be marvelous."

"If there's anything I've learned, it's that money is the only real form of power. Even the power that Terry has bows before the money men. And I don't want to be bowing and scraping to anyone anymore."

CHAPTER 15

Arthur and the Agent

ARTHUR WAS ENJOYING AN AFTER-DINNER CIGAR IN THE SMOKING lounge of the Niagara Club when he spotted George McKnight, who ran the insurance agency down the hallway from Arthur's office. He walked over and pulled George aside by the sleeve.

"Say, George, if you have a minute to spare this week, I'd like to drop by your office."

George backed away as Arthur's smoke rolled over his face. George hated cigars: the smoke, the messy ash, the disgusting taste they left in his mouth the morning after. And as a dealer in life insurance, he knew the statistics. Like it or not, though, in his line of work, cocktails and cigars were a way of life. As much as he detested both, he smoked and drank as much as anyone he knew. Had to.

"For you? Any time. Everything's all right, I trust?"

"I'd like to take out a life insurance policy."

"A very wise decision, Arthur. Life insurance is the only thing a man can be sure of after his demise."

"Well said."

"Do you know how much coverage you'll want?"

"$100,000, I'd say."

George's eyes bulged a bit involuntarily. The commission on that much coverage would put his eldest son through college. He reeled himself in just in time.

"Did you say *a hundred thousand*?"

"Yes. Life and accident."

"You realize . . . that's as much as Spencer Kellogg has."

"I'm certainly not the Linseed King," Arthur said. "If something happened to him, he'd have his oil factories and so on backing up his estate. Cassie and I have all our assets tied up in real estate and the market. Which means mortgages, loans, and so on. If something should happen to me, my income stops, but the bills keep coming."

"All too true," George said, regaining a measure of his composure. "Still, that would be an enormous amount of coverage. Especially for a man your age."

"I have large aspirations," Arthur said, puffing on his stogie. "And I'm thirty-six now."

George chuckled. "As they say, youth is truly wasted on the young! When I was your age, I certainly wasn't preoccupied with mortality." He was not quite five years Arthur's senior.

"My father died at sea when I was a boy. We were left in a difficult way after that. I won't put Cassie in a similar predicament should the worst happen."

"No, and that's commendable. All too many men don't think much about how their wives will manage after they're gone."

"Not this man." Arthur waved his hand with such dismissive force that he knocked off a large chunk of cigar ash, which, like a tiny comet trailing smoke, arced onto George's sleeve and stuck. It seemed still to be smoldering, but George didn't dare look or brush it away. Too much at stake.

"Er . . . every fellow has his own reasons. Come by my office anytime you like. We're neighbors, after all."

The insurance man swore he could scent burning wool, but steeled himself to maintain eye contact.

"I'll drop by this week, then." Arthur clamped his dead cigar between his teeth and shook George's hand. Mercifully, the smell of sizzling lanolin seemed to have dissipated.

No sooner had Arthur sauntered away into the crowd than George examined his sleeve. Sure enough, the ember had burrowed clear through the worsted to the white cuff of his shirt. Damn cigars. A brand-new suit, too. Then he started calculating the commission on $100,000 of insurance and felt better.

CHAPTER 16

Room Two

June 6, 1901
Thursday

ALICIA HAD BEEN IN AN UNCHARACTERISTICALLY GIDDY MOOD for a week and a half after their automobile excursion. She could think of little else but Arthur's revelation about having met his soulmate in the Ferry Street Tunnel. This led her fancy into ever more baroque conjectures about what sort of man a soulmate might turn out to be, and in various situations. With Edward, she babbled about how much fun she and Cassie had had, the girls too, and did he have a good time? She avoided mentioning Arthur, though to such degree it made him all the more conspicuous by his absence.

And though his time had been consumed with stock investments and plans for financial fortune, in every unoccupied moment Arthur's mind had strayed into very similar paths.

Alicia had hoped to see Arthur at the Ashwood Social Club dance the Saturday after their automobiling jaunt, but the Pendles had not shown up. She'd spent most of the evening watching the door, hoping that every new arrival might be Arthur, only to be a dozen times disappointed. And so the evening had passed, and she'd gone home with Ed again, drunk again, and had lain in bed alone and touched herself, dreaming of Arthur, again.

Since then, she'd mulled endlessly over her options, rehearsing, weighing words. After four days of driving herself nearly to abstraction, it was already noon on Thursday. Come Friday, who knew whether Arthur would be in his office at all? If the weather was fine, he'd probably be out in his automobile. With Cassie, too. At last, tired of debating with herself and disappointed that he hadn't made contact, she decided to swallow her pride and make the first move.

She'd looked at the entry in the Buffalo City Directory so many times that she knew it by heart. "Arthur R. Pendle, Esq., Attorney at Law. Room Two, Aston Building. Bell 1553." She wondered what mysteries Room Two might hold, imagining the smell of wood and leather and the ranks of hefty volumes of statute and precedent. Clients, like supplicants, coming to solicit Arthur to explain the arcane language of the law in that rich baritone of his . . .

If she could have seen Room Two through the telephone wire, however, she might never have called. Room Two was nothing more than a nook carved out of Room One, a large space on the ground floor of the Aston Building. Room One was occupied by a busy real estate firm and, most of the time, was a hive of activity, with brokers coming and going, doors slamming, the hubbub of simultaneous telephone conversations. When Arthur and Terry parted company, Arthur rented a desk in Room One, hoping to keep costs down while resurrecting his practice. It turned out to be like trying to think in a hurricane. He had prevailed on the realtor to partition off what became Room Two and filter out the worst of the din.

In Room Two was an oak roll-top desk, a desk chair, a guest chair, and a telephone stand. That was all. No art on the walls, not even a calendar. The main attraction was a slightly grimy window that looked out on Franklin Street. On the rare occasions when Arthur was there, he enjoyed putting his feet up on the desk, looking out at the passing crowds, and daydreaming.

He did have need of his Spartan quarters from time to time. There, he could close the door and count the monthly collections, make out deposit slips, write correspondence, all in perfect privacy. The real estate agents on the other side of the partition made so much noise that they paid no mind to what Arthur was up to in his little lair. They wouldn't have known or cared whether he was on the telephone, meeting with someone, or lying dead on the floor. That gave him a certain peace, hiding in plain sight.

The ring of the telephone made him jump. Thursdays were slow, and so it was the best day of the week to be in his office. Sometimes Mr. Babcock at the automobile garage would call to ask if he had need of his machine that weekend so that he could wash and spiff it up before then. On Fridays, he generally didn't go into the office in the morning, preferring to sleep late and ready himself for his weekly lunch with Penrose.

"Hello?" he said, picking up the receiver. "I mean to say, Pendle speaking."

"Arthur?"

It took him a couple heartbeats before he placed the voice, distorted and tinny.

"Allie," he said. "What a pleasant surprise."

"I hope so." Her voice seemed strained. "I thought I might call and say what a fine time I had automobiling. It would be so nice to do that again sometime."

"It would indeed," he said faintly. "Such a pleasant memory." God, the second time I used 'pleasant' in ten seconds, he thought.

"I hope I'm not disturbing you."

It seemed that Arthur, only recently so talkative, eloquent even, had already relegated her to memory.

"Not in the slightest," he said, picking up on the hint. "I'm sorry to say, but I'm terrible on this thing. I simply have never gotten the hang of the telephone. I either talk too softly or too loudly. I don't know when to stop and start. It's dreadful."

Alicia felt as though she could breathe again. "I know. It's so true. It's not a natural way to communicate, wouldn't you agree?"

"Completely. It would be so much better to do our talking face-to-face and not over this infernal contraption."

"Are you free this afternoon?" she heard herself asking.

"This afternoon?"

"I'm sorry, that was rather forward of me, wasn't it? I'm sure you're very busy—"

"Not too," he replied. "I was just now finishing up—a case I've been working on."

"That sounds exciting."

"All in a day."

"I could perhaps come downtown, to your office?"

Arthur looked around Room Two. "Uh, no, there's so much going on here, we'd not have a moment of peace. How about instead we meet in Lafayette Square? It's a beautiful day, and I'm tired of being cooped up. Would that be acceptable? Say, half-past two?"

Alicia looked at the hall clock. She'd have just enough time to make herself presentable and get downtown. "Yes, that's perfect," she said.

She hung up the receiver and sprinted upstairs to her bedroom.

At her dressing table, she examined herself in the mirror. What could he possibly see in a woman six years older, she thought. She turned to see as much of her profile as she could manage. Her nose had always been a little too straight, a little too long. Her chin's outline was softer, the neck's fuller than they used to be. No matter how she dieted or slathered on the latest beauty creams, the skin seemed to droop a tiny bit more every day. And her hair . . . where to begin?

This doesn't help, she thought as she began to apply her makeup. He called me his *soulmate.* That would be a terribly cruel thing to say if he hadn't been sincere.

She wondered what stance to adopt with him. Cool and distant?

What a little fool I am, she thought. I called *him,* at his office. I can hardly affect disinterest now. And what would be the use? She puckered her lips to redden them a bit. No, she thought, I'm not going to play coy. Whatever he wants, I'm giving him, and more. He might well find himself surprised.

She took a new lavender dress from her armoire and laid it on the bed, looking at the flat, empty garment and trying to imagine what he would think of it with her inside. She slid it on and scrutinized herself in the cheval mirror. Not too bad, she thought, smoothing the fabric over her curves.

Alicia took up her little handbag and scanned the room for her new parasol, a beautiful one in ivory eyelet lace she'd purchased only two days before at Hengerer's. It must still be downstairs, by the door. At the foot of the stairs, she found the dainty thing still in its box and paper wrapping.

"Mother!" she shouted back up the stairs. Mrs. Hall poked her head out of her sewing room at the top of the flight, from which lookout she could see anyone who came or went.

"Why are you dressed up?" Mrs. Hall said.

"I'm going downtown for a few hours."

"Oh dear," Mrs. Hall said, "will you be back when the children get home?"

"Can you watch them for me? It's important."

"I suppose I will have to," her mother said. "I'll have Annie make them a snack."

"Thanks, mother. 'Bye!" She took the porch steps as quickly as she could and hurried toward the trolley stop. She just knew that Mrs. Stoddard was watching her, wondering where Mrs. Miller could be going, all dressed up, on a Thursday afternoon? It was all so wearying, the constant scrutiny. From the neighbors, from Ed, even from her mother and the children. All of them, always looking at her, evaluating, judging.

❦

She stepped down from the creaking streetcar at Terrace Station and walked past City Hall and up Main Street toward Lafayette Square. The early afternoon sun had at last burned away the dampness that had persisted through lunchtime. Arthur was waiting for her when she arrived. He was standing near a bench he'd staked out, a good one facing east, to keep the sun out of their eyes. He smiled broadly as she came up.

"Fancy meeting you here," he said.

"Quite a coincidence," she said, trying to master her breathing.

"May I offer you a seat?" Arthur said, gesturing to the bench. She folded her parasol neatly and sat.

"You look beautiful in that dress, if I may say so."

"Why, thank you." That didn't take long, she thought. I could have walked into the room engulfed in flames, and Edward would never have noticed.

"And the parasol. Is that French?"

"Oh, no. I got it here, downtown."

"Looks French."

"Thank you. I thought it was pretty."

"I'm delighted you called me," he said.

"I hope I wasn't being too forward."

"Not at all. It was a very pleasant surprise. I'd wanted to call you, but—well, I didn't know how that might go over. Be perceived. By others in your house."

"You could always write."

"To your home address? Mightn't that be a little irregular?"

"I suppose so, if I didn't collect the mail."

After a few seconds, he turned toward her with a sly look. "I have an idea!"

"What's the idea?"

"About how we could write to each other. I'll go to the post office and take out a numbered box. You write to me there. I'll give you the combination for the lock, and I'll write to you at the same box."

"That's very clever," she said. "But if the box is in your name, would they deliver mail with my name on it to your box? They might forward it to my home."

"Good point. We need an alias. A *nom de guerre*. And it can't very well be Mr. and Mrs. Pendle."

He looked at her and blinked slowly, almost as though bringing her into focus.

She was taken quite aback. "I wonder what name we could use," she managed to say through the lump in her throat.

"I've got an idea. How about Mr. and Mrs. Arthur Ashwood? We are wealthy visitors from New York City."

She laughed. "That's ideal! Mr. Ashwood, it's a pleasure to make your acquaintance." She extended her hand, and he shook it. "Mrs. Ashwood," he said with a bow of his head.

"If you want to know the best thing about this little postal conspiracy of ours," he said, "it's the relief I feel about not having to manage talking on the telephone."

"Me too. Now with that obstacle out of the way, Mr. Ashwood, where do we go from here?"

He stroked his chin in mock contemplation. "If we're sharing a post office box, there should be many more things we share, don't you think?"

"Such as?"

"Oh, all our secrets. Our hearts' desires. Our innermost longings. Whatever you want."

"That could take a long time."

"Not if we hurry." He gave her another one of those slow, sleepy blinks.

"You are a dreadful tease."

"Not in the slightest. When I know what I want, I don't hesitate. Teasing would be just a waste of precious time. Life is too short already."

Alicia gathered up her courage. "And do you know what you want?"

"Oh yes," he said, closing his eyes. He extended his legs and placed his hands on his thighs. "I know. I've always wanted to be an explorer."

"Like Baldwin? To the polar regions?"

"No. Maine was cold enough. I want to explore something warm. Do you have any ideas?"

"Come on now," she said. "Let's not play games. I telephoned you. I came here to meet you. I know you're having fun, but if you go on this way, you'll only hurt me."

"I never want to hurt you," he said. "But you're right, I find it hard sometimes to be as plain as I might be. What I want to explore is *you*. And I don't want to stop exploring until I know everything, every detail. Even things you may not know about yourself. Unless you stop me, which is your right."

Alicia said nothing, feeling the sun caressing the back of her neck.

"Now that I've told you what I want," he said, leaning close, "are you going to tell me if you'll let me have it?"

"Yes."

"Yes, that you'll tell me, or yes, that you'll—"

"The latter. Do I get to explore you too?"

He put his hands behind his head. "As much as you like. But first, we need to get you out of Buffalo so that we can study each other in a different environment."

She tilted her head.

"Next week, Cassie and I are going to New Haven for the commencement weekend. Be our guest."

"How can I do that? With Ed, you know."

"You'll have to invite him, of course. But I predict he won't want to come along. That's not his cup of tea. You'll be with both of us, so there's not a whiff of anything improper. He'll tell you to go. Watch and see if he doesn't."

CHAPTER 17

Commencement

"THE PENDLES ARE GOING TO THE NEW HAVEN COLLEGE COM-mencement next week," Alicia said as flatly as she could manage.

"Is that right?" Edward mumbled over his newspaper. "That'll be nice for them."

"Yes. And they asked us if we wanted to come along. Sounded like fun."

He put his paper down in his lap. "With them? To a college commencement?"

"It's not all about that. It's a series of parties and events over the weekend. And a boat race. He used to be a rower."

Edward's mouth took on the sarcastic curl that she hated.

"I think I'd rather have my eyes gouged out."

"That's unambiguous. Somehow, I'm not surprised. But I thought I'd mention it. I'd hoped you might want to go."

His eyes opened a bit wider. "Why don't you go? I'll stay here. I've got lots of work to do."

Arthur had been right. "You wouldn't mind?"

"Not in the slightest," he said, taking off his glasses and rubbing the bridge of his nose, where they always left an imprint. "You like that sort of thing. So why not? It's not like you'd be going unchaperoned."

"That's a good point."

He caught her slight smile. "See? I can tell you like my idea. Tell them you'll go! Don't think another thing of it."

"Why, thank you, Ed, I will. As long as they don't mind having a third wheel along."

"I'm sure they'll be delighted." The paper went up again.

❦

The threesome left Buffalo after lunch, changing trains at Albany, and from there south toward New Haven.

Alicia had never been to a real college campus before. And New Haven's was everything she'd imagined or read about. Stone walls, ivy, wide expanses of lawn, well-dressed and well-heeled young people. And this weekend, a couple hundred slightly older people on an endless round of parties and dances.

Over the following two days, the festivities continued in high spirit. Allie's head seemed always to be pleasantly misty with champagne, and she found it equally intoxicating that several of Arthur's classmates mistook her for Mrs. Pendle, congratulating her on her excellent match. Cassie stood by quietly, enjoying a laugh about it when the blunderers learned, to their embarrassment, that Mrs. Miller was merely the Pendles' guest for the weekend.

The second and final night of homecoming was the Sweetheart Ball, the gala event and capstone of the weekend. It was for graduates and their wives only, so Allie would have to sit this one out, although there was a smaller, separate soirée for guests. Though disappointed that she could not be announced to the distinguished graduates of the Class of 1887 as Mrs. Arthur Pendle, she took a little comfort that Arthur might, at least, see her in her finest dress before they went their separate ways.

That evening, Cassie walked into their shared dressing room as Alicia was pinning on her hat and putting the final touches on her evening attire.

"You look simply beautiful," Cassie said.

"Not so lovely as you. You'll be the belle of the ball tonight."

"Oh, I don't have your looks or grace, Allie."

"Hush."

Cassie sat at the next dressing table, began primping up her hair, and said, "When do you have to go?"

"I have to leave in just a minute. I'm not entirely sure of where I'm to go."

"I know where your event is. You go down to the main common

area, turn right, and then go through the gateway at the far end. Yours is the building on the right after that."

"Thank you. That'll save me from looking like I don't belong here. Any more than I already do, that is."

Allie took a final look in the mirror. Her thick, almost black hair, which had been streaked with auburn growing up, now had more than a few wisps of grey sneaking through. She tucked as many of them as possible under the brim of her hat.

"Well then," she said, getting up, "See you later! I'll want to hear all about it."

"Me too. Have fun."

Alicia left their dressing room and walked down the echoing hall to the staircase. She was almost to the bottom when she realized that she'd left her handbag behind in the dressing room. "Darn it all," she muttered, and started back up the stairs. She arrived breathless at the door of the dressing room and, expecting that Cassie would have already been gone to meet Arthur, barged right in without so much as knocking.

Cassie was still sitting at her dressing table, looking intently at herself in the mirror and moving her head slowly from side to side, to one shoulder and then the other, like a pendulum. She must have heard Alicia open the door, but didn't seem startled, nor did she turn to see who had entered the dressing room. Her silk lace sleeve was drawn up above her left elbow, and the pale skin on the inside of her forearm was dotted with tiny pink spots, like poison ivy or chickenpox. Open in front of her was a small Russia leather manicure case. Resting on it was a hypodermic syringe.

Leaning forward to look in the mirror at the door, Cassie dropped an embroidered handkerchief over her medical kit.

"You're back already," she said, as if the whole evening had already passed.

"Oh . . . yes. I forgot my handbag."

"Don't you just hate it when you forget things?"

Alicia tried her best, but found she kept staring at the handkerchief in front of Cassie.

Cassie noticed. "Is this what you want to see?" she said, pulling the handkerchief away. Beneath it was the little red leather case and the glass and metal syringe. Inside the open case, a few small vials were neatly arranged. "I hope you don't think me terribly wicked," she said slowly, with a languid smile. Her ice-blue eyes looked huge, a tiny black dot in the center of each.

"Should—should I call for a doctor?" Alicia blurted out, not knowing what else to say.

Cassie laughed. "Dear Allie. Heavens no. No doctor could make me feel better than I do at this moment."

"Cassie, what have you taken?"

"Please, dear, calm down. It's nothing to worry yourself over," Cassie said, her eyes half-closing. "I have had a grain or two of morphine to settle my nerves, that's all. I get a bit high-strung at these social events. I can't face all those cannibal eyes without a little something. Dozens, hundreds of them, all looking at me, wondering what a man like Arthur sees in me."

"Oh, that's not so," Allie said.

The newspapers were full of gruesome stories about morphine fiends, hop-heads, and every other manner of drug addict, which always ended badly and with the expected moral. So far as she knew, however, Allie had never actually met a drug-fiend, and certainly not one in the process of injecting herself in an Ivy League dressing room. In the newspapers, drug users were lowlifes, safely confined to the red-light district, locked away in jail, or lying dead in the gutter.

"Does Arthur know?" she asked at last, looking toward the leather case. "Isn't it dangerous?"

"He does. And he knows that I'm careful. I don't want you to worry yourself, or him, about this. Let's make it our secret, and you never have to think that there's anything going on that isn't completely above board." She began carefully packing up her dainty little set. "You see, I am my parents' only child, and they are religious people," she said, neatly fitting the syringe next to the vials and gently closing the leather flap. "I wasn't introduced to society as many girls are, and so I never became accustomed to it. Arthur is much better about it than I am, but we have to go to so many of these sorts of things. If I didn't have something to take the edge off—I don't know what I'd do."

This seemed strangely reasonable to Alicia, although she had a hundred questions she wanted to ask.

Cassie seemed to understand. She stood and took both of Allie's hands in hers. Allie found her eyes beguiling and peculiar, each tiny pupil like a poppy seed in an ocean of blue. "I'll tell you more anytime you like," she said softly. "Anything you want to know. There's nothing to be frightened of. Nothing at all. Chloral, opium, laudanum . . . belladonna. Don't you simply love their names? They're musical, aren't they? Each its own particular note. Each divine in its own way."

"I see—I mean, they are nice names."

"And do you know where I get most of it?" Cassie said, leaning close to whisper in Alicia's ear.

"Where?"

"Seth Payne," she murmured. "Sarah's husband. Dentists are stocked with everything imaginable, dear."

"I had no idea," Alicia managed.

Cassie raised her left hand to Allie's cheek, caressed it with the backs of her fingers. Her lace sleeve, still unbuttoned, sank to her elbow, revealing the line of red dots.

"We can share everything now, you and I," Cassie whispered.

Allie pulled away, startled. "Let's do talk more sometime. For now, though, I take it you're—"

"Everything's perfect. Don't think another second about it. Go and enjoy your event. I'm going to have to go soon—in just a few minutes—to meet Arthur."

"If you're sure."

"I'm quite sure, dear."

"Then I'll get on my way and see you in the morning."

Cassie blew Allie a kiss. "Until then."

Gathering up her forgotten handbag from the dressing table, Alicia trotted down the stairs again and hurried out into the evening. She didn't know how to digest what she had seen, but the Pendles were sophisticated people, and maybe she was just being provincial. After all, Cassie had been quite unfazed by the whole thing. She'd made it seem as natural to take morphine as to have a cocktail before going out on the town. And she was robust, perhaps a little bit pale, but certainly not anything resembling the withered, jaundiced wrecks the newspapers went on about. Maybe on the train, I'll ask her more, Alicia thought. For now, I need to put it aside and concentrate on making a good showing.

In the vast common area, the air smelled like clipped grass and cigar smoke. A few hovering gaslights, honey haloes along the dark pathways across the lawn, reminded her of the fireflies that used to flit behind her parents' house, when she was a little girl, and how she would catch them if she could and marvel at the tiny winking light trapped in her fist. How sad she'd been one time, though, when she gripped one too tightly, and the little glowing creature had quietly sputtered out. Whenever she saw fireflies, both memories would flood over her: one a bright, sunny thought, dogged close behind by its shadow.

It was a little cooler than she'd expected, especially after such a warm day. She drew her wrap around her and hastened toward the huge, arched gateway that joined two stately buildings at one end of the commons. It looked very much like the Bridge of Sighs in Venice, which she'd seen in a stereoscope view. So many places she'd like to go. So many wonders in this world.

"May I offer you an escort, miss?" came a voice from the darkness off the pathway, startling her.

"No, thank you, I'm fine," she said, picking up her pace.

"What if I insist?"

She turned, fully prepared to give this masher a piece of her mind. She laughed when she saw Arthur's mischievous smile. He was twirling his mustache like a theatre villain.

"Oh, it's only you," she said, stopping.

"*Only* me, is it?"

"I didn't mean it that way. What are you doing here? Aren't you supposed to be at the Sweetheart Ball? With . . . your sweetheart?"

"Now, don't be jealous."

"Don't flatter yourself."

"As you wish," he said, extending an arm. "But let me at least show you some proper New Haven College chivalry and see you to your destination. No respectable lady should be walking alone out here."

"Who said I was respectable?"

"Be that as it may, I insist on safeguarding your honor for the remainder of your walk," he said.

They took their time, slowly crossing the commons, her glove resting lightly on his forearm. She leaned against him just slightly, saying nothing, feeling the firm curve of his body. At the entrance of the arched gateway, she stopped and looked up at him. "This is my stop. And you've got a party to go to."

"What if I don't want to say goodnight?"

"Then don't," she said.

The arch loomed above them, blocking out the moonlight. They had taken two steps into its shadows when he stopped and leaned toward her. He kissed her, somewhat tentatively. If she'd objected, he could have claimed that he meant it as a chaste kiss on the cheek, gone astray in the darkness. But she didn't. She kissed him back, and he pulled her deeper into the shadow of the archway and kissed her again, this time with intent.

"Why, Mr. Pendle," she whispered. "You can't be trusted, after all."

"That's the nicest thing anyone's ever said to me."

He leaned down to kiss her again, but this time she pushed away. "We have another little secret now. And in our second tunnel. That'll have to last us."

"I don't see how it can," he said, extending his arm again. She took it, and they passed through the arch to a court of buildings beyond. One of them was draped with banners welcoming Homecoming guests. Yellow light spilled out of the doorway, inviting.

"Good night, Mr. Pendle," she said, for appearance's sake. "Thank you for the escort."

"The pleasure was all mine, Mrs. Miller," he replied, giving a courtly little bow.

"Not *all* yours," she said in a stage whisper and disappeared into the light.

❦

"Must say I've missed the breakfasts at the old *alma mater*," Arthur said the next morning through a mouthful of pancakes.

"How was the Sweetheart Ball?" Alicia asked.

"It was magical," said Cassie. "The dresses some of the ladies had! Why, I felt like an old shoe. And they had the whole ballroom strung with tiny electrical lights—like so many snowflakes, but in summer."

Alicia nodded. "I wish I'd seen that. But soon, I hope to see millions of them at the Exposition, at least."

Arthur took a sip of his coffee. "And how was your event, Mrs. Miller?"

"It was fine, but I certainly missed having an escort." She looked at Arthur quickly, who glanced back. She thought she detected a grin as he stabbed another forkful of pancake.

"Poor Edward, always at work," Cassie said. "I'm so sorry he couldn't come."

"Business never rests, you know. What would people do without envelopes?"

"Nothing would be private," Arthur answered. "The envelope serves as the seal of the confessional. Once a letter goes into one, the contents are sanctified."

"I suppose," Alicia said.

They ate in silence for a little while. "Since we'll be on our way soon, I'd better go find a telephone," Alicia said. "I said I'd let the children know everything is well."

"Do you know where it is?" Arthur asked.

"No," she said, "but I'll find it easily, I'm sure."

He stood up and put his napkin on his chair. "Let me show you. I'm an old hand around here, you know. We'll be right back, Cassie."

Allie took his arm, and they walked out of the dining hall and toward the main reception area. Arthur leaned over slightly.

"Have you—thought about last evening?" he said.

"What about it?"

"You know what I mean."

"Perhaps we had best forget about that."

"I can't forget it. I don't want to forget it."

"You know that's not what I meant."

"You're sparring with me."

"I am not sparring. But last night doesn't lead anywhere, so it's probably best put aside."

"It does lead somewhere. To a thousand more like it."

"Arthur," she said, without looking at him, "since we arrived here, I can't stop thinking—what could a man like you possibly want from a woman like me? You're a man of the world. I'm a girl from Buffalo. Look at this campus of yours." She pressed closer against him. He could feel her breast against his arm.

"Where would I begin?" he said. "I've already told you, you're my soulmate. You're beautiful. And mostly—you're fascinating."

"So you say."

"I mean what I say. I want to learn everything there is about you. I want to know every thought you have. Every desire. You were on my mind constantly before we came to New Haven, but after last night I am completely at loose ends thinking about you."

She stopped and looked at him with soft eyes. "You may find that there's less to me than meets the eye. But if you are serious—and you genuinely want to know me—I'll play along."

"Then I am to be serious, but you get to play, is that it?"

She smiled. "In a nutshell."

"I thought you said 'no games?'"

"Perhaps I was playing a game when I said that."

He drew her aside into a nook near the phone booths. "Do you have any idea how much I want you?" he whispered, his nose in her hair.

She slipped her hand down along his trouser front, not caring if anyone saw. "I think I have an inkling," she said.

❦

When Allie returned home, Edward didn't seem interested in a detailed report on the New Haven excursion, and likewise, she didn't feel compelled to force one on him.

The weekend after their return from New Haven, the four of them—Cassie, Arthur, Alicia, and Edward—met for a round of team golf at the Red Jacket Golf Club. The lovely, manicured course was finally dry enough to play after all the spring rains, and Edward suggested that a foursome with their new friends would be just the thing to kick off the golfing season. On the links, Edward and Cassie were decisive winners, mostly because Alicia seemed unable to concentrate and sent her drives and putts off the mark. Arthur, an intense and competitive player, humored her as best he could. Ed was so invigorated by victory that he proposed a little stroll around the grounds before lunch.

"That'd be delightful," Cassie said.

"Old boy, I'm going to sit here by the lake and lick my wounds," Arthur said, plopping down on the bench where they'd piled their golf bags. "I'll stand guard faithfully over everyone's gear."

"I'm bushed, too," Alicia said. "I'll stay behind and take in the view."

"Your loss is our gain," Edward said, extending his arm to Cassie. "Shall we? How about we leave these sore losers to brood, and you and I work up an appetite."

Cassie took his arm, and she and Ed headed up the gravel path toward the clubhouse.

Arthur was sitting with his arms splayed out in exaggerated exhaustion, but he straightened up immediately and patted the bench next to him.

"Thank you, sir," Alicia said, sitting next to him.

They looked out over the shimmering water. This was one of the best viewpoints in Buffalo, on a little bluff that concealed the muddy Erie Canal and the wharves below but gave an unobstructed view of Lake Erie. From their vantage point, they could see a few little steam ferries plying back and forth to Canada, and some heading downriver for the season's first flush at the Grand Island summer resorts. The breeze from Erie, though, seemed still to be carrying with it the last of the spring damp. Arthur took off his jacket and draped it over Alicia's shoulders.

They talked idly for a few minutes before Arthur worked up the courage to broach the topic he'd been mulling all morning.

"What I said in New Haven—"

"About what?"

He looked around to make sure that Ed and Cassie were well out of earshot. "About you know what."

"Oh, please. Just get on with it. Quit stalling."

"I'm not stalling."

She punched him in the arm. "Out with it. What's on your mind?"

"I think you know. About us wanting each other."

"I thought that might be it. Guilty as charged."

Arthur nodded gravely. "Now that you've entered your plea," he said, "what do you—what are we going to do about it? I almost can't bear—"

She looked away, observing the swollen river surging around the piers of the bridge in front of them.

"—I don't know what I'm trying to say," he said. "I thought I did. Now I'm just tongue-tied."

"And right when you said you needed to lick your wounds, too."

"You're not making this any easier."

"Don't be a crybaby. No need to beat around the bush. I'm not exactly a virgin anymore, you know."

"You might be, in a way."

She rolled her eyes. "Funny virgin I'd be—a married woman with three children."

"On the contrary. I believe that many people—men and women— live their whole lives as virgins. In the sense that they've never known what it's like to be loved. Truly."

"Doesn't Cassie? Love you?"

"That's a more difficult question to answer than you may think. She and I have an—alliance. We each get something from our bargain."

"I understand," Allie said. "I've lived that life."

She took a deep breath. "Then let's don't be so shy about it, if we both know where this is headed. I'll wager that we've both already been to that place in our minds. Where the mind goes, the body ought to follow out of courtesy."

"I like the sound of that."

"Then let's not think about it too much and spoil it. This happens, and it's happened to us. I'm not entirely sure why or how, but it has. And now, perhaps we should consider it our civic duty to do something about this plague of virgins. Because to be honest, Mr. Ashwood, I can barely sit still until we do."

"All right," he said, trying to maintain some composure, "but what about our spouses? Where do they fit in?"

"Who, by the way, are liable to walk up any second. I don't think they're going to be a problem—unless we make them one. We don't let them cut in on our little *pas de deux*."

"Won't you feel guilty?"

"About what?"

"About committing a sin. I know I'm arguing against my own interest here, but it's best to be above board."

She sniffed. "Sin. Let me think about that a minute." She folded her arms and looked at the lake. He waited expectantly.

"Here's what I think about sin," she said. In the distance, Edward and Cassie could be heard crunching down the path.

"Better hurry up," Arthur said.

She shook her head. "No, this is too important to rush. What I think is that the first time we sin—we'll probably feel guilty. Or strange, somehow, like shedding our skin. But I think like anything, after the second or tenth or thousandth time, it'll feel quite normal and won't bother us a bit. My opinion is to get on with it, and without delay."

"Will you look at those two lazybones!" Cassie's voice said as she and Edward strolled up. "Why, we've made an entire circuit of this club while the two of you have been putting your feet up like a couple of tourists."

"Looks to me like they've just sprinted across the bridge," Edward said. "Look at those red faces."

"It's this stiff wind off the lake," Allie replied, smoothing her hair. "Leaves one rather breathless."

Arthur smiled to himself. Stiff wind, indeed.

They packed up their gear and headed back up the hill to the clubhouse. Arthur was afraid to look at Allie, but the one time he did, she gave him a wink.

❧

Two days after the golf game, Arthur was going through the mail at his office and spied a small envelope addressed in a familiar hand. "Now, what's this about?" he thought, slitting it open.

In the envelope were two small sheets of ladies' writing paper. One was blank and had been used only to cover the other one folded inside it, to protect its contents from prying eyes. He unfolded the inner sheet and read:

Loved our recent foursome, but it's obvious that you and I need much more individual practice. Perhaps we should schedule some. Let me know a time and place. – AA

He smiled. So she had already become Alicia Ashwood. He smelled the paper. No trace of perfume, but that was good, and like her. This was between them and them alone. That was enough. But I do need to get the post office box set up before things heat up, he thought.

❧

The consummation came two days later, at 123 Whitney Place, a slightly crooked-looking foursquare that rented by the week or month, furnished. Under his *nom de guerre,* Arthur took it for a week. Who knew whether there would be a second one?

Yet after their very first rendezvous, Alicia declared emphatically that she was, in fact, no longer a virgin. Something dead or dormant was moving again in her, and in short order, 123 Whitney Place became a regular hideaway. The first week's rental became a month, and then another. In their new post office box correspondence, the house even acquired its own soubriquet: 'One Two Three.'

As much as One Two Three was their refuge from husband or wife or real life, they remained sensible that there were other people living on the periphery of their private world. Being found out would be very bad for everyone, so they took precautions. Varying their schedule, meeting on market days, or on gloomy afternoons when most of the world chose to stay inside. Then they could lie together peacefully under the eaves, listening to the rain drumming on the roof, and seem very far away. Until it was time to break the spell and go home again.

The post office box made it easy to be intimate while keeping up appearances. They would write to each other at that address, often merely to arrange a time to meet at One Two Three, but just as often to pour out thoughts and emotions that they hadn't time or words to express in person. They wrote about everything, creating a shared diary of the flow of their feelings and a catalogue of the more elaborate yearnings that they planned to explore, in the fullness of time, on Whitney Place. Arthur knew it wasn't wise to commit so much to writing, but he made her swear to burn everything after reading it, and after a while, he didn't hold anything back.

Meanwhile, Montana Copper shares, like the broader stock market, continued to climb. The price swelled from $40 a share to $60, then to $80, almost without taking a breather. Every morning, even if he knew he had dirty work ahead, he enjoyed the warm and pleasant feeling of opening the newspaper to the stock table and running his finger languorously down the long column of companies to stop at Montana Copper. Each day he was inching closer to the thing he wanted most: freedom. That was the only decent thing that money could buy. Freedom from Penrose's control, freedom to be his own man, and, though the idea was still new even to him, freedom to be with Allie. He had begun to believe that being with one's soulmate was worth whatever it might cost.

CHAPTER 18

All Knotted Up

ALLIE'S MIND HAD BEEN STUCK IN A PARTICULAR RUT SINCE BE-fore daybreak, and around 9:30, she decided to take a chance. She had been having so much fun at One Two Three that she thought it would be thrilling to introduce something riskier.

It was Friday, and Arthur would probably not go downtown until just before his lunch with Terry Penrose. And Friday mornings were Cassie's favorite shopping day, since she had an aversion to the weekend crowds downtown. So it was likely that Arthur would be at home, by himself.

Throwing her silk dressing gown over her shoulders, she tiptoed down the stairs in case Annie hadn't yet left. With no sign of life de-tected on the ground floor of 101 Ashwood, she picked up the earpiece of the hall telephone and clicked the hook for the operator.

"Pendle residence, please," she said when the girl picked up. "Cleve-land Avenue, in Ashwood." If, by chance, Cassie answered, Alicia could always tell her that she was calling to ask if the two of them could go shopping together. After four rings, she was about to hang up, frustrated, when the line connected with a sharp click.

"Pendle here," said Arthur's familiar voice. "Who's calling, please?"

"I'll give you one guess," Alicia whispered in her huskiest and most lubricious tone.

"Allie? Has something happened?"

"Not yet," she said. "Can you come over? To the house?"

"Are you alone?"

"Of course I'm alone, you ninny. Ed's in Cleveland until tonight, the girls are at school, my mother went to the church to help them set up for the bazaar. And Annie told me a few minutes ago that she was going downtown to pick something up. She took Ed's automobile. At least she's allowed to drive it."

"Why do you want me to come over? Is everything all right?"

"Why do you think? I've been wanting to try something. I'd rather not entertain the Bell operator with the details, if you don't mind."

"I'll be right over."

"You'd better walk. I don't think leaving your automobile in the drive is a good idea, without anyone here. And come in through the back door. I'll leave it unlatched. I'll be waiting upstairs."

"On my way," he said.

Alicia hung up the earpiece and walked into the pantry, where she located the thing she'd been obsessing about, and went back upstairs to wait for Arthur. She left her bedroom door ajar so that she could hear him arrive, and threw herself down on the bed to wait.

The Pendles' place on Cleveland Avenue was almost a mile away from the Millers', but only seven impatient minutes had dragged by when she heard the quiet rattle of the rear door. Admirable time, Alicia thought. At the first creak of the stairs, she jumped up and was standing by the door when Arthur sidled into her room. He was quite red in the face and breathing hard after his jog.

"So what's this all about?" he said, panting.

"This," she said, and let her dressing gown slip off her bare shoulders and ripple to her feet.

"Mother of God," Arthur breathed as best he could.

"I thought of something a little naughty," she said, grabbing his lapels, "and the more I thought of it, the naughtier it became. It was either telephone, or explode."

"I'm glad you didn't explode," he said. "And you're sure we're alone?"

"I may be horny, but I'm not insane."

He laughed despite himself, clearly nervous about being alone with Alicia in the Millers' house, and in broad daylight, at that. "I'm not going to argue with you," he said. "What did you have in mind?"

She reached under her pillow and brought out a hank of clothesline. "Can you guess?"

"I can't think of a single thing arousing about laundry," he said dryly.

Alicia stepped close to him again, rubbing her naked body against him. "I want you to tie me down," she said. "To the bed."

"Why?"

"Are you completely daffy? I want you to tie me to the bed and fuck me. Why else?"

Arthur looked mildly surprised but gamely began shedding layers of clothing.

"Seems you like the idea too," she said when he'd gotten everything off.

"Oh, I do. I need to cut this into lengths first." He picked up his trousers from the floor and retrieved a rather large clasp-knife, which he opened and used to cut four sections from the hank of line. Allie flopped on the bed, face up.

"Hurry up," she said. "I'm about ready to bust."

She extended her arms over her head, one toward each side of the headboard. Arthur affixed her right arm to the bedpost and then bent over her to secure the left.

"Be careful, will you? You almost put my eye out with that thing," she laughed, nodding at his cock.

"Take it as a compliment."

She spread-eagled and let him tie each of her feet to the footboard posts. "Let me take a look at you first," he said, admiring her firm, perfect body, her round breasts, the neat patch of hair between her legs. "God, you're beautiful, Alicia."

"You don't look half bad yourself. Now let's go while we still have time."

He was almost on top of her, both of them breathless, when she had another idea.

"Wait," she said. "You have to gag me, too, to make it real."

"With what?"

"Is that a dirty joke? Over there, in my bureau," she said, raising her head to indicate a tall piece of furniture across the room. Get a hand-kerchief or something out of the top drawer. Whatever you find." He complied and returned with a large square of white lace.

"Well done. Now stuff it in my mouth." He hesitated. "Come on, I can't wait all day. Jam it in there, good and hard. I'm not kidding. You're wasting time."

She opened her mouth. Arthur wadded up the lace and packed it in.

"Can you breathe?" he said.

"Mmm-hmm," was the muffled reply. She lifted her head again, nodding toward his penis. "Mmm-hmm," she said again, more urgently.

Arthur climbed onto the bed. When he entered her, between the thrill of the thing and Allie's obvious delight, it took a supreme effort of will not to let go immediately. He knew that he would be able to surrender soon enough, but only when Allie was ready and on Allie's terms.

They had been at it for a few minutes when Alicia opened her eyes wide and began shaking her head violently and emitting stifled, urgent sounds. Arthur thought she might be suffocating and yanked the wad of lace out of her mouth.

"Are you all right?" he said.

"No," she gasped. "Someone's outside. In the drive."

"You're imagining things," he said, desperately wanting to get back to business. "Relax."

"Look out the goddamn window and tell me if I'm imagining things!"

He pulled out of her regretfully, from deliciously warm and wet to cold and damp in an instant, and waddled to the front window overlooking Ashwood Street. He parted the curtains cautiously.

"Holy shit!" he said. "It's Annie!"

"Annie? *My* Annie?"

"Yes. She's in the drive, in Edward's machine."

"She said she was going to pick something up downtown," Allie moaned.

"And she did," he replied, picking up his trousers from the floor and yanking them on over his collapsing erection. "Your husband."

"Edward?"

"Yes, that's what she meant by picking something up. She must have picked him up from the station. God *damn!*" In his haste, Arthur had neglected to put on his underdrawers, and now he'd cinched up his belt and so had to stuff them in his trousers pocket. He was fumbling his shirt on when Allie started thrashing on the bed.

"Hurry up and untie me, will you!" she said.

"Oh, of course," he said, leaping onto the bed. He reached into his trouser pocket, but the clasp-knife must have fallen out in all the ruckus. He began feverishly working at the knots with his fingers as Allie lay there naked.

"What is taking so long?" she growled as he struggled with the clothesline.

"You must have pulled the knots tight when we were—I can't get them undone!"

"You're a fucking *sailor*, for chrissake," she said. "They're knots!"

"I was never any good at it," he muttered. "There, I've got one."

He had finally untied the last one, her left foot, when they heard the front door bang.

"Shit!" she said, jumping up and scrabbling for her abandoned dressing gown. "You've got to get out of here. I'll get downstairs and stall them, and when you hear me talking with them, go down the back staircase and out the way you came. And don't put your shoes on, or they'll hear you!"

He stuffed his collar, cuffs, necktie, and studs into the pocket already bulging with his underwear. Half-tucking in his shirt in, he picked up his heavy brogans and shook his head. "Edward is going to murder me," he said.

"You're the least of my problems right about now," she said. "Now be quiet, will you? I'm going downstairs."

She padded down the stairs. Annie and Ed were chatting in the foyer.

"Ed!" she said. "I thought you weren't coming home until tonight."

"Finished up my business yesterday," he said. "I decided to get the early train this morning. Didn't you see my telegraph?"

"You were still in your room when it came, ma'am," Annie said sheepishly. "I thought that rather than disturb you, I'd pick up Mr. Miller myself."

"That was very considerate of you, Annie," Alicia said, wanting to knock the girl out cold. "What a surprise all the way around!" She gave a phony little clap of joy.

Ed squinted at her. "You look awfully flushed. And what happened to your wrists?" he said, pointing. Around each of her wrists was a livid rope burn.

"Is someone at the back door?" Annie said, looking down the corridor. "It sounded like the door slammed."

"I tried some stupid electric wristband thing yesterday," Allie interrupted, moving in front of Annie and blocking the hallway. "There was a fellow downtown selling them, claiming all sorts of health benefits. But this morning, I found they'd left a mark."

"All that electric stuff is overdone," Edward said. "Does more harm than good, if you ask me."

"I've certainly learned *my* lesson," Allie replied. "An experiment not to be repeated."

"I have some unguent you can put on them," Annie said. "Why don't I take Mr. Miller's valise upstairs, and I'll fetch it for you?"

"Oh no, no," Allie said, not entirely sure whether Arthur had made his escape. "It's nothing, really. And leave the bag here for now. I'm famished. Ed, would you like some breakfast?"

"I suppose I would," he said, "but I can get myself a bowl of cereal—"

"Nothing doing," Alicia said. "Annie so enjoys cooking. Annie, what do you say you make some of those delicious eggs you do, the ones with the cheese?"

Annie smiled. "I'd love to. I'll have them up in no time."

"Then I'll pop back upstairs and make myself decent," Allie said. "Ed, you relax in the breakfast nook after your early trip. I'll take your case upstairs with me."

"If you insist," he said. Alicia smiled, picked up his valise, and ran up the stairs.

Ed and Annie exchanged looks. "What in the world has gotten into *her?*" he said, shaking his head.

❧

The following afternoon, while Cassie was napping upstairs and Arthur was enjoying a cigar, the postman delivered a letter addressed to him from the Miller Envelope Company. "What the hell?" he muttered out loud, turning it over. Ten dollars says that the jig is up, and I'm fucked.

He took the envelope into his private office and closed the door. Taking a deep breath, he reached for his letter opener. Here goes, he thought, and slit it open. Inside was a single sheet of letterhead, on which Edward had hand-written:

My dear Arthur:

I've been remiss in not having you to the factory long before this. Can you stop by at 11 in the forenoon on Tuesday? I mean to show you the works. I shouldn't think it would take more than a half-hour, which I trust you'd find time well spent.

Awaiting your favorable reply to my home or office address.

Yours sincerely,

E. L. Miller

'Show me the works?' Arthur thought. The *works?* What does that mean? Maybe it means his suspicions he's going to lay out for me. I heard his voice when I was sneaking down the rear stairs, and I swear he sounded like he knew more than he was letting on. I wonder if I should tell Allie. No, that might alarm her, and she might give it all away.

He took out a sheet of his writing paper, dipped a pen, and wrote back to Edward, thanking him for the kind invitation and that he would naturally be delighted to meet him on the coming Tuesday, precisely at 11.

PART 2

RUMORS OF WAR

CHAPTER 19

A Visit to Miller Envelope Company

THE MILLER ENVELOPE COMPANY WAS ONLY SIX BLOCKS' WALK from the front door of Arthur's office, but it felt like the longest six blocks of his life. He'd been dreading this visit since Saturday—indeed thinking about it had ruined what was left of his weekend, and all of Monday too.

Miller Envelope—which occupied three-quarters of the ancient, grimy Cashton Building—was one of a surprising number of manufacturing enterprises that fumed and roared in the very heart of downtown, cheek by jowl with department stores, homes, and churches. Arthur's streetcar passed by Miller's factory every morning and evening, so he knew the spot well, an uninspiring pile of brick, six stories tall. The tired, red façade facing Washington Street was crusted with scabby deposits of soot spreading patchily, like lichen.

A giant American flag flew from a stanchion on the roof, and the words 'TRUST MILLER ENVELOPES' were painted in enormous white letters on an exterior wall facing the new and showy Main Post Office, barely a year old but already one of the crown jewels of Buffalo architecture.

Edward was waiting on the sidewalk when Arthur strolled up as calmly as he could manage. Together they took a swaying elevator to the third floor, where in the rear corner was a large anteroom furnished with a broad desk with a telephone on it. The glass door pane read

E. L. Miller.
President.

They were greeted by a very attractive young secretary and walked into the paneled office.

"Cup of coffee before we go over and see the works?" Ed asked, gesturing Arthur to a chair and sitting down neatly behind his desk.

The works, Arthur thought. Of course, he means the factory. "Coffee?" he said, almost as though hearing the word for the first time.

"Or something stronger, if you'd rather."

It was eleven in the morning, but why not, Arthur thought. He was nervous, a feeling he didn't often experience. How could he know whether Edward might know what mischief he and Allie had gotten up to? It might be well to fortify himself.

"Why not?" he said. "I don't mind joining you in a nip."

"I'll stick with coffee. Machinery and all that, you know." He pressed an intercom button on his desk. "Abby?" he said when his secretary picked up. "Coffee for me and a glass of our best rye for my friend."

Arthur felt a little strange holding a tumbler full of whiskey as Ed blew on his tidy little cup.

There seemed to be nothing particular to say, so Arthur offered, "Very kind of you to invite me. I've been eager to see—the works for some time."

"You may be disappointed," he said. "Allie may have poisoned you against them."

Arthur bit his lip. "Not in the slightest. I'm sure Mrs. Miller is very proud of your success, Ed."

"She's more interested in professional men. I'm a yokel who knows how to make money." Ed gave a bitter chuckle.

"Ed, I'm sure that's—"

"You're probably wondering why I asked you to come by today. Other than to see the works."

"Oh, that's more than enough reason," Arthur said.

"I asked you here because I wanted to talk with you—about Allie, in fact."

"Is everything all right, Ed?"

Edward studied the coffee in his cup, thinking.

"We haven't known each other very long, you and I."

Arthur took another generous sip of his whiskey. On his empty stomach, he felt it immediately.

"And we're as different as night and day. Yet at the same time," Ed continued, "somehow I feel we have more in common than we suspect."

"I'm sure that's true," Arthur said uneasily.

"Even so," Edward said, again examining his cup, "this is a bit awkward. Maybe even slightly out of turn."

"Probably best to come right out with it," he said, steeling himself. Arthur hoped that Ed wouldn't see his Adam's apple bobbing like a cork under his stiff linen collar, which suddenly felt especially tight.

Edward took a deep breath. "All right then, I'll stop dilly-dallying. Buffalo's a small town, you know. And Ashwood, even smaller. It's awkward to say, but I'm sure you've heard the stories about Alicia's fits."

"Fits? Is Mrs. Miller unwell?" Arthur said, floundering.

"She has a very passionate nature, let's say."

I won't disagree with you on that, Arthur thought.

"And moody," Ed went on. "I wanted to be out in the open about an episode that you may have heard about. Or may hear about."

"I'm sure I don't know."

"Not too long ago, Allie and I had a rather bad spat and"—he rubbed the spot on his head where the monkey had landed—"she threw a paperweight in my direction, and as bad luck would have it, it beaned me. The story's made the rounds of the neighborhood three or four times by now. I was concerned you'd hear it out of context and form the wrong opinion about me and Allie. All over such a silly little nothing."

"I would never do that. What sort of the wrong opinion?"

"That we're unhappy. That's what people say whenever a couple has a quarrel. But Allie and I have been married for seventeen years, and I'm sure we'll be married 'til death do us part."

"I've no doubt of it, Ed."

"Lately, too, things have been much, much better at home. Allie's been unusually affectionate. Cooperative."

Oh, she has, has she? Arthur thought, feeling flushed. I'm going to have to ask her about that.

"More whiskey?" Ed said.

"No thanks—I don't have to be around machinery, like you, but I do have to get some work done today." He forced a laugh.

"I won't keep you. I merely wanted to make sure you heard this from the horse's mouth. And I also don't mind saying that I think you may have a little something to do with Allie's better mood, Arthur."

Arthur shifted in his chair. Here we go.

"How so?" Arthur regretted the words immediately. He had no idea where this was headed, and he recalled his legal training: Don't ever ask a question you don't already know the answer to.

"You seem to have given her an outlet."

I am not asking another thing, he thought.

Ed cleared his throat. "Allie loves art and poetry and music—subjects that are more in your line than in mine." He seemed to be either slightly wistful or merely nonchalant. "People need other people of like mind to talk with. Then everyone is happy."

"Everyone's happy," Arthur murmured.

"Exactly. Well, enough about this sore subject. I feel better for having cleared the air. Now how about we show you how envelopes are made?"

The tour was mercifully brief. Arthur faked a deep interest in the whirring and clicking machines and the towering stacks of various kinds of envelopes in every conceivable size, shape, and color. At last, they made it to the shipping department, near the front door.

"Glad you could come by, Arthur," Edward said, shaking his hand. "Thanks again for hearing me out."

Lost in thought and still a little tipsy as he headed back to his office, Arthur walked right by his building and, if not for the urgent clanging of a trolley bell and the shouting of passersby, was very nearly run over by the express car on its merciless route down Main Street. He jumped back from the tracks in time to see the horrified faces packed inside the machine thundering past, so close that he could smell the hot, metallic oiliness of its running gear. A full five minutes afterward, he was still breathing heavily when he sank into his familiar desk chair.

❦

"Last week was a bit too close for comfort," Arthur said later that afternoon, as he was tying Allie to the iron bedstead upstairs in One Two Three.

"Now that's an understatement," she said, pulling gently on her bonds to test them. "I was just about to come, too."

"*You* were? You'll forgive me if I can't muster up much sympathy. I think I may have ruptured something down there."

"Oh, you poor, poor dear. What happened after you went out the back door?"

"I hoofed it across the backyard, carrying my shoes. I dropped one and had to double back a few steps to pick it up, and by then, I wasn't sure if there was time to open the fence door without being spotted. So I chucked the shoes over the fence and vaulted the thing. And came down flat on top of a row of ashcans. I thought sure you'd hear all the racket."

"No, but we were in the front of the house, thank God."

"I ran all the way to Bryan in my stocking feet, then pulled on my shoes and got home. I'm sure someone along that alley behind your house saw me."

"I don't think so," she said. "I would have had three telephone calls and five unannounced guests, if someone had. Word travels fast on Ashwood Street."

"Well, good," he said, finishing his knots and kneeling between her legs. "But my heart won't stand another close shave like that one. Especially since Ed summoned me to his office right afterward. I was sure our goose was cooked."

"He's clueless. But I certainly didn't expect it to play out that way. I thought it would be fun and a little naughty."

"And so it would have been."

"All's well that ends well," Allie said. "Now let's go. We've got some catching up to do."

Arthur was kissing her stomach when she said, "Wait! You forgot something!"

"What now?"

"The gag. Muzzle, whatever you want to call it."

"Right," he said, getting up and pulling a handkerchief from the pocket of his coat, which was draped over a chair near the foot of the bed. "Got it."

"Now this time, jam it in there good and hard," she said. He was balling up the hankie when she laughed. "Actually, that goes both for the gag and"—she raised her head and looked down—"that thing of yours, too."

The two of them laughed and picked up where they'd left off the week before.

CHAPTER 20

In the Spotlight

ON THAT WARM JULY EVENING, NO ONE WOULD HAVE BELIEVED that in only two months, a young man with an unpronounceable Slavic name would obliterate the happy fantasyland of the Pan-American Exposition as utterly as a wayward comet.

The Exposition's chaotic Midway, in all its noise and color, was an outdoor pleasure palace, a zone of enchantment tucked away from the real world outside the gates. Despite a month of unseasonably cool and rainy weather, which had dampened spirits and attendance, the Midway had not failed to live up to its billing. Everyone who came, left enthralled.

As she and Arthur strolled the Midway together, though, it was Allie who felt that disaster was imminent. She scanned the crowd for familiar faces, dreading bumping into someone she knew. She had taken up this new pastime unconsciously as soon as things with Arthur had gotten complicated. It wasn't so much the sin, it was the secrecy—fragile and crystalline, which could be shattered by the intrusion of a single familiar face.

Only a few months before, she would have walked guiltlessly with him, even proudly, secure in the knowledge that they were nothing more than friends. She could have spoken those words without shame to anyone, even to Ed. One Two Three had changed all that overnight, and now she couldn't shake the thought that something in their manner—a wrong expression, a single misplaced word—might give them away. Uppermost among those threats was the irrepressible smile that stole across her face when she replayed in her mind their conversations, their kisses, their other antics. No married woman smiles like this, she thought.

Arthur, on the other hand, seemed his usual imperturbable self. So much so that from time to time, he would casually place his hand in the small of her back as they walked to direct her this way or that. When he did, she pulled away reflexively, as if from an electric shock. At those moments, too, a jealous thought had begun to take shape: He has far less at stake than I do. No children. A profession, a substantial income. A wife preoccupied in pursuit of what—drug visions? If *he's* exposed— yes, it would be embarrassing for a while. But *his* life would eventually go on, more or less the same. *Mine* would be made barren, sown with salt. I would become a nonentity—no money, no children, no home. No future.

Still, the atmosphere of the great Pan was so festive that she set aside most of her uneasy thoughts and walked with Arthur as nonchalantly as she could manage. She liked the Villages best—a large section of the fair dedicated to the arts, customs, and industries of far-off, exotic lands that most people could never hope to see in person. Each village was a country in microcosm, idealized perhaps, but peopled with actual natives of whatever land was featured. Arthur was particularly keen to see the Japanese Village. As a boy, he'd been to Japan on several of his father's voyages and had found the place fascinating. The pair lingered in the village to participate in a tea ceremony, hear some traditional music, and give Arthur a chance to dust off his rudimentary Japanese.

As they were about to leave the serenity of the Japanese Village to return to the teeming Midway, Arthur pulled Alicia into a little booth selling handicrafts.

"Let me buy you something," he said. "Something to remember the day."

"You don't have to do that. I'll never forget it."

"A little keepsake. I insist."

She looked over the wares displayed on the shelves, and a cheerful Japanese salesgirl walked over to help.

"If it's to be a *keepsake*, then this little keepsake box would be ideal," Allie said, picking up a shoebox-sized wooden chest with a little hasp and some Japanese characters carved into the lid.

"I wonder what it says?" she wondered aloud.

The salesgirl leaned in. "It says 'may life last only so long as love does.'"

"Perfect," Arthur said. "We'll take it."

❦

"We'd best be getting going," Allie said. She was weary of scanning faces, and in a half-hour, it would be dusk.

"Leave now? Before the lights come on?"

"I can't get home after dark."

"Allie, the only reason to do the Pan at all is to see the electric lights. The fountain, the Electric Tower, all these buildings—it's supposed to be like a fairyland. We can't miss that."

"What would I tell Edward?"

"He thinks Cassie is with us, right?"

"Yes."

"Well then? What's the problem? Tell him how much Cassie enjoyed the light show. I'll make sure she backs up our story."

Alicia seemed skeptical. "Why would Cassie lie for us?"

"It's not a lie if she believes it," he said, which Alicia found impenetrable. In truth, she wanted to see the lights, and relented.

"If you say so. It would be fun to see them. I've seen them in the rotogravure, but I'm sure that doesn't do them justice."

As twilight gathered, they made their way over to the center of the fairgrounds, to the Court of Fountains, a long reflecting pool at the foot of the soaring Electric Tower. They staked out a prime location at its edge.

"What does the guidebook say about the lights?" Arthur asked.

"Too dark to make it out." She had a small pair of reading spectacles in her bag, but she didn't want Arthur to see her in them.

"So much the better," he said, giving her waist a squeeze and making her jump. "We'll just have to wait and see for ourselves."

Like an upturned bowl of embers, the scarlet sunset cooled to dusty rose and then to purple. And as the sky's energy drained away, tens of thousands of incandescent lights—in daylight carefully hidden—started to glow faintly, like swarms of fireflies. From barely detectible droplets of honey, by degrees they grew brighter until each of the colossal buildings of the great Exposition was adorned with a glowing necklace of warm, yellowish light.

Then in a single, piercing flash, the soaring Electric Tower exploded into a shaft of brilliant white light. From its summit, a hundred carbon-arc lamps blazed down on the unsuspecting crowd. In the sharp electric glare, the dancing fountain itself appeared to freeze, becoming a giant wedding cake of marshmallow meringue. The blinded crowd gasped and blinked.

Some stared up at the source of the beam, transfixed like druids at a solstice. Others instinctively ran for cover, frightened by the sudden, unaccustomed return of daylight. And others—like Arthur and Allie— reflexively clasped each other tightly.

"Kiss me," he whispered in her ear.

"What if someone sees us?"

"Then I suggest you close your eyes," he said.

He didn't wait for an answer. In front of the churning fountain, he kissed her—and not a peck, but the way he kissed at One Two Three. She kissed back with all the pent-up desire of a whole day spent leaning on his arm and the stress of scanning for lurking danger. He put his hand into the curve above her backside and pulled her close to him, so that she could feel how much he wanted her.

This welcome release would have attracted little attention were it not for a favorite game played on romantic couples by the lighting operators. Spotting Allie and Arthur in the crowd, they aimed one of their spotlights directly at the kissing pair. Arthur and Alicia, lost in each other, felt the tingling heat of the beam before they realized what was going on.

People around them hooted and applauded. Squinting up into the spotlight, the mortified Alicia gave Arthur an involuntary shove that sent him reeling, almost into the fountain. This made the onlookers laugh even harder, and caused the lighting men to keep the beam focused in their direction.

Alicia put her tiny handbag in front of her face and turned, and Arthur looked at the pavement, pulling his hat down over his eyes. He grabbed her arm with his free hand and tugged her out of the reach of the searchlight and back toward the Midway. The tittering of the crowd died away as the lighting men looked for fresh victims.

In the shadows of the Midway, Allie burst into tears. She had forgotten herself for one moment, one second, and punishment had been swift and sure.

"How mortifying," she mumbled.

Arthur leaned down and kissed her on the cheek. "I know. But it was only a second or two. No one knew it was us."

He pulled her through the maze of buildings toward the West Amherst Gate. They got turned around a couple of times—exactly what the fair's designers had in mind—but instead of carefree meandering, it made for an irritating delay in making their escape. At last, ahead in the shadows of the Midway, they could make out a three-story-tall, plaster face of a sleeping lady. This slumbering giant was the entrance portal to Dreamland, the Exposition's maddening hall of mirrors, hard by the West Gate. Dreamland was deserted now, and the distant aura of the main light show made the colossal, slumbering face seem pale and nightmarish. They scurried by without looking up, turned left, and were soon out of the park.

Back at the Court of Fountains, the light show had finished, and the crowds were beginning to thin. A smartly dressed couple sitting on the rim of the fountain stood and smoothed their clothes.

"Now, don't you say anything to anyone," Sarah Payne said to Seth. "I'll call Edward in the morning. Don't go starting any rumors."

❦

When Allie got home, Ed was reclining on the divan in his den, shrouded in darkness, his face illuminated by the gas fixture like a capsized boat in a lagoon of ink.

"How was the light show?" he said without getting up.

"More exciting than I expected."

"Did Cassie enjoy herself?"

"Oh yes, we all did. Cassie and Arthur both." She tried to speak his name as flatly and without affect as she could. She felt again like she was under that horrible spotlight.

"Oh good," he said, still looking at the ceiling. "I'm glad you had fun."

"I can tell you more about it at breakfast if you like," she said, putting her hand on the newel post. "I'm exhausted."

"Sleep tight," he called after her from his divan.

❦

The carriage dropped Arthur off on Cleveland Avenue around 9 p.m. By now, Cassie would be worried, or angry, or both. As he swung open the front door, he hoped he wasn't carrying with him the scent of perfume. He sniffed his sleeve.

When he entered their parlor, Cassie got up from her chair, swaying slightly. She blinked at him with glassy eyes. Her pupils were tiny poppy-seed dots again.

"Look who's back, my knight in shining armor," she said, slurring her words. "How was the Exposition?"

"Cassie, honestly. You have got to slow down."

"I wish you weren't such a fuddy-duddy," she said, her eyes glazed. "Did you have fun? I did." She giggled.

"It was fine."

"Did Allie enjoy herself?"

"She seemed to."

"I'll bet the two of you watched that old moon rise together." She gave a weird titter.

"Come on, let's get you up to bed."

"Yes, off to bed, Cassie! You come home and send me off straightway to my room."

"I'm not sending you off anywhere. You might better lie down, though."

"Would you like to dance?" she said. "Why don't you put some music on the gramophone?"

"You don't like to dance, and I'm tired."

"You like to dance with Alicia."

"Cassie—"

"And it is something to see, how you two move. What's it like? Umm—when you dance with her, I can't help wondering what it's like—when you're—*you know.*"

"For God's sake," he said. "You're out of your mind."

"I'm quite sane, most of the time anyway. And have I told you to stop whatever it is you're doing with her? No, I haven't. In fact—oh, why tiptoe around it, we've been married a long time—I've even thought, next time you fuck her, do it upstairs, so I can hear the two of you rutting."

Arthur grabbed Cassie's shoulders and shook her, none too gently. She giggled again.

"That's disgusting. I know you don't mean it, but it's still disgusting."

"Is watching *Swan Lake* disgusting?"

"You're not yourself right now."

"But, Arthur—this *is* myself. It's the rest of the time that I have my false face on."

"Let's go," he said, losing patience. "I hate that you take this stuff. It makes you crazy."

"Arthur," she said. "You know what makes me crazy?"

"I'm sure you'll tell me."

"The only thing that makes me truly crazy is the thought that seeing her and being *with* her won't be enough for you. That you'll have to *have* her, all to yourself. And not be with me."

"Will you stop?"

"You know if you leave me, I'll promise you I'll take everything I have all at once. And I've hidden a lot of it away where you can't find it."

"That's not funny."

"You may do as you like. I don't mind. A man like you has needs. Which apparently I can't satisfy. But I'm warning you"—she wagged her finger in his face—"don't think for a second that you'll leave me alone in this world without you."

CHAPTER 21

Harry Price

THE LAST DAY OF JULY PROMISED TO BE A BIG COLLECTION DAY after a long, hot month of fevered hell-raising in the gambling parlors, brothels, and drug dens of The Hooks. Shipping was at a peak, the waterfront packed with men, and the dives all flush with cash. Arthur should encounter no grousing or quibbling from tight-fisted owners. He had only to get through the next five or six hours and would have two days to himself.

He had one account, however, that might spoil his perfect plan—the All-in-One Saloon. They'd paid only half of their debt on the previous collection. Arthur had taken what they had and let them off with a warning. But over the intervening weeks, a couple other neighboring saloonkeepers had tipped him off that the All-in-One would try to short him again. So Arthur did what he always did in such circumstances. He took along Harry James Price.

It wasn't entirely clear whether Price was his real name. Some said it had been Leonard or Lloyd, something Welsh. He claimed to be from north-central Pennsylvania, where he'd been a logger, clearcutting white pine and hemlock from the mountaintops. When whole counties of old-growth timber had been reduced to barren hillsides, Leonard or Price or whoever he was in Pennsylvania appeared in Buffalo and thereafter was known as Harry Price or, though not to his face, No Limit Price.

The whispered moniker 'No Limit' was said to have come from Harry's penchant for high-stakes card games. That may have been partly true, yet there were others who knew differently. The name had stuck because Harry Price was a man who could and would bring astonishing and limitless violence to bear when he, or those who paid him, deemed necessary.

He didn't look the part. He had a compact frame and stood about 5 feet 8, by no means the hulking brute that was the usual type of muscle people would hire. His sandy hair was always neat and cleanly parted down the middle, and even his fingernails were clipped and fastidious. The only thing mildly unsettling about the man was a pair of clear, blue eyes that seemed never to quite focus but rather stared off into the middle distance as if Harry were mulling over something, even when gouging another man's eyes out.

Years spent in the logging camps, swinging an axe, working in a two-man sawpit twelve hours a day, and sleeping rough had made him hard, physically and otherwise. Men died every day in the lumber camps, cut in half by whirling circular saws as tall as a man, hands lost or destroyed by an errant axe strike or sledgehammer blow, attacks of meningitis, and by the dozens of other maladies caused by living in what might as well have been the Stone Age. Being soft was a luxury that men didn't have. They toughened up, or they died.

Why Harry had such a positive enthusiasm for violence, though, wasn't clear. There were lots of strong, wiry types who would fight if they had to, to defend themselves or avoid the horror of being thought a sissy. But few of them loved it, and many who had seen or tasted real violence usually would try to avoid doing so a second time. Harry Price's hair-trigger, it was believed, likely arose from the fact that the man had syphilis, and had for years. A few men had seen his cock, scarred and deformed, when Harry had taken a victory piss on a fallen combatant. As the disease progressed—and no amount of mercury or the other tinctures peddled in every drugstore could stop it—the mind of the syphilitic became less and less inhibited. Sometimes it was shocking verbal outbursts, waves of ungovernable emotion, or more rarely—and in Harry's case—a propensity for cruelty.

On an overheated July 31st, Harry James Price, or whatever his name was, accompanied Arthur to the All-in-One, down on the aptly named Fly Street. The All-in-One was the owner's tongue-in-cheek way of advertising that the joint served up the trifecta of alcohol, gambling, and girls. Neither the booze, the games, nor the women were on the level.

Why the All-in-One had been skimping on their payouts was a mystery. The place was always thronged with people. Arthur assumed that the Black Hand or some other criminal organization was getting a big cut, and there was only so much protection money to go around. The owner's name was Mario something, obviously Italian, and so he must have thought that the District Attorney was the safer fellow to short than the Sicilians in the Black Hand, who had a nasty reputation.

Mario had made a grave tactical error, however. The Black Hand would cut your throat and throw you in the Canal, but that was the end of it. It was impersonal, quick, and done mainly to send a signal to other people paying out protection money that the money was for protection, not only from the cops but from the Black Hand itself. The organization didn't mind writing off a debt so long as they could make a point. And dead men couldn't rat about who had done them in.

Arthur and Terry saw it differently. No one was going to rat out the DA, and if a man had wanted to, to whom? Besides, that would only make things worse for the tattletale. And the city graft operation wasn't about to write anything off. The money would be collected, come hell or high water, and even after that, you still might find your operation closed for 'health violations' or some other trumped-up, minor infringement of the ever-expanding ripples of new regulation. It was a dead certainty that everyone in Buffalo, great and small, was transgressing multiple laws every day and simply didn't realize it—until the DA chose to drop the hammer.

Enter Harry Price. Harry might end your miserable life with a swift, ear-to-ear stroke of a straight razor, if he felt like it. That was messy, true, but you were dead before you hit the floor, for all intents and purposes. But if your luck ran bad, Harry would make you suffer. It would be almost as bloody, but you would live on to clean up your own mess as best you could with missing digits or a single working eye. And you would still make good on your debt or be served up another helping, and another, until you did.

Arthur normally had cops with him, and while Buffalo cops didn't mind cracking heads, most of them weren't temperamentally suited to Harry's specialty. They were for protection, not punishment. Harry came along when things were getting out of hand.

Arthur and his two cops strode into the All-in-One around 5 p.m., before the barflies started getting too thick. Harry rolled himself a cigarette with his beloved Five Brothers tobacco and waited outside.

Mario was behind the bar, as usual, and he began stammering as soon as he saw Arthur and the cops.

"Mr. Pendle, Mr. Pendle, hello, sir," he said, "I been expecting you. I know I was a little shy last month . . . but good news, today I pay all of last month."

"And what about this month?" Arthur said.

"So many things wrong. Roof leaked during those storms last week. Some things stolen."

Arthur looked up at the ceiling. "I don't see any leak." Of course, he knew that had the All-in-One no roof at all, business would likely not even have slowed.

"Upstairs, the girls' rooms," Mario said, smiling. "You like to see for yourself? Your friends too." He was offering Arthur and the cops a free ride.

"I think we'll take a rain check, pardon the expression," Arthur said. "So that I'm clear, though. You don't have this month's payment? None of it?"

"Not today. I have all I owe from last month."

"You're *sure* about this, then? Because I'm giving you one more chance. Make sure you're sure."

The cops always enjoyed this part.

"Mr. Pendle," Mario said, "I am very sorry. Next month I promise I will have everything. Maybe in two weeks I have more for you."

"I won't be here in two weeks, Mario." Arthur cupped his hand behind an ear. "Now, I want to make absolutely sure I heard you right. Nothing more today? Except the balance of what you owed last month?"

"Yes, sir. It is the best I can do."

"All right, give it to me." Arthur smiled at him like a benevolent uncle.

"Thank you, thank you, Mr. Pendle," Mario said, extending his hand to Arthur, which Arthur ignored. "You are very kind."

Arthur and his escort waited while Mario went into the back and rummaged around, or made it sound like he was rummaging. He returned with a wrinkled envelope. Arthur glanced inside it and put it into his bag. He made a careful notation in his pocket notebook. Mario stood there, sweating copiously in the heat.

At last, Arthur looked up and put away his notebook. "Thank you, Mario," he said. "It's distressing that I have to remind you, though, that there are consequences to this repeated failing on your part."

"Don't shut me down, please, Mr. Pendle," Mario said in a low, pleading squeak. "I make good on it, I am. I promise."

"I won't shut you down, Mario. I need your establishment open to pay what you owe. But last month, I gave you a warning. I can't let this go a second time."

Mario mopped his forehead with a filthy handkerchief he took from his pants pocket. "Of course. I pay interest or—even—an extra fee to you, sir."

Arthur looked at the cops, who were now smirking openly. He crooked his finger at Mario, leaned over the bar, and whispered in the man's ear.

"How is it that you can pay me an extra fee if you don't have enough to pay your bills?"

"I mean—next month," Mario stammered.

"Oh, Har-ry!" Arthur called over his shoulder in a musical singsong voice.

Harry Price sauntered in with a very unusual expression, somehow childlike and full of wonder, the look of Christmas morning.

It wasn't clear whether Mario soiled himself at that moment or sometime later. Not that it mattered. He understood fully that his bluff was about to be called in a way he'd never forget. Ever.

"No, Mr. Pendle," he pleaded. "No. Please. I know this man. He—"

The cops started laughing out loud.

"Boys, go see if Mario's got anything else around here that would help satisfy his obligation," Arthur said to the cops, who nodded and left to ransack the back rooms and maybe enjoy a free one upstairs in the process. Arthur and Harry and Mario were left alone in the barroom.

"Mario, now my friend Mr. Price here is going to explain to you why you can't do this sort of thing to me anymore," Arthur said. He nodded to Harry.

Mario was opening his mouth to protest, but Harry, nimble as a cat, had already picked up an oak chair from one of the tables and hurled it over the bar and toward Mario. Mario ducked but took a glancing blow from the flying furniture, and the plate-glass mirror behind the bar dissolved into a million pieces. Mario straggled back to his feet, bleeding from the forehead, his shoes crunching on the bits of broken mirror.

"I understand—I have the message!" he shouted.

"Too late," Arthur said, with the finality of a judge.

Harry took off his hat and coat, laid them neatly over the back of a chair, and walked around behind the bar. He picked up the oak chair where it lay between the back wall and the bar, raised it over his head, and brought it crashing down on Mario. Mario crumpled. Harry raised the chair again and, with perfect calm, smashed it into pieces on the bar top. He sorted through the wreckage and selected one of the turned legs.

"Get up," he said to Mario, still on the floor. Mario either couldn't or wouldn't comply, so Harry grabbed him by the collar and dragged him upright with one hand. Mario was burbling through a mouth full of blood—the descending chair must have knocked out a couple of his remaining teeth—but neither Arthur nor Harry could make out what he was trying to say.

"Probably speaking Italian," Arthur said to Harry.

"I fucking hate Italians," Harry said. "I know a lot of 'em. Every one of 'em's a swine."

He folded Mario over the bar and pulled an arm out straight across the wooden surface. He held the forearm in place with his free hand and, swinging the chair leg as regularly and dispassionately as a metronome, pulped Mario's right hand. Despite the man's howls, he switched sides and finished the job on the left, bashing the fingers over and over with the chair leg.

"Who told you to stand up, you dago prick?" he growled, and with a sound like a firecracker, two decisive blows of the chair leg busted one of Mario's, sending him tumbling to the floor again, writhing in pain on the carpet of mirror shards.

Harry smoothed his hair back. He took from his pocket a large folding knife.

"Harry, now don't get carried away," Arthur said. "We need him earning."

"Not a bit of it, Mr. Pendle," Harry said cheerfully.

He rolled the groaning barkeep onto his stomach and, with the knife, cut away the man's suspenders, then slit the back of his pants. He pulled down the man's underdrawers around his knees. There was visual confirmation that Mario had soiled himself by this time, and Harry looked over the bar at Arthur and held his nose in mock disgust, but also with an infectious glee. Through the haze of pain, Mario understood and began wailing something. Harry picked up the chair leg again.

"This'll help things a little," Price said, working up a big hawker of snot and spitting the viscid goo on the end of the chair leg. Then he bent low behind the bar and disappeared for a few seconds. Then Mario started screaming. Not a human scream, exactly, something quite different. Almost mechanical, like the squeal of tearing metal.

"All right, Harry, that's enough," Arthur said.

Harry straightened up, smiled, and smoothed his hair back again. He walked back around the bar and put his jacket back on, straightened his trousers, replaced his hat. "Thank you, Mr. Pendle," he said.

"All done, fellows?" Arthur called up the stairs.

The cops came down, looking slightly flushed in the face. "Look what we found," one of them said, holding out a little bag.

Arthur hefted it. "Feels like gold to me," he said. He opened it and dumped it on the bar. Coins tumbled out, some silver but mostly $5 and $10 gold coins.

"He was holding out on us," one of the cops said.

"What a surprise," Arthur said.

He slid two $5 gold pieces down the bar to the cops. "Well done, boys." They pocketed the coins. Arthur knew they'd likely already taken a little off the top, but that was their secret. Besides, there was more than enough to square Mario's account, with some left over.

Arthur counted out $20 and handed it to Harry. Harry nodded, gave him that odd cherubic smile.

Arthur peered over the bar at the prostrate form, grimacing as he saw the chair leg protruding like a tent-pole. The cops took a look too, and winced.

"He's still breathing, right?" he asked Harry.

"Unless he's trying to breathe out of his asshole," Harry said, smiling.

CHAPTER 22

Spotlight and Shadow

THE PRIVATE PHONE RANG IN EDWARD'S OFFICE. HE WAS STAND-
ing at the filing cabinet and reached over to pick up the earpiece. It was
Sarah.

"Eddie! How is my little envelope man today?"

"I'm doing pretty well," Ed said. "You sound like you have a big smile
on your face today."

"I always smile when I hear your voice."

"Same here. And to what do I owe the pleasure of this call?"

"There's something I need to tell you. Before you hear from anyone
else."

"This doesn't sound good."

"I'll come right out with it. Seth and I were at the Pan last night for
the light show."

"That's a coincidence. Allie was there last evening, too."

"That's what I wanted to tell you. I saw her there."

"She didn't mention seeing you."

"If she had, I don't think she'd tell you."

"Why is that? Because she was with the Pendles?"

"You might say that. But it wasn't the Pendles, plural."

"I don't follow you."

"No Cassie anywhere in sight."

Ed was quiet.

"Arthur and Allie were there alone?"

"Yes. And Eddie—during the light show . . . I saw them *kissing*."

"You saw them *what?*"

"Kissing."

"Now, Sarah, I know you wouldn't—"

"I would never say something like that—to you anyway—if it weren't the God's truth. They were kissing. I saw it with my own eyes. So did Seth."

"Well, well," Edward said.

"What does that mean?"

"I don't know what it means. Let's not say any more on the phone, though."

"I know this is upsetting, but I'd rather you heard it from me."

Edward was breathing hard, felt like he needed to sit down, but then thought he might not be able to stand again. "Of course. It was the right thing to do—to tell me."

"Please tell me we'll talk about it. Not now, but sometime. Don't keep this bottled up inside."

"No—I mean, yes, we'll talk about it. I have to travel this week, though."

"Where are you going now?"

"Cleveland," he said.

"How exotic! I'll miss you, Eddie. Then we'll meet next week at Lang's? Five Fours day, as usual?"

"I'll be there," he said. "And Sarah—thanks again for telling me about all this."

Edward gently set the earpiece back on the telephone, staring at the device as if it might start talking again. He steadied himself against his desk, his legs weak and wobbly.

❦

Edward's business put him on the train at least a week a month. It was usually the same trip, snaking down the Lake Erie shoreline to Cleveland, then to Indianapolis, and back again. Occasionally to Pittsburgh. Dull, but he knew the territory well.

He missed the girls when he traveled, but only Millie, the youngest, still treated him like daddy. The other two, Mary Anne and Caroline, were teenagers and fast becoming young women. Since Mrs. Hall had joined forces with Alicia, a wave of coldness toward him had overtaken the two older daughters. If he heard laughter coming from their bed-rooms, it decayed into a whisper as his footsteps approached. Little by little, he had felt at home only when alone in his den, with the door closed. Late at night, he would sneak out to the kitchen for a bowl of cereal, put coal on the furnace if it was chilly, and then go up to bed. Sometimes he'd just fall asleep in the den, on the long Turkish divan tucked under the north windows.

"I have to go to Cleveland this week," he said to Allie that evening, after Sarah's call had had some time to sink in.

"Cleveland again?" Allie said.

"Yes, there's a situation there I need to tackle."

"Maybe you'll tackle Helen Warren while you're at it."

"Wouldn't you like that?" he said. "You could get rid of me for good, then."

"Oh, Ed, my life would be barren and joyless without you. You know that."

"Uh-huh. In any case, I'll be gone a few days. Maybe most of the week."

"If you must, you must," she said. He tried to detect any duplicity, but she was as cool, normal, unaffected as always.

The next morning, though, Edward didn't go to Cleveland but in-stead hopped the Express to New York City. After Sarah's report, he'd placed calls to several New York detective agencies. He hated spending the ridiculous long-distance charges, but there wasn't time to waste. Some of the firms had flatly turned him down, claiming to be too busy—'divorce has become quite a fad these days,' one said. Others fo-cused mainly on corporate work.

He found the New York agencies' attitude dismissive and a little rude until, on his seventh try—'lucky seven!' he said aloud before plac-ing the call—he reached the Mooney & Boland Detective Agency. Bo-land had a good reputation, divorce work was a specialty, and they didn't seem to look down their noses at miserable married men from the sticks. They agreed to meet, and after a peaceful train ride and evening away from the simmering tension at home, on Wednesday morning Edward sat with two of Boland's agents, Detectives Williams and Reitz.

Williams was a nondescript fellow of middle height and sandy hair, who dressed like any middling businessman. Reitz was a big German, either off the boat or first generation, with a pronounced accent. He would be perfect in certain parts of Buffalo, where the dominant ethnic group was still German.

Edward had never worked with detectives before, and given the exorbitant fees he'd be paying—$20 a day for the two men, plus expenses—he wanted to do all he could to help.

"The most important element in sleuthing," Detective Williams told him, "is surprise. We can't have your wife knowing that you have engaged us to shadow her. Nor can any man who may be paying her unwanted attention."

"I understand completely."

"Who is the gentleman in question?" Williams asked, opening his notebook.

"Arthur Pendle. He's an attorney in the city."

Williams jotted while Reitz listened.

"Your families are friendly? You and the Pendles?"

"We're on good terms," Edward said. "I wouldn't say that he and I are close, but everything is quite cordial. In fact, I only recently gave him a tour of my factory."

"Good," Williams said. "Keep it that way, as far as you are able. Cordial. The more sociable you are with him, the less he's going to suspect."

"I've done that to a fault. Like an idiot, I even told the man—I'm not sure why—that my wife enjoys his company. I meant it as a compliment, not an encouragement."

"Don't upbraid yourself, Mr. Miller. That may work to your advantage in making him believe that you suspect nothing. That gives us the best chance of gathering evidence if anything is going on."

"Thanks. I feel a little better about that."

"Do you have any evidence of wrongdoing now?" Williams asked.

"My wife has neglected me for quite some time. Earlier this year, she attacked me with a brass monkey—"

"A monkey?"

"Not an actual monkey. It was a paperweight in the shape of a monkey. She threw it at me, and beaned me in the head. Took twelve stitches."

"Ouch," Williams said.

"And this weekend, she was observed by someone I trust, kissing Pendle in front of God and everybody."

"That's good," Williams said, scribbling. "Not good, I mean—good evidence. Anything else?"

"Only suspicion. She's sunnier now than she's ever been. That's a tip-off, for sure."

"Got it," Williams said. "The only other thing I need to know—is what exactly is your objective?"

"My objective?"

"I wasn't being clear," Williams said. "What I mean to ask is—if we do uncover wrongdoing, what do you want to do about it? Do you want your wife to come home and be good to you? Would you prefer to seek a divorce? Do you want to damage the reputation of the other man in question?"

"Yes, I should like a divorce," he said. "I don't care to live the way I'm living. Though I don't care to do any harm to Mrs. Miller, nor to Mr. Pendle, for that matter. I'd probably be happiest, for the sake of my girls, if they went off quietly together. It would be a halfway respectable outcome."

"That's very helpful, Mr. Miller. And very magnanimous, if you don't mind my saying. Not every man would be so broad-minded in your situation."

"I'm no saint," Edward said. "Alicia has more than a few reasons to be disappointed in me."

Williams smiled, and so did Reitz, who revealed a mangled set of teeth that had seen their fair share of brawling.

"It's refreshing to hear that from you," Williams said. "Though I would like to caution you about something. The evidence we may collect can provoke very unexpected emotions. It's one thing to suspect—even know—that something is going on. It's quite another to see the proof."

"I'll do my best to maintain my composure," Edward said.

"We'll make it as easy for you as we can. We can come to Buffalo around the last week of August and get started."

"The last week of August? Is that the soonest you can manage?"

"I'm afraid so. We have a couple of matters we need to wrap up here, and it'll be better for your case if we can focus on it without distraction."

"Very well. Give me a few days' notice before you arrive. And stay at the Iroquois, if you can. Pendle hangs around that place a lot. You'll pick up his scent easily there."

❦

As her marriage to Edward had slowly curdled, Alicia had become ever more attentive to her mother. Mrs. Hall was small, like her daughter, but her size was no mark of frailty. The same unshakeable physical constitution that had served her so well in the stew of disease along the waterfront was matched by an adamant mental attitude that wasted no time in adapting to changed and changing circumstances.

After Mr. Hall's fatal slip on the ice, Mrs. Hall almost immediately moved in with the Millers. The new widow quickly set about disposing of her husband's clothes and personal effects. She'd offered Edward his watch, which he politely declined, so off to the jeweler it went, along with the man's wedding band, cufflinks, and sundry items. Within a few short weeks, it was as if Mr. Hall had never existed. Edward found it unsettling how quickly his mother-in-law's grief had dissipated, and wondered whether Allie had inherited the trait.

Mrs. Hall had never particularly liked Edward, but he served a purpose. A boring envelope man wasn't going to do anything crazy, such as spirit his wife out West or seek his fortune in the Klondike. With a man like Edward, Alicia would stay close to home, where she belonged.

But when Arthur took center stage, Alicia seemed to forget her mother as quickly as her mother had forgotten her late husband. Allie spent every spare moment out of the house, leaving her mother to look after the girls, make sure the grocery orders were placed, supervise Annie, and so on. That was not what Mrs. Hall had bargained for when she'd moved in with her daughter. She wished Allie would make up her mind so that life could return to normal. Arthur or Edward, it didn't matter much.

What gave her the sweats was the very real possibility that while Alicia was having the time of her life, she was, in reality, playing a dangerous game. She might lose both men, and wind up alone, Mrs. Hall in tow. Allie had already given away the two things that men cared most about—children to Edward and the other thing to Arthur. There was nothing left to surrender except her reputation, and that was hanging by a thread.

CHAPTER 23

Batavia

WHEN SHE ARRIVED AT SETH'S BATAVIA HOUSE, SARAH LAID OUT A little snack for them: crackers, cheese, and grape juice. She would have liked a glass of champagne, but putting alcohol in front of Seth wasn't a good plan. Maggie was snoozing in the back bedroom after the trip from Buffalo.

"How about a cocktail to go with this?" Seth said. "Something to cool us off. It's damned hot today."

"There's no such thing as 'a' cocktail with you. One becomes five, and five becomes however many you can manage before you pass out. Think of this as unfermented wine."

"Since when did you join the Temperance bandwagon? I don't see you all week, and you arrive looking so pretty. That's cause for celebration."

"You're a grown man," she said with a sigh. "Pour yourself a cocktail if you want. I'm not going to."

Seth went to the vice cabinet and opened the door.

"Eeny-meeny-miny-mo," he murmured, "Let's see, what would be nice with those crackers?"

Sarah rolled her eyes.

"Let's try this."

He brought over to the table a bottle of Monarch bitters and a pint of Old Overholt rye whiskey.

"We're drinking the good stuff to celebrate my wife's return," he said, pouring the rye into two glasses and topping them off with the bitters.

"To you," he said, raising his glass.

She clinked hers against his and sipped the drink, grimacing. "How can you stand this? It's horrible."

"We don't have any ice," he said. "Let me add some water to yours."

"I thought you wanted to cool off," she said. "I feel like my whole head is on fire now."

He diluted her potion, and she took another sip. "That's a little better," she said. "Not by a lot, but it's drinkable. Now then, what have you been doing with yourself since the Pan-American?"

"Same thing as always. Seeing patients."

"You don't look like a man who's been seeing patients. You need a bath, and you smell terrible."

Seth's sallow complexion made his dark hair, already streaked with grey, and copious mustache seem to float in midair, as if the man himself were gradually vanishing.

He tossed back his glass at a gulp.

"We could take a bath together," he said.

"You'd have to take one first," she said.

"I know you don't believe me, but I have had some new patients."

"Who? Most of the locals don't even have teeth."

"I had a new one this week—whom you know."

"Who's that?"

"None other than Cassie Pendle." Seth refilled his tumbler of rye.

"Cassie? There's not a thing wrong with her teeth. And even if there were, why would she come all this way?"

"It's a new procedure. On her gums."

"On her gums."

"That's right."

"You didn't say anything to her, did you? About Arthur and Alicia Miller?"

Seth mumbled something into his glass.

"Did you?"

"No, I didn't. But we got to talking about the Pan, and I said we were there on Saturday night, and she said that so were Arthur and Allie. And I said, yes, we saw them there."

"What did she say?"

"She said something weird. That they make a beautiful couple."

"Are you serious?"

"Yes, something to that effect."

"Good night," Sarah said. She took a tentative sip of her drink and thought for a minute. "It didn't make sense that a lady like Cassie Pendle would take the train all the way out here for her gums or your gossip. Until it hit me a second ago."

"What hit you?"

"Why she was here to see you."

"It's bad enough you think I'm a rotten husband," he said morosely. "Now you don't even think I'm a good dentist. 'Oh, no one would come all the way to Batavia to see you.'"

"Boo-hoo. Cassie certainly wouldn't. My guess is that she was here to buy narcotics."

"Narcotics?"

"Don't play innocent with me. What are you selling her? Is that how you're making your money now?"

"If I were, it's a hundred percent legal. I'm licensed."

"How pathetic," she said. "My husband, the dope peddler." She pushed her glass away from her in disgust.

"If you don't like your cocktail, I may have something else you will like," Seth said, sliding her glass in front of him.

"I don't want anything else, thank you."

Seth got up and disappeared into the room where Maggie was napping. He emerged again holding an apothecary bottle, stoppered with a cork. He took out his handkerchief and sat down at the table, working at the cork.

"You must try this," he said. "You'll love it."

He eased out the stopper, held his handkerchief under the mouth, and carefully sprinkled it with a few drops. Then he sealed the bottle up again. He waved the handkerchief a few inches under his nose and inhaled deeply, closing his eyes. In a few seconds, the air was filled with the odor of burned cotton candy.

"What in the world is that?" Sarah said. "Is that the ether again?"

"Try it," he said. "Hold this under your nose." He held out the handkerchief. "Quick, before it all evaporates."

"Not until I know what it is."

"More for me." He sniffed the handkerchief again and had to put his head down on the table.

"Seth?"

"What?" he said drunkenly into the table.

"I keep asking you—is that ether?"

"What else?"

"And you're sniffing it why?"

He raised his head off the table and said, "Try it for yourself. You'll see."

She shook her head. "I don't think so. You look like you're going to pass out."

He laughed. "I might, at that. Come on, try it. Don't be such a stick-in-the-mud."

"I can't believe you had that stuff in the room where our daughter is sleeping. It's dangerous. Flammable. And as I've said before, not something to be sniffing for fun and games."

"Oh, you," he slurred, waving his hand. "You're such a killjoy."

"I am not a killjoy."

"Look," he said. He unstoppered the bottle again, added a few drops to his whiskey, and drank it down. "You can drink it, too. But sniffing's more tame." He dripped ether on the handkerchief again. He swayed to his feet and came around the table to Sarah. "I'll hold it for you. All you have to do is breathe."

She pushed him away with one arm. "I don't want to, Seth. Go away."

"Go away? That's a hell of a thing to say to your husband you haven't seen for a whole week. Be sociable for a change."

"I am sociable, but for the last time—"

Seth stepped behind her chair and, with his forearm, trapped her head against his stomach. Then he pressed the handkerchief against her face. She struggled, tried again to protest, but opening her mouth only filled it with fumes. As the vapor swirled upward, it shed its sickly-sweet disguise, became hot and acrid. Yet as vile as it tasted, the feel of it—a numb, pulsing vibration roaring like a grass fire from her face to her fingertips, wedded to a harrowing sense of both supreme confidence and insuperable lethargy—made her seize Seth's hand, not to pry it away, but instead to bury her face in the handkerchief more deeply. She inhaled, hungrily, and never felt herself hit the floor.

❦

Seth was out cold on the davenport when Sarah came to. She was lying supine on the hardwood, looking up at the underside of the table, with a pounding headache that made it hurt to draw a breath. Good lord, she thought—Maggie. She crawled out from under the table and used the chair to wobble to her feet. She peered bleary-eyed into the bedroom, where Maggie was still peacefully napping. I wonder how long I was out?

The bottle of ether was sitting guilelessly on the table, the dragon inside again contained beneath the tiny stopper. I've got to get Maggie out of here, she thought. And I'm not leaving this for him to kill himself. She snatched up the apothecary bottle and tucked it into the pocket of her dress. Padding softly into the adjacent room, she gathered up her carpet bag and the little girl's frilly traveling case and gently shook Maggie awake.

She put her finger to her lips. "Come on, dear, we're leaving," she whispered. "Don't make any noise. We want to surprise Daddy when he wakes up."

She bustled Maggie in front of her and, at the front door, looked back over her shoulder. Seth was snoring peacefully on the davenport. Sarah eased the door open and slipped out, walking quickly toward the station.

On the train, she stowed their gear on the rack above their heads and got Maggie situated next to her. Sarah watched the platform anxiously, heart beating hard, afraid that Seth would discover them gone, follow them to the station, make a scene. But when the train jerked into motion, there had been no Seth, and she relaxed. Maggie was already fast asleep, her head pillowed on Sarah's lap. She felt something digging into her leg and realized that Maggie was resting on the ether bottle. Easing a hand under her daughter's curls, she fished out the bottle and transferred it to her other pocket.

Sarah's head throbbed all the way back to Buffalo, in time to the rhythm of the locomotive. At home, she and Maggie had an early supper and went up to bed almost as soon as the sun vanished, still without any word from Seth. In her bedroom, Sarah slowly combed out her thick hair. She knew now, beyond question, that Seth was lost and that she was powerless to stop his self-destruction. She looked at the bottle of ether sitting on the dressing table, considering where to hide it, away from an inquisitive child. She set her hairbrush down quietly and picked up the bottle, wiggling the cork to test the seal. And it took everything she had not to put a drop or two on a cloth and hold it under her nose— if only to feel invincible again for a few, fleeting seconds.

CHAPTER 24

The Keepsake Box

BACK FROM THE POST OFFICE, ALICIA WAS PUTTING AWAY AR-
thur's latest letter in the little keepsake box he'd bought her at the
Pan-American. She knew it was wrong to keep the letters; he'd been emphatic about that. He'd reminded her, again and again, to burn them.
But she simply hadn't the heart to destroy letters that said so eloquently
what she'd always wanted to hear.

She'd started keeping them all. It'll be like our diary, she thought,
and one day we'll read them together. There were so many now—after
only a few months—that she could barely close the lid and secure the
lock.

"Who are those from?"

She whirled around to see Edward leaning against the frame of her
bedroom door.

"You're home early."

"Had a meeting that ended early. I thought I'd come home for a
change and see what I've been missing."

"What are you talking about?"

"Who are all those letters from?"

She said nothing.

"Don't bother. I know."

"Oh, you do?"

"Yes, I do. From *Arthur.* Am I right?"

"I don't go through your correspondence, do I?"

"You're not denying it."

"Why would he write letters to me, anyway?"

"I don't know. Why wouldn't he?"

"He'd have nothing to say to me. He's an educated, worldly man."

"Not a rube like me."

"You're so tedious. Will you please go away?"

"Let me see them." He gestured with his fingers.

"I will not. What I keep in the privacy of my room is none of your business."

"Anything that happens under this roof is my business. Hand me the box, Alicia."

"Shoo. Go back to work, where you belong."

"I will not."

"Then we'll stand here forever, like a couple of dodoes."

"Give me the box," he said. "I'm not joking around."

"Over my dead body."

He wasn't smiling anymore. His eyes were cold, full of menace.

"Don't tempt me," he said quietly.

"Get on with it, then. Put us both out of our misery."

"Too easy," he said. "I'd rather see you miserable than dead."

"We differ in that, then."

"Very droll. For now, I'll let you have your way. I will go away, gladly, and give you the evening to yourself. I'll be staying at the Genesee tonight. I'll call the girls before bedtime to say goodnight."

"I'll make sure someone else answers," she said.

❦

Edward wasn't a half-block down the street before Alicia was on the phone, ringing Arthur's office.

"Hello, my dear."

"We need to meet," she said. "Urgently."

"I like the sound of that."

"It's not always about *that*. Can we meet downtown in an hour?"

"Of course," he said. "There's some work going on around One Two Three today, though. Too many people about. How about instead . . . the lobby of the Genesee?"

"Anywhere but there."

"As you wish. I have a better spot. I just rented an office in the Ellicott Square. Second floor. My name is on the door. I'll be there when you arrive."

In less than an hour, Alicia rapped gently on the glass of the oak door, off the iron staircase leading from the grand lobby to the second floor of the Ellicott Square Building. The pebbled glass window in the door read

Arthur R. Pendle, Esq.
Collections.

Collections? she wondered.

Arthur answered the door. He was wearing a brocade vest, a heavy gold watch chain, and a crisp white shirt.

"Fancy meeting you here, Mrs. Ashwood," he said.

The office was rather plain, just a desk, a Mission-style settle, a couple of chairs. He could sense her surprise.

"I only recently engaged the space," he said. "I've not had time to furnish it properly."

"Since when have you been in the collections business?" she asked.

"Not long. But I think it'll be a good business."

"You seem to have the Midas touch."

"I don't know about that. Now tell me—what is going on? You seemed rather distraught."

"It's Ed. He saw me with—one of your letters today."

"One of my letters? Was he at the post office when you checked our box?"

"No," she said slowly. "It was at home. It was a letter—I'd kept."

"One you'd kept?"

"Now don't be cross, Arthur."

"You know you're supposed to destroy those."

"I know, I know. And I did, most of them. A few I kept."

"Did he *read* it?"

"No, it's not that bad. He saw me putting it into my Japanese keepsake box. The one you bought me."

Arthur exhaled hard. "Is that it?"

"That was only the beginning of it."

"How so?"

"He became enraged. He demanded that I give him the box and the key."

"That scoundrel! It's your private property. You didn't, I hope?"

"Never. I'd die before I'd—but that's the part I need to tell you."

Arthur leaned toward her on the settle.

"When I refused to give him the box, he said, 'I could strangle you!' and he charged into my room, and—he put his hands around my throat—"

"He didn't!"

"He did! I was terrified he would throttle me. Look," she said, pulling down her collar, "I'll bet you can see his handprints."

Arthur craned over, looking at her creamy white skin, smelling of gardenia. He didn't see any marks.

"I believe I can," he said. "This is monstrous."

"Arthur, what am I to do? I don't feel safe. He could kill me in a fit of rage or harm the girls."

"I should teach him a lesson, man-to-man."

He savored this for a second, picturing the scene.

"You do love me, don't you, Arthur?"

"More than anything, dear. You can't know how much."

"Will you always?"

"Always."

"What should I do now—about the letters, and Edward?"

"Are the letters still at your house?"

"Yes, in the keepsake box. Edward left in a huff, and I put them back and 'phoned you."

"You need to go back there right now and burn them. All of them, before he gets ahold of that box."

"I will. I promise."

Arthur stewed a little, wiggling his foot back and forth, as he did when he was agitated.

"You oughtn't to have kept those letters."

"I know. But they were dear to me."

He put his hand gently on her shoulder and leaned over. "This is where that miscreant grabbed you?" He brought his lips close to her neck.

"Yes," she whispered.

He kissed the spot, once, and then again. He was tempted to do more, but then thought better of it. The time was better spent getting rid of those damned letters.

"You'd better go," he said.

She gathered up her purse. "Yes, you're right."

"And make sure you tell me if he ever lays a hand on you again. I'll make him pay dearly for it."

"Sue him for damages, you mean?"

"A lawsuit would be the least of his problems. Suffice it to say that I know plenty of people that would be willing to help me settle the matter more dramatically."

❦

The keepsake box seemed to be safe and untouched when she got home. She weighed it in her hands. It had become surprisingly heavy, this chronicle of their love. She opened the lid. They were all there, and in the order she knew from riffling through them a hundred times. She looked at the fireplace in her room. She knew it was the right thing to do, but the thought of all that joy, all poured out for her, over her, going up in flames and lost forever, was almost unthinkable.

The mantel clock chimed 2 o'clock.

Two o'clock. A private smile spread over her face. Buffalo Savings Bank closes at 3, she thought. This is something that he'll wish he'd thought of, himself.

She tucked the keepsake box into a carpet bag and hurried to the trolley on Bryan Street. At the downtown stop, she alighted and walked a block to the Buffalo Savings Bank. There, she rented a safe deposit box and locked all of Arthur's letters in it. She took the empty box home and put it back into her armoire. I hope he does pry it open now, she thought, with some satisfaction. I'd love to be a fly on the wall.

❦

After their argument, Ed went downtown and checked in at the Genesee, a decent-enough business hotel, where he flopped supine on the bed with the afternoon sun streaming in, to calm down and nurse a throbbing headache. When he awoke, the sun was long gone, and it was too late even for supper.

The next day, late morning, he called his house. Annie answered and, as expected, told him that Mrs. Miller had left for a luncheon with some friends and would be back by mid-afternoon. No need for her to call me back, Edward said. Nothing urgent.

He hopped aboard a trolley and rode back to Ashwood Street, where he watched his house from a safe distance. No sign of Allie. He walked up the front steps and let himself in and, keeping an eye out for Annie, tiptoed upstairs.

When he lifted the keepsake box from Alicia's armoire, he could tell it was empty, its incriminating contents gone. He put it back quietly and looked in the fireplace. No ash. The only other place, he thought, was the coal furnace in the basement. He went softly down the stairs and down again into the cool dampness of the cellar.

A little light was coming in from around the door of the coal chute. He felt for the box of matches and the kerosene lamp that he kept on a little shelf at the bottom of the stairs. It was his job to add coal to the furnace in the winter, shake the grate for the cinders to fall through to the collecting bin. Then, once a week, an ash-man would come to carry them away. Fortunately, the furnace had been cold and clean since April. He opened the coal door in the side of the hulking, black furnace and stuck the lamp in.

No trace of fresh ash. No smell of burned paper, either. So she hadn't burned them, not here anyway. He turned out the lamp and replaced it on the shelf. Back upstairs, he thought of one other possibility and walked back to the kitchen to rummage through the trash bin.

"Mr. Miller?" He turned around to see Annie wondering at why the man of the house would be elbows deep in refuse.

"Annie," he said. "You startled me. I was missing a—piece of paper I'd written some figures on, and I thought maybe it had gotten into the garbage."

"Where did you have it last?"

"I think it was in my den, but I'm not sure."

"I haven't been there yet today, so it may be still in the trash bin."

"Oh, good. I'll check in there next. It might be at my office."

"Very well. Let me put all that rubbish back for you."

"Thank you," he said. "I'm going to get downtown now for the rest of the day. I'll see if I can find it there. Oh, and I'll probably stay in the city again tonight since it'll be late."

On the way back to Miller Envelope, he swung by the Iroquois Hotel and left a message for the Boland men, who had arrived in Buffalo and had started snooping around.

❧

Williams called him back in less than an hour.

"Mr. Miller?" he said. "I was about to call you myself. We have some interesting news."

"I have some too. If you're at the hotel, I can walk over and meet you in the bar downstairs."

At the bar, Edward and the two detectives holed up at a corner table.

"You go first," Williams said.

"Mrs. Miller and I had a no-holds-barred spat over a box she has stuffed full of letters. I'm sure they're from Pendle."

"Were you able to get a look at them?"

"No. By the time I could, she'd already disposed of them. I checked the grate in her room, and the furnace as well. No ashes. No smell of anything having been burned."

"You're a good detective," the usually silent Reitz said.

"Trying to help," Edward said. "But I can tell you she was rather sensitive about them, so I doubt she destroyed them."

"Very interesting," Detective Williams said. "And I think we know where she hid them."

"Where?"

"Yesterday afternoon, we picked her up around half-past two."

"That would have been shortly after our argument."

"She got down from the streetcar and walked to the Buffalo Savings Bank."

"That's odd," Edward said. "We don't have any accounts there. Could she have opened an account for herself?"

"I followed her in," Williams said. "She engaged a safe deposit box. She went into the vault with a bag that seemed quite full, and when she came out, it looked to be empty."

"I'm sure it was the letters," Edward said.

"The two puzzle pieces do fit together."

"Is there any way we can get our hands on them? Short of bank robbery, that is," Edward said.

"We do have an idea," Williams said. "No bank robbery required, either. But we are going to need your help."

"Whatever you need," he said.

CHAPTER 25

It Pays to Advertise

LANG'S WAS BUZZING WHEN SARAH AND EDWARD TUCKED INTO their chocolate fudge, which had a gooey butterscotch ribbon winding through it. He'd also gotten each of them a gigantic vanilla float with strawberries and cream.

"It's been a while," she said. "How were things in Cleveland?"

"The way they always are. I'm sure Batavia was more interesting," he said, putting his palms flat on the marble top of the table, which felt delightfully cool after the blazing heat outside.

"That's one way to put it."

"That good?"

"Seth is getting worse, that's all."

"Are you and Maggie all right?"

"Yes, we're both fine."

She looked down at the table, then back into his eyes. "I feel lonely when I'm with him, and that makes me sad."

He so wanted to tell her it would all be all right. Instead, he took a big swallow of his ice cream float and was silent.

"Do you disapprove, Eddie? Perhaps I'm being too forward."

"Nothing of the sort," he said. "I'm flattered when you tell me things." He stared into his ice cream.

"Let's change the subject," she said.

"We don't need to change the subject. It's—well, I don't know quite what to say."

"Then we'll wait until you do." She reached over and tugged at his cuff. "Did you know you're missing a cufflink?"

He looked at his sleeve ruefully. "Yes, I was getting dressed today and couldn't find it."

"One of your nice gold ones, too. With your initials."

"I know. It's distressing."

"Were they a gift from Alicia?"

"No, if they had been, I wouldn't mind. My sister gave them to me when I started the business."

"That's a shame. I hope you didn't lose it on your trip."

"If I did, it's lost forever. Well, nothing to be done about it," he said.

"Still, it's too bad. I hate losing things." She settled back in her chair. "You must have some news for me. You look like the cat that ate the canary."

He laughed. "I suppose I do, at that. I hired a detective agency. To see what Allie is up to."

"You didn't!"

"I did indeed. Boland Agency, out of New York."

"You said you'd gone to Cleveland."

"I did, but I made a quick trip to New York first."

"You sneaky little man! And you kept me in suspense until now?"

"I know how you like surprises."

"Tell me all about it," she said, nibbling at her fudge. "Don't leave out a single detail."

"They'll come to Buffalo in late August and follow them around. Other than that, I don't know if they have a plan."

Sarah leaned over the table so far that she could have sampled Edward's float. "I'm sure they'll see something going on. Those two can't resist each other."

"I blame Pendle more than I do Allie. I'm not sure he can control himself."

"Allie could stop him if she wanted to."

"I suppose," he said. "Though men do seem to find her bewitching. I was her first victim."

"You were a boy. What could you know of life or women?"

"I don't know much about either, still."

"Are you fishing for compliments?"

"No," he said. "Women mystify me, that's all."

"Women mystify everyone, dear. We mystify one other. Don't think it's only a man thing."

"That's refreshing to hear."

"I hope your detectives catch them red-handed," Sarah said.

"Things do seem to be heating up. In fact, I found Allie stuffing some letters into a box she has in her room. I'm sure they're Arthur's."

"And?"

"She refused to show them to me. Later on, I went to check the box, and they were gone."

"She's hidden them somewhere!"

"No doubt. But if they can be found, these detectives will find them."

"I don't suppose you know that one day I intend to have my own detective agency," she said.

He sat back in his chair. "You're joking."

She scowled, her pretty face looking as mean as she could make it. "I am not *joking*. I've wanted to do it since I was a little girl. I even have a name for it."

"What is it?"

"I plan to call it the 'Avenging Angel Detective Agency,'" she said proudly. "Maybe Angels, plural, if one day Maggie will join me."

"You would be good at it," Edward said.

"If only I could figure out what makes *you* tick, Mr. Miller."

"That should take all of five minutes," he said. "I'm not complicated. Allie says I'm boring."

She shook her head. "That's because Allie doesn't realize what she has."

"Yes, she does, and that's why she wants Arthur. He's everything I'm not. Educated. Tall. Byronic."

"I'll agree he has a lot to offer. On the surface. But on the inside, he's got a tapeworm eating his soul."

"You do come up with the most appetizing comparisons," Edward said, looking at the butterscotch ribbon slinking out of his piece of fudge.

"Don't be such a namby-pamby," she said. "I think anyone would consider herself lucky to be married to a man like you. I'm sorry to say it, but you deserve better."

"Do you have someone in mind?" In the next heartbeat, he regretted saying it. Too much, too soon.

Sarah blushed. "Why, it does pay to advertise, after all." She batted her long lashes at him in mock-coquette fashion.

He looked away. "I didn't mean to be presumptuous—"

"Will you *stop*? Don't apologize for being honest. It's a relief to know that—certain thoughts—have crossed your mind. I've been hanging out on a limb all by myself, until now."

"I'm not in the habit of saying things like that."

Sarah put her hand on Ed's arm. "Now that you've broached the subject about what kind of woman you deserve—I *do* like Helen Warren, I do, but she's much too old for you."

"Helen Warren? What brings up Helen Warren?"

"You were in Cleveland, and that's where the Warrens are now, so I suppose she was rattling around in my head. Rumor has it you two have something going on. Or had."

"That's ridiculous," he said, looking down.

"Surely you know how people used to talk."

"They should keep their dirty thoughts to themselves."

"Don't shoot the messenger," she said. "And as I say, she's too old for you anyway."

"She's a year younger than I am," Ed said. "She's 40."

"And I'm 27." Sarah gave a low chuckle.

"Sarah, I can't even begin to think—"

"You don't have to think. I've already done all the thinking."

"About what?"

"About the future. I've given Seth nine years of my life, and that's my limit." She held up a dainty hand. "And it's long past time you wriggled out of Allie's clutches. Soon enough, your detectives will have plenty of dirt on her."

She put her hand on his and looked around quickly. "And when they do—you know what we ought to do?"

"What?"

"Run away together."

"You're a funny one."

"I'm dead serious. We take Maggie and your girls with us and start over—maybe in California, where everyone goes to start over, and the weather is always nice and not cold and gloomy like it is here. We get a little bungalow in Santa Barbara—that's my first choice, but I promise to keep an open mind—and start fresh. They must need envelopes there, and I'm learning stenography, so I could be your secretary, and you could call me into your office in your mean, old gruff voice, 'Sarah, come in here, sit on my lap and take a letter!'"

"You've thought this through in some detail."

"I have. I think about it all the time."

"You're pulling my leg."

"Don't call me a liar. We both need a fresh start."

"I don't deny that. But running away to California?"

"Close your eyes for a minute," she said. "I'm going to hypnotize you."

"What?"

"Don't always be so contrary. Close your eyes."

He closed his eyes.

"All right," Sarah said softly. "You and I are sitting in the garden of our little bungalow, far, far away from here, in California. The sun is shining on our faces, and flowers are blooming everywhere, and birds are singing. We're watching our little ones playing. The ocean is crashing in the distance. And I reach over and take your hand and squeeze it a little, but I don't say anything at all. We sit like that for hours and hours."

Ed sat there with his eyes closed.

She snapped her fingers. "Now you can open your eyes. Well? What did you think?"

"It looked wonderful."

"Doesn't it? If you want to know another secret, I picture that scene every night before I fall asleep. It makes me happy."

"Too bad it's only a dream."

She looked wounded. "That is about the rottenest thing you could ever say to me."

"I don't mean it badly. I meant that—it *is* a dream. It's not reality."

"Everything's a dream until you do something about it. If we were, for one minute, one *second,* truly serious about changing our lives, we'd get up from this table, go home, collect our things and our little ones— and catch the next train west."

"That sounds lovely, but I have a business, and marriages are still marriages, even if they're no good. Those are complications, you know."

"Complications or excuses, Eddie? Complications can be eliminated, one by one. Excuses will eat up our whole lives."

"I don't know," Edward said. "Sometimes I think I can never be happy again."

"Are you happy now? At this moment? Yes or no."

"Yes."

"Then you can be happy. But we can't wait for happiness to arrive on our doorstep. We have to go to it."

"I wish I had your confidence."

"Don't you worry. I'll wear you down, throwing myself at you week after week, plying you with sweets. I can be very persistent."

"That I know," he said. "But Sarah—"

"What?"

"It's a bit awkward."

"As if we're not both up to our ears in awkward."

"All right. Let's say my detectives do find what I need to break free. What about you? You don't have grounds for a divorce. In New York State—it's adultery or nothing at all."

"You'll have to come up with a better dodge than that."

"It's not a dodge, Sarah. It's the law."

"There's more than one way to skin that particular cat, Eddie," she said, giving him a wicked little leer. "Today, you and I finish our sweets, go anyplace you want, and get busy. A knock-down, drag-out adultery session. Until we're nearly dead."

"Sarah, please," he said, looking around. "Keep your voice down."

"I'm not kidding, buster," she whispered, not quietly at all. "It's been far too long since I've broken a commandment. One of the big ones, too. And we'd be partners in crime."

"You are a firecracker," he said, shaking his head.

"Think about it. Promise me only one thing, though."

"What's that?"

"Whenever you think of a complication, ask yourself if it's an excuse. Will you do that for me?"

"I'll try."

"Look me in the eye. You promise?"

"I promise," he said without looking away.

"Good. And remember, breaking a commandment is one thing, but breaking a promise to me is quite another."

"I wouldn't dare."

"Smart man," she said. She glanced at a tiny watch dangling from a diamond-set pin on her lapel. "My, I must get going, or I'll be late for my tailor, and he doesn't take that sort of thing very well. Finish my float, if you like. My lips were on the spoon." She blew him a kiss over the table and stood to go.

"And when you get a report from your men," she said, "anything, big or small, I want to hear about it. I'm not going back to Batavia, so you can call me at any hour. And"—she leaned down to whisper in his ear—"if you change your mind about the commandment, I'll be two blocks away at Hill's tailor shop. And I don't mind saying you wouldn't regret it, either." She brushed her lips against his cheek, so close to his mouth that he could taste butterscotch. Then she rustled out of Lang's.

CHAPTER 26

The Toughest Cut of All

THE BOLAND MEN'S OBSERVATIONS HAD CHANGED EVERYTHING. Until they joined the cause, he hadn't been sure whether to believe Sarah about what she'd seen at the Pan. She liked to play detective, and she had a personal axe to grind. These men were professionals and could not be doubted. Only this week, they had nearly captured Allie and Arthur on camera, emerging from a house on Whitney Place, but the pair had somehow eluded them.

There was no longer any rush to get home, so after work, Edward walked three blocks to his favorite spot, a wood-and-iron bench facing St. Paul's Cathedral, and let darkness drop over him. Here, in the heart of downtown, the scent of oil, timber, and burning coal wafted over from the harbor like incense.

He loved the smell of the city and the sound of great things happening. It had been so different, growing up in the country, only the scent of hay and the chirp of crickets. In this little city park, an urban orchestra supplied the background, the clang of trolley bells from Main Street, the distant bass thump of steam-dredges mucking out the harbor. The lights were winking on through the stained-glass windows of the cathedral. A cop on his beat strolled by but took no special interest in Edward, a tidy little man in a derby and blue serge suit.

The patrolman disappeared around the corner onto Pearl Street. A minute or so later, Edward saw a young woman steal toward the side door of the church, directly across from his bench. She was carrying what looked like a crate of fruit, which she placed delicately on the step. She pulled the doorbell and scurried away. A few moments later, the Gothic door swung inward, spilling golden light onto the step. A robed silhouette leaned down and examined the crate, then picked it up and retreated with it into the cathedral.

A foundling. Probably some poor prostitute from down in The Hooks got knocked up, and then what could she do? She knew that St. Paul's would find some good church family to take the child in, give him a chance at a decent life. And—another blessing—her baby would never even know that mother had abandoned him. Or would he?

Too much to think about. Let it go, he thought. Better to imagine a happy ending for a change.

❦

"I might need another pair of hands to help me get through this steak," Gaines said the following day, over supper at the Swan Restaurant near the factory. He was sawing away at a particularly resistant piece of beef.

"That does look rather firm, even for here," Edward replied, blowing on his soup. "You ought to know better than to order steak at this place."

"When you say you're picking up the tab," his partner said, "I order steak."

"I admire your honesty."

"What are friends for? Anyhow, what's on your mind? You must have something rolling around up there."

"I need your advice on something."

"I've been wondering about how things have been going lately but didn't want to pry."

"It's about those detectives I hired. From Boland. It's worse than I thought, Howie."

"I'm sorry to hear that."

"They saw them walking together downtown, and then they disappeared. The next day they were spotted coming out of a block of rental houses on Whitney Place, but they were too quick for the detectives to get a photograph."

"They're a couple of crafty ones," Howie said.

"My detectives said they are two of the smartest characters they've tailed in quite some time. Especially considering that they're amateurs."

"I hope you catch them quickly, and you can put this all behind you."

"Thanks," Ed said, sampling his soup. "I hope so, too. Oh—you know another thing the detectives told me?"

Gaines raised his eyebrows while working away at a piece of his steak.

"They watched Pendle's office for almost a week and saw him there only one time. Checked the court dockets, too. Not a single pending case with his name on it."

"So?"

"Come on, Howie, think."

"I am thinking."

"If he's never in his office and has no pending cases . . . where does he get all his money? He lives life on a grand scale. Twenty thousand a year."

Gaines whistled softly. "I know he has a reputation as a big spender, but that big? Wow."

"That's what I've heard."

"Inherited, maybe."

"Doubtful. His father was a ship's master."

"Married into it?"

"Possibly, though Cassie's parents are still alive."

"Then the only other thing I've got, pal, is that he's playing the market."

"Maybe," Edward said.

"But what's the difference? Who cares where he gets his money?"

"My point is: What if it's ill-gotten? He used to be law partners with the District Attorney. He's cozy with the cops, too. My men told me that one cop at the courthouse warned them to stop nosing around in Pendle's business."

"It's possible," Gaines said, putting down his fork. "But even if he's as crooked as a dog's hind leg, you're better off not poking a hornet's nest. People mixed up in that sort of thing will cut your throat without a second thought."

"I want to find out what he's up to," Edward said. "If I can dig up some dirt on him, it would give me a great deal of leverage."

"You said you wanted my advice, right?"

"I did."

"Then my advice is to file for a divorce when you have enough evidence and be done with it. Don't worry about what Pendle is up to. Let him do whatever he does, and let Allie deal with it. Get on with your life."

"I don't disagree with you," he said. "But what if Pendle is mixed up in something criminal? Do I want my girls being raised, part of the time anyway, by a man like that?"

Gaines chewed gamely on another wad of his steak. He raised his eyebrows, pointing at his mouth, and grunted.

"For the love of God, don't talk with your mouth full," Edward said. "Sorry," Gaines said, swallowing hard. "Look. What if you divorced your wife like any other fellow would? That is, without knowing anything about whoever her next husband might be? You can't control who she winds up with."

"True, but if I *do* know, I can't pretend I don't know. If I went to trial, I could name him co-respondent, and he'd have to defend himself. It'd all come out then—any criminal stuff he's up to. He'd be finished."

Gaines shook his head. "Jesus, Ed. I don't think that's a good idea. If Pendle is dangerous, it's only going to rile him up."

"Right. I can't *wound* him. I can't make a move until I can *finish* him."

Gaines finally gave up on the steak, putting his knife and fork across the carcass. "You asked for my advice, Ed. All I can do is say it again—let it go. Don't go walking into quicksand."

"And I appreciate it, Howie, I do," Edward said. "I knew I could count on you to give me sound advice. That's more than worth the price of a steak."

"I wish you'd thrown in a dental appointment with it," Howie said, pushing with his thumb on a molar that he suspected might have loosened.

CHAPTER 27

Arthur Calls It Quits

September 7, 1901
Saturday

"OF COURSE," ARTHUR SAID, TOSSING HIS NEWSPAPER ON THE TA-
ble. "Now he'll be a genuine hero, on top of everything else. McKinley's
shooting is the best thing that could have ever happened to him."

Cassie looked up from her magazine. "I don't think you ought to say
such things. The President has been shot, Arthur. Right here in Buffalo,
no less. He may not survive. I'm sure Terry isn't happy about that."

"Don't kid yourself. I've never met anyone half so lucky as Terry
Penrose. In school, it was the same story. He never studied, always had
something fun going. At the last minute, he'd ask me to help him. And
he made it through. I was *magna cum laude*, and he—"

"It doesn't help to go over all that again," she said. "You only put
yourself in a blue mood when you do."

"A would-be assassin, of all things, falling into his lap? Open and
shut case, national recognition. He'll be lionized. And meanwhile, what
am I doing? Shaking down the scum of the earth—and for him. What
a waste."

"Life isn't always fair," Cassie said.

"Fair isn't the half of it," he said. "If you'd seen what I saw only a week
ago, you'd throw up."

"I'm sure, Arthur. I'm always worried for you."

"Worrying that I'll get home in one piece is one thing. But the real
worry is what happens if any of this comes to light. If it does, guess what

happens to me? I get disbarred, certainly. I probably go to jail. And what would happen to him? Nothing. I'd be the one hung out to dry."

"Terry wouldn't let that happen to you."

"Oh no? It's every man for himself in such a case."

"He'd be in trouble, too."

"He might not get reappointed, but with all his triumphs, he'd go right back into private practice. With all the people he knows and the favors they owe him, he'd be rich."

Cassie was growing tired of the topic. She'd heard it before, too many times.

"You know what?" he said. "Terry could kill someone and get away with it."

"You know that's not so."

"Sure it is. The cops would arrest some dimwit and pin it on him. I tell you, they would."

"Enough for now, dear. Calm down."

"I am calm."

"If this is bothering you so much, working with Terry, then stop doing it. Our shares of stock have gone up. You can do enough legal work to keep things going while we wait to sell it. Tell him you've done as much as you care to do."

"I've thought about that a thousand times. But our bills—the premiums on the life insurance alone are almost $500 a month."

"I have some money set aside that my parents gave me when we were married. We could live on that until we sell the stock. How much longer do you think that'll be?"

"Maybe six months, a year, Baker said."

"Then we have plenty to last us until then. Tell Terry you're through."

"You wouldn't be disappointed in me?"

"Disappointed? I could never be disappointed in you."

"He won't be amused. I can tell you that."

"Isn't that too bad?" she said. "You're not an indentured servant."

"Then I'll telephone him right now," Arthur said. "I'll ask to see him at his house."

❦

When Arthur arrived, Terry Penrose had a half-dozen lawyers milling around, all looking terribly serious. Arthur waited nervously for at least thirty minutes before the DA joined him in the private office tucked in a corner of the house.

Penrose quickly ran a hand over his shiny head as though smoothing down the hair that had disappeared long ago.

"What's this all about, Arthur? On a weekend, and the day after the President's been shot, to boot. It's been a madhouse around here since yesterday."

"I understand you're busy. But you'll be busier come Monday. What is the President's condition?"

Terry shrugged. "Hard to say. The doctors were naturally very concerned at first, but the current sense is that he'll pull through. He'll probably carry around one of Czolgosz's bullets in his body for the rest of his life, though."

"It's a shame," Arthur said.

Terry shook his head. "No kidding. This is going to finish off the Exposition. Anyway—I need to get back to these other men, so tell me what's on your mind."

"I'll come right to the point. I would like to step back from the work I've been doing with you."

"Step back?"

"We've been at this together for more than two years now," he said, "and Cassie and I have started investing in the stock market. And real estate, too."

"Is it your share of the money? A *third* isn't enough?"

"It's not about the money. I simply need a change."

"A change."

"Yes, a change. And Cassie doesn't approve of the nature of my work."

"I see." Terry stared at him. "How does she feel about the nature of your lifestyle?"

"That's not at issue here," Arthur said. "I'd like to start stepping back."

"I heard that already."

"I'll give you plenty of time to replace me, of course."

Terry tapped on the blotter with his fingers. "That's mighty white of you," he said. "You do know, though, I can't exactly take out a classified ad to replace you."

"I'll do anything I can to make it easier on you."

"Why, thank you. Let me think—I've got it. You know what would make it easier on me, Arthur?"

"You name it."

Penrose's straightened up in his armchair. "What would make it easier for me is to pretend that we never had this conversation. Chalk it up to a very bad day for both of us, and go on as before."

"Terry," Arthur said, drying his palms on his trouser front, "we go back a long way—"

"We do indeed. All the more reason not to have things end in an ugly fashion."

"I don't see why this has to be ugly."

"Did it ever occur to you that leaving your best friend in the lurch, at the moment he's about to start prosecuting the attempted *assassin* of the *President*, might be an ugly thing?"

"The timing can never be perfect."

"And it couldn't be worse. It's as though you're trying to assassinate me, too. Instead, why don't you stop pissing and moaning and letting your wife lead you around by the nose? While I'm DA, you make more money each year than you'd make in a whole career drawing up deeds and such."

"And I don't have any choice in the matter?"

"You always have a choice. But choices have consequences. When I leave my office—for bigger things—I want to have dinner with you and toast how we got things done together. As a team. Don't leave a sour taste in my mouth."

"What am I supposed to say to that?"

"For one, you can say, 'I'll stand with you, Terry. By your side, through thick and thin.' There are at least a dozen things I can think that you might say. Do you want me to go on?"

Arthur looked away, at the inkstand on Terry's desk.

"No, you don't need to go on. You've made your point."

"Arthur, now don't pout. Take it as a compliment—you must know that there's no other man that the District Attorney can trust as much as he trusts you. The question is: Do you trust me? Do you, Arthur?"

"You know I do, Terry."

"Then I'm asking you to trust me again. I'll always look out for what's best for you, but right now, I can't afford to lose you. If, in a year or two, if you still want a change, let's discuss it again. Deal?"

"All right," Arthur said.

"Now that's a load off my shoulders," Terry said. "I can turn my attention back to Czolgosz, where it belongs."

"I'll let you get back to it," Arthur said.

"No hard feelings?"

"No hard feelings." Arthur stood to go. "Good luck with the Czolgosz thing. Let me know if I can help. Now that's a fellow who does deserve the Chair."

"And he'll get it," Penrose said. "Talk soon, Arthur. Always good to see you."

When Arthur got home, he breezed by Cassie and slammed the door to his private office. He sat down hard in his chair, staring at the desk. On it in a place of honor was a Tiffany fountain pen, inkwell, and blotter set his mother had bought him for his graduation, with a shiny 1887 $10 gold coin set in the base. He picked up the pen like an ice pick and studied the sharp, gold nib, wanting to plunge it into his thigh. Instead, he brought it down point-first onto the desktop, hopelessly crumpling the nib and sending a rain of ink onto his shirtfront. He cursed and threw the mangled body of the pen angrily against the wall.

CHAPTER 28

Hares and Hounds

ARTHUR'S UNFAILING CURE-ALL FOR DAYS WHEN NOTHING WENT right was to take his automobile out for a drive. After being rebuffed by Terry on Sunday, he decided to let his machine take him as far from Buffalo as its batteries would allow.

In the garage, the gleaming Babcock was sitting connected to the man-sized battery charger, a tall, black obelisk. It looked like something out of Dr. Frankenstein's laboratory, complete with a big knife switch, oscillating needle gauges, and a big knob to regulate the current as it seeped into the heavy lead-acid storage cells in the rear of the vehicle.

He rarely drove his machine less than flat-out once he was out of the city and sometimes when he was still in it. His little Stanhope model, with the weight of only the driver, could make 20 miles per hour, a mind-boggling speed. And, being electric and equipped with solid rubber tires, it was as silent as it was swift. He loved hearing only the sound of the wind rushing by his ears, bringing the bracing chill off the great lake or the scent of distant factory smoke.

The Babcock ran so quietly that people, dogs, and other critters often didn't know that it was coming at all. He rather enjoyed the startled looks on the faces of children playing jacks or hopscotch in the street as his machine whooshed by them. One time, on the outskirts of Buffalo, a little brown rabbit had been sitting in the middle of the road, idly nibbling a bit of grass that had taken root in the packed dirt. The creature never sensed the danger it was in as he barreled silently toward it. It took the slightest twitch of the steering lever to run it down. The rabbit gave a squeal, and when Arthur glanced back over his shoulder, he saw the little thing lying in the road, the life crushed out.

At first, he'd felt angry at the rabbit, a stupid creature without enough good sense to flee. Such a weak and mewling thing didn't deserve life. Yet his little spasm of violence had given him no release. Instead, as he drove, he kept feeling the bump of the animal's soft body going under the wheels. After a few more miles, he turned around. At least he would throw the remains into the ditch. When he got to the spot, though, there was no sign of the rabbit. He stopped the automobile and got down. Maybe the thing had only been wounded or stunned and had hopped away to safety. Was this even the spot? He walked up and down the dirt road, covering his pant legs and perfectly shined bulldog shoes with a layer of sticky brown dust that would probably never come out. At last, he found what might have been a few spots of blood but no further trace. It was as if the rabbit had ascended directly to Heaven.

When he climbed back onto the driver's bench, heavy with dust, he steered toward Buffalo. About halfway there, the silent Babcock began to develop a little intermittent squeak. Within a few miles, the sound became a rhythmic whine and then a relentless, tormented squeal. He pulled over, and the mystery was quickly solved when he saw oily smoke rising from one of the wheel hubs. A wheel bearing had gone dry, and driving further would do neither him nor the car any good. He set the brake, put the top up in case it rained before the Babcock people could come and haul away the lifeless thing, and, trailing a little cloud of dust, walked all the way back to the city.

❦

While Arthur was making his dusty way back to Buffalo, Allie was sorting the afternoon mail, putting Edward's in a pile on the table. Among them was a letter addressed to him and marked with a rubber stamp, "Personal." It had been addressed to his office on Division Street, but the post office must have thought that a personal letter might better come to the Millers' home address. The return address was

Mooney & Boland Detective Agency.
130 Broadway.
New York, New York.

"What in heaven's name?" Allie muttered to herself, turning the letter over. She held it up to the fanlight above the front door, but she could make out nothing. Annie was busy in the parlor, so Alicia hastened to the kitchen in the back of the hall. There she held the letter up to the window to see if the afternoon sunlight would reveal anything. Again, nothing. The envelope seemed to have security printing on the inside.

She tapped her foot, thinking. She left the letter on the countertop and walked back to the parlor. "Annie," she said, "I'm going to make myself a cup of tea. Would you like one?"

"Oh, no, ma'am," the girl said. "Let me make it for you."

"No trouble at all," Alicia said, holding up her hands. "I'll be fine. You carry on."

Back in the kitchen, Alicia put on the kettle, knowing now that the whistle wouldn't summon the servant girl. She paced the tiles until the kettle started to wheeze, then flipped the whistle up and grabbed the letter.

She'd read about this trick, unsealing an envelope with steam, but had never had occasion to try it. It proved considerably harder than she'd imagined. The paper warped and wrinkled; the ink began to run. Still the glue held firm. Not one of my husband's cheap ones, that's for sure, she thought.

After considerable frustration, she managed to ease a fingernail under the edge of the sealed flap, little by little adding some steam as the glue became treacly. She coaxed the letter out and unfolded it. It was a single sheet of letterhead, elaborately engraved with an all-seeing eye in the center of the masthead. It read:

Dear Mr. Miller,

Yours of Wednesday to hand. Can confirm that AHM and ARP were seen together, again on Whitney Place. Pair disappeared into one of the houses, though may have exited from the rear as not again observed. Please advise if you wish both men next week to continue surveillance.

Yours very sincerely,
J. Wagenfuhl, Manager.
Mooney & Boland, Detectives.

Why, that little bastard, Alicia thought. He's got detectives following us around! She wanted to tear the letter to bits, trample it underfoot, stuff it down Ed's scrawny throat.

Her hands were shaking as she carefully replaced the letter. Resealing the envelope was easier but still sloppy. She set the finished product on the table and examined her handiwork. It looked like a letter that had been amateurishly steamed open, read, and then resealed. Oh hell, she thought, I should just burn it. But what was the point? Another one would come. She left the mangled thing on the table, grabbed her handbag, and walked out the front door. She had to talk with Arthur before Ed got home and saw what was left of his letter.

❦

"Allie," Edward called from his den as the dinner gong sounded.

"Yes, Edward?" Alicia called back.

"Can you come here a minute?"

Here we go, she thought.

"Yes?" she said as innocently as possible when she got to the den. She didn't enter but leaned against the doorjamb. She didn't like his weird little room, all done up with heavy embroidered curtains and vaguely Moorish décor.

He was holding the wrinkled envelope from Mooney & Boland in one hand, the letter in the other. He put them on his desk and took off his pince-nez, rubbing the bridge of his nose.

"I take it you read this letter." He nodded toward the table. "Before you answer—remember, I know a thing or two about envelopes. Not that it would take an expert to know this one had been opened."

No point in lying about it. "I did read it. I was rather surprised, to say the least."

"And why would that be?"

"Detectives, Ed? Really?"

"The way you've been carrying on? You're surprised?"

"The way I've been 'carrying on'?"

"Yes. Most people would call you and Arthur Pendle going into a rented house on Whitney Place 'carrying on.'"

"It's nothing of the sort. I bumped into him when I was downtown doing some shopping. He said he wanted my opinion on a piece of real estate he and Cassie are thinking of buying as an investment."

"Bumped into him, eh? Like you 'bumped into him' at the Pan-American?"

"What is that supposed to mean?"

"Let's say that a little bird told me that a woman who looked very much like you was kissing a man who looked very much like Arthur."

Alicia was stunned but recovered quickly. "That's simply—it was one time. It was an overwhelming experience, the lights. A stupid, imprudent thing, nothing more."

"Though not the only one of its kind, I'm afraid," Ed said. "I don't need to go into all the detail. I know more than you might think."

"Someone spreads a rumor about me, and you go and hire detectives? You could have asked me instead of going to the trouble and expense of private eyes."

"You must take me for an idiot."

She looked at the ceiling. "What now, Edward?" she said. "What do we do about all this detective nonsense?"

"That depends on you," he said. "But a word to the wise—knock it off. Neither you nor Arthur wants to get into a divorce battle with me, I assure you."

She didn't reply for quite some time. "It's time for supper, you know," she said. "Are you quite finished?"

"In a manner of speaking, yes, I am."

❦

He was waiting for her, as she'd requested, near the perfume counter at Meldrum's. It was a spot she knew Edward would never go.

When she mentioned detectives, he pulled her aside. "You can't be serious," he said.

"And they're New York spooks," Allie said. "I don't know what they know, but Ed seems to think—"

"Stop," he said, raising his hand. "I get the picture. I'm surprised they don't have a camera mounted over our bed."

"At least that would give Ed his money's worth."

"Not funny. You know they're collecting evidence."

"Evidence that we've gone walking together," she said in a whisper. "Not that we've been *fucking*. Though, of course, we have been."

"Stop it, will you?"

"Oh, don't be such a nancy. You like it as much as I do."

"That's not the point."

"Fine. What do we do about it, then? He told me if we're not careful, he's going to file for divorce."

"This gets better and better," Arthur said, looking at the ceiling. "We're only having a little fun. If he files for divorce, that would destroy my reputation entirely, and his, too."

"If it came to that?" she said in a little growl. "Where the hell did you think this was leading? You've been saying for months that you're going to ask Cassie for a divorce. What happened to that brave resolution?"

"This is not the place," Arthur said.

"All right, then. Where is the place?"

Arthur smoothed his mustache. "Of course, he may be bluffing. This could all be a ruse. To rattle us."

"I know when he's bluffing. He wasn't. He was preening. You should have seen him."

Arthur thought a moment, then nodded.

"Let's meet at One Two Three tomorrow," he said. "Eleven-thirty. You take Virginia Street to Whitney Place, and I'll take Carolina, so no one sees us together. I have an idea that I want to discuss with you."

"What?"

"A talk with Edward. Man-to-man."

❧

"Are you sure you weren't followed?" Arthur said as they settled down on the sagging, overstuffed couch at One Two Three.

"I grew up six blocks from here," Allie snapped. "I think I know this neighborhood better than a couple of New York stiffs."

"Fine, I didn't mean anything by it. Now, to tackle this little problem with Edward. I need to know what he knows."

"You want to meet with him?"

"If I do say so myself, I think I can coax him to tell me what those detectives have learned. The more we know, the better we can respond."

"He might not tell you."

"I think he will. Especially if the conference is in his offices, on his home field. He'll think he has the advantage."

"If you think so. What can I do?"

"Tell him I would like to meet with him. Man-to-man. Set aside our differences, all that."

"He hates the sight of me. He won't do anything that I ask."

"I'm sure he hates me more. With you, he's got three children."

"All right, then," she said. "I'll ask him."

❦

The meeting was arranged for Friday at Edward's office. Arthur steeled himself for the conversation as he walked toward Division Street from the Aston Building on a crisp, clear day. At least it's man-to-man, he thought. If worse comes to worst, he's a pipsqueak.

Yet when Arthur was ushered into the office, he found himself facing Ed and two other men, looking none too friendly.

"Good day, Edward," Arthur said, holding out his hand.

Edward didn't take the proffered hand but instead gestured to the men flanking him.

"You remember Mr. Gaines," he said.

"Of course. Gaines," Arthur said, giving a little bow of his head but not offering to shake hands.

"And my attorney, Mr. Hartshorn."

"Haven't had the pleasure," Arthur said. "Though I've heard you speak at the Bar Association."

"They let me out of my cage every once in a while," Hartshorn said.

"Why don't we sit," Edward said, "and get down to brass tacks. Arthur, you wouldn't be here, I'm sure, if you hadn't heard about Mooney & Boland."

Arthur shook his head. "On the contrary. I've thought for some time that we were past due for a man-to-man talk."

"Have you seen the letter in question?" Hartshorn asked.

"I have not. But Mrs. Miller has described it."

"Then you understand why I'm considering a divorce," Edward said.

"I most certainly do not," Arthur said. "There has been nothing of a criminal nature between myself and your wife. Your detectives claim to have seen Mrs. Miller and me walking together. If that is so, I'll grant you that was imprudent. But there's no law against that."

"Nor is there a law against abusing someone's friendship," Ed said. "But that doesn't make it right."

"Ed, you yourself have encouraged my friendship with Mrs. Miller. You've cultivated it."

"And that ends today," Hartshorn said. "My client requires that you cease immediately any unchaperoned contact with his wife."

"Rather a dramatic shift in the wind, don't you think?" Arthur said. "But she's his wife. That's his right."

"Then there's only one other thing we require as a precondition for setting this matter aside without legal action."

"Which is?"

"You will leave Buffalo permanently for some other place suitably distant as soon as practicable."

"What?"

"You will leave Buffalo—"

"I'm not hard of hearing," Arthur said. "It's absurd. Who would agree to exile—for walking with someone in public? Imagine explaining that to my clients, my friends—my wife."

"You might not want to explain our draft complaint for divorce to your wife, either," Hartshorn said.

"You and I both know that a complaint can be stuffed with all manner of nonsense." He turned to face Edward. "Ed, I hope this is your attorney's wild idea?"

"The idea is to eliminate temptation, Arthur," Edward said. "Yours—or hers."

"So your answer is to make a fugitive of me?"

"Actions have consequences," Hartshorn said.

"Yes, they do," Arthur said. "And this trial balloon of yours isn't something I'll soon forget."

"Arthur," Ed said, "why don't you make it easy for everyone? Leave the city, have nothing further to do with Alicia, and that will be the end of it. Otherwise, it doesn't end happily for you. You don't want all this becoming public." He picked up a thick sheaf of paper and waved it in the air.

"Is that the detectives' report?" Arthur asked.

"It is."

"If you want me to consider your ultimatum, I need to read it."

"That's not going to be possible," Hartshorn said.

"Let him read it, Bert," Edward said, handing the documents over to Arthur. "I'm not making any of it up. It's all there, in black and white."

"Thank you, Ed," Arthur said. "At least you are behaving like a gentleman. Would you mind giving me some privacy while I read this?"

"Take as much time as you need," Edward said, getting up and motioning to the others. "I don't need your answer today. I recognize this is a matter that requires careful consideration. Telephone me next week."

Alone in Edward's office, Arthur didn't start reading right away. Instead, he looked around the room, at Ed's tidy desk and Gaines' next to it, which looked as though a great wind had swept everything off Ed's desk and deposited it on his.

After musing for a few minutes, he opened the file and began to read. It took him three minutes to make up his mind.

❦

"I think we put him on his back foot," Hartshorn said after Arthur had departed.

"I'm not so sure," Edward said. "He seemed a little too agreeable. Arthur is the most intelligent man I know. He's got something up his sleeve."

"Wondered about that myself," Howie said.

Ed took off his glasses and rubbed his eyes. "I think we may have overplayed a weak hand."

"I don't agree, Ed," Hartshorn said. "I am confident we did the right thing at the right time."

"If you say so," Edward said. "But somehow I think Arthur Pendle isn't going away without a fight."

CHAPTER 29

Mocking the Time

"YOU AGREED TO HIS TERMS?" ALICIA SAID, NONE TOO AMUSED.

They were lying together in the upstairs rear room of a different bolt-hole on 7th Street, watching the sun decline through the window facing the bed. Arthur had hurriedly arranged the new spot, and they had been especially careful about being followed.

Arthur kissed her on the forehead. "My dear, don't be upset. I haven't the slightest idea of following through. I needed to know what he knows. I told them what they needed to hear."

"What did the report say?"

"They've seen us walking together in Buffalo a dozen times, and going into an unidentified house on Whitney Place twice. There were eight or nine other meetings here and there."

"That little shit. What should we do?"

"We don't panic. That's what they're hoping we do."

"I don't want to live my life under a microscope, Arthur. The Pan was bad enough, and now this. Let him file. I'll give him his divorce. I can't wait."

"Now's not the time, Allie."

"Why not? I don't understand what's come over you lately. I was going to leave Edward, and now he's saving me the trouble."

"I have to get Cassie in line first."

"You told me that she would either agree to a divorce, or that you'd go out to Dakota and get one if she didn't."

"Sometimes she seems amenable, sometimes she doesn't. I need to give her time. She's a little fragile right now."

"Fragile?"

"Yes, fragile. Her nerves."

"Because of the drugs?"

Arthur leaned up on one elbow and frowned. "What do you know about that?"

She pulled the sheet over her face. "I oughtn't to have said anything. In New Haven—I found her with her—apparatus."

"I see," he said, lying back again. "And what did you think about that?"

"You want the truth?"

"When have I not?"

"I very nearly asked her if I could try it."

Arthur heaved a long sigh. "I hope you didn't."

"No, but the look in her eyes . . . "

"What about it?"

"Like she was having a prolonged climax."

"You already have plenty of those without starting on that stuff. That dope has hollowed her out. Stay away from it."

"Don't worry. But I don't know what good it does waiting for Cassie to sort out whatever mania the drugs are causing."

"That's only part of it," he said. "The other part is related to the work that I do."

"As an attorney?"

"You know I trust you completely, Alicia," he said.

"I certainly hope so."

"Then if I tell you something about myself, will you promise not to hate me?"

"Unless it is that you've been stringing me along this whole time. Then I think it's fair to say that I'd hate you."

"Thank God it's not that, then. You see, I don't do a lot of standard legal work these days. I do other things."

"Like what?"

"I take care of problems. For the District Attorney."

"Penrose?"

"One and the same."

"Well, you've been friends a long time."

"True," he said slowly. "But what I do now is a little different."

"Are you playing a guessing game with me?"

"No, I'm not. I simply don't know how to put it delicately."

"Then don't."

"I fix problems for Penrose. I collect money—money that not-so-good people pay so they can stay this side of the law."

"Am I to assume that this is not, strictly speaking, legal?"

"That would be an understatement."

"And what does that have to do with getting a divorce from Cassie? Because frankly, if you think that whatever it is you do is worth doing, I couldn't care less about whether it's illegal. Most of the laws are stupid anyway."

He kissed her impulsively on the cheek. "Why do you always surprise me, still?" he said.

"Maybe because you expect so little of me. Or you think I'm just a good fuck, and I don't have a brain. Could be either."

"It's neither."

"Then I do not know."

"You *are* a good fuck," he said, leaning up again and running his fingertip along her neck.

"Ah, the words every woman longs to hear. But don't try to change the subject. What does doing your work for Penrose have to do with getting a divorce?"

"Simple. Cassie knows about it. And if I don't let her down easy, she could turn on me. She could go public with it."

"Ahh," Alicia said. "The little woman scorned."

"More or less. I want to stop working for Terry, but I need to make enough money to—be all set—before I can. That's why I need time."

"I wish you had come out and said it," Alicia said. "All this beating around the bush. I was worrying that you'd cooled off."

"I'm sorry, dear."

"I'll wait for you, Arthur. For as long as I need to, so long as we have a plan. I want to be the center of your life, not someone kept at a safe distance."

"What did I ever do in some former life to deserve you?"

"It must have been awfully good," she said, laughing. "Now what's next? How do we keep from making matters worse than they are?"

"We write to each other at the post office box. We burn our letters as soon as they are read. And when we meet, we plan very carefully and ensure we're not followed. It would be best if we could meet outside of Buffalo."

"I'd love that. Could we go away somewhere together for a few days? It would do us both so much good."

"I was going to mention that very thing. I read in the paper this morning that in a couple weeks, the Women's Suffrage League convention is taking place in Atlantic City. To prepare for the elections. It's going to be quite a shindig."

"Good for them," Allie said. "But you know I don't go in for that horseshit."

"I do know. But does Edward know?"

"Are you joking? Edward doesn't know—or care—what I think about politics. Or most anything else."

"Well? Tell him that you want to go, and then slip away and meet me in New York for a few days."

"Oh . . . I like that idea."

"There's always some pretext I can use to get away to New York. Besides, there's something I want to tell you about, and I want to do it in a special place."

"I love surprises," Allie said. "Ed will be happy to have me gone, anyhow."

"Also, if you're convincing about it, those detectives are not about to chase you to Atlantic City. Ed won't pay for that kind of surveillance. And even if he does, you won't be there, anyway."

"I can be very convincing, you know."

"I do know. Then let's go a week or so after Labor Day. I'll make the arrangements and mail you the particulars. Just be cautious. If we aren't caught out again in the next month or two, Ed will think he's won the day, and passions will cool."

She rubbed her foot against his. "Mine won't. And if I'm not mistaken," she said, looking down, "yours haven't either."

CHAPTER 30

Sell in May and Go Away

"THERE'S AN OLD SAYING ON WALL STREET," ED BAKER SAID. "'SELL in May and go away.' But in this case, it's September instead of May. But that doesn't rhyme."

"Why so soon?" Arthur said.

"I don't like the look of the market right now. Volatility, prices moving up and down, sometimes dramatically. You've done well. Cash in and see what happens for a while."

"I'd hoped to let it rise at least another year."

"I'd like that too, but the market's looking too unstable. I recommend you sell now."

"But what if I sell, and it keeps going up?"

"There's another old saying—bulls win, and bears win, but pigs get slaughtered."

"Haven't heard that one either."

"You can always sell some and hold some," the stockbroker said. "Pay off your margin loan, set your principal aside someplace safe, and let the rest ride. Put it in a different stock entirely. That way, you're only risking your gains."

"If you think so," Arthur said grudgingly. "When should we do this?"

"Your stock has already more than tripled. You're sitting on a little more than $600,000. I'd sell it now—all of it. You've done beautifully. Take your gains and move on."

"Let me talk with my wife. I'll telephone you tomorrow."

"Why not give me the sell order now? I won't put it through until tomorrow. That will give you time to inform the missus."

"I'd rather talk it over with her first."

"Now don't forget. Trust me on this, Arthur."

"I won't, I promise. I mean, I do trust you. And I will telephone."

He made a note in his pocket diary to call Baker as soon as he got back from New York. Oh well, he thought. I'd hoped we'd make an even million, but there's enough now to afford a divorce from Cassie, and live in style with Alicia. And I'll be free of Terry and be my own man again.

How odd it was, he thought, that the very words 'Montana Copper' sounded so promising, like the bright and shining new frontier almost within his grasp. Odder still was the notion that he would owe this prosperous new future to people he'd never met, in a company he'd never worked for, in a place he'd never visited. How strange and wonderful life can be.

"I have to make a quick trip to New York," Arthur said to Cassie over coffee the next morning.

"What for?" she asked. "I thought your last-minute travel was a thing of the past."

"Mostly. An old friend of mine from college needs a little legal advice. Said I'd get a nice steak dinner for my fee."

"Will you see your mother and brother?"

Arthur hadn't considered being asked that question. "Not this time—too hurried, I should think."

"Perhaps I could come along and enjoy the city? If you don't have free time, I could take your family to see a show."

"Not this trip, dear. I'd find it distracting if I couldn't spend time with you or them. Next time, I promise."

CHAPTER 31

Nymphs & Satyr

ED TOOK THE GIRLS AND MRS. HALL TO CHURCH ON SUNDAY, AND then afterward to lunch downtown. Allie said that she wasn't feeling well and would rather stay home and avoid the crowds. It wouldn't make the weekend pass any more quickly, having to spend more of it with Ed than required.

She had picked up a letter from Arthur the day before, proposing a Sunday get-together at One Two Three. She'd turned that down too. They'd see each other soon enough, and Ed had been a little too accommodating of her absences from the house, almost cheerful when she would say that she was going out for a few hours. Until recently, even though he didn't care much about the answer, he would nevertheless ask her where she was going. Lately, he had said only to 'have a good time.' *Have a good time?* Obviously, he was baiting his detectives' hook.

She spent the day in her room, reading, listening to her gramophone, and writing in her diary. Nothing that she wouldn't want Ed to read—the keepsake box had been a close enough call—although, over the years, Alicia had developed a rather elaborate, private code that would read quite innocuously to anyone other than herself. Yet there was no need to take chances, not now. Arthur's letters were safe, and she sensed that Arthur was edging toward a commitment. Tomorrow morning, the two of them would be speeding east on the New York Central Express to arrive in New York in plenty of time for dinner and the theatre. And three days of heaven.

❧

"Have fun in Atlantic City," Ed had said when the coach arrived at 101 Ashwood. Allie thanked him, kissed the girls and her mother, and hurried out to leave before anything inconvenient might come up. She'd felt relieved only when the coach had turned left on Summer Street and was out of Ed's hypothetical line of sight.

Arthur and Alicia discreetly avoided each other at the Exchange Street Station, and on the platform nodded only briefly—Arthur giving her a little wink—when they boarded the 8:10 a.m. Eastern Express to New York. The train would arrive in Grand Central Station at 4:15, where they would idle away a half-hour to allow the Buffalo people to disperse into the teeming New York streets. They had arranged to meet at the cab stand. They would still arrive at their hotel—Arthur had steadfastly kept the location a secret—in time to get reacquainted in the room before the evening fun began.

Both were in First Class, but in different compartments, which reduced the temptation to spy on each other, or be spied upon. Alicia did notice Arthur walk by her compartment a few times, ostensibly on his way to the washroom, and he glanced in at her each time with a look that gave her a little shiver. Four hundred miles, and eight and a half hours, would be a long wait to touch him—but that was the way it had to be.

❦

When Arthur settled into his seat, he opened his morning newspaper to catch up on the share price of Montana Copper. $125 a share at the previous close of market, up another two dollars. We are in clover now, Arthur said to himself. What's that, 5,000 shares at $125? Six hundred twenty-five thousand dollars. We started with $100,000, borrowed another 100, so that's a profit of $425,000 after everything's said and done. Not bad at all.

He leaned back in the plush. When the porter came down the aisle with his cart of drinks and snacks, Arthur ordered a flute of champagne. These are going to be the best few days of my life.

❦

A couple of hours after their front door had closed behind Arthur, the phone rang at the Pendle house. The maid was nowhere to be seen, so Cassie picked it up.

"Mrs. Pendle? This is Ed Baker."

"Mr. Baker, yes. How can I help you?"

"Is your husband at home? I tried his office, but there was no answer."

"No, I'm sorry. He left this morning for New York."

"I see," Baker said slowly. "Can you tell me where he will be staying? It's quite important that I speak with him today."

"Heavens, I didn't even have time to ask him, Mr. Baker. He usually tells me, but today he was in a hurry and forgot, I guess. He likes the Waldorf. Or the Hoffman House. You might try him there tonight."

"Tonight may be too late. Do you know if he will be there this afternoon?"

"I doubt it," she said. "The Express train won't get there until 4 or 5 o'clock."

"That's unfortunate," Baker said quietly, almost to himself. "I'll try both hotels. And if for some reason he has a stop and rings you this afternoon, will you please tell him to call me, pronto? It's important that I speak with him. Right away."

"Yes," she said, a little put off by Baker's persistence. "Is everything all right?"

The line was silent for a moment. "I'm afraid that the account is in Mr. Pendle's name only, so it's something I'll have to discuss with him."

"It's my money too, Mr. Baker," Cassie said, now feeling genuinely annoyed. "I have a right to know what's going on."

"I am truly very sorry, madam, but I can't."

"How absurd. If that's the way it is to be, then all I can do is give him your message if he calls."

They hung up, and Cassie wanted to throw the receiver against the wall. She'd been starting to relax, and now it was all spoiled. She was angry and somehow frightened, and had no way to release the torrent of emotion. With no other outlet, she picked up a pillow from the parlor and screamed into it until she thought she'd pass out.

At Grand Central, Alicia whiled away the agreed-upon thirty minutes in the grand arrival hall, with what seemed like half the world swirling by her. Each of these people has a family, she thought—somewhere they've come from, someplace they're going. Each one a story, but did any have one quite like mine? Would it be interesting or disturbing to meet someone else in my situation?

She hailed a porter to carry her bag to the cab stand, where Arthur was waiting. He tipped the porter and kissed her warmly, right in public—like normal people, she thought. Around them the indifferent city surged and roared, creating an anonymous intimacy that was intoxicating, and so unlike little Buffalo, where there were familiar eyes on every block.

"Will you tell me yet where we are stopping?" she said in the carriage.

"I'll give you a hint. It's on Madison Square Park."

"I don't know New York like you do," she said, swatting him with her gloves. "Fine. I'll have to wait and see."

"You won't have long to wait. It's only 15 blocks or so from Grand Central."

The carriage took them downtown, straight along Madison Avenue, until turning west on 26th, skirting Madison Square Park. They followed the perimeter of the large, green park—even along its border, the air felt cooler than in the rest of the city—and at 25th and Broadway, pulled up in front of an enormous palace hotel. The massive stone structure rose eleven stories above the sidewalk, the first two levels defined by peaked Moorish windows. Piled on top were eight plainer levels. The whole mass was surmounted by a double upper floor, under which huddled a row of paired cathedral windows, set under arched limestone lintels, looking like so many raised eyebrows.

"My dear, welcome to the Hoffman House," Arthur said, hopping down and offering his hand to assist Alicia. "The best in the city, I think. Better than the Waldorf, even."

"It's magnificent," Alicia said, looking up and nearly losing her hat. "I've seen stereoscope views of it."

"It's rightly quite famous. Wait 'till you see the inside."

He tipped the coachman, and two bellboys took their cases.

"Shall we?" Arthur said, offering his arm.

"We shall."

Stepping off the sidewalk and into the shaded hotel, they entered what Alicia had always called a lobby. Yet this was nothing like any hotel lobby she'd seen. Every surface of the cavernous room seemed to be covered in gold, the entire glittering expanse punctuated by giant, floor-to-ceiling mirrors.

"The Grand Salon," he said.

"Gives new meaning to 'Gilded Age.'"

"And Twain was right in more ways than one. Half a block in any direction from all *this*—you'll find someone begging for a nickel to keep body and soul together."

The Grand Salon was quieter than the street outside, but still bustling and noisy. Arthur found Allie a seat and left to arrange their room.

"Everything's in order," he said when he returned. "While the bell-boy takes our things to the room, let's have a quick look around. I want to show you something."

They strolled over to the entrance of the Grand Saloon, the hotel's ornate bar, where a man was guarding a velvet rope. "I'm sorry, gentlemen only," the man said.

"Only a glance," Arthur said, pressing a gold quarter-eagle coin into the fellow's palm. The man unfastened the velvet rope and made a little bow.

The Grand Saloon was thronged with men, talking and smoking. There was a knot of them standing in front of a huge velvet drapery behind the bar.

"We're in time," Arthur said. "Go on, push up to the front. Tell them you want to see the painting."

The men at the bar seemed a bit shocked to see a woman in their midst, but obediently parted to let Allie pass. She had been standing for less than a minute, unsure of what she was supposed to do, when the bartender pulled on a tassel dangling from a thick gold cord. The curtains parted to reveal a huge painting, at least ten feet on a side, depicting four stark naked nymphs coaxing a reluctant goat-legged faun into a pool of water. One of the nymphs was tugging suggestively on the creature's horns. There was a collective chuckle and murmur among the men crowded around the spectacle. The painting was on view for a minute or two, and then the bartender drew the curtains again.

"You're fortunate to see the painting," Arthur said when they were back in the Grand Salon and walking toward the elevators. "Before the end of the year, it'll be gone."

"Gone? Why? It's quite beautiful."

"The Puritans, of course. Public decency and all that. That's why they put the draperies in front of it a few years ago, but that didn't stop the braying. So it had to go."

"Such a shame," she said.

"The world will never be free until people can throw off all of their phony morality."

"Floor?" the elevator operator asked when they boarded. He shot a glance at their wedding rings and lapsed back into his bored trance.

"Penthouse," Arthur said.

"Penthouse?" Alicia mouthed silently.

On the elevator lobby of the top floor, a small brass sign greeted them. An arrow pointed to the restaurant, and an opposite one said 'Suites.' They took the latter direction to the Broadway side of the building and stopped at the door of the Hoffman Suite.

"Welcome home," Arthur said, pushing open the door.

The Hoffman Suite looked out through two sets of double cathedral windows over the endless stream of comings and goings on Broadway. The windows swung open to allow the cooler air, eleven stories up, to flow through the brightly lit suite. Even the noise was tempered at their altitude, a pleasant background chorus of distant shouts and hooves and the occasional policeman's whistle. The great room itself was a pastiche of Rococo and Moorish styles, hung with heavy draperies and furnished with velvet upholstery, lacquered tables and chairs, and paintings in heavy gilt frames. A pair of man-high lampstands in the shape of black-amoors flanked a wide, curtained archway into another room beyond.

"What's through there?" Alicia asked.

"Our bedroom, of course."

"And you've stayed here before?"

"Not in this suite, naturally. But in the hotel, quite a few times. For Bar Association meets, and the New Haven Alumni Club has an annual meeting here."

"How did you manage to sneak me past the desk man?"

"There wasn't any sneaking required. So far as they are concerned, we are Mr. and Mrs. Ashwood of Buffalo."

"Of course we are."

"Now that we're cozy in our little room," Arthur said, "I have a gift for you. Sit down."

"Little room," she laughed, sitting on one of the big velvet couches. "What is it?"

He reached into his bag and took out a square, flat box wrapped in gift paper. "Here you go. I hope you like it."

"How about we order some champagne first?"

"That's a capital idea. I'll find the house phone."

"Well, get a move on, because I want to open my gift."

Arthur bounced up from the couch and darted out the suite door, almost knocking over a man standing in the corridor, smoking and chatting with another man.

"I beg your pardon, sir," one of the men said indignantly.

"You beg *my* pardon?" Arthur said. "Why don't you loiter outside someone else's door?"

The man scowled, but quickly mastered himself. "You are quite right, sir. I wasn't paying attention. Apologies."

Arthur bowed. "I didn't mean to be abrupt. You startled me, that's all."

Arthur walked to the top of the staircase, where a house phone was sitting on a little gilt table. He picked up the receiver and rattled the cradle until the desk clerk answered.

"This is Mr. Ashwood in the Hoffman Suite. I'd like a bottle of good champagne and some fruit and crackers brought up. And a rose for Mrs. Ashwood, if you would."

He hung up the receiver and turned to go, and again almost bumped into the pair of gentlemen who were walking toward the stairs.

"It's going to be one of those days, I suppose," Arthur said, and headed back to their room.

The champagne and snacks arrived almost as soon as he'd closed their door. After the bellman had completed the interminable process of opening the bottle, filling two flutes, and setting out an absurd array of silverware for a small service of fruit, Arthur tipped him and sent him on his way.

"At last," he said. "My dear." He handed the rose to Allie.

"Why, thank you, sir. Now may I open your present?"

He nodded, and she tore the paper away. Inside was a large, square, velvet box.

"It looks like jewelry!" Alicia said.

"You guessed that right, but you'll never guess what kind."

She tilted the lid open. "Oh my," she said. "It's stunning."

Inside the box was a heavy, gold torc—a thick neck-ring—in the form of a snake consuming its own tail.

"I've never seen anything like this," she said, holding it up.

"It's an ouroboros," he said. "That's the word for a serpent eating its own tail."

"It's astonishing. It must have a meaning."

"It does. It's very ancient—it symbolizes eternity, no beginning and no end. And I thought it reminded me of us—that it's difficult to tell where you stop and I begin."

"I love it," she said. "Put it on me!"

"I can't. Tomorrow, we'll go to Benedict Brothers, the jeweler who made it for me. They're in Lower Manhattan, in the Financial District. They have to put it on."

"They do?"

"Yes, it's rigid, and it doesn't have a clasp in the usual sense. He'll solder it on for us, and then you never take it off."

"Day or night?"

"For the rest of your life, Alicia. Think of it as a wedding ring around your throat."

"But won't Edward see it?"

"And what if he does? You can wear a high collar most of the time, and if he sees it, he doesn't have to know that I gave it to you. Tell him you bought it yourself."

She ran her fingers around the circumference of the torc. "I love it, Arthur," she said. "Nothing could be more perfect."

"I'm so happy, darling. I saw the design in a book I have about the ancient Celts, and I immediately knew I had to have it made for you. You are my Morgan Le Fay."

❦

Cassie sat limply in the parlor, spent after screaming into the pillow. She stared out the window for an hour, but there was nothing to see. Ed Baker's call had upset her severely. She was lonely, too, with Arthur away. She enjoyed his company, his ideas, the physical security of having him around. It wasn't a perfect marriage, but it suited her.

After a while, she went back into the hallway, picked up the phone again, and clicked the hook for the operator.

"Dr. Sherman, please," she said. "On Pearl Street."

Dr. Jeannette Sherman was the lone female dentist in Buffalo, maybe in all of Erie County. She lived on the second floor of a creaky old building downtown, above her office. Cassie had first met her at a suffrage event several years before, and they'd become good friends. Jeannette was a tall woman in her mid-thirties, who might have been striking, had she been more filled out. Jeannette was rail-thin, with a hollow face and dark eyes set deep behind prominent cheekbones.

"Jeannie?" Cassie said when her friend picked up.

"Cassie! How very strange, only a moment ago I was thinking about you. I was worried that I might be having a premonition. Are you unwell?"

"Fit as a fiddle. Arthur's gone again, though. I suppose I was sitting here feeling a little sorry for myself."

"You poor dear. When is he due to return?"

"A few days. I never know."

"Why don't you come over, then? Stay with me tonight, and we'll have some girl talk."

"Would you mind terribly?"

"I'm all by myself, too, you know. I'd be delighted to have some company."

"I'm on my way!"

She called the livery stable to arrange a carriage, threw a few things into a bag, and went outside to wait.

I must have hired the world's slowest driver, she thought as the carriage went south from Ashwood at a plod. I could have walked and worked off all this nervous energy. She fidgeted the whole 45 minutes it took to cover the couple of miles, picking at her nails, which she knew she shouldn't do. The slow clip-clop of the hooves, usually soothing, made her want to jam her fingers in her ears. She kept thinking about Mr. Baker's call, Arthur's whereabouts, what sudden business had taken him away to New York. I've a headful of flies tonight, she thought.

At long last, the conveyance lurched to a halt outside a slightly cock-eyed, board-and-batten house crammed between two much newer brick buildings. Jeannette's dental parlor-cum-home was a survivor of Buffalo's canal boom days, a frame building stubbornly holding at bay the brick closing in. Cassie liked the building. It reminded her of her childhood in New Haven, the rickety ship chandlers' stores lining the harbor.

Cassie alighted from her carriage and paid the man, who, as expected, started grumbling about his meager tip. Ignoring his whining, she glanced up and saw Jeannette watching out one of the upstairs windows, and then saw her vanish.

A few seconds later, the front door opened, and there was Jeannette, wearing a mohair dressing gown in a shade of blue that was very nearly black.

"Shoo," Jeannie said to the driver, who was still droning on. "Cassie," she said, embracing her friend. "Come upstairs."

They walked through the dental parlor and up the back stairs to Jeannette's living quarters. She had four large rooms, the whole upper floor above her office. No husband, no children, and a solid dental practice had allowed her to furnish the place with a degree of opulence. Her parlor boasted William Morris wallpaper, silk taffeta draperies in a soothing shade of green, and a long divan angled out from the wall, piled high with pillows in Oriental style, with a long, low table next to it.

Cassie had been there before, a dozen times at least, and as usual, her eye wandered to the divan and the low table.

Jeannette took Cassie's hand gently. "We'll get to that, dear," she said. "Why don't I get us a cocktail in the meantime?"

Cassie settled into an overstuffed chair, or tried to. She couldn't sit back because of her tight corset. Jeannette must have seen her from the kitchen. "Why did you wear that silly thing to our slumber party? Go to my room and take it off. You'll be much more comfortable."

Cassie took her bag with her and did as instructed, and when she returned in a long undergown, the cocktails were laid out with some crackers and a little cheese.

"Now tell me," Jeannette said, "where has Arthur gone off to this time?"

Cassie took a sip of her drink. "He said New York."

"But you don't believe him."

"You know me all too well, Jeannie. I don't know, he could be anywhere. He's taken a mistress, you may have heard."

"I didn't."

"Alicia Miller," Cassie said.

"Ah yes."

"A bit of a climber, as you know. Just Arthur's type. She sees him as a real man-about-town. An aesthete, too."

"Does it bother you very much, dear?"

"Not too much. I'm a little afraid that he's getting notions about her, though. About divorcing me and being with her. He thinks I don't know what he's thinking."

"He's underestimating you, then."

"I don't need any scandal. I'm not like you, a professional woman. Living on my own—people would talk. Now, they don't. I disappear."

"I can understand that. He'd be mad to divorce you, though. Surely he knows how wealthy your parents are?"

"He knows they have some money, but no, he has no earthly idea just how much."

Jeannette laughed and took a big drink of her cocktail, her long throat undulating like a fishing bird. "Good for you, dear. Some things are best kept to yourself."

Cassie was feeling calmer now, safe, a million miles from anyone and anything in Ashwood.

"Jeannie, what about you? How are things for you?"

"Same as ever. Repairing teeth. I'm going to the shore next week, I think. I need some time away from the city."

"Good for you. You deserve it."

They sat in silence, enjoying their drinks and the quiet companion-ship.

"Dear," Jeannie said after a while, "would you like me to light the lamp?"

"Do you want to?"

"When you said you were coming over tonight, I couldn't stop thinking about it."

"Then yes, let's do!"

Jeannie got up and, from the storage compartment of her sideboard, took out a small tin box, a rolled cloth, and an alcohol lamp. She set these on a japanned tray and brought them over to the low table next to the divan. She made another trip to the sideboard and returned with a bamboo pipe, about two feet long, as thick as a child's wrist, and blunt on both ends. A pottery bowl, shaped like a squatty onion with a tiny hole in the top, sprouted from the top of the tube, about a third of the way from the far end.

Jeannie sat on the divan and patted the upholstery next to her. "Slide over next to me, now."

Cassie obeyed. Side by side, they looked at the tray, with the box and lamp and cloth roll so neatly laid out, and the pipe set diagonally across.

"You have such a lovely layout," Cassie said.

"It's our magic carpet, dear."

Jeannie unrolled the cloth, spilling out onto the tray what looked like metal crochet needles with delicate porcelain handles. She struck a match and lit the lamp, and set it flickering to one side. Picking up one of the crochet needles, she opened the tin box and expertly speared a little pea-sized blob of a dark, gooey substance, the consistency of thick mo-lasses. She made sure this was affixed carefully to the end of the needle.

Then, taking up the pipe in one hand and the needle in the other, she held the needle near the flame of the lamp until the blob of goo began to sizzle and bubble. With a practiced air, she spun it rapidly be-tween her fingers, removing it from the flame when the sizzling blob threatened to ignite, and then twirled the molten mass deftly around on the top of the pottery pipe bowl. As it cooled, she formed it into a little cone and thrust it into the orifice of the bowl. She withdrew the needle and set it on the tray again.

"You first," she said.

Cassie stretched out on the divan, on her side, facing the table. Jeannette got up and sat cross-legged on the floor near Cassie's head, still holding the pipe. "Let's put some pillows under your head, dear," she said.

When Cassie was comfortably reclining, propped up at a slight angle, Jeannie moved the lamp to the end of the table near Cassie's head. She then handed Cassie the pipe. Cassie flipped the pipe over, the bowl pointing toward the floor, and then positioned it so that the pinhole in the bowl hovered over the flame of the lamp. She waited a few seconds, and when she heard a soft hiss, put the other end of the pipe to her lips and took a deep draw. The overturned bowl made a sharp crackle and a slight whistling sound in the quiet of Jeannie's apartment.

"Oh, that's a good one," Jeannie said appreciatively, stroking Cassie's hair. She took the pipe from her friend's hands and laid it on the tray. Cassie had been holding her breath the whole time, and at last exhaled. There wasn't much smoke, just a thin, sour vapor with a slight blue tinge, like burned oil.

"Oh my God," Cassie said, gasping and squeezing her eyes shut. "I have never—"

"It's the best I've ever had," Jeannie said. "And I got it from the laundryman, of all people. Sometimes you get lucky."

Cassie was blinking slowly and looking at the tray. "I didn't want to let it go."

"Would you like another, dear?"

Cassie nodded.

Jeannette repeated the process, and again. After the third little blob of opium had disappeared into her lungs, Cassie lay back. "Now you, honey," she whispered to Jeannette.

"You poor thing, you're the one who needs taking care of," Jeannie said, her face close to Cassie's, which was dreamily sinking into the pillows. She stroked her hair again. "How are you feeling?"

"Like I could just drift off forever," Cassie said. "But, I must say . . ." she said slowly and with some effort in forming each word.

"Yes?"

"I don't want to go to sleep quite yet."

Jeannie laughed. "I'm afraid you won't be able to stay awake too much longer. But perhaps there's one other thing you might like before you drift away."

Cassie looked at her friend and shifted onto her back. Although quickly going numb, she felt Jeannie's hand reaching under her hem, tracing a slow course along the inside of her leg. She opened her eyes, already going glassy, when the hand stopped moving.

"My, you *do* want something, don't you?" Jeannie whispered, gently lifting Cassie's undergown. "Now you relax and let Dr. Jeannie look after you, dear."

Cassie smiled softly and murmured words that didn't make any sense to her anymore. And for the first time in hours, the flies in her head quieted, and there was no thought of Arthur or Ed Baker or anything but the snow-soft blanket of sleep falling over her, and the tender ministrations of a friend.

CHAPTER 32

Panic

ALICIA WAS ALREADY AT A TABLE IN THE SUNLIT BREAKFAST PAR-
lor of the Hoffman when Arthur came downstairs, a newspaper tucked
under his arm.

"Long time, no see," she said.

"I'm moving slowly this morning."

"So am I," she said.

"Do I flatter myself that I had something to do with that?"

"You do. Flatter yourself, that is."

"You do know how to keep me humble," he said.

"Someone has to."

"Say, would you mind if I took a quick glance at the paper? I picked
up the evening edition when we got in last evening, but after we got to
the room"—he leaned over the table and whispered—"I was distracted
and didn't check it."

"Go right ahead. I'll order some coffee."

Alicia waved the waiter over as Arthur opened his newspaper. The
evening edition of the Brooklyn *Eagle* had only sketchy coverage of the
day's doings on Wall Street. It seemed like there had been quite a bit of
volatility, wild price swings in some big-name stocks. Ed was right about
that, he thought. Yet whenever the market is down, Montana always
seems to go up. He found the list of stock quotes and ran his finger down
the long column. Here it is. Montana Copper, at the close. $30 a share.

He looked again, running his finger over the chalky newsprint, making sure he was on the right line. That's what it says. $30? Must be a mis-
print, he thought. Probably supposed to be $130, up another five dollars.

He folded the paper neatly next to his plate and rubbed black ink onto his napkin. It left an ugly smudge on the crisp, white linen.

"Everything good?" Alicia asked.

"As good as the news ever is."

When breakfast arrived, he dived in with his usual enthusiasm, but the Montana Stock quote nagged at him, misprint or not. He ought to telephone Baker. It had been a little shabby of him to promise to call the stockbroker and then skedaddle instead, but he'd been eager to get out of the house before Cassie could ask any probing questions.

They lingered over breakfast until almost 10 o'clock, when Arthur felt that he could gracefully excuse himself, saying that he had to make a couple of quick calls. Alicia said she'd meet him in the Grand Salon.

"A grand place to talk about new beginnings," he said.

He had wanted to tell Allie last night about his imminent stock windfall, but one thing had led to another. On this fine morning, in the most opulent palace hotel in New York City, he would surprise her. As soon as he got this call out of the way.

Arthur spoke to the concierge and arranged to place a long-distance call to Bartlett & Frazier. He waited in the little booth, wiggling his foot back and forth. After a few minutes, the phone rang, and he picked up the earpiece.

"Bartlett and Frazier. Baker speaking."

"Mr. Baker? Arthur Pendle here."

"Finally!" Baker said.

Arthur was perplexed. "It's nice to hear your voice."

It was difficult to tell who was trying to speak on a long-distance telephone line that had barely enough capacity for one conversation, let alone hundreds. Ed's voice crackled through the noise, but it was faint.

"Mrs. Pendle got ahold of you, then?"

Arthur was confused but played along. "What can I do for you, Ed?"

"Have you seen the news? There was a panic on Wall Street yesterday. I've been trying to reach you. I called the Waldorf and the Hoffman yesterday afternoon, but both said they had no Mr. Pendle registered."

"Panic? What do you mean, panic?"

"Gee, you'd think it'd be the talk of the town there."

"It's still early, I guess. Haven't been out."

"Have you checked Montana Copper?"

"Yes. For heaven's sake, that's why I called you," Arthur almost shouted. "The evening paper said it closed yesterday at $30, which I assume was a misprint. I thought it best to check it out with you. And authorize the sale we talked about. I had to run out of town yesterday and hadn't time to call you."

There was some popping and what sounded like a deep sigh, or could have been noise on the line. "I wish it were a misprint. Things started deteriorating before the open yesterday—a big short squeeze brewing in railroad stocks—"

Arthur pretended to know what a short squeeze was. "So? I'm not in any railroad stocks."

"No, but people who were short those stocks had to close out their positions and sell anything they could to raise cash. They sold anything that wasn't nailed down. Including Montana Copper. It went down as low as $15 a share yesterday before recovering a bit, to close at $30, which you saw."

"You tried to call me about this?"

"Yes. I called your office right after the market opened. Then called your home and spoke to Mrs. Pendle. She said you were in New York and would get a message to you. I thought that's why you were calling."

If Arthur had not been sitting down, he would have collapsed.

"What does this mean for me?" he asked, feeling nauseated. This faint, crackling conversation on a device he hated to begin with was almost unbearable.

"What does it mean?"

"I mean, what happens now!" he yelled.

"When I couldn't reach you, we obviously didn't take any action on your shares. Things held steady for a while, and I thought we might be in the clear, but then all hell broke loose. The market was like a falling knife yesterday afternoon. We held on as long as we could, but then we had to liquidate your position to satisfy the margin call."

"You sold our shares?"

"Yes. We had no other choice."

"All of them?"

"Yes."

"At what price?"

"We had to sell to cover the $100,000 note, so we sold your 5,000 shares at $20 a share. It wasn't easy to move, because it was a big block, and the market was in freefall. But we got you out, and your lender will be repaid in full."

"What possessed you to sell everything? At such a loss?"

There was a pause, and then Baker's voice came back over the line, but colder and harder.

"Mr. Pendle, I don't need to remind a man like yourself about the terms of the agreements we have, including your margin loan. The lender has the right to sell collateral to prevent a loss of his principal."

It seemed as though the phone booth was getting smaller, and Arthur was having a hard time getting his breath.

"What's it at now?" he stammered. "The stock."

"There's been a good recovery going on this morning since the open. Give me a minute. I'll check the tape."

The line was silent for more than a minute, so long that Arthur thought the connection had dropped. He began bellowing in frustration, "BAKER! ED! ARE YOU THERE?"

After an eternity, Baker's voice came back. "For God's sake, man, I'm here! I can almost hear you all the way from New York. I was checking the tickertape. It takes time."

"I thought I'd lost you. Where is it now? Can we buy back in?"

"The whole market's bounced up strong today. Looks like Montana Copper is up to about $90 now."

"$90? We sold out at $20, and it's $90 now? Why the hell didn't you just hold on? A few hours, for Christ's sake!"

Baker's voice was decidedly chilly. "Had you been trading on your own account, it would have been entirely up to you whether to sell, hold, or buy more at a lower price. But as I said, when there's a lender involved, who will not take a loss on your behalf, our hands are tied."

"This must be a terrible joke. Please tell me you're—"

"I fully understand this isn't good news."

Arthur almost laughed at that despite himself.

"I must apologize for my haste, but I have other calls I need to make," Baker said. "We can talk more when you are back in Buffalo. Since the account was liquidated, we will need you to send us a draft for our brokerage fee. The sales charge was fifty cents per share, making it $2,500 due us."

"The brokerage fee," Arthur mumbled. "Yes. I'll come by your office when I return. Thank you for calling," he said, forgetting that he had placed the call himself.

"I wish I'd had better news," Baker said. "Believe me, I did try my best to locate you yesterday."

Arthur was numb. "I'm sure you did."

"Try to enjoy your time in the city. What's done is done. In investing, there's no looking back."

"All too true," Arthur said, and was about to hang up. But as the receiver was almost back on the hook, he recovered a little of his composure and thought of something. "Ed!" he yelled into the device. "Are you still there?"

"Yes, I'm still here."

"I was wondering—Is there any way to undo the trade? Say it was a mistake? I'd be willing to share any—recovery—with you. Split it with you, even."

"I can't do that. If I did, we could both go to jail."

Arthur was accustomed to dealing with situations where the outcome could be changed or even reversed with the application of a sum of money. It wasn't going to work here.

"I meant no offense." He took a deep breath. "Ed, you won't tell Mrs. Pendle about any of this, will you?"

"She's not on the account. That's why she couldn't give me instructions yesterday. You ought to know that she seemed more than a little irritated that she had no discretion in the matter."

"I understand. I'll speak with her when I get back."

❧

He spent a few minutes, sweating and shaking, trying to compose himself in the phone booth, ignoring the irritated line of men outside the folding glass door, glaring in at him. At last, he gathered up his courage and stepped out, muttering apologies to the fellows waiting their turn. He didn't even care to think that they'd probably overheard the whole thing.

Mechanically he retrieved his coat and hat from the checkroom and went to find Allie. The long hallway from the back of the hotel to the Grand Salon echoed hollowly under his feet, like native drums. He hadn't even considered what to tell her about what had just happened. It was probably best to keep it to himself until he figured out his next move.

"At long last," Alicia said when she caught sight of him. "The concierge told me that there's a downtown omnibus stand adjacent to the hotel. May we go to Benedict Brothers?" She held up a cloth bag. "I have my snake thing."

"Ouroboros," he said mechanically.

"Yes. My ouroboros. May we go?"

"Of course," he said.

He gave her his arm, and they walked out onto the swarming avenue, the impassive city folk parting around them as they made their way to the omnibus.

"Penny for your thoughts," Alicia said, snapping him out of his trance.

"I am terribly sorry, Allie. I was a bit mesmerized there, I think. New York does that to me."

"Do you think you'd want to live in New York?"

"If I were starting over again, maybe. My livelihood is in Buffalo."

"What about Maine?"

"Maine doesn't seem like a place to live anymore," he said. "I expect it's where I'll be buried, and that's about all."

At the omnibus stand, he looked up Broadway, avoiding Alicia.

"Is something wrong?" she said. "You seem rather distant."

"Business things weighing on my mind, that's all. Nothing for you to be concerned about."

"You said last night you planned to ask Cassie for a divorce as soon as you got home."

"Do we need to talk about this in public?"

"May we talk about it later, then?"

"Allie, please. Let's just enjoy ourselves, and not be so serious all the time. Have some fun."

"We have had loads of fun since Valentine's Day," she said. "But now it seems to me we have to be a little more serious. You mentioned new beginnings, and I want to get going on them."

Arthur tried to smile. He looked down at her upturned face and felt his sadness turn inexplicably into a blaze of sudden anger. Not her fault, he reminded himself. It's all mine.

CHAPTER 33

Ruin

"BUFFALO MAIN!" THE CONDUCTOR CALLED AS ARTHUR'S TRAIN pulled into the station two days later. The ride back from New York had been the longest eight-and-a-half hours of his life. He would have to tell Cassie, and right away. Might as well get it over with. As the cab drew closer to Columbus Avenue, he couldn't help thinking: This must be what Bobby O'Shea felt when he realized that his faith in me had been misplaced.

❦

"If you'd only told me where you were staying, this all might have been avoided," Cassie said.

"I thought I did tell you."

"Don't insult my intelligence. Surely if you can tell me that we are ruined, you can at least tell me where you were when our ruination came."

He exhaled deeply. "I was at the Hoffman House."

"With Alicia?"

"She needed my help. Her husband's considering a divorce."

"And naturally, one has to go to New York to discuss that."

"If Edward sees me with her, even in my office, he'll name me co-respondent. And that's beside the point, anyway. Alicia Miller doesn't mean anything to me. All that matters is to find a way out of this money situation before any of our investors start asking questions."

"A way out? You mean a way to pay back all the money we borrowed. If that's even possible. How are we ever going to come up with $100,000?"

"I'll figure it out," Arthur said.

"I'll believe it when I see it," she said. "And I should add that until every penny of everyone's money is repaid, don't even *dream* of asking me for a divorce. You can tell Allie that whatever hope she had of being the next Mrs. Pendle flew right out of your hotel window. Though I do wonder what she'd think—if she learns you're bankrupt."

"I haven't asked you for a divorce."

"And you won't get one if you do. Imagine how the current facts of our domestic finances would reflect on your precious reputation."

He bristled. "I've suffered a shock too, you know—"

"Let me tell you about suffering. Ed Baker calls here, looking for you. Clearly, there's something wrong, but he refuses to let on what it is. I tell him you're in New York, although you hadn't bothered to tell me where you were staying. Then all I can do for three days is while away the time, hoping these terrors of mine will prove to be imaginary. But no! You walk in, stinking of pussy—and tell me we're broke."

"Cassie. Don't say that."

"Oh, get off your high horse. We both know very well what pussy smells like."

"I meant that we're broke. We're not broke. I still make a lot of money."

"Doing work you hate. It's a lucky thing that Terry didn't let you quit."

"Maybe you'd be happier if I did away with myself? You'd get my insurance, and everything would be paid off. I'm worth more dead than alive."

Carrie cocked her head. "Spare me the self-pity. The way I live, I could drop dead any day. But you wouldn't get a dime if I did, because my life was never worth insuring."

"That's not—"

"Arthur, take some comfort in the fact that you're worth more dead than alive. I'm worthless both ways. Imagine how that feels."

❦

The house was quiet when Alicia got home from the station. Ed's probably still at work, she thought with some relief. What a strange few days it had been. It had started so well. Arthur had wanted to show her all the sights, tell her something special, and the first night everything was simply glorious. Then suddenly, the wind had shifted, and he'd become morose, moody, almost despondent—and, to make it worse, had gone strangely silent. He'd refused to provide a reason or even acknowledge the obvious. He'd even insisted that they take separate trains back to Buffalo, and that he'd be happy to wait in New York for a later one. She'd made the long trip back in silence and alone.

There was no mail of interest, and she was a little hungry after the journey, so she walked back to the kitchen to have a snack. She walked into the bright, tiled room and found Edward sitting at the table, a thick manila folder in front of him.

"Welcome home," he said, though without any warmth.

"Good to be home." She opened the icebox.

"How was your trip?" he said. "Was New York pleasant?"

"The convention was in Atlantic City," she replied, into the icebox.

"I know."

She shut the icebox and faced him, feeling warm. "What are you talking about?"

"Is the Hoffman House really as magnificent as they say it is?" he said with a smirk.

"How would I know?"

"Why don't we ask Mr. Eastman?" he said, undoing the string on the manila folder.

"Who is Mr. Eastman?"

"He saw you at the Hoffman. Well, not him—one of his Kodaks." He opened the top flap of the folder and spilled a dozen photographs out onto the tabletop. Photographs of Alicia and Arthur in the bar, eating together, walking arm in arm, even one of the two of them going into Arthur's suite.

"Is there nothing you won't stoop to?" she said.

"That *I* won't stoop to? This from a married woman who runs off to New York City with her lover."

"He's not my lover."

"There's no point debating it. The court will decide. You should know that I'll be seeking a divorce as soon as I can get the papers together."

"If that's what will make you happy, then do it."

"It doesn't make me happy. Not a bit. But I do think it'll make me a little less *un*happy."

"Are we through talking?"

"Yes, I would suppose we are, Alicia. Or should I call you Mrs. Ashwood from now on?"

"I'm sure you've called me far worse."

"Oh, and"—he shoved the photographs and the manila folder in her direction—"you can keep these. They're copies."

❦

As rattled as Arthur was by the sudden reversal of fortune—and by Alicia's call, informing him that Ed's detectives had spied on them in New York—he regained his footing quickly. He recalled something his father had told him years before: Nothing can keep a man in a state of panic for long.

When Arthur was a boy, Captain Pendle had related how he'd once put down a mutiny in some lonely quarter of the South China Sea. With a few loyal sailors, he'd beaten back the mutineers and clapped them in irons. Of the two ringleaders, he hanged one directly after the man had pissed himself when shown the noose. The second one, though, had shown no fear of the rope, counting on a quick and painless death.

Then one of the common seamen piped up that what this other sailor was afraid of was *rats*. There was no shortage of rats aboard any ocean-going ship, so many that few nights passed without one running across the sleeping men dangling in their hammocks. Yet even the hardest seafarers dreaded a visit to the bilge to repair a pump or recaulk planks. The dark, cramped netherworld was the one part of the ship outside the captain's authority—a kingdom ruled by rats.

Thus had Captain Pendle fixed upon a novel punishment, one more terrifying than a quick snap of the neck at the end of a rope. He ordered the man cast into the bilge.

The hatch had scarcely closed over the mutineer's head than he began to scream, wail, keen, whatever shriek a human being could manage. In an hour, the screeching weakened to a hoarse croak. In another hour, that too stopped.

The next morning a party was sent down to recover the body. Lanterns lit, they descended the ladder to the bilge but saw no immediate sign of the man. Then they heard ragged breathing. The man was sitting waist-deep in the lapping bilge water, propped up against one of the iron posts running up from the bilge strakes to support the decks above. Rats by the dozen were swimming and scurrying around him, and the mutineer had more than a few bites on him, but when the light of the bullseye lantern fell on his face, he squinted into its beam quite calmly.

That taught me a valuable lesson about what a man can bear, Captain Pendle told his son. In a matter of an hour or two, this man's worst fear had become tolerable, or had driven him comfortably mad. Remember that, boy, if you ever find yourself in a really tight spot. Hold on, and it will pass.

Thus, after the initial shock of losing a king's ransom, Arthur began to think. At first, he tried to pin the blame on Cassie, on Ed Baker, on Terry Penrose—but without success. Like a pesky compass needle, the more he tried to nudge it away, the more the finger of blame kept swinging around to point back at him. He had liked Cassie's scheme, had yearned for the level of wealth that would buy him freedom, even from her. That seemed unfair, but it was the truth. True, he did terrible things for Terry Penrose, but he'd willingly taken the king's shilling, and now he was hooked. And Baker? Ed had wanted him to sell, and yet he'd put it off, to his great detriment.

It wasn't an easy verdict to accept, that he was the only person culpable for the collapse of his dreams of wealth, power, freedom, and Allie. Yet his father had been correct. After a day or two of raging, even this storm would blow itself out. It had swept everything away, including hope, and that was a relief. Now he was free to do as he pleased.

Not that there weren't constraints. With no immediate prospect of a divorce, he'd have to mollify Cassie. That would entail keeping her well-supplied with dope and lies.

Allie would have to stay with Edward for a time, kept on ice while he continued to enjoy her. It wasn't the worst thing. Her hatred of Edward fueled her hunger for him. As much as he loved fucking her, he loved it all the more because each time, he knew he was fucking Edward too.

And he would need Penrose. The DA's dirty work could bring in enough money to satisfy their investors and give him a place to direct his rage. Besides, he thought, if there's one person who can help me think my way out of this, it's Terry.

❦

At their Friday lunch at the Dainty Restaurant, Penrose ordered chicken and dumplings, one of his favorites. He liked it so well, he ate it at a clip exceeding even his usual blistering pace. Arthur only pushed his food around on his plate.

"What's eating you, old man?" Penrose said. "These dumplings are scrumptious."

"You can have mine," Arthur said, pushing his bowl away. Terry immediately reached over with his fork and stabbed one of the two huge dumplings—each the size of a small orange—soaking in Arthur's steaming bowl of broth.

"Terry, I'm nearly at my wits' end!" Arthur said, bringing his hand down on the table with a smack. While only trying to be emphatic, the gesture was hard enough to jostle Penrose's arm as he eased the outsized wad of dough over to his bowl. The dumpling hopped off the tines of his fork and fell squarely into his lap. With a steaming-hot lump of batter burning his crotch, Terry jumped back in his chair, and the escaped dumpling plopped with a sticky smack onto the scuffed linoleum floor.

"Now look at what you made me do," Penrose moaned, looking down between his legs. "Goddamn it, Arthur, that was a perfectly good dumpling." He ducked under the tablecloth and emerged with the giant dumpling between his fingers. "Fuck it," he said, "I'm eating it. I don't care." He dropped it into his bowl and scrubbed his pants vigorously with his napkin.

"Now what's this about your wits' end?" he said, after he'd regained his composure and taken up his spoon again.

"It's the whole Miller thing," Arthur said. "Edward's detectives spotted me and Alicia."

"Hopefully only on a tandem bicycle in Delaware Park."

"No, in New York City."

"You took her to New York?"

"So? But of all the lousy timing, his men were on the same damn train, returning to home base. And then proceeded to follow us around for three days."

Terry shook his head. "Remind me not to stand next to you in a thunderstorm," he said.

"And, of course, now he wants a divorce. And he's threatening to name me co-respondent."

"What do you expect? You're screwing his wife, Arthur."

"So? I'm sure he's screwing—someone. I don't know who, but someone."

"You know it doesn't work that way, chum," Terry said, digging into the recovered dumpling. "Men can do that sort of thing, but women can't. He's within his rights." He stuffed half of the dumpling into his mouth, almost choking himself. Arthur watched him slowly chew the thing down to a manageable size, and was relieved when he saw the bolus move down the DA's throat, like a cormorant swallowing an eel.

"Anyway," Terry resumed, gulping his muscatel, "what do you care? Let him get a divorce."

"I care because I already have a wife."

"Not to be indelicate, but that hasn't stopped you from trying something from the sample case."

"Point taken, but it was never a matter of divorce. We wanted to have a little fun. No complications. If she is cast off, what am I going to do then?"

"You've lost me," Penrose said. "I don't see why you should give a shit."

"Because I love her," Arthur said quietly.

Penrose swallowed a mouthful of wine. "And Paris probably loved Helen, too," he said. "But he might better have left her alone."

"I appreciate the classical allusion. What's next, the *Aeneid?*"

"If you give me until tomorrow, I'll have one of my clerks précis it for me."

"Poke fun all you like. But I don't want to see her turned out of her house, her reputation in tatters. Without two nickels to rub together. All because of *me*."

Terry wiped his mouth with the soiled napkin. "How very tender of you," he said. "But she made her bed. You're not to blame for the consequences. But, mind you"—he pointed at Arthur with his spoon—"let this be a lesson to you. Don't fall in love with anyone you are banging. It's quicksand."

"I'm telling you, Terry, if"—he lowered his voice to a whisper—"Alicia is divorced, she's going to expect me to do the honorable thing and marry her. That means either I will have to seek a divorce from Cassie, or Cassie will divorce me over the shame of it."

"Why don't you just pay Mrs. Miller off? Give her enough money, and she'll go away."

Arthur sat back in his chair. "She's not a *whore*, Terry. I can't do that."

"Does it ever strike you as funny," Penrose said through a mouthful of dumpling, "how every woman in the world is quite plain about her desire to marry a rich man—presumably because he has money—but no one ever calls them whores for it? But some poor woman, down on her luck, who accepts a few coins in exchange for a workaday blowjob—not something nearly so serious as marriage—everyone thinks that's a different thing entirely. She's a whore."

"You've been in your world too long," Arthur said. "You can't distinguish between respectable women and the demimonde anymore."

"Maybe. But I'm not sure the demimonde and the regular monde are all that far apart."

"Don't take me down one of your rabbit holes. I know you like this game, but right about now, I don't want to play. All I can think about is how to keep Edward from filing for divorce. At least for a while, until I get things figured out. With—everything else I have going on, I can't have this heaped on top. I can't take it."

"Then there's only one thing you can do," Penrose said.

"What's that?"

"Beg. Plead. Kiss his ass. Go to Miller on bended knee, and promise that you'll never lay a finger—or any other appendage—on his wife again. Tell Mrs. Miller that your wife isn't ready for a divorce quite yet, and have her ask her poor, dear husband to take her back. That she's seen the light and will be a good girl again."

"That's unseemly," Arthur said. "Undignified."

"The alternative's pretty bleak, my friend. I don't think you have another choice. It's not pretty, but you're a persuasive fellow, and you know as well as I that a divorce would cost Miller a fortune. In his heart of hearts, I'd bet he'd prefer to pursue his outside activities and keep his wife around the house for the sake of appearances."

Arthur shook his head. "You may be right."

"I am. I have only one other question," Terry said.

"What's that?"

"Are you going to eat your other dumpling?" he said, pointing with his fork.

CHAPTER 34

Digging Out

ARTHUR WAS ALMOST ELATED THAT PENROSE HAD CONFIRMED his plan—as least so far as his friend knew the story. Arthur well understood what Terry could not, that he had to address the investor problem first, on which rested the whole house of cards. Cassie, Alicia, and even Edward could wait for a little while. First, he needed to buy some time before their investors started asking questions. He could then work on the other problems.

Having to rub up against the underbelly of Buffalo's population, for so long a source of deep discomfort, now seemed a stroke of immense good fortune. Over time, Arthur had worked with at least one of every species of felon in Buffalo, digging them out of their idiotic scrapes. Now the tables were turned. They were going to bail him out for a change.

In the rabbit warren of workers' homes huddling behind the giant Larkin Soap factory lived a man for whom Arthur had gotten a forgery and false pretenses charge bumped down to a lesser offense. The man had, wisely, gone straight after his sixty days in the penitentiary and was now doing engravings for the Larkin mail-order catalogues. Arthur found him at work in his little shop, in the back of his house on Seymour Street.

The man looked up from the piece of metal he was scratching on. "Hey, what's this all about?" he said, agitated when he saw Arthur. "I've been keeping my nose clean."

Arthur took off his hat and laid it on the man's work table. "I'm not here about that, Mr. Bracken. I need some work done."

"What sort of work?" Bracken said, squinting.

"I need you to do up some deeds and certificates for me."

"Oh no, you don't," he said. "You'll have me do whatever, and violate me back to prison, and get yourself another payday. I'm not getting trapped by you lot again."

Arthur took out his leather billfold from his breast pocket and removed several notes. He laid them on the work table long enough for Bracken to get a look, and then carefully covered them with his hat.

"I won't do that—you have my word," Arthur said. "This is a personal favor, and you'll be paid well. You do owe me."

"I don't owe you shit."

"Mr. Bracken, if you please."

"I paid you every cent of what you asked. And I still did two months in the joint. No thanks."

"You did. But you know how it is. Sometimes things don't stick."

"Christ," Bracken muttered. "It's a life sentence with you guys."

"This one little job, only, and then I promise—you'll never see me again."

Bracken let out a hiss of frustration. "What do you need done?"

"Get out a piece of paper, and I'll go through what goes on these. They have to be good, too."

The forger rolled his eyes. "I—" He didn't go on, but instead got a pencil and paper and took notes as Arthur read from his pocket notebook.

"There, that wasn't so hard, was it?" Arthur said after he had finished with the list of names, addresses, and numbers. "When can I pick these up? I need them right away."

"I don't know. Jesus. Next Friday?"

"Thursday would be better."

"Thursday, then. I won't sleep between now and then. Is that good enough for you?"

Arthur picked up his hat, revealing the bills beneath. "I'll see you then. In the meantime, a very good day, Mr. Bracken."

Bracken exhaled in disgust. "Same to you," he said.

❦

The day after Arthur picked up the fake documents from Bracken, he and Cassie mailed them to the investors. Bracken had done some of his best work, and Arthur had mostly made up the addresses, on lonely streets that would one day be developed into housing. No one outside of Buffalo would know.

Neither of them liked doing this, but under the circumstances, what else was there to do? They could hardly tell their relatives and family friends that they had taken a swing and a miss at huge gains in the market, and with their money. The better part of valor was to live to fight another day. He had solidified things with Penrose. After the bills were paid and the insurance premiums satisfied, there would still be plenty of money left over that they could squirrel away and hope, with time, to make back what they'd lost.

There was, however, one small fly in the ointment. To certain investors, they had promised quarterly dividends, and the first two payments were already past due. They'd made the usual excuses, but now the anxious letters were beginning to arrive from investors who feared that their money wasn't ever going to earn anything. Or worse, had been lost.

The surplus income that Arthur had from his work with the DA fixed that problem, at least for a while. He simply wrote checks from his own account to the most skittish investors and trued them up. That bought them another three months to figure out where the next payment would come from. If the Penrose money continued strong, they could manage that.

How long they could keep up the shell game, they didn't know. At least until Penrose was no longer District Attorney, which would be five years, barring some political misfortune. That should give them enough time to make everything right.

That part of Arthur's problem, at least, was now in hand. He could turn his attention now to the Millers. It had been relatively easy to temper Alicia's expectations for their future. But to handle Edward, he would need help from an unlikely place—Cassie.

That was not going to be easy. He'd expected his wife to be frosty after his return from New York, but she had gone into something more like a deep freeze. The $2,500 check to Ed Baker—for shares of stock they no longer owned—cleaned out their bank account. When he told

Cassie that, she'd shook her head in silent disgust and said only that this was adding insult to injury. Then she disappeared upstairs. He rapped on her bedroom door several times over the next day, either to no answer at all or to a curt, 'go away, Arthur.' When she did emerge, she seemed especially drawn, as if some vital force had been siphoned from her body. He dared not say anything about the drugs, but when he tiptoed upstairs after she'd sat down heavily in front of a large cup of coffee, the sour scent of stale opium smoke hit him before he'd reached the landing.

Days passed without any conversation worthy of the name. It wasn't like her at all. She'd been furious with him before, of course. Yet this was the first time since he'd known her that she was simply indifferent. He had always been the center of Cassie's world, at least until she fell in love with narcotics. At first, that made him sad.

Then his sadness soured and became anger. The more he stewed, the angrier he became. If she thought she was teaching him a lesson, she would find herself sadly mistaken. Two could play at her game, and he would have been content to let Cassie continue to give him the cold shoulder but for the fact that he needed to enlist her in his mission to return Allie to Edward, if only temporarily.

That said, he didn't know whether Alicia would call the whole affair off, if she knew he had not only no money but had dug himself a crater of debt that would take years to fill. Since she'd known him, he'd been a lavish spender, a welcome contrast to her cheapskate husband. When a man has a mistress, he can't afford to economize.

Cassie was the only one on firmer ground now that the Pendles were broke. Her greatest fear—that Arthur would abandon her entirely—had burned away like a morning fog. Financially, divorce was impossible, for now, and maybe for good. And she had in her quiver another arrow—information. If the money problem was eventually solved and Arthur moved to leave her, there was plenty she knew about him that he wouldn't want made public. That wasn't something she wanted to do, but if it came to that—the end would more than justify the means. Arthur may not have fully accepted it, but he had no chance of ever being free of Cassie unless she willed it so.

❦

The following Thursday, George McKnight stuck his head into Room Two, where Arthur was sitting with his feet up on the desk, reading a novel.

"Sorry to disturb," George said.

Arthur quickly put his feet down, nearly pitching off his chair. "No trouble at all, George. What's the latest?"

McKnight looked as genuinely disappointed as an insurance agent can. "We gave it the old college try, but the underwriters have refused to increase the coverage limits on your life policy."

"You suspected as much."

"They're pulling in their horns for a while. Too many claims for suicide after the market crash," George said.

Arthur thought he was joking and was about to laugh along, but saw that he was serious. "That's surprising."

"Not at all. It happens every time there's a collapse. In my line of work, you see these things. They run in cycles."

"I was only surprised because I didn't think life insurance generally covered suicide."

"A common misperception," he said. "Most do, with an exclusion period of a year or two. If a policy has been in force for longer than the exclusion, then it pays out, same as for any other cause of death. That said, the companies will still sometimes fight it. They don't want people taking out insurance only to make away with themselves."

"Grisly business you're in."

"It can be. Thank heavens you're a young, healthy fellow with a long life ahead of you. You haven't a care in the world."

If you only knew, Arthur thought.

"I wouldn't feel too bad about our being turned down if I were you," McKnight said. "You still have excellent coverage. A hundred thousand death benefit, double indemnity for accident. And only a six-month exclusion period, should you decide life's not worth living." He laughed. "Seriously, we could *never* get that policy written today."

"That's good news, I guess." Something occurred to him. "I do have one question, come to think of it."

"What's that?"

"If something happened to me—I know the benefit's paid to Cassie, but what about any personal debts?"

"Your death benefit is payable to Mrs. Pendle as your sole beneficiary. Since she's also your executrix, she would make any payments to your creditors. When she passes away, your brother takes over. He would then have that authority."

"But what if I owed money to, say, my mother? Would Cassie have to pay that debt?"

"I'm sure you would know the legal ins and outs better than I. My understanding is that, as executrix, your wife would have full authority to decide who gets what and when, so long as she lives. Now, if—haha—you both got struck by lightning simultaneously, then your brother becomes executor, and it's his responsibility."

"Then here's hoping I haven't angered Zeus too much. Can't have any stray thunderbolts heading my way."

George laughed a little too hard. "Even so, there's a bright side. If you do get hit by one, it'd be an accident claim. Double indemnity. A big payout then."

Arthur chuckled. "Funny way to make a fortune," he said. "Anyway, George, thanks again for trying. You're a good man."

CHAPTER 35

The Pieces Move Again

ARTHUR WELL KNEW THAT ED MILLER WAS SUSCEPTIBLE TO FEMI-
nine persuasion and that he had a special fondness for Cassie. If she
would only speak with Edward, Arthur thought, that would tip the
scales in my favor. What better advocate for the blamelessness of both
Arthur and Allie than the man's supposedly wronged wife? It would
reek of credibility.

He had asked her several times if she would speak with him. Each
time, all she did was laugh. She refused to tell him why and continued
stubbornly not to reply. He implored her to set aside her feelings long
enough to help him fix the mess with Allie, and then she could go back
to giving him the silent treatment. She'd done as much when they sent
out the fake documents. But that too didn't work. Stymied, he racked
his brain as to what inducement he could offer to secure her assistance.

There was nothing he could give her that she would want or that she
couldn't get on her own. Then the obvious struck him. He wouldn't *give*
her anything. He would *take* something *away*.

While Cassie was at the market one morning, Arthur mounted a
thorough search of her bedroom. He spent a full hour carefully collecting
an impressive array of intoxicants from her desk, dressing table, and wardrobe. He put them all carefully in a large wicker basket and was about to
declare victory when he thought of one last place that he'd seen a few of
his delinquent payers use. Sure enough, there was a full, sealed bottle of
laudanum submerged in the water tank above her toilet. He rearranged
everything in perfect order and went downstairs to await her return.

She was never gone long, and right on time, the front door creaked.
Cassie came in, walked to the back of the house, passing Arthur's small

office without acknowledging his cheerful 'welcome back.' She put her parcels in the kitchen, where the maid would find them before supper. Then she went upstairs.

He heard her footfalls on the boards directly above his office, quiet at first and then louder and faster. He could trace her path from stem to stern, picturing every little secret nook he had invaded. He couldn't help but grin at her frustration.

The frantic searching on the floor above stopped abruptly. He heard the rattle of the doorknob to her bedroom and then heavy footsteps coming down the stairs, rounding the corner, coming down the hall toward his office. She stood in the doorway, her face flushed. He looked up calmly.

"Hello, dear," he said.

"Don't you 'hello dear' me."

"Is something wrong?"

"You know what's wrong. You went through my room when I was at the market."

"I was looking for something."

"I'll expect you to give everything back. Now."

"Can't do that, dear. Your hobby is not a healthy one."

"That's none of your concern."

"On the contrary."

"I'm going to ask you one more time. Are you going to give me my things back?"

"I can't, even if I wanted to. They've been disposed of where they can do no further harm."

"You know, Arthur, you can go fuck yourself. We'll see who gets the last laugh." She turned on her heel and walked quickly down the hall. Perfect, he thought. I know exactly where she's going.

When he heard her bedroom door slam, he raced up the stairs, key in hand. At her door, he quietly inserted the key and secured the lock. Then he listened. As expected, he heard her clamber up on the toilet lid and the hollow clank as the top of the tank was removed. Then some splashing. Then silence.

Still listening at the door, he heard her leave her bathroom and race across the floor. The knob rattled.

"Arthur! Open this damn door, right now!"

"Sorry, dear, I can't do that," he said through the oak.

The sound of her fist thudded against the inside of the door, so loud that it caught him by surprise.

"You bastard. You won't get away with this."

"In a few days, you'll thank me. You'll be right as rain again. I need you to be thinking clearly if we are going to fix the mess we have gotten ourselves into."

"You mean *you've* gotten us into. Open the door!"

"I'm going downstairs now to finish up my paperwork."

He heard her banging and kicking at the door as he walked downstairs, and the crash of glass shattering. At the bottom of the steps, he paused and cocked an ear. There were two loud thuds and a loud creak, and then quiet, the sounds of Cassie throwing her shoes against the wall and herself onto the bed. He pulled his watch from his vest pocket. Plenty of time for a little spin in the Babcock while she stews a bit, he thought.

❦

For September, it was cold as hell and damp, but for a Mid-Coast Maine boy, that wasn't hard duty, and he found the gloom conducive to thought and reflection.

The only time he had to pull his astrakhan collar around his ears was in one fast straight along East Delavan, heading out of the city. Despite the sparseness of the area, the Street Department had paved the whole stretch, either from great expectations for the future or, more likely, some successful horse-trading in City Hall. It was like riding on rails, and he pushed the Babcock to its limit, yelling into the wind with a wild joy. He then kept going, past the tidy little village of Lancaster, and turned around at the weather-beaten hamlet of Alden, a little more than twenty miles from home. The pavement petered out there, anyway, and he'd use up almost his full 50-mile range by the time he wheeled back up Columbus Avenue.

The house was quiet when he got there. Cassie was probably sleeping. He stamped his feet in the foyer to knock off some wet leaves but also, he hoped, to rouse Cassie and gauge her receptiveness. It worked because he heard her voice calling his name from upstairs. He went up and leaned against her bedroom door.

"Did you call, dear?" he said.

"Where have you been?"

"I went for a drive."

"You've made your point, Arthur. Now let me out of here."

"I'm only trying to be responsible."

"Responsible," she said, the bitterness in her voice seeping through the door. "That's rich."

"I'll be the first to admit I've made mistakes."

"And the last to do anything about them."

"Will you talk with Ed Miller?"

"No. I feel sorry for him. He's been duped enough by our family."

Arthur studied the grain of the wood of the doorjamb. "If you help me, you'll be helping him at the same time. You can persuade him that this was all a terrible misunderstanding. You and I are in this together."

He heard her walk over to the door so that they were separated only by a half-inch of wood.

"That's where you're wrong," she said softly. "I am not telling another lie for you."

"It's not a lie. I want to put this all behind us."

"And how do you propose to do that, after locking me up in here like a prisoner? Do you think I'll simply forget this?"

"I'm trying to help you with your problem."

"You're the one with a problem. Actually several problems. You're stuck with me, you're stuck with Allie, you're stuck with Edward, and you're stuck with paying back a hundred thousand dollars of our families' money."

"God damn you, then!" Arthur shouted, and punched the door so hard that he could hear her take a step back. "Do you realize that if Ed names me as a co-respondent, all of our relatives will call in their investments? Which don't exist?"

"It would be a relief if they did."

"Brave talk. Let's see how you feel tomorrow."

"You should be ashamed of yourself," she whispered.

"Not even a little," he said. "Have a good evening."

Arthur made for the staircase.

"You asshole!" Cassie screamed after him. She began hammering on the door, then pelting it with anything she could lift. Shoes, cosmetic bottles, the little footstool by the bed were all hurled against the door in a squall of fury.

She'll calm down soon enough, he thought. No one can remain in a state of panic for long.

❦

He rapped gently on her door the next morning.

"Good morning, dear," he said.

"Don't you 'dear' me. Are you going to let me out of here?"

"Are you going to help me with Edward?"

"Arthur, I am starting to feel very unwell. I need my things."

"That's the problem. You *need* them."

"If I will agree to talk with Ed, will you give me back my things and leave me alone?"

He made her wait a few long moments. "Yes," he said. "I will. So long as you give me your promise."

"Fine, if that's what it will take. 'I do solemnly swear.' Is that good enough?"

"Wait a minute," he said.

"Where are you going?" she shouted after him. He trotted down the stairs and retrieved the wicker basket from his office. She was waiting on the other side of the door when he unlocked it and snatched the basket out of his hands, eyeing it hungrily. Her face was pale and streaming with sweat.

She slammed the door in his face, but he had put the toe of his boot over the threshold, and it bounced back.

"Remember, you gave me your word."

"I'm not like you. I'm not one to go back on a promise. Now go away!"

He nodded and pulled his foot back, and she slammed the door again, with feeling.

❦

Cassie called Edward at his office but wouldn't go into any detail over the line—the phone operator would be listening in—but she said he knew what the topic was, and could she come by his building tomorrow?

The next day she arrived right on time, and Edward escorted her to the little lunchroom so that they'd have privacy.

"Ed, this trouble with Arthur and Allie has got to stop."

"As it shall," he said. "The more I've thought about it, the more convinced I am that I need to seek a divorce."

She put her hand on his arm. "Now don't be hasty. Think about what you'll be doing. You'll be destroying not one but two families."

"*I'll* be destroying them? I'm the injured party here. As are you, for that matter."

"It would seem so, but I'm not injured. I know that Arthur and Allie have been foolish, but nothing criminal has happened between them. Poor judgment, and that's all."

"You believe that?"

"Believe what?"

"That this is all innocent."

"Yes, I do. The love they have for each other—"

"*Love?*"

"Yes, there's no doubt in my mind that they love each other. In a high-minded, poetic way."

He shook his head. "There's no such thing outside of fairy tales."

"You know Arthur's romantic nature. He's the type of person who could have been born in another time."

If only, Ed thought.

"Let's say you're right, and they do love each other," he said. "If that's so, I don't see how to remedy the situation. I can't go on living with a woman who loves another man."

"I know it seems that way. But we must be more broad-minded, more progressive, these days. Because we use a single word—love— doesn't mean there's a single *kind* of love. The love Allie has for your children can never be Arthur's, for example."

"Of course the love for a child is different from the love for a husband, even if the word is the same. The problem is that Allie seems to want two husbands."

"Arthur has told me, and I believe him, that their actions have been entirely innocent."

Ed looked away. "I'm sorry to say it, Cassie, but I find that very difficult to believe."

"You don't know Arthur like I do. Arthur's word is sacrosanct to him. He told me that he will give you his word of honor to avoid contact with Allie. I know him. If he agrees to something, you can depend on him to honor it."

"He's given me that very assurance once already. Apparently, without any intention of honoring it. What's changed?"

"You know that assurance was made under duress. Facing you, your partner, and your attorney?"

"Then he oughtn't to have said it."

"Ed, you've done a noble thing in standing by Allie. I know that can't have been easy. But one more thing will not be hard. For the sake of the children, at least, please say you'll consider what I'm saying. Your forgiveness alone can save everyone."

"My forgiveness? I'm not Christ. I'm not so heroic as to give up my whole life for others."

"Of course you're not Christ. What I mean is that you have the power to put an end to all this. I want you to see that. Hasn't Arthur agreed to your terms? What more can you want?"

Edward cleared his throat.

"I'll give what you say my full consideration. That I can pledge. That's the most I can do."

"And that's more than enough for now," Cassie replied. "Thank you, Ed. Think about it. Talk to Allie. She still loves you, you know."

❦

They had decided to meet at a neutral location, the dining room of the Genesee. Edward ordered a piece of sole and Allie a lamb chop. She enjoyed it cooked very rare—'*saignant,*' she told the waiter, showing off what French she knew. Edward tried to avoid looking at her plate. The sight of all that blood seeping out of the meat made him queasy.

"I'm more than a little surprised you want to talk about a reconciliation," he said. "But I'll take you at your word. I hope you'll take me at mine. And that is that if I'm to consider letting this all go, I'll need to know what has happened between you two. Without any redaction."

"That is only right," Alicia said. "To answer your question directly, Arthur was always a perfect gentleman. Nothing ever happened of a criminal nature between us."

Edward thought for a moment that it sounded as though Cassie and Allie were working from a common script.

"Then what have you been up to in those houses around town, then? And in his office in the Ellicott Square? It's all in the reports. Don't deny it."

"I don't deny it. You won't believe me, Ed, but I'm telling you before God. Arthur and I talk. That's what we do. *Talk.*"

"Talk."

"Yes, talk. About books and ideas, all the new things that are happening in the world these days. I'm interested in those things, and so is he."

"The New Woman and the New Man, is that it?"

"You've always been cynical about what it means to be a New Woman. But we are living in a progressive time. Much of what women aspire to today will be the day-to-day reality of the 20th century."

"I can hardly wait."

She let it go. "Arthur is passionate about what's going on in society. He's a very interesting person. Very well-educated. And that's the extent of it."

"Much better educated than I am."

"And far better than I am. You and I grew up in different circumstances. Do you know what it takes to be admitted to New Haven College? Let alone graduate?"

"Can't say I do."

"Latin, Greek . . . logic, rhetoric. I'd be foolish to pass up a chance to learn from someone who knows those things and how to apply them to the problems of today's society."

"And now you want to break it off with this college genius? And come to live at home with boring old me? Seems like a lot to give up."

"I wouldn't be giving up something, I'd be gaining something back. Peace of mind. A calm house. I never foresaw the problems this would cause. How upsetting it would be for everyone."

"Cassie doesn't seem particularly upset."

"You know Cassie. She's an angel. But do you think for a moment, if she thought that anything improper was going on, she would want Arthur still? You know she has a higher opinion of herself than that."

He stabbed a piece of his sole and chewed it slowly.

"Ed, I am guilty of something."

"Now it comes out."

"I'm guilty of being foolish. I thought there could be no reason why a man and a woman of similar interests and temperament could not be friends. But whether it's in business, or war, or love—men must have conquest. It was only when Arthur kissed me at the Exposition that I realized it."

"Since then," she went on, "he and I have been looking for a way to repair the damage we've done. He's too proud to admit it, but Arthur feels terribly about this whole misunderstanding. And Ed, you and I have a duty to our girls. You and I cannot divorce without doing them irreparable harm."

"You've always been persuasive, Allie," Edward said. "But I'm not going to be a fool. If you love this man, and he loves you, how can I have confidence that you won't go to him or he to you? Besides, unless you suddenly become a hermit, you're bound to see him here and there, around the city. That is going to be a terrible temptation for you both."

"He's pledged to not interfere with me—or you—in any way. Ever again."

"It's *your* pledge I need," he said. "That you can give him up. I can and will sacrifice a great deal for our children, but I cannot live with a woman who is constantly thinking of the love she has for another man. Imagine yourself living under those conditions."

"It won't be like that. I still love you. I always have. We've had some difficult times recently, but you'll see—things can be good again. I do pledge it. I swear it."

Edward swallowed the last of his sole. "If you are being square with me, then I will consider it. I find I can't hold a grudge against you, as much as I'd like to. But I'm risking the rest of my life if I decide that I'm willing to start all over again."

"You will never regret it," Allie said. "I promise."

When they got home from the Genesee, it was late, and the house was quiet.

"I'm going to go up," Allie said. "Don't stay up too late."

"I won't."

"Allie—" he said when she was halfway up the stairs. She put her hand on the banister and half-turned. "Yes, Ed?"

"Thanks for your honesty," he said.

Allie smiled and blew him a kiss. Then she disappeared upstairs.

Later, lying in his den, Edward mulled over their conversation at the Genesee. One thing kept tripping him up—her assurance that he would never regret his decision. She might very well be right about everything else, he thought, the children and Arthur and even that she still loved him. But she's most definitely wrong about regret. Either way I go—toward Sarah or back to Allie—the rest of my life will be filled with regret. It's far too late to escape it now.

❦

After Cassie's and Allie's barrage, Edward needed a clarifying emotion to help him cut through the fog of war. Anger might do, so he turned to the detective reports, which detailed Arthur and Allie's comings and goings, their cozy tête-à-têtes, the expensive gifts. They contained enough to inspire anger, even rage. What awaited instead was one of those unexpected emotions that the Boland men had said he would experience, and he had scoffed at. What he found was that he wasn't especially angry. He was *jealous.*

Jealousy? Over a woman he didn't love and wasn't sure he had ever loved? Not too long ago, the notion that he might fob her off onto Arthur Pendle seemed somewhat attractive, even fortuitous. Lately, despite careful study of the detectives' catalogue of Allie's transgressions, he felt as though she'd called his bluff. She had done the impossible. She had found someone else who loved her. This he found intolerable.

In his honest moments, he had to admit that he didn't truly want her back, but it rankled to lose her to a stripling like Arthur Pendle. Hadn't taken long, either. Six months? He and Allie had been married for 17 years, and he'd been faithful, give or take, the whole time. Not quite as enthusiastic as he might have been, perhaps, but steady. Three children, an excellent income. He'd been better to her parents than they'd deserved. True, he liked work and being at his factory, but what man didn't? Men weren't made to sit around the house.

Then there was Sarah. Could he be sure that Sarah was serious about running away with him? She was playful and sometimes more than a little flippant. And how long would it be before she, like Allie, would find herself the object of other men's attention? Younger men, richer men, more interesting men. It seemed almost arrogant that at 41 years of age, he could offer her much in the way of a future. By the time everything was settled, would he want more babies at age 45, when he would be almost old enough to be their grandfather?

During this endless round and round, trying to think his way out of the dilemma—which was his way—what he tried hardest to suppress was that he knew deep down what he wanted to do. When he gave himself permission to dream, it brought him peace. And then, in the next eye-blink, back would come the old, rational businessman's brain, the columns of pluses and minuses, endless if-this-then-thats, all the while believing that there had to be a logical way out of the labyrinth, if he could only think it up.

At last, he decided that he couldn't break through the logjam on his own. It was time to invoke a higher power.

CHAPTER 36

Ed and the Palmist

"WHICH ONE WILL YOU CONSULT?" GAINES ASKED.

"Not sure," Ed replied, poring over the newspaper spread open on his desk. "There must be twenty of them here."

"Under what? Fortune-tellers?"

"Category is 'Clairvoyant.' Two cents a word."

"I'll say this, if you want privacy, you'll get it. No one would ever think to look for Ed Miller in one of those joints."

"There are two of them within a couple blocks of here," Ed said, ignoring the joke. "How about this one?

"*'Madame King, astrologist, clairvoyant, palmist, trance medium. Acknowledged by the press as the star of her profession. Tells all from cradle to grave regarding business, love, sickness, divorce, lawsuits. 81 Swan Street.'*"

"Sounds pretty fair to me," Gaines said. "Business, love, divorce, the whole shebang."

"Here's another one," Edward said.

"*'Madame Vondroll, world's greatest clairvoyant and trance medium, 51 Elm Street. Speaks German.'*"

"That one's even closer. But German? You don't need some old Dutchwoman telling you what's what."

"That's a good point. Look, I'll try the one on Swan. Three minutes' walk and 50 cents. What have I got to lose?"

Gaines shrugged. "Nothing. I never knew there were so many of them, so people must be finding them useful, or they'd all be out of business."

"Lots of people in our club have been to séances and fortune-telling sessions. Though mostly women. I wonder if I should find a man instead?" He ran his finger down the crinkling newsprint. "There's only one man.

"Francis—Greatest living communicator. Guaranteed advice on law, health, love, business, divorce. Gentlemen, special price. 101 Niagara."

"You don't want that one," Gaines said. "Way too public, down on Niagara Square."

"All right then, at lunch, I'm going to stroll down to Swan Street and consult with Madame King."

Gaines snapped his fingers. "This is going to be marvelous, Ed. I can't wait to hear what she has to say."

❦

Madame King's reading room was on the top floor of an old, brick boarding house set back from Swan Street. Edward climbed the three flights of groaning stairs, on every tread wondering if he might better turn back and forget his foolish notion. No, he thought, I've made up my mind, and I'm going through with it.

At the top of the staircase, he turned left and walked down a hallway filled with the smell of cooking onions. He walked all the way down to the end and saw nothing to indicate that the world's greatest clairvoyant lived behind any of the battered doors. He went back the other way, and near the staircase, he spied the correct door. On it was a colorful rendering of a human palm, with lines and numbers and symbols printed on it, and a small sign that read 'Madame King, Clairvoyant.'

When he knocked, the door was part opened by a short and somewhat dumpy, middle-aged lady. "Hello?" she said, without any trace of the exotic gypsy accent he'd expected. She looked at Ed with a somewhat skeptical expression.

"Mrs.—Madame King?"

"Who wants to know?" She said, plainly not expecting a smallish, tidy, well-groomed gentleman standing at her door, hat in hand.

"I understand from your advertisement—"

The door swung open wide and Madame King grinned broadly, showing a much-neglected set of teeth. "Welcome," she said. "Come in." She gestured for him to go into a side room that looked out over Swan Street.

Even if Madame King hadn't done much in the way of costume, she'd tried to make her reading room look the part. In the center of the room, there was a small table and four chairs, with decks of cards arrayed atop a red tablecloth. A few moth-nipped brocade curtains were draped over the cracked plaster walls, and the heavy scent of incense—combined with the onions wafting in from the hallway—was cloying but exotic.

"Please, have a seat," the great clairvoyant said, motioning.

Ed looked for a place to hang his hat but, finding none, slid it under his chair.

"How may I help you today, sir?"

"You know," he began, "I've never done this before, but—I've heard that one can find out what the future holds."

"From start to finish," she said gravely. She then sat quietly, looking at him.

"Should I show you my palms?"

"It's fifty cents."

"Oh, of course. Sorry," Ed said, pulling a little pouch of reddish leather from his waistcoat pocket. He counted out some coins.

"Now then," she resumed, palming the coins, "are you right- or left-handed?" She glanced quickly at his hands, noticed his gold wedding band.

"Right."

"Then we'll start with your right hand, if you please."

He extended his hand, palm up.

Madame King bent over the hand. "Let's see. You have a very interesting hand."

Ed felt strangely flattered and a bit reassured that the palmist hadn't recoiled in horror from something dire.

"That's good, I suppose."

"Your head and heart lines are joined," she said. "That means that you have a very strong sense of purpose. When your mind is made up, you don't change it easily."

"That's very true. Is that a good thing?"

She shrugged. "It can be good or bad. Good if you are very determined and are doing the right thing, but bad if you are doing the wrong thing." She chuckled. "You understand?"

"Yes," he said, feeling somewhat less encouraged.

"Marital problems?" she said, quite out of the blue.

Ed was taken a bit aback.

"Your secrets are safe with Madame King," she said, looking at him intensely. "The more I know, the more I can help."

Ed considered this for a moment. He wanted to take his hand back, but the Madame was holding it quite securely.

"Yes, my wife—she's—"

"She is in love with another."

Ed looked down and nodded. Madame King scrutinized his palm again and then looked up with the same strangely direct expression.

"Gentlemen come here only for this reason. Let me see your other hand."

Madame King studied both of Ed's hands, turning them over, tugging on the fingers, rubbing the skin on their backs.

"Your marriage will end, but not by divorce," she said.

"Not by divorce?"

"Not by divorce. By death."

"Death?"

"Yes. You and your wife will be married until death. I am certain of it. You are not fated to divorce. The vow that you took to be together until death will hold fast."

Ed pulled his now sweaty hands back and wiped them on his trousers.

"How could I not divorce if my wife—" he trailed off.

Madame King looked at him as she might a child. "That your hands cannot tell me. Perhaps the cards could . . . "

"No," Ed said, a little too loud. "I'm sorry. I mean, thank you, but I'll have to think about that."

She nodded. "I understand. I hope you can take this as good news.

Although your wife may have given love to another that she owes to you, it will not cause a divorce."

"Yes, thank you. I will try to see it that way." He scooted back his chair and stood. "Thank you for your time today, Madame King."

"You're more than welcome, sir. Do come back. The cards can help us get deeper. It is very affordable, too."

He gave her a little nod of acknowledgment and turned to go. The onion odor in the hall now seemed to have been replaced by incense clinging to his coat. He wiped his hand over his face and realized he'd left his hat under his chair. He turned to go back to Madame King's parlor and came face to face with her, standing in the hallway, holding his hat in front of her.

"You left your hat," she said, handing it to him. "But your head is so perfectly shaped, you could do without one. Perhaps come back for a phrenological reading. The bumps on your cranium can often tell me more than your hands."

Ed took his hat back and put it quickly on his head to hide it from Madame King's gaze. "Thank you, I'll give that some thought," he said and hastened down the stairs to Swan Street.

When he got back to his building, he pounded up the stairs to his office, smashing his feet against the treads. His was throbbing with fury at the thought of spending the entirety of his life with Alicia. He'd hoped against hope that she would tell him that divorce was inevitable. It would have been so easy then.

"Hey there! How'd it go?" Gaines asked as Ed walked red-faced into their office and plopped down heavily in his chair.

"Bunch of claptrap," Ed muttered, picking up one of his sharp pencils lined up neatly on his desk. He had a strange urge to impale his hand on it. "Waste of half a buck."

❦

It wasn't a topic easily broached, so he tried his usual strategy: to avoid it entirely. Instead, he kept the conversation light and breezy, this and that, Maggie, his girls.

Sarah, though, wasn't easily put off by what she saw as a ruse to avoid the topic that was on both of their minds.

"Eddie," she said, making a little whirlpool in her egg custard with her straw, "why so much small talk today? Something on your mind?"

"Nothing's on my mind."

She rolled her eyes. "You want some advice? Stick to making envelopes. You're good at it. You're an atrocious liar."

"I'm not lying!" he said, trying not to laugh.

"Now there's my Eddie peeking through. Now what's on your mind? I know it's all this mess with Allie."

"That's always on my mind, it seems. It must be so tedious for you to hear."

"Of course it's tedious, dear. The fact that you're married to Allie is tedious. It's not forever, though. As soon as we can pry you away from her, things get a lot more interesting."

"You know," he said slowly, "Cassie and Allie both talked to me this week. They both want me to do my duty and make a new start of things. And Arthur will give his word of honor, as a gentleman."

Sarah sat back in her chair. "Please tell me you didn't fall for it. Surely you realize the three of them are up to something."

"The three of them?"

"God, Eddie, sometimes—really. It's as plain as the nose on your face. They're obviously in cahoots."

"Come on. Allie and Cassie don't even talk anymore."

Sarah let out a long sigh. "Arthur Pendle is like Svengali. He's pulling both of their strings. There's something he wants out of this, and he's got them both to do his bidding. And everyone's getting something out of it—except you, that is."

"I don't believe in conspiracies."

"There are lots of kinds of conspiracies, smarty-pants," Sarah said. "Most of them aren't explicit—as in people sitting down agreeing on a plan. What happens instead is that people act in a certain way because each of them is getting something out of acting that way. That's what keeps their actions coordinated—they only *appear* to have been pre-planned."

"So who's getting what?"

"Cassie's motive, I think, is easy to decipher. For her, she's twisting your arm so that she can have her husband back. Why she'd want him, who knows, but I'm sure she does. The woman's become a wreck in the past six months, so whatever she had in the way of a marriage before all this started must have been better than what she's got now."

"What about Allie? And Pendle?"

"As far as that pair are concerned," she continued, "now that I'm thinking about it . . . they have something very profound in common. I'm not sure why I didn't think of it before."

"What is it?"

"In a fundamental way, Allie and Arthur are the same person. They care only about themselves. They can't, or won't, care about anyone else. That's my theory."

"That's intriguing."

"It's more than that. It's true. And if it is true, there's a reason they don't want you to file for divorce, and it has nothing to do with you, let alone your happiness. It has to do with them and theirs. If I had to guess, it's that if you reconcile with Allie, you'll be giving her a good, safe place to be while she waits for him to wriggle out of his marriage. Then she leaves." She sniffed. "One other thing. You'd better be careful with her. If there's one thing I know, it's women. And Allie is a dangerous one."

"It sounds as though you might be frightened of her."

Sarah's pert, little mouth pursed up in scorn. "I'm not afraid of anyone. Least of all Alicia. I'd knock her into next week if she so much as looked at me crosswise."

"And what am I supposed to tell her?"

Sarah fixed a stare on him that would have melted his ice cream, if he hadn't already finished it.

"It's not for me to tell you what you should say to your wife. You're a grown man, and you should have figured this out by now. I will say this: Don't think that because I like you that you can take me for granted too long. I might just disappear one day, and then you'll be in your cups, saying, 'boo hoo hoo, poor me, why did I ever let Sarah go?' But Sarah will be long gone, and for good too, because I'm not sticking around this podunky place to watch you and your wife cozy up again."

"I'm sorry, Sarah. I'm a little confused."

"I'm sorry to say it, but it oughtn't to be so confusing. You know what you want. The confusing thing is why you spend so much of our precious time worrying about what other people want. And especially those three characters. I want to make you happy, and I think you'd like to do the same for me. It's astonishingly simple when you think about it. Maybe you should take a page from their book and think about yourself for a change."

She paused. "I've said too much, perhaps, but I'm the only one honest enough to lay it out for you. You'll find I'm right, but I hope you don't find out the hard way." She gathered up her bag. "Thank you for the delicious custard. I'm going to have to walk all the way home to keep that from settling on my hips."

Edward remained in Lang's for another half an hour, at a loss, as he often found himself when tussling with Sarah. It was different from when he sparred with Allie, though. With Allie, his rage quickly bubbled up, and he could barely stand to look at her face. With Sarah, he felt that he wanted just to get lost in those violet eyes, even when they were angry with him. And he knew that while she wouldn't shy away from a fight with him, when necessary, she wouldn't hesitate to fight for him, either.

Even knowing all that, he was still about to make the single worst decision of his life.

PART 3

RECKONING

CHAPTER 37

The Italian Joint

October 1901

"I'M SORRY, ARTHUR, BUT I DON'T HAVE ANYTHING FOR YOU YET," the DA said on a beautiful autumn Friday, over a tasty plate of squab. "I haven't had a spare moment with the Czolgosz trial."

"You've been under siege for a month and a half. But an excellent outcome—congratulations are in order," Arthur said.

"Thank you, my friend. Though it wasn't terribly challenging. The man murdered the President in front of a hundred witnesses and boasted about it throughout his trial."

"Still—they tried to claim that he was insane. I thought that might succeed in sparing his life."

"Public opinion, when it's behind you, is an amazing thing," Terry said. "But the insanity defense was doomed from the start. Anyone who has met Czolgosz will tell you he's one of the sanest men on Earth. Not saying what he did wasn't crazy, but his reasons for doing it were sound as a dollar. To him."

"Nonetheless, he's going to the Chair," Arthur said.

"You won't believe this, but he didn't have to. We offered him a life sentence if he'd rat out his accomplices. He turned it down."

"Certainly has the strength of his convictions. When is the electro-cution scheduled?"

"The 29th, at Auburn. I'll be there as a witness. I could probably get you a seat if you wanted to join me."

"Very kind of you, but I think I'll sit this one out."

"Let me know if you change your mind. Now I can get back to the real job, but just now, I don't have anything big for you."

Arthur was crestfallen. He had hoped that Terry would have a few more big fixes for him. Those big lumps in the gravy, as he called them, were what would help him pay everything off.

"Nothing?"

"Not unless something turns up. You know how these things go. Happenstance."

"Yes, I know. It's fine."

"Are you bored?"

"No, not bored. I'd like to buy Cassie something special for her birthday. Some extra money would be useful."

"It always is," Penrose said, slurping his champagne. "Must say, though, I'm a little surprised. Not so long ago, you were rolling in it. When you were going to throw me over, remember?"

"Will you stop bringing that up?"

"Did it not happen? Am I fabricating it?"

"Don't take me wrong," Arthur said, ignoring him. "I don't *need* the money, but my cash is tied up in the markets."

"Make sure you don't get too tied up. The markets are a fickle mistress."

Arthur took a bite of his pork chop, cutting around the perimeter to avoid a big raw spot in the center.

"How much do you want something else to do?" Penrose asked. "It would pay well, but it's not without risk."

"Can't be any riskier than some of the recent work. What are you thinking about?"

"You know that lately we've not been collecting from more and more of the Italian places."

"They're paying the Black Hand what they used to pay us."

"So what? The Black Hand's not giving us a cut."

"True."

"The problem is, Arthur, is where does this stop? The rest of the wops will stop paying once they see they can get away with it. Then the micks will follow suit. And so on. It's like that story about the Dutch kid with his finger in the dike."

"*Hans Brinker.*"

"Right, Brinker. Great story. Stopped the whole dam from giving way by putting his finger into the little hole. If you're looking for something to do, you can be my little Dutch kid."

"Get the Italians to pay?"

"They're herd animals, all these foreigners," Penrose said, swallowing with some effort. "If you can grab one of them by the nose, you can lead all of them around. Go put the fear of God into one of them who isn't paying, a visible one—the toughest one of them all would be best. And don't leave until you have what they should be paying. Then watch how fast the rest of them fall into line."

"I could manage that," Arthur mused.

"Might be dangerous," Penrose said through a mouthful of squab. "Are you sure?" He paused and then pointed at Arthur with his fork. "I'll tell you what, though. If you can manage it, I'll give you half of whatever we collect from the Italian places through the end of next year. Think of it as hazard pay."

"Can you spare a couple cops one night next week?"

"Tell the Chief when you want them and that it has my blessing."

"I'll do it, then."

Arthur dived back into his lunch with a renewed appetite.

❦

The toughest of the dive bars didn't have names. People knew where they were—whether to find them or avoid them. The typical resident of The Hooks—poor and Irish—kept a full block away from them, and it took careful planning to stay a block away from anything in that crowded part of the city.

The worst of the worst, as everyone knew, was an Italian joint on Commercial Street, so-called because of a row of squalid structures backed up against the Commercial Slip. The slip was a jutting arm of the Erie Canal where boats could be wharfed and cargoes loaded and unloaded without interfering with Canal traffic. This no-name Italian joint was one of many so-called 'free theatres'—a saloon in front and a rough music hall in the back, where girls danced naked and could be rented out for the price of a couple of drinks. The girls expected a couple for themselves, too, or a little toot of powdered cocaine to keep them at the ready as the night wore on.

This Italian joint hadn't paid a penny of tribute in months, though it was plainly prospering. It catered to Italians only, and if you couldn't pass yourself off as one, you might well end up floating face down in the Commercial Slip. It was to this establishment that Arthur, his two cops, and Harry Price steered late on Friday night. Arthur reasoned that the busiest night of the week would be the perfect time for a crowd to witness the lesson he hoped to teach the Italians.

The cops cleared a path for Arthur and Harry through a gaggle of well-lubricated and rough-looking Italians, yammering away in their native tongue. The men stared at Harry and Arthur, two rather unprepossessing dandies accompanied by the burly cops. Out-of-town swells going slumming, most likely. Too bad for them, they'd soon learn they'd picked the wrong place to sample the low life.

Arthur's two cops that night were a burly Irishman and a smaller patrolman, who was one of the relatively few Italians on the Buffalo Police Force. Arthur was not taking any chances that someone would give them the runaround, claiming they didn't understand English. "Tell me everything they say," Arthur told the Italian cop. "And don't let on that you're Italian unless we absolutely need to."

It was deafening in the front saloon, reverberating with music from the dancehall in the rear and the thudding of women's shoes on the suspended wooden stage.

"I'd like to speak with the proprietor," Arthur shouted to the barman. He looked over the man's shoulder into the dancehall. It was packed shoulder to shoulder with men, all watching the spectacle. This could be tricky, he thought.

"No English," the barman replied, shaking his head.

One of the men drinking at the bar said something in Italian to the barman, who replied in kind.

The Italian cop tugged Arthur's sleeve gently. Arthur turned to face the street, and the Italian cop turned too. "The man at the bar asked how we got in here. The barman said that he'd buzzed the owner and that he'd take care of us."

The barman obviously had an electric buzzer concealed behind the bar someplace so that he could discreetly summon help when necessary.

"Tell the others to get ready," Arthur said.

He had only gotten the words out of his mouth when a small man stepped toward them, flanked by a couple of muscular, hard-looking types. The small one said a few words to the men at the bar, who scattered immediately. Then the big fellows squared off against Arthur's group, pinning their backs against the bar.

"What do you want?" the little man said in heavily accented English.

"Tell him this," Arthur said to his Italian cop. "And say it loud enough so people can hear. 'I'm here to collect your fines for running an unlicensed establishment. Payment is due immediately.'"

The Italian cop dutifully translated this, taking the owner and his men somewhat by surprise. Then their eyes narrowed, making a mental note of the young cop's face. One of their countrymen working for the cops was a betrayal that would merit special punishment.

The small man laughed and said, this time in very capable English, "And I'm here to tell you to fuck off." His bodyguards took half a step forward, crowding Harry and the patrolmen.

"I hope you don't expect me to take any shit from these goddamned dagoes," Harry said out of the corner of his mouth. "They get any closer, and they're going to be picking their teeth up off the floor."

"Hold your horses, Harry," Arthur said.

Through his translator, Arthur told the man that if he didn't come current with $500 here and now, he was going to shut the place down. The man replied (although Arthur was sure the young cop gave him a sanitized version) that Arthur was sadly mistaken in such an expectation.

"There's no cause to be rude," Arthur said. He turned to Harry and nodded.

That strange beatific smile spread over Harry's face, which puzzled the three Italians, who were used to seeing people on their knees pleading by this part of the show.

Harry's hands were jammed deep in his pockets, as usual. He stood like that, walked like that, rarely taking them out except to eat or teach someone a lesson. It was just his way.

The big men made a serious error at that moment. They hulked a few inches closer to Harry.

Harry's right hand flashed out of his pocket, in one movement whipping open a straight razor. Before anyone realized what had happened, a curtain of blood was flowing down the front of the big Italian closer to him. With a deft continuation of the same stroke, Harry slashed the razor across the inside of the other bodyguard's upper arm, laying the flesh open to the bone.

The man whose throat had been cut dropped like an anvil. The other man, his forearm flopping around like it was made of rubber as he tried to raise his hand to fend off another stroke, began to howl as he realized what had happened. Harry calmly stepped to the side, shoved Arthur out of the way, and with a quick forehand, slit the second man's throat. That one didn't go down, not for a few long seconds, but instead clutched at his neck, trying with almost humorous futility to cap the red gusher with his fingers. Like Hans Brinker, Arthur thought oddly, and almost laughed.

Harry Price's deadly sleight of hand caused a general and immediate uproar. Men started yelling, the hired women screaming, and the barflies knocking over chairs in their haste to get away. Most of them either made a beeline to the exit or at the very least tried to dodge the arterial spray from the second man, who seemed to be possessed of an astonishing amount of blood. By the time he collapsed, gurgling to the filthy floor, a sea of red was lapping against the bar and running along the uneven floorboards toward the front door. The first man's head had gonged against an absurdly large and full brass spittoon, overturning it. A layer of thick, brown slime was bucking up against the spreading pool of blood.

Word spread quickly into the dance hall. The music stopped, and a crowd of rubberneckers crowded the doorway, gawking at the two men seeping out their life onto the floor.

Harry calmly folded his razor and put it and his hand back into his pocket. His left hand had never left the other pocket, and Arthur wondered what the hell could possibly be in there. Harry nodded at Arthur, and his strange smile faded.

"Now tell this gentleman," Arthur said to the Italian cop, "it's $500 to get current and an additional $250 each for us to dispose of these two.

THE ITALIAN JOINT

That makes $1,000 cash right now—or I'll make sure he spends the rest of his life in jail for murder. Oh—and tell him that we'll fucking well fill the Commercial Slip with dead Italians if he doesn't keep paying. Say it loud."

Which he did. The owner, splattered with blood and obviously terrified, held up his palms, nodded, and ran off to parts unknown. He returned with a fat leather pouch, which he handed over to Arthur like a live coal. "Take it!" he said. Arthur put the pouch into his satchel without opening it. The temporary catalepsy following the killings was already starting to dissipate, and sticking around much longer could be lethal.

"Tell them I've got five dollars in gold for each of the first four men who toss these"—he gestured toward the bodies—"into the slip." The Italian cop relayed the message, and a fight very nearly broke out among an eager knot of men jockeying to do the honors. It took them only a minute or two to hustle the limp and dripping corpses through the dance hall and out the back. Two distant splashes, and they were back to collect their fee. The proprietor had the barkeep throw a few coal buckets of sawdust on the blood and spittle, and the barflies alighted again, going on with life as before.

"Let's go," Arthur said after paying off the pallbearers. "Keep an eye out for anyone hiding outside the door."

And with that, the message had been sent. Two men were dead, and in an evening, Arthur had made $500, three times what a laboring man could make in a year. While it was not enough to fix his money woes, word would get around, and it would increase the monthly collections. That said, Arthur had very likely made an enemy of the Black Hand, who wouldn't take this affront lying down.

Terry would give him some guff about excessive force, but Arthur knew that would be just for show. Besides, it was a moot point—the stakes had been raised. He knew that from now on, he was a marked man, and yet the knowledge of danger nourished his pride, aroused something in him. He'd seen too many men—like Edward Miller—turned into contemptible chumps, waste their lives digging a moat of false security. As one of his father's sailors had told him once: In America, you'd better keep a weather eye out, because someone always wants what you have—your money, your job, your wife. And he's coming for it.

CHAPTER 38

Duty or Dishonor

HE PUT IT OFF FOR A DAY, THINKING IT WOULD GIVE HIM TIME TO consider what he'd say to her. Edward hadn't counted on the speed of Ashwood gossip, though, and his private line was jangling even as he walked into the office the next morning.

"The damn thing's been ringing off the hook for an hour," Gaines said as Edward hustled for the phone. "It's been driving me half crazy."

"You could have picked it up."

"Private line means private."

Ed picked up the phone. "Edward Miller speaking."

"I assumed you were avoiding me," came Sarah's voice across the wire, and not with its usual playful, cheery tone. It was stern and cool. Ed felt his stomach drop.

"No—I wouldn't—"

"I'm on my way now, so don't move a muscle. You owe me an explanation. I'll be there in 15 minutes." The line went dead.

He slowly returned the earpiece to the receiver. "Howie," he said, "I've got someone coming over. I'm going to need the office for a bit."

"Got it," Gaines said. "I'll do the morning rounds in the factory."

❦

Sarah made it to his office in twelve minutes.

She walked in without so much as a hello and came to a halt in front of his desk, her hands on her hips. She stomped her foot so hard it made the pens in Edward's desk inkwell dance.

"After all this," she said, red in the face, "you're taking her *back?* You're letting that *creature* waltz back into the home she couldn't abide? I must say, I'm flummoxed. I don't know what to say. I—honestly— don't. I thought I understood you a little better than I suppose I do." Sarah sat down in the chair so hard, it seemed she was trying to break it.

Edward was at a loss. He'd reassured himself that Sarah would understand his duty was to his family, pleasant or not, and that she would support whatever decision he made.

"Sarah, please—"

"Don't 'Sarah, please' me, if you please. I could throttle you right now, and unless you tell me that this is nothing but a cruel practical joke—in which case I'd still want to throttle you, but for a different reason—I don't have anything further to say."

"You must understand—it's my duty," he said feebly, not fully believing it himself. "The children."

"Duty is something that is supposed to inspire courage, not cowardice," she said. "Need I add that hiding behind children isn't very upright, either? Those girls of yours deserve more than that witch of a mother coming back and poisoning their heads against their own father. Have you completely taken leave of your senses?"

"I don't know anymore. Please—"

"If you think you're going to get any sympathy from me, think again," Sarah said. "I couldn't have been plainer with you about my wishes unless I had jumped into your lap. We could have had a beautiful, *wonderful* life. With real love in our home that children could see and feel. My Maggie would have had a proper father, upright and sober. Your children could have been with us half of the time, maybe more. And yet you threw all that away, without so much as consulting me before doing it. Which has changed both of our lives forever, and not for the better. Oh—and which I had to learn about from a goddamn woman at the market."

Edward put his head in his hands. "I feel like I'm going mad," he said. "I don't know what to do from one minute to the next. I don't know which way to go. I thought you'd understand that I'm only trying to do the right thing."

"Again, with the self-pity? You don't need a detailed street map to get someplace. You and I had a destination in mind, and then we could have figured out the rest together. Instead, you struck out in some other strange direction. It's a good thing you didn't decide to become a polar explorer. You'd be a frozen block of—fucking ice by now."

"Then what do I do? Put yourself in my shoes."

"I told you what you should do, and you did precisely the opposite. Almost as if you were trying to spite me. And believe me, I'm way too hot under the collar to give you any more advice. Perhaps one day, but not today."

"Sarah—I know how you must feel—"

She smacked the desk with a dainty hand. "Don't insult me, Edward Miller. You can't possibly know how low I feel. I am dead certain that we would have had a long, happy life together." She jabbed a finger at him. "And don't you think for a minute you'll grow old and gray with that hellcat, doing your precious duty by her the whole time. She'll drop you like a hot potato as soon as Arthur Pendle can extricate himself from his drug-addled wife. You know what you are, Mr. Miller? You're gullible. I'm sorry to say it so bluntly, but that's what you are."

"I know I've disappointed you," Edward said. "I am only trying to do—"

"I know, I know. Your duty. Go on, sell your eternal soul for duty if you like. I'm not going to be a slave to duty for anyone who doesn't deserve it. Seth doesn't, and Allie doesn't. I never thought I'd say it, but I wonder now whether you do, either."

He slumped in his chair. Gaines appeared at the doorway but immediately felt the tension and kept right on moving.

"I've said what I came to say. I'm sorry if I lost my temper, but to be quite honest, I am not at all sure I'll ever get past this. Don't get up, Ed. I'll see myself out. I know the way."

CHAPTER 39

Goodbye and Amen

MUCH MAY HAVE CHANGED IN EIGHT MONTHS, BUT ONE THING remained the same: On the first morning of every month, Arthur would awake with a jittery, angry edge—the lingering effect of another long night in The Hooks. A year before, he could clear his head by taking his automobile out for a spin, weather be damned. The fresh air and a couple of strong cigars would soon dispel the stink of the slums. But this, too, had changed since the woman not then known as Alicia Miller had passed him in the Ferry Street Tunnel. No amount of fast driving or cigar smoke could restore his mood. These days, the only never-fail nerve tonic for the first of the month was Alicia, on her back.

She had not failed to notice how especially eager he was on the first, and learned to cultivate and prolong the intensity of the day. The bedroom door at One Two Three would no sooner shut than Arthur would attempt to dispense with any preliminaries and get right to business. Allie would have none of it. Instead, she'd strip down to her undergarments and plead with him to tell her about the previous night. Her soft, probing questions would at first meet with irritation and impatience. Then, as she egged him on, Arthur would become frustrated, then furious, red-faced with rage at how he was being used, how a champion athlete and scholar was now defied, disrespected, defiled by lowlifes—all for the benefit of Terry Penrose ...

Once her taunting had gotten him good and worked up, she would lie back, lift her hips slowly, and slide her bloomers down.

One time, Allie had thought to up the ante by telling him that Edward thought Arthur was nothing but a coward, a dandy with a big mouth who would get his comeuppance someday. It had been a gamble on her part, but it had paid off. As she knew he would, Arthur had brushed it off when she first said it, as befitted a man of his breeding. Then it became an earworm. He ruminated on this slight during his drives in the Babcock, and recalled it when his mind wandered when reading the newspaper. When he did, he felt the urge to walk over to the Miller house, bust down the door, and give smug little Edward a tutorial beating. *There's a reason his wife wants* me *and not him.*

This month would be the last time for this particular ritual, though. As much as it pained them, he and Alicia had to separate for some discreet period to allow Ed to cool off and forget about the divorce. After breakfast, he addressed a note to Alicia asking her to meet him at One Two Three. He checked their box several times the next day, until in the last post of the afternoon, there was an envelope waiting for him.

> *YKW left for Indianapolis and will be gone at least three days. Instead of One Two Three, how about Niagara Falls tomorrow? If you can secure a room at the Prospect House, we can stay the night. Mother can watch the children. – A.*

'YKW,' he chuckled to himself. You Know Who. He read her note a half-dozen times, deeply sniffed the paper her hands had touched, and then struck a match and set it afire in the ashtray on his desk. He watched the paper curl and blacken. Then he wrote out a note to confirm that he would arrange things at the Prospect House and gladly spend the night. He ran his tongue over the strip of glue, moistened a stamp, and popped it into the letter box at the trolley station.

❦

He met her at the International Railway Company's trolley stop on Riverway, a short carriage ride away from the Prospect House Hotel.

"Mr. Ashwood, all the way from Maine," said the desk clerk when they arrived at the hotel. He glanced at Alicia's gold wedding band. "And Mrs. Ashwood. Welcome to you both. As you requested, your room has a view of Luna Falls."

They followed the bellman up the curving staircase of the grand old inn. After the obligatory room tour and a generous gratuity—a good investment in discretion and selective memory, if either should be required—Arthur threw open the draperies, and they took in the view, his hand gently around her waist.

The Prospect House sat on a low bluff above the American Falls and their much smaller, more delicate neighbor, Luna Falls. Its celestial name derived from a fortunate alignment with the full moon, which in summer rose directly over its crest. The moonlight seeping through the hovering mist from the Falls created a moonbow—a rainbow at night. Luna Falls had thus become a favorite spot for lovers, kissing in the dark as the silver water sparkled endlessly past. Now that summer was long gone, not a soul could be seen braving the chill, soaking mist.

They sat down on the loveseat by the window. Alicia leaned her head on his shoulder.

"I'm going to miss you," he said, burying his nose in her hair.

"How long do we have to be apart?"

"A couple months? Three, to be on the safe side."

"It's been only a little more than eight months since we met. On Valentine's Day."

"A lot has happened since then."

She rested her head on his shoulder for a while, watching the water slide over the jagged crest of the Falls.

"Two months will seem like forever," Allie said.

"I did get you a little something to remember me by," he replied.

"Something else? What a coincidence. I have something for you, too!"

"You first," he said, pulling a little velvet box from his coat.

She opened the box. Inside, gleaming on a tiny satin pillow, was a gold ring.

"Why, this looks like—" she said, somewhat taken aback.

"That's what it is."

She scowled. "This better not be a joke."

"God, no! It's hardly a joke. For heaven's sake, Allie."

"It looks very much like a wedding band."

"That's the point. How many times over these eight months have we said that people are only married when they feel that they are married?"

"That's very thoughtful," she said. "But you know I can't go home wearing your ring."

"You don't have to wear it on your finger. Wear it on a chain around your neck, or keep it in your pocket."

Allie looked at the open box sitting on Arthur's palm. "This is either the most romantic gesture in history or the craziest," she murmured.

Then to Arthur's surprise, she tugged Edward's ring off and set it on the window ledge. Her finger looked odd without it, with a thin, pale scar where the ring had rested for seventeen years and where she'd once thought that it would stay forever. She held out her left hand to Arthur.

He slipped his ring over her naked finger.

"That's that," she said. He nodded back.

"My present for you isn't near so grand," she said. "But I hope you'll like it all the same."

She got up, opened her valise, and took out a small silk bag tied with a drawstring. "Here you go," she said, handing it over. "I recognize you're not too good with knots, but you can take your time here."

He chuckled and worked away on the string. He opened the mouth of the bag and let the contents spill into his hand. It was a gold chain with a locket pendant.

"Open it," she said.

He pushed a tiny spring-loaded button on the long side of the oval pendant, and it sprang open to reveal a tiny photo of Alicia on one side and, on the other, flowing cursive letters:

AA from AA.
With Love, 10/15/01

"Mrs. Ashwood," he said, "it's magnificent. I love it."

"If you ever forget me, you can open it up and remember."

"I could never forget anything about you, Alicia."

"Good. But there is one other thing we need to get straight before we say goodbye."

"What's that?"

"You can do anything you please with Cassie, but you'd better not fuck her."

Arthur rolled his eyes. "Cassie and I haven't done that for years. I don't think there's any danger of our starting up again at this late date."

"Good," she said. "Because your mind is your own, but *that*"—she pointed to his crotch—"belongs to *me.*"

❦

The sound of her voice over his private office line startled him.

"May I come over?" she said.

"Of course," Edward said.

She arrived in his office within a half-hour, dressed to the nines, beautiful as always. But she gave him only a tight smile. She declined to take the chair he offered.

"Thanks," she said, "but I can't stay long. When I left a couple days ago, I promised myself that I wouldn't see you again, but then it felt like I was punishing myself without having done anything wrong."

"I'm glad you changed your mind. I've missed you."

"I told you some time ago that I wouldn't stay in this podunky town one second if you holed up again with Alicia. It wasn't a bluff, so I'm leaving for Batavia. Which I recognize is even podunkier, but I never said I was consistent."

"Seth will be happy to have you and Maggie nearer."

"When he's not stupefied. Anyhow, I came to tell you that I'll be leaving, and to do something else I promised myself I'd never do. And that is to tell you I forgive you. You are doing what you see as your duty, and I can't hate you for that."

Ed bit his lip. "That's kind of you to say. I know you disagree."

She paused, her words caught momentarily in her throat. "I wish you the very best, Eddie. Don't forget me entirely."

"I could never forget anything about you," he said, suddenly blinking back tears.

She smiled at him. "Anyway, I brought you a little parting gift." She held out a flat package wrapped in floral paper and tied with a pink bow.

He took it from her, untied the ribbon, and removed the paper. It was a framed photograph of herself, taken in one of the downtown studios. In it, she was smiling—at him.

She read his mind. "Put that in your little den," she said, "and you'll have someone watching over you every evening."

"Sarah," he said, clutching the photograph, "I don't know what to say."

"I suppose 'goodbye' would come next."

"But there's so much more I want to say."

"It's better to leave some things unsaid. That leaves room for imagination."

"But I need you to know that I—"

She reached out, put her forefinger on his lips, and shook her head.

Ed looked down at the floor and at the photo in his hands.

"I have to go," she said, "while I can. Goodbye, Eddie."

"Goodbye, Sarah," he mumbled, afraid to look up. When he did, she had gone.

❦

Batavia seemed like the best of bad alternatives. Sarah rented rooms for the two of them a couple blocks from Seth's office. Maggie would be able to see her father, and shielded from the worst of his addictions. She had wanted to stay in Buffalo, where she had playmates and school, but Sarah had told her that for a while, they had to be near Papa.

Sarah continued her stenography courses at Bryant & Stratton Business Institute. Once she became proficient, she would try to supplement Seth's dwindling income. Yet her main interest in stenography was to prepare for the eventual establishment of her detective agency. When or where that would be accomplished were open questions. Without Eddie, her dream of clear sunlight and the salt tang of the ocean only gave her pain. Until Seth died, or until they were divorced—whichever came first—Batavia would have to suffice.

As to Edward, Sarah felt disappointment, pity, and disgust—but strangely little sadness. On principle, she had resolved not to cry over him. Tears were sacred and not to be wasted. To her mind, he had mistaken obligation—a dull and plodding thing—for duty, a noble and triumphant urge, or was trying to fob off self-interest as altruism. To return to a dead marriage that had no prospect of resurrection suggested that he had chosen himself, not Allie. Losing Edward to Allie would have been mournful. Losing him to his own vanity was deplorable.

❧

A month trickled past. With each passing day, the silence became even harder for Arthur to bear, even though it had been his idea to suspend contact. Several times each week, he'd ride his automobile down Ashwood Street, past the Miller house. He gave himself some credit in that he hadn't rung the automobile gong but instead silently wheeled past, trying not to cast a sidelong glance at the front upper window. Driving past her house satisfied part of his craving, but only part, and only temporarily. And he knew that if he persisted in trolling past her place, eventually he'd be spotted by one of their nebby neighbors.

He checked their post office box daily, but there was no reason to expect anything from her. Nor had he seen her there. He knew that Alicia liked to go downtown for shopping on Wednesdays, so every midweek, he walked up and down in front of her favorite haunts in hopes of bumping into her accidentally. This had proven to be a complete waste of time and shoe leather.

The fruitless pacing on the cold sidewalks of downtown Buffalo made him so tense that a few times, he'd popped into a druggist and asked the fountain clerk for a 'corn bloom,' a sweet soda with a stiff shot of whiskey. Twice—driven almost to distraction by the itch to see her—he'd asked quietly for a 'millionaire,' which was the same sickly soda but with a few grains of morphine sulfate added. He drank it down and promptly went numb from head to toe, which felt so good it frightened him. That had been enough of a peek through the keyhole at what Cassie was becoming, inside her chrysalis.

Which was worse, he thought, becoming a dope fiend or just having a quick, harmless conversation with Allie? Hearing her say hello would be enough. He would be able to tell so much from one or two words. So on the one-month anniversary of their farewell, after his morning shave, he sat down in the phone booth at the Iroquois and placed a call to the Miller residence.

Edward had gone to work that day having left some business papers behind in his den, so after going through the morning mail, he had to go back to Ashwood Street to pick them up. The house was empty when he arrived, Annie probably out doing the marketing.

Edward listened to the silence, broken only by the dry ticking of the mantel clock in the adjacent parlor. He thought about the evening ahead. As usual, he'd finish up at work, take the trolley home, walk through the front door with a half-hearted smile. They'd eat dinner, read, and then when Alicia went to bed, he'd stretch out in his den. Since their reconciliation, it had been the same as it had always been, less quarrelling but the same indifference. Still unaddressed was the longstanding question of intimacy. God only knew how long it had been since he thought of her like that, or she him. Making an advance—or her making one—seemed out of the question, queasily incestuous, a place where his mind simply could not go.

Besides, he couldn't un-know that Allie wasn't the cold fish he had thought she was, that she was fired with passions hot enough to risk her home and reputation to satisfy. And there was no denying, either, that it was another man who had stoked them. He could blame duty, or shame, or Madame King for his predicament, but after Sarah's departure, he had to consider that it had arisen mostly from a craven desire not to feel so utterly and so easily vanquished by a fashionable cad he barely knew, and a wife who, it turned out, he didn't know at all.

He was jolted out of his musing when the phone rang. He trotted down the hall to the telephone table and picked up the earpiece.

"Miller here," he said.

The line went dead with a sharp click. Edward slowly replaced the earpiece on the hook. He thought for a second and then got the operator back on the line.

"Operator," he said, "I missed a call just now. Can you tell me who was trying to reach me? It may have been important."

"Let me ask the other girls to see who put that call through, Mr. Miller," the operator said.

She was back in a few seconds. "Mr. Miller, that call came from the Iroquois Hotel, but the caller didn't provide his name."

"Thank you, miss," Edward said. He took out his watch and checked the time. Nine-thirty. Yes, around this time, Pendle has his shave with his favorite barber at the Iroquois, having finally got up the gumption to get out of bed and get downtown. The Boland men had documented his routine, and it was the one thing utterly dependable about the man.

On the other end of the line, when he heard Edward's voice, Arthur threw down the earpiece as though it were red-hot. He shot out of the phone booth and walked quickly out of the hotel and up Main Street. His thoughts refused to slow, running frantically here and there in a sealed maze. Where was she? Why was she not at home this morning? And why was Edward there at this hour of the day? He was always in the office long before. Perhaps they had slept late. Together. Then they had laughed and lingered over breakfast, and of course, he'd been reluctant to leave, even for his beloved envelopes.

His skin crawled to consider what he had lost and—worse—what Edward had gained. Her eyes, with that hungry look only he had been able to conjure, now reflecting some other man's desire—little Edward's, at that. The son-of-a-bitch probably came home, took her laughing by the hand upstairs, bent her over the bed, the way she liked it, and had his way, his silly gold nose-glasses swinging from his lapel like a pendulum. A thousand dark fantasies became ever more baroque as he brooded.

Moreover, there was no work in The Hooks until the end of the month, nothing to immerse himself in. He couldn't even talk with Cassie. Since the return of the wicker basket, she had been quite content to retreat into her dream-world, like a snail.

Pale and sweating, worked up into what felt like a fever, Arthur left the Iroquois lobby and stalked back to his lair in Room Two. He threw himself into his rickety office chair. I can't do this any longer, he thought. He leaned over the desk, pulled out a sheet of letter paper, and began to write. If she still cares, she'll check the post office box eventually.

And at almost the same moment and with a creeping sense of dread, home in the echoing emptiness of 101 Ashwood Street, Edward was placing a long-distance call to the Mooney & Boland Detective Agency.

CHAPTER 40

Alicia's Brother

ALICIA HAD INDEED BEEN CHECKING THE POST OFFICE BOX, SOME-times twice a day, though after a month without so much as a postcard, she was beginning to wonder whether Arthur felt the same itch that she did. It had taken all her resolve not to write, not to call his office.

On today's visit to the box, when she entered the combination and opened the little door, Alicia fully expected to see the same emptiness mocking her. She would take only a quick glance, which helped her manage the disappointment. She stood on her tiptoes—theirs was on the top row of the block of identical boxes—and peered in.

A letter!

She slid the envelope out of the box, recognized his handwriting. Quickly shutting the little door and twirling the dial to lock it again, Alicia folded the letter and put it in her bag.

On the sidewalk, catty-corner from the Miller Envelope Company, she couldn't hold out any longer. She'd at first assumed it would be one of his gushing missives, but in the next heartbeat, she worried about the scanty thinness of the thing. Perhaps he was saying goodbye for good?

She slid her finger under the flap and lifted the seal, reading avidly, consuming the words. It was indeed short but made her giggle. He could sometimes truly sound like a fool in love, which she found mainly en-dearing, if occasionally slightly annoying. However short, though, this letter was significant. For the first time, he'd proven to possess even less willpower than she had. He wanted to meet, and soon. *We'll laugh over this one someday,* she thought. From the post office, she took a leisurely walk to Buffalo Savings Bank to squirrel away her latest treasure.

This lonely part of late fall is my favorite time of year in Buffalo, she thought. And she thought so without a trace of her usual apprehension about the inevitable snow. With any luck, her dream would come true—she would not have to endure another new year with Edward. The thought warmed her considerably. She had found peace in simply not caring anymore. Arthur's torc encircled her neck, day and night, as did his ring on her finger. Ed had asked her about her ring—apparently, he observed more than she'd thought—and she'd dissembled. Hers was in for resizing and polishing. This one was a loaner.

We *will* be together, she thought. It's only a matter of biding our time.

At the bank, she fairly skipped across the marble lobby to a barred window adjacent to the vault. By now, she had the ritual perfected: show the clerk her key fob, sign a card, follow him into the vault, and open the door with his key and hers. As usual, the clerk set the inner box on a table in a small booth and told her to press the button on the table when she was done.

Now came her favorite part. Sit down, square up the metal box neatly, and slowly lift the lid to reveal her cache. If she had time, she would linger, read a random letter or two, and relive the memories they brought back. Today, she'd have time only to deposit the latest arrival and go. But still, she took her time arranging the box. She flipped open the lid, smiling with anticipation. She placed the new letter, the opening page in the next chapter of their lives, right on top. She closed the box, pressed the little button, and the clerk put the box away again.

Alicia left the bank feeling as optimistic as she thought she'd ever felt. Only a few more weeks, with any luck, and I'll be rid of that runt of a husband.

She wrote back to Arthur immediately. She heard nothing over the weekend, but on Monday, there was a return message in the box suggesting a date and place to meet again. She confirmed by return mail and put his new letter in her safe deposit box, along with all the others.

That was her biggest mistake.

❦

On Thursday, there was another letter from Arthur. They were back in a rhythm, and on Friday, she'd meet him at One Two Three, now that he was sure that the heat was off. They'd passed three full hours together under the eaves, saying little. But when the afternoon sun had burned it- self out, and he reluctantly left her, it hurt as much as anything had hurt in her life. She never wanted to feel that kind of emptiness again and was sure she couldn't survive it.

But the past was the past. Once again, her heart was full of him and the sound of his words, shared one page at a time, each new letter a fresh secret to be carefully unsealed and savored. Everything was ahead of them now. So from the post office, she very nearly skipped all the way to the bank to add the newest letter to her trove. She crossed the lobby, smiled at the clerk behind the window, and settled into her little booth. Eager for her few sacred minutes at this shrine to their love, she slowly raised the lid.

The box was empty.

The blood left her head and plummeted down somewhere far below. She sagged into the chair. There's been some mistake. This must be some- one else's box, put into my slot. But where are my letters? In someone else's box? She pressed the button, then hit it with her fist, again and again.

The clerk showed up right away, jolted out of his chair by the frantic buzzer.

"May I be of assistance, madam?" he said, looking worried. "Is every- thing all right?"

"No, everything is not all right. We have the wrong box here. All of my contents are—missing."

"I'm sure there's an explanation. Let me see your fob."

He checked the fob against the numbers embossed on the box, locked and unlocked it again. "This is the correct box," he said. "If it weren't, we wouldn't be able to open the door, nor the inner box itself."

"I was in here only two days ago—and all of my things were here, as usual. And they're definitely not here now. I wish to speak to the man- ager. Right away."

"Of course, ma'am," the clerk said. "I'll show you to his office."

Alicia waited outside the manager's office for the longest few minutes of her life, pacing back and forth in a daze and almost knocking the man down when he did at last arrive.

"Good afternoon, Mrs. Miller. I'm Mr. Truesdale. I understand there's a problem with your box?"

Almost out of breath and fighting her rising panic, she explained the problem.

"Let me get the records for your box," he said, attempting to calm her. "If anything is amiss, I assure you we'll find it."

Truesdale gestured to a chair at a large oak table. She wanted to pace but sat down anyway, drumming her fingers on the tabletop. Soon he reappeared with a file folder. "Our file for your box," he said, patting it. "This is where we keep all your account documentation, the papers you signed to open the box, and a signature card for each entry going back twelve months."

"Yes, yes," she said.

He withdrew from the folder a thin stack of cards. "These are the signature cards. What day did you say you were in?"

"Monday, it would have been."

"Yes, here's the card for Monday, as you say," Truesdale said. He shuffled to the next card. "The next one is from Tuesday"—he shuffled again—"and then the one for today."

"Mr. Truesdale, sir, something's wrong. I wasn't here on Tuesday. Only on Monday and then today."

The manager looked closer at the second card. "Yes, I see now. It appears that your brother accessed the box on Tuesday."

"My brother?" Alicia said. "I don't have a brother. I'm an only child."

Mr. Truesdale looked puzzled and opened the file again. "You would have to provide a signed consent form for anyone other than yourself to access your box," he said, paging through the documents. He withdrew one with a flourish that made her want to smack him silly. "Here we go," he said, putting it on the table. "Our standard consent form. This is your signature?"

"Yes, it is," Alicia said, dumbfounded. "It looks a little hasty, but yes. That's my signature."

"And it says here that 'I'—that would be you—'until further notice, do hereby grant access to the contents of Safe Deposit Box 521 to my brother, Edward L. Miller.'"

It was the closest Allie had ever come to screaming in a stranger's face, because nothing else could possibly have expressed the emotions causing her chest to heave so strangely.

"I need to place a telephone call," she murmured. "Urgently."

"Yes, of course. You may use the phone in my office."

She called Arthur immediately and said she wanted to see him right away, at his office the Ellicott Square.

"Not tomorrow, at One Two Three?" he said.

"That's different. I need to see you now about something else. I can't talk about it here."

❧

"What in the world were you *thinking?*" Arthur said a quarter-hour later in his Collections Agency office. "How many times have I said: 'destroy the letters, Allie'?"

"I know. You have every right to be upset. I should have burned them."

"Goddamn it, Allie." He groaned and looked up at the ceiling. "Just—*goddamn*. I don't even remember what all is in there. Things about my *work*. My most private thoughts, without any redaction. I don't know what all. Things I ought never to have put on paper. And now the person who's reading it—of all people—is your husband!" He put his head in his hands.

"I don't know what to say, Arthur. I meant no harm. I thought one day we'd want to read them together and remember everything we'd been through. I couldn't bear to part with them."

"I ought to have known better. I ought never to have written them. Do you know the kind of trouble we're in now?"

"Arthur, it can't be—"

"Allie. We are *fucked*. That's all there is to it."

"I know you're angry, but it can't be so bad."

"Those letters are *evidence!*" he said, hitting the table with his fist.

"Until now, whatever Ed knew wasn't enough direct evidence to force a public trial. Now he has a whole library of it, all in my own hand. Each of those letters is a signed confession. Of adultery, and a *lot* of other things too. Do you have any idea what Penrose is going to say? He is going to hit the roof."

She was silent, looking down at his foot, which was doing that little quivering dance.

Arthur bit his tongue. "No use crying over spilt milk. What's done is done. I'll have to figure a way out of this. I have to get those damned letters back, somehow."

"Can't Penrose swear out a warrant or something? They were stolen from my bank box. Isn't that a crime?"

"Even if it is, the letters would be the evidence of the crime. That would mean everyone from the cops to the court gets to read them. I'm going to have to think of another way to get my hands on them. In the meantime, don't breathe a word about this to Edward."

"Don't say anything?" Allie said, her face going crimson. "How am I going to face the little shit tonight and not say anything? I'd like to kill him! That bastard!"

Arthur took her hands in his. "Allie, we won't get anywhere losing our heads. If we can remain calm, we have the upper hand. We don't know for certain that he has them."

"Who else would have them?"

"I don't mean that he isn't behind it. It could be that his detectives have them, and he hasn't seen them yet. Let's wait and see if he says anything first."

"I don't know if I can do that."

"You can, and you must. When we see each other tomorrow, we'll know more. And I'll have a chance to think through what to do next."

❦

"The mother lode," Williams announced, placing a shoebox on Edward's desk. He removed the lid and tilted the box so that Ed could see the contents. It was full of small bundles of letters, each tied in a lavender ribbon.

"Are those what I think they are?" Edward said.

"When you asked us to follow her again—the first thing we saw, on Monday, was your wife taking a letter from the post office to her box at the bank. The next day we followed our plan from before and got everything. Like taking candy from a baby."

Ed frowned. "If these letters predate our reconciliation, it hardly seems fair for me to have them. I said I'd give her another chance."

"Unfortunately, there are letters here less than a week old. It would appear they have been lying to you."

Edward's face drained of color. "They lied? All of them? Cassie and Allie—and Arthur, who gave me his word of honor?"

Williams looked at his lap. "Seems so, sir. In the letter she deposited on Monday, Pendle suggested a meeting at the house on Whitney Place, but we don't have her reply, so we don't know the date. But soon."

"Those goddamned—"

The detective looked up at him across the desk without emotion. "I'm sorry to say it, but promises from straying spouses aren't typically worth the powder to blow them up with."

Edward sat back, breathing hard. "I should have known it was all for show."

"Don't blame yourself. These two are shrewd."

They sat quietly, Edward tapping on the desk with a pencil.

"I suppose you ought to get Reitz back," he said.

Williams looked puzzled. "I can shadow them myself."

"Not that," Edward said. "If you find them together at their little love-nest, I want you to teach Arthur Pendle a lesson he won't forget."

"Oh yes, I see. We can do that."

"Uh-huh," Ed said. His face had gotten very red. "Keep me informed."

CHAPTER 41

Falling on His Sword

HE HAD ALREADY FOLDED THE PAPER, SLID IT INTO ONE OF HIS best envelopes, addressed and stamped it. He was about to seal it up when he thought he'd better read it over one final time. It would probably be the only chance he'd have, and with long odds, it had to be good.

Dear Sarah,

You'd be well within your rights to tear this up unread, though I hope you won't. I ought to have known better than to believe A&A; they had already richly furnished me with proof that they could not be trusted. Worse than that, though, I ought to have believed you, without requiring any proof at all, merely the faith in you that you deserved. You knew I was making the wrong decision, and now I do too.

I want you, I need you. I beseech you to come back. Come back to me, and help me finish this. It's not something I deserve, but it's the thing I want more than anything else.

Yours very sincerely, Edward.

It'll have to do, he thought. It's as much as I can put into a letter that might be intercepted. If she doesn't come back, I'll live with it as best I can. He sealed the envelope and tucked it into his jacket. Now it was on the knees of the gods.

❦

Three days after, he had almost made it to his building when a cold gust tore Edward's hat off his head and sent it sailing down Division Street, rolling along on its brim like a runaway tire. He was about to chase after it when a teamster driving a wagonload of rubbish ran it over with undisguised glee.

"Thanks a whole lot!" he shouted at the passing teamster, who tipped his cap, smiling.

Edward walked over to where his derby was lying in the grey slush. He bent over and saw that the rigid, shellacked crown had cracked like an eggshell.

"You know, you very nearly knocked me over again," said a voice behind him as he stood examining the battered hat.

He turned around to see Sarah Payne standing on the sidewalk alongside Division Street. Even in the blustery wind, she managed to keep an unusually large hat perfectly balanced atop her Gibson Girl hairdo.

"Sarah?" It was all he could do not to pick her up and kiss her.

"Is there anyone else matching my description roaming around Buffalo these days?" she said. "You spoiled my surprise. I was going to stroll into your office like it was any other day."

He trotted over to her, wanted to embrace her, but instead offered her his arm. "I can't believe it's you," he said. "Let's get out of this wind." They strolled the last block to his building, Sarah gripping his forearm through the soft skin of her gloves. The leather had a little fur ruff at the wrist.

They sat down in the conference room down the hallway from his office. They looked at each other for quite some time, neither knowing how to begin.

"You came," he said.

"You asked me to. You *beseeched* me, if I remember it right."

He looked at her as though he might be an apparition. "I'm so relieved you did. I'm sorry, Sarah. Truly."

"Eddie—"

"I promise, Sarah, I'm going to make it up to you."

"I'll believe it when I see it, but it's nice to hear."

"You can count on it," he said.

"So do I read correctly between the lines of your artfully obscure letter? You have evidence that something is still going on?"

"She and Arthur were lying to me the whole time. They had no intention of breaking it off."

"Some temptations are harder to resist than others."

"Yes," he said. "You knew it, but I didn't listen."

"I'm not going to scold you. You made a mistake, Eddie. It was a whopper of a mistake, but a mistake all the same."

"I've been so gullible and stupid. You must hate me."

"Eddie, please," she said. "I don't hate you. But maybe you are stupid if you don't know that I love you. Always have."

"Good heavens," he said.

"Why, you look like you've seen a ghost, instead of hearing a woman tell you she loves you."

"I didn't expect to hear that," he said. "Not today, and maybe not ever."

"Life is full of surprises. Now, don't you think it would be polite to tell me that you love me? If you do, that is."

"Oh, I do love you," he said. "More than anything."

"What a relief that we've got that out of the way."

Ed laughed. "I can hardly believe you're sitting here."

"Neither can I, to be honest with you."

"You won't regret it," he said.

"Good. Now how can we get you freed from Allie, once and for all?"

"I think I may have just the thing," he said. "Give me a minute. I'll be right back."

Edward disappeared down the hall, the sound of his footsteps receding. He was back in a couple of minutes with the box of letters and set it on the table, lifting the top grandly. "Look what the Boland men got their hands on."

Sarah shuffled through the envelopes. Most had handwritten addresses, all to the same address. "Mrs. Ashwood?" she muttered. "Queen City Detective Agency?" she said, holding up one with a typewritten address.

"Read it," Edward said.

She slid the folded paper from the envelope and scanned it. "You mean to tell me that Arthur's had detectives following you around? This is a report on your comings and goings. Our little chats at Five Fours."

"Seems he decided two could play at the detective game. But read some of the ones to Mrs. Ashwood."

She read through a couple of Arthur's letters. "Strong stuff," she said, shaking her head. "He doesn't leave much to the imagination."

"I'm so ashamed," he said.

"It's *their* shame, Eddie. Not yours. But how in the world did your detectives get their hands on these?"

"She took out a safe deposit box at the bank," he said. "The Boland men couldn't get at them without authorization, of course, so they suggested a scheme. Allie was in a hurry to get downtown one afternoon. Probably to meet Arthur. I had any number of documents that needed her signature that day. Bank drafts, things for the children's school, and so forth. I slipped a consent form to access the box among those documents—in plain sight. She glanced at it, and signed it like all the others. I was a bit shocked—I had expected only to use it to confront her about the existence of the box. Then the Boland men took the consent form in and raided the box."

"Oh, Eddie," Sarah said. "I'm sorry to say it, but that doesn't seem right. Even if the letters are nefarious, they're Allie's private property."

"I don't feel a shred of remorse. They should never have been written."

"That pride of yours is going to get you into trouble," she said. "You can't do anything you please because you feel wronged."

"What would you have me do? Let this all go?"

"You can't very well now. In stealing—I'm sorry, but that's what it is—in stealing these letters, you've taken a wolf by his ears. Once Arthur and Allie know these are gone—you don't know what they'll be willing to do to get them back."

"Don't you think that's a bit overblown?"

"I do not. Arthur is a very cunning man and has powerful friends. And I am sure he's got some unsavory connections."

He sat a minute, thinking this over.

"I see those wheels turning," she said.

"What if I could somehow get to the bottom of that? What he's up to?"

"You've already stuck your nose far enough under his tent. It's not a good idea."

"But what if I could find something incriminating?"

"What do you want here? Divorce or revenge?"

"After what they've put me through? Both. I made—I almost made the biggest mistake of my life, because they played me for a fool. I'm allowed to keep my pride."

"Let it be enough that I'm proud of you. You've handled yourself like a gentleman. Let them be the nasty ones. We need to keep a cool head and stay focused on our objective. Being together. We don't need more trouble."

"He started it."

"Don't be schoolboyish. If you're going to use these letters at all, use them to trade for a quiet, private divorce."

"Whose side are you on here?"

She fixed him with a caustic squint.

"I'd better go lock these back up," he said. "You've made me a little nervous about them, now."

"Do you have copies?"

"I had Abby typewrite a few of them, and then I stopped her. Some of them—I was embarrassed."

"I'm sure they're hard to read."

She tapped her finger on the box. "No, don't lock them up here. Give them to me until we can get this sorted out. No one in a million years will think I have them."

"Mightn't that put you in danger?"

"Not if you don't let on that I have them. That said—if Arthur has detectives watching you, you can bet that they've seen me come here. If I leave with a satchel that I didn't have when I came, that's going into their report. He'll suspect I have the letters."

"Should I mail them to you, then?"

"Way too risky. They could get lost or intercepted. I have a better idea—I'll conceal them on my person and take the trolley home as usual. That won't arouse suspicion."

"On your person? Where are you going to hide all these packets of letters?"

She winked at him. "Well, I never! We've been reunited for all of a half-hour, and you already want to know what's under my clothes."

"I didn't mean—"

"Oh, look, he's blushing! That is so cute."

"I simply meant—"

"I know what you meant. Don't you worry, I'll find places. With all this fabric, corset, overcoat . . . trust me. I'll take them home and read them. Then we should talk again."

"I can call you," he said.

"I haven't a telephone at my house yet. I'll call you as soon as I've read these through. And in the meantime—consider what I said about giving them back. Let them go and be miserable together."

"I don't know if I can do that."

"But you will think about it, won't you?"

"I would do anything for you," Edward said.

"I like the sound of that. Now, unless you want to watch me while I find places on my *body* to put all this paper, you'd better run along. I'll find my way out."

"I'll go right back to my office."

"Made you blush again! I must say, it never fails. But I don't mind if you do stay and watch. Might be fun, you know. Wouldn't you like to have a peek at what's inside the wrapping?"

"Oh, stop," Edward said. "I'm going."

"Eddie, one last thing."

"Yes?"

"In all seriousness. You'd better keep your eyes peeled—for Pendle or one of his minions. He's not going to take this lying down."

Edward nodded and held out his hand awkwardly as if to shake hers.

"Oh, you dear little man," she said, leaning in and giving him a peck on the cheek. "Now go. My disrobement begins in ten seconds, with or without an audience."

Back in his office, Edward sat down at his desk, thinking he might do some paperwork, distract himself. He was so overjoyed that Sarah was back, though, he couldn't concentrate. But then his mind wheeled around again to Arthur Pendle.

He picked up the telephone and asked the operator for long-distance, New York.

CHAPTER 42

More Evidence

ALTHOUGH HE CHOSE NOT TO INFLAME SARAH WITH HIS PLAN, Edward arranged to have the Boland men arrive in Buffalo on the 29th of November. He passed a very quiet Thanksgiving at home, mainly because Allie didn't say a word to him, nor did her mother. The girls had picked up on the mood and stayed in their rooms.

On the evening of the 29th, he met with the detectives downtown at the Genesee.

"I wanted you here now because the last day of every month is somehow important to him," he said. "I've noticed that he always makes sure he's in the city, no matter what. And I want to know why. Tomorrow is our best chance of finding out."

"We'll do the best we can," Williams said. "We have all day and all night. Twenty-four hours, if necessary."

Williams and Reitz spent most of November 30th cold and frustrated, popping into stores and bars where they could pass themselves off as friendly, working class fellows from out of town, looking for a friend of theirs. As dusk was gathering, they were beginning to despair when Reitz got to talking with a fellow German in a saloon near the Terrace Station. The German told him that about an hour earlier, he'd steered clear of a man matching Arthur's description walking with two policemen toward The Hooks, only a few blocks away.

❦

He had disappeared into The Hooks, as usual, around half-past five. It was a miserable evening to be tramping from place to place. All day the mercury had stayed hidden, and about sundown, wet snow flurries had started to fall. Around 10 o'clock, a soggy, surly Arthur and his two cops checked in at the first of their last five stops that evening, a dive bar on Le Couteulx Street, just off Canal, in the innermost circle of The Hooks.

In front of the place, the usual mob of semi-intoxicated men was lolling around in the doorway, smoking and swearing, breath steaming in the damp cold. As soon as Arthur and his men opened the door, they were assaulted by the usual warm wave of stale smoke, beer, and sweat belching out of the old brick row house. It was something impossible to get used to, especially in the cold season.

By this time of night, Arthur had usually attracted a little entourage, who straggled a few yards behind, like a school of scavenging fish following a shark. The hangers-on tailed them into the dive. Arthur's mood had continued to worsen along with the weather, and the little coffle of freeloaders boxing him in this fetid place was the final straw.

"Get the hell back!" he yelled, pushing his cops out of the way to confront them. "I'm not going to tell you twice."

"Big man," said one of the voices. "And if we don't?"

The cops were starting to look worried but put on their best front, prodding the ringleaders with their sticks.

"You heard him. Back off!"

"Buy us a drink!"

"Let us see what you've got in that bag!" said the first voice.

"Come on, Mr. Pendle," one of the cops said to Arthur. "We'd better get out of here."

"Not until I get what this place owes," Arthur said. "I'm not letting these types push us around."

"We'll push you, all right," said one big fellow, who was emboldened by his group's resistance.

Arthur snapped. "Get back, or I'll have you hauled in front of the District Attorney myself. I'm his goddamned guard dog, understand? You want a drink? If it weren't for me and him, this place and all the rest"—he waved his hand to indicate the whole of The Hooks—"would be burned to the ground."

There was muttering among the bunch of men, who were unsure what to do with this bit of information.

"Stand these men a round," Arthur said to the cops, "while I finish my business." A few of the men gave out a hoarse cheer.

Arthur disappeared into the back of the place and was back almost immediately, scowling. The men were milling around, drinking their watery whiskey, looking sidelong at Arthur. "Let's go," Arthur said when they were back on the crumbling sidewalk. "I've fucking had it for tonight."

In the crappy dive bar, two of the shabby hangers-on clinked their glasses. This evening they'd earned a lot more than a free whiskey in a dirty glass. There was a hot bath and clean clothes waiting for them back at their hotel, where they would relax over a proper cocktail with their steak. Working for Boland could be hard, but the perks were good. Tomorrow's report to Mr. Miller was going to be a humdinger.

❦

While Williams and Reitz were picking up Arthur's trail, Sarah was reopening her house on Norwood Street. She and Maggie had brought only a couple of trunks of clothes and essentials, so moving in was simple. By bedtime, she happily tucked her little daughter into bed in her very own room. Then Sarah changed into her nightgown, brushed her hair and perfect teeth, and propped herself up in bed to begin reading Arthur's correspondence.

The earliest ones seemed innocent enough, if a bit florid. There was one that went into considerable detail about a kiss in an archway at New Haven. Others talked about meeting at a place called One Two Three and were carefree and effervescent. Clearly, the pair had been enjoying themselves, having fun.

The tone changed as the weeks and months went by, however. The letters became more fraught, erotic, urgent. If more than a day or two passed between letters, Arthur would relate checking their post office box several times a day, even pestering the postal clerks to check if there were any mail not yet sorted and put into the boxes. And his accounting of their intimacies was, in places, strong medicine, and she skipped through many of the details, feeling like a common peeping Tom.

The sex then gave way to spite, directed at Edward, Ashwood neighbors (there was some nasty gossip about Sarah and Seth in at least a half-dozen), Arthur's professional colleagues—and, oddly, quite a bit centering on District Attorney Terence Penrose. Notably absent from this surging tide of bile, though, was Cassie. Both of them seemed to consider Cassie as an ally, someone aiding and abetting, willing to accept whatever dregs of a marriage Arthur or Allie would permit her.

The corpus of their correspondence also had throbbing through it a vein of deadly venom. 'Sometimes your husband's manner of treating you makes me feel that I want to kill him, but I hold my temper, knowing that any expression on my part would probably lead to a quick and violent end,' wrote Arthur in one. One of the most recent missives outlined in some detail how much they would relish the expression on Ed's face when Allie told him that she was leaving him. In another, Arthur proposed that they send Ed a photograph of the two of them taken as— why, even a young, married lady like Sarah had to blush.

And buried within several of the letters were dark hints that confirmed Sarah's hunch that Arthur was involved in some form of racket. 'I have to be back by the 30th so that I can pick up TP's payments,' one said; another, 'if I keep fixing things for TP at my current pace, you and I will be free in a year.' 'I am sorry I was so surly last evening,' Arthur wrote in another. 'I am brought down sometimes by how rotten the whole legal system is—justice sold to the highest bidder.' In yet another, Arthur lamented, 'giving up my legal practice entirely to fix things for Penrose.' These would be difficult letters for Arthur, or the District Attorney, to explain away, should they become public.

Two documents were most damning of all, though for different reasons. One was in Allie's hand, a list of the places, dates, and times she and Arthur had met, gone away together, spoken on the telephone, or even passed a word on the street. And in each entry was a description, sometimes quite explicit, of what had transpired. It was as close to a diary of their affair as could be imagined.

The other was a document in Arthur's practiced script, a long list of names, dates, and sums of money—sometimes preposterously large— collected from various and sundry individuals in Buffalo over more than two years. The tally was kept on the front and back of four pages of yellow legal paper. There was no detail about what the money was for, nor any reason Sarah could determine why Allie would possess this document at all. It was clearly a private record that—in Sarah's suspicious mind—could only have been purloined by Allie as potential leverage over Arthur, should things go against her.

Sarah read all of them, twice, and studied the tally document until her eyes began to blur. She then stowed the whole mess into an empty hat box and slid it under her bed. Whether it was simply being in a new home, or whether the box of letters below her mattress was emitting some unwholesome air, she spent the rest of the night sleepless and staring at the ceiling. She was tormented by the persistent notion, like the buzz of bottle flies, that Eddie was in grave danger.

❦

The following week, Sarah returned to Edward's office. She rather liked the old place. It smelled of timeworn brick, wood, and a little bit like his sandalwood aftershave. There was something comforting about Miller Envelopes, Edward's private world, which told so much more about him than did his grand home on Ashwood Street. She felt close to him when she observed the precision of the machinery, the neat pallets of finished envelopes.

"I find his repeated references to the District Attorney very worrisome," she said. "I'm sure you saw the document in there listing what seem to be payoffs from various people."

"And the Boland men saw him in The Hooks, collecting money from a bunch of miscreants—"

"Excuse me?"

"I had him followed. He's nothing but a bag-man, Sarah, shaking people down for the DA. That's why the last of the month is so sacred to him. It's collection day."

Sarah shook her head emphatically. "Eddie, what did I tell you about meddling in that man's private business? We already know he's up to no good."

"But I have him by the—I have him dead to rights now."

"'Dead to rights?' Dare I ask what you intend to do with this new information?"

"I asked the Boland men to pay a visit to Mr. Penrose and let him know some of what we've learned."

"You didn't."

"I did. Why not?"

"Why not? I hardly know where to begin. This is beyond rash. If Arthur is doing something for him that he shouldn't, you can bet the DA isn't going to want that to come out."

"And if the DA knows that we know, he'll let Arthur take the fall."

"You don't know that. This world these people inhabit—it's not your world. Our world. It doesn't follow the same rules. I'm not sure it follows any rules at all."

"The legal system is supposed to be about rules."

"You're too old to be so naïve. Rules are for people like you and me. The people who make the rules don't follow them. Period. That's the way it works."

Edward shrugged. "I don't know that I want to live in a world like that."

"Don't believe me, then. At the very least, though, why did you tip your hand? You don't know what lengths these people will do to hush this up."

"Sarah, please. I've made up my mind."

"That's what I'm afraid of. I like you better when you do what I tell you to do."

"I'm not afraid of Arthur Pendle, or Terence Penrose, for that matter," Edward said. "If Arthur tries anything, he's in for a big surprise. Look what I got at Walbridge's."

He opened his drawer and took out a blued steel revolver, a cheap Iver Johnson. He set it on the desk, muzzle pointing toward Sarah. She reached over and pushed it with a finger to aim toward the brick wall instead.

"You don't know how to use that thing," she said. "You'd be better off buying a dog."

"I bought three boxes of shells. I'm going to take them to Wheatfield and do some target practice. It can't be that hard."

"You've lost your mind," she said.

"You say that because you want me to let this all go by without sticking up for myself."

"You've more than proven that you are willing to stand up for yourself. But you're not the only fellow willing to stand up for himself, and some of the others have a lot more at stake. Don't back them into a corner. You may not be afraid, but I am. Corner them, and you'll see how dangerous they can be."

"He's a coward," Edward grumbled. "Nothing but a little sneak-thief."

"I think you have him wrong. Dead wrong. I've read every one of his letters. Twice. He's shaking down ruffians for a living. Do you know what sort of person can manage that? He may look smooth, but he's as tough as they come."

"The detectives said he had two cops along for protection while he did his dirty work."

"He's a coward, then. And so are rabbits. But when I was a little girl, I saw my father's dog trap one against the woodshed, and that little thing fought like a tiger and sent that dog away with his tail between his legs. That's what I'm afraid of. You run them to earth, and they are going to turn on you. And you aren't going to like what they look like then."

PART 4

HARVEST

CHAPTER 43

Mene, Mene, Tekel, Upharsin

"BIRDS HAVE THEIR NESTS, AND FOXES HAVE DENS," ARTHUR SAID, crooking his arm under his head.

"A couple of fine foxes we make," Allie said.

"You don't like being here with me?"

She shifted and fixed her dark, dreamy eyes on him. "Oh, these stirrings you give me are almost enough to live for," she said. "But things are soon going to get worse. I'm not looking forward to being Buffalo's most notorious harlot."

"I won't let that happen."

She was quiet for a few moments. "That might not be within your control."

Arthur flopped on his back. "I'll figure it out."

"What if you can't? If we couldn't be together, I wouldn't even want to go on living."

He looked at her. "I've thought the very same thing."

"You have?"

"Disgraced? Shunned? Not much of a life. No thank you."

"Then what do we do?"

He shifted up in bed to catch the last sliver of the red sun as it disappeared behind the house on the other side of Whitney Place. "We have a nice dinner, then come up here and take morphine. Go to sleep. Forever."

She murmured something he couldn't make out.

"What was that?"

"How would that work?" she said. "I'd want you to watch me die."

He looked out the front window again. "It's easier than you might think. I'd inject you and then myself. God knows I've seen how it's done enough."

"We'd fade away together," she said. "No more hiding."

He stared into her eyes, close to grasping something that had thus far eluded him. "Would you truly do that? For me?"

"I would. I'd do it now if we had the morphia."

They lay quietly next to each other as the shadows in the room thickened.

"I suppose we ought to be going," he said. "It'll be dark soon, and—"

The hollow sound of heavy shoes coming up the wooden porch steps below their room silenced him.

"Who's that?" she said.

Arthur jumped out of bed and peeked out the front window.

"Well, fuck me," he said, letting the curtains fall closed. "It's Edward's spies."

"It's not!"

"But it is. We must have been spotted coming here. You better get dressed," he said, yanking on his pants.

The doorknob below them began rattling, hard. "Go down the back staircase," Arthur said. "The alley behind the house—go left, to the church. Wait a while there, then go home. They won't follow you—it's me they want."

Alicia was throwing on layers of clothes as quickly as she could. The front door was now shuddering, reverberating through the frame of the house. "Hurry up," he said. "They're going to break down the door."

"I *am* hurrying," she said. "You try getting all of this shit on quickly sometime."

"Put the rest on, on the stairs. Check our box tomorrow."

Allie hurried to the door, still in her stocking feet. She looked back at him and then raced down the back stairs. At the bottom, she stepped out of a long window into the narrow alley behind One Two Three. She didn't dare look back but locked her eyes on the Unitarian Church. During the week, the church left the sanctuary doors open for those who needed to pray. At the church, breathless, she slid into one of the pews in the rear of the sanctuary. Winter light filtered in through the stained glass, and the air smelled faintly of incense. It would have been a peaceful place to reflect and to pray. But reflection was painful, and prayer was only so much wishful thinking.

☙

While Alicia was hurrying toward the church, the Boland men were kicking at the front door of One Two Three, which was more solid than expected.

"I'm going to beat that little *scheisser* to a pulp," Reitz said, huffing, puffing, and angry after a full minute of kicking futilely at the door. To make matters worse, he'd fallen on his ass twice, slipping on the icy threshold while trying to kick his way in.

"Miller wants him schooled," Williams said.

Inside, Arthur knew there was no way out, and was too proud to run from the likes of these. "Will you stop?" he yelled through the vibrating door. "I'm opening up!" He threw the bolt and stepped back into the parlor to let the two red-faced detectives barge in.

☙

Even though he'd seen dozens of other men make the same mistake, Arthur tried to get uppity with the Boland men. He told them they could both go to Hell, that he would be damned if he would entertain their impertinence. That had given Reitz all the excuse he needed to give him a more thorough working over. Williams got a couple of kicks in if only to boost his credibility with his larger partner.

After it was done, they crushed his derby flat and sailed it after him as he was picking himself up from the front sidewalk, where the detectives had tossed him. His jacket collar was torn, both knees were out of his trousers, and when he wiped his runny nose, his sleeve came away soaked with blood. He picked up his crumpled hat and stumbled away from the rented house, across the crust of dirty snow.

☙

"May I ask where you have been?" Edward said the second Alicia walked through the front door, her skirt and coat and shoes stained and splattered with the fly ash spread on the streets to give carriage wheels a little bit of winter traction. He was waiting for her outside his den. He must have been looking out his window and had seen her approach.

"I was at church."

"Normally, I'd give you high marks for such a fantastical lie. But incredibly, in this case, your story checks out."

"Meaning?"

"Meaning that I got a call a little while ago at my office from my operatives. They told me they caught you red-handed this time. And please, don't try to deny it. Because Arthur didn't. He gave the fellows a full confession. Haha, while I suppose you were making yours in the church. I had barely enough time to get home and make arrangements."

"What arrangements?"

The front doorbell rang.

"Would you mind getting that, dear?" Edward said in a honeyed voice.

Grateful for an escape, Allie turned and opened the door. A neatly dressed young man was standing on the porch.

"Hello," he said. "Mrs. Edward Miller?"

"Yes, that's me," Alicia said.

The man handed her a large, sealed envelope. "Ma'am, please accept this summons from the Erie County Court of Common Pleas to defend yourself in a divorce action. You've been served." He turned and stepped carefully down the porch steps.

Alicia stood in the vestibule, holding the envelope, frozen. She wanted to flee, but there was nowhere to go. She couldn't run into the cold, and she felt equally loath to stay. She turned back to the hallway. Edward was standing where she'd left him a few seconds ago, watching with a slightly amused look on his face. She longed to bloody that smug face of his.

"Now that the legal niceties have been observed," he said coldly, "you will leave my home immediately."

"Leave? *Your* home?"

"You heard me. Leave. Go. Get out. Should I continue?"

"Be reasonable, Ed."

"I have been too reasonable for too long. That ends today. You may have an hour to pack some of your things. I'll send the rest wherever you like, once you get settled. While you are doing that, I'll arrange a hack to take you wherever you like. Maybe the Pendles will take you in."

"You can't be serious. You can't send me away from my own home. My mother—my children are here. I'm not going to go. I refuse. I'm going up to my room. Leave me alone."

"One hour," he said. "If you are not ready to go in one hour—" he took his gold watch from his vest and flipped it open—"I'll have my detectives remove you bodily. I doubt very much you'd want the neighbors seeing you carried, kicking and screaming, out the front door. Not that I'd care, though, because they already know what you've put me and this family through the past year. So don't test me. One hour. Not a second more."

She ran up the stairs without saying another word.

❦

"Time to go, Allie," Edward called up the stairs precisely one hour later. "Your driver is waiting."

She came down the stairs with all the bitter grace she could muster. A heavy-set hackman was waiting in the vestibule.

"Good day," she said. "There's a trunk and a carpet bag upstairs. In the front bedroom."

The hackman grunted and clumped upstairs.

"This was all your doing, I'm sorry to say," Edward said to her back, as Alicia stared out the window next to the door, anything to avoid looking at him.

"It took you quite a while and a lot of work, Allie, but at last you succeeded in killing whatever love I had for you. But after everything, believe it or not, I do sincerely wish you well."

She gave a little snort and didn't turn around. "Of course you do, Edward."

"Um, I'll just go put this in the hack," said the driver, who'd been standing uncomfortably on the staircase, trunk on his back, uncertain about what he was walking into. He thudded back down the rest of the stairs and out the front door, surprisingly nimble for such an ungainly fellow.

Allie whirled around, finally, ashamed of her tears. "What about the children?" she said. "What are you going to tell them? And my mother."

"It's not for me to tell our children about your misbehavior. I'll tell them that you went away for a little rest. I'll leave it to you to tell them anything else. Blame it all on me, if you like. You've alienated them almost entirely from me as it is. As for your mother, I'm sure she knows more about all this than I do."

Alicia wanted to find some cutting remark, some triumphant quip, but she came up empty. She turned to go.

"Oh, Alicia," Ed said as she opened the door, "the hack is prepaid. Everything else from now on—Arthur can pay for."

Alicia wiped her eyes with the back of her glove and walked carefully down to the waiting hack. She told the driver to take her to the New York Central station. There, she planned to call Arthur.

❦

Arthur pressed an ice bag against the side of his head with one hand. Cassie was kneeling next to his chair.

"Arthur, what happened? Were you in The Hooks?"

"No," he groaned. "I was at a house with Alicia, and Ed Miller's detectives found us."

"And they beat you like this?"

"I certainly didn't fall down ten flights of stairs. They kicked the living shit out of me."

"And you hurt your head?"

"There was a big fellow who was sitting on my chest and slamming my head into the floor. I blacked out after about six or eight times. Lost count. Jesus, it hurts like hell."

"They could have fractured your skull!"

He touched the back of his head with two fingers. "Thank goodness I have a hard head."

"I'll call our doctor."

"Don't. I'm not about to tell a doctor that I was beaten up while with another woman. It'll be all over Ashwood in five minutes. What's he going to do, anyway?"

"At the very least, you ought to lie down."

"That I will do."

He was gingerly getting up when the telephone rang, making them jump.

"One guess who that is," Cassie said. "Not a moment's peace from her."

"I'll get it," he said, easing himself out of the chair.

"You stay put." She picked up on the third ring.

"Hello?"

"Cassie?" said the voice on the line. "This is—"

"I know very well who this is. What do you want?"

"I'm sorry to bother you. Is Arthur at home?"

"He's not feeling well," she said. "Is this urgent?"

"Very urgent," Allie said. "Please. This is the last time I'll call your home."

"Hold the line," Cassie said. "Arthur, Mrs. Miller wants a word." She set the earpiece on the table.

Arthur hobbled to the phone.

"Allie?"

"Edward has sent me away. I'm at the Exchange Street Station. I've been banished. What should I do?"

Arthur knew he had no good option. "I'll be there shortly."

"I knew I could depend on you."

"Give me a half-hour."

"And so it continues," Cassie said hollowly from behind him. "Even after all this. You're going to her, again."

"I have to go to her now. Edward threw her out."

"Serves her right."

"Cassie, if anyone is at fault here, I am."

"Is that an apology?"

He said nothing.

"How long will you be gone?"

"Overnight. I'll get her to Niagara Falls and come back in the morning."

"Good, good," she said, sneering. "At least you'll get to fuck her a few more times. Get good and emptied out."

"I'm not going to touch her. I need to get her calmed down. She can do us a lot of harm."

"Some things you can't fix, Arthur."

"Well, this, I can."

He limped toward the foyer, grabbed his overcoat and hat, and inched down the steps to Columbus Avenue.

❦

The New York Central train chuffed and rattled through the bleak landscape between Buffalo and Niagara Falls.

Other than a startled outburst from Allie, quickly stifled, when Arthur's battered face had appeared at the Exchange Street Station, they'd been quiet the whole ride. It seemed like days, not hours, had passed since One Two Three, and that something brittle and hard had forced its way between them.

In Niagara Falls, they hailed a coach for the Prospect House.

"Now, will you finally tell me what happened after I left?" Alicia asked when the bellhops deposited her trunk and left them alone in their room. "You look terrible. Are you in shock?"

"They gave me a beating, but good. Forget about that. I want to hear about Edward. That's why we're here, isn't it?"

"I waited in the church for a while, as you said, and then went home. By the time I'd gotten there, his men must have told him they caught us. He was waiting for me there and told me to get out. He'd hired a driver. And I left."

"That's all?"

"He did say you'd given me up and made a full confession."

"If by 'giving you up' he means that I told them you had left to go to the church, yes, I did. He's right about that."

"Why in the world would you tell them that?"

"Are you being serious? Those men of his—I had no choice. You have no idea what I endured. God knows what all is broken. I feel like I was thrown out of a ten-story building."

"What did they—"

"I don't want to talk about it now. Let's get settled in, and we'll talk things over in the morning."

"But I want to talk about it."

"Even polygamy can be monotony," he muttered.

"What?"

"Let's go to bed," he said. "I'm tired. Everything fucking hurts. I can't think straight, and I need to. Tomorrow."

"All right, I understand. I'll get ready." She disappeared into the bathroom.

He sat down at the writing desk, overlooking the column of cold mist rising from the Falls. It hurt to sit up, slump over, take a breath. He put his aching head in his hands. He sat there staring down at the blotter, which was covered with backwards writing and reverse signatures, like one of Leonardo's notebooks. Looks like some forgotten alphabet, he thought. Akkadian? Babylonian? Like Belshazzar's feast.

Alicia emerged from the bathroom in a silk nightdress, clinging to her shoulders, kissing the peaks of her breasts, flowing down sinuously along the lines of that beautiful body. In the gaslight, the golden torc, his ouroboros, was molten gold encircling her throat. All the way from Buffalo, he had wanted to be angry with her, to loathe her for the pain, the hell he was in, but he had lost the thread. She was blameless. She hadn't set the Catherine Wheel in motion—it revolved around her.

Is this the face that launched a thousand ships, he thought.

"Make me immortal with a kiss," he whispered out loud, to her surprise.

It had all been worth it.

❦

The next morning, they sat in the forlorn dining hall of the Prospect House. Stubble was taking root on Arthur's swollen cheeks, but in his haste, he had brought no razor, no anything with him. Just as well, he thought on looking in the mirror earlier. It's going to hurt like hell to shave over that.

The space was penetratingly cold. The misty December damp of the

Falls sifted in through the old walls, and with so few guests at that season, it was too costly to heat the whole place. They huddled at a table close to one of the few working radiators, warming their hands on their coffee cups.

"What do we do now?" she asked.

"I have to go back to Buffalo. And we need to get you out of here," he said. "This place is depressing."

"Where should I go?"

"New York is cheerful at Christmas. I'll get us a hotel."

"Us?"

"Yes, us. I need to take care of a few things at home, and then the two of us will go to New York together."

Alicia felt like she might weep but didn't want to appear weak. "That would be so very welcome, Arthur," she said. "I know I oughtn't to, but I feel terribly lonely."

"That bastard wants you to suffer. That's why he separated you from everything dear to you at the holidays. We won't let him win, Allie."

He kissed her hand. "I'd better go. Cassie's angry enough with me, as it is—I'll need to settle her down so I can get away to New York. I've paid for everything here for a week, so try to keep your mind off things as best you can. I'll telegraph you as soon as I know more."

❦

Two days later, Alicia was beginning to worry. She had received no word from Arthur and was running low on funds, but she wasn't about to call his house again.

Sitting in her dressing gown by the window, she watched the mist rise from the frozen Falls, the occasional carriage creeping by, the few souls brave enough to stand by the iron railing to watch the ice whirling past them in the Rapids.

There was a slight rustle behind her. She turned around to see an envelope hiss under the door. She got up and retrieved it. Finally, something from Arthur.

My Dearest—The first chance I have had to write you. I decided to come to Maine for a day or two. Harpswell is beautiful tonight, the skies clear and the moon shining full upon the water. I look up at it and think of you, but then try to think of something else, because my mind is not at ease.

I very nearly called you yesterday, in hopes of hearing your dear voice even for a few minutes, but then thought better of it. Sometimes I think it would be better if I let you alone, instead of making so much trouble for you. But leaving you alone is the one thing I can never do.

There was one thing I learned after I left you in the Falls. A very good friend of mine told me—he oughtn't to have done so—that Edward has revised his will. He has cut you out of it entirely. If he prevails in a divorce, then other than any alimony we may secure, you will get nothing on his eventual death. And his business is worth a lot of money, at least three hundred thousand. He knows that only through divorce can he hurt you this way, since by N.Y. law, so long as you are married, you are entitled to a widow's dower of 1/3 of his total estate for life. The children would get another third. Another good reason for us to settle this thing before he can succeed in cheating you entirely of what is rightfully yours.

Enough of this unpleasantness, but it is something we must think about.

I have things in New York arranged. I'll be in Niagara Falls late tomorrow, and we will go together.

Love, your Arthur.

CHAPTER 44

At the Victoria

ON DECEMBER 20TH, THEY TOOK THE OVERNIGHT TRAIN TO NEW York from Niagara Falls.

"I'll get us a couple of sleepers," he said as they stood in the line in front of the ticket window.

"Why two?"

"Obvious reasons. Appearances."

"Appearances be damned," Allie said. "I've been banished, and so far as all these fuckers go"—she gestured around to the milling crowd in the station, without bothering to lower her voice—"anyone who knows me already thinks I'm Jezebel. We might as well enjoy ourselves."

Arthur was unaccountably exhausted, his throbbing head ringing all the time, and wasn't about to argue with her. For the first time since they'd met, a sleeper would be for just that. Sleeping. Thinking about the simple rhythm of the train made him dizzy enough, and the notion of adding a vigorous in and out atop a moving woman was almost enough to make him queasy.

"You do have a point," he said, and purchased a single Pullman compartment for the two of them.

A hint of winter dusk was already gathering when the train pulled out of Buffalo, an hour late. As the train chugged eastward, Arthur and Allie whiled away the time in their compartment, reading and watching the bleak countryside rush by. Arthur couldn't seem to stay awake.

"Have you been drinking?" she asked him one time when his head lolled over onto her shoulder and woke him with a start.

"Wish I could say so. I can't seem to shake this woozy feeling ever since that walloping your husband's men gave me."

"Would you mind not calling them 'my husband's men'? I want to make those bastards pay," she said.

"My fault. I mouthed off, and they let me have it."

"If I'd stayed, they wouldn't have dared." She looked out the window at the passing scene. "They haven't heard the last of me," she said. "That, I promise."

He took her hand and kissed it. "My lioness," he said.

"Where are we staying this time? The Hoffman again?"

"No, the Victoria. I tried to get a room at the Hoffman, but everything was booked. Christmastime."

"No matter. The Victoria's beautiful."

"Would you like me to order some champagne?" he said.

"I don't think you should have champagne."

"I'm fine, Allie. Don't worry so much."

"No means no, Arthur. No champagne. We'll have something to eat soon, and then you can get some rest."

❦

Overnight, their train made up for lost time. Arthur tossed and turned much of the night, and seemed to be troubled by disturbing dreams. Yet by sunup, when the porter brought around hot towels, he seemed somewhat improved.

"Are you still dizzy?" Alicia asked.

"Not if the world would stop spinning."

"You're not being helpful."

"Right now, all is well. I'll let you know how it goes when we get moving again."

"How long will you be able to stay with me?" she asked, finally getting up the courage.

"Through Christmas. I'll probably return to Buffalo a few days before the end of the month."

"We'll get to spend Christmas together?"

He smiled. "Unless you send me home early."

"This year is going to end with a new beginning," she said. "As I dreamed it would."

He put his arm around her. "Dear Alicia," he said. "I wish that your every day from now on could be a happy one. But I fear sometimes that Fate has a different outcome in store."

"I don't believe in Fate," she said. "And even if I did, I'd have to believe we can change it. Otherwise, what are we but machines?"

"It would be easier to be a machine," he said. "I'm tired of making choices for myself."

❦

The hansom cab came to a stop in front of an enormous, red brick wedding cake of a building, in the Second Empire style, topped with an impossibly steep, mansard roof of grey slate. A filigreed, cast-iron balcony five stories up completed the effect, lending the Victoria Hotel a strange aspect halfway between royal palace and factory.

"Room's ready," Arthur said after visiting the concierge desk in the cathedral lobby. "Let's get you settled in."

They took the elevator to the fifth floor. When the doors opened, they were greeted by a stern, beefy woman stationed in a chair facing them.

"Name?" she said.

"Mrs. Alicia Miller," Arthur said. "Room 521."

"And you are?"

"Her brother. I'm getting her settled."

"521's that way," the woman said, gesturing with her head. "There's a ten-minute grace period. Leave the door open."

Arthur nodded, and Allie followed him down the corridor, full of questions. They turned a corner, out of sight of the scowling matron. Almost at the end of the row of rooms, near a large window with an iron frame, was Room 521. Arthur left the door standing open, as instructed, put Allie's case away in a closet by the door, and sat down on the end of the bed, rubbing his neck.

"What's wrong, Arthur?" Alicia said.

"Dizzy again. I need to sit for a minute and let my head settle down."

"Perhaps I should call the house doctor?"

"Absolutely not."

"Who was that woman in the elevator lobby?" Allie asked.

"That's the floor matron. This is a ladies' floor. Since we're not Mr. and Mrs. Ashwood this time, I can't stay with you. I'm one floor down, but they let me in here for a few minutes because it's midday."

"We can't stay together?"

"There's nothing I can do about it, Allie. House rules."

"Can't you sneak past her?"

"I'm not the fucking Invisible Man," he snapped. "And I can't very well have myself rolled up in a carpet. Leave it to me, will you? I'll think of something. I always do."

"No need to get all worked up. I was merely asking."

He pulled out his watch. "Speaking of which—I need to get out of here before that hag starts barking at me. How about we meet downstairs in an hour, and we can see some of the Christmas decorations?"

"That will be lovely."

"I'm sorry we have to live in a world full of idiots," he said.

"Go on, Arthur," she said gently, pushing him toward the door. "Don't get yourself in an uproar."

After he left, Alicia stripped off her traveling clothes and threw herself on the bed. The pillows smelled faintly of damp feathers. The room was luxurious, even sumptuous, but starting to show its age. The dark, lacquered furniture was copiously chipped and dented from hard use, and shiny trails were worn into the floral carpeting.

Only three months before, and two blocks away, the Hoffman had been all sparkling gilt and tinkling crystal. But in those days, she had been having fun, and now everything had changed. Edward, for sure, but now Arthur too. New York itself seemed altered—harder somehow, less welcoming. It was no longer a place of escape but rather a place of exile.

❦

In the lobby, Arthur looked more like his old self—was freshly shaven and faintly smelling of Jockey Club cologne. "Nice day for a tour if we bundle up," he said. "I have a coach waiting, and the driver has plenty of blankets and a foot warmer."

They piled into the open coach, mufflers wrapped over their faces, so only their eyes peeked out under their hats, and spent a blissful hour in a leisurely ride around the Madison Square area. The broad square was alive with street music, the scent of roasting chestnuts, a big Christmas tree—even the spreading arms of the bare elms were festooned with ribbon and tinsel. They passed slowly by the grand façades of the palace hotels—the Albemarle, the Fifth Avenue, the Hoffman, and the Gilsey—all competing to out-decorate one another.

Arthur was unusually expansive, as though the city's energy had reawakened something vital. And his voluble mood persisted through a long afternoon conversation in the reading room of the Victoria. He seemed optimistic about the future—not his natural disposition—and it was infectious. For the first time since Ed had sent her away, Alicia felt a glimmer of hope that things might just work out after all.

At dinner, though, the winds had shifted, and he seemed distant and melancholy. He pushed his food around on his plate, mumbled into his water glass with inexplicable irritation at the service, the temperature of the room—too hot, then too cold—and grousing about his failure to secure a room at the Hoffman.

"Will you *please* let it go about the Hoffman, for God's sake?" Allie said, at last losing patience with his grumbling. "It doesn't matter. This hotel is excellent."

"I'll be goddamned if they keep me away from you all week. What an idea. Treating us like we're a couple of spooney youngsters." He raised his voice. "They must know that grown-ups like to fuck, every now and again."

"Jesus Christ, Arthur," she said under her breath. "Will you put a lid on it? You're going to get us thrown out of here."

"It gets under my skin, that's all."

"And you cursing like a sailor in a place like this gets under mine. Cool down and eat your food. You said it yourself—you tried, but there was no room at the inn. We'll be together all day and all week. Not at night, but we'll make the best of it."

"We'll see about that. Make sure you keep your door unlocked tonight, because I'm determined to find a way onto your floor."

❦

He noticed that his palms were sweating profusely as he waited in the genteel elevator lobby, impatiently watching for the arrow that indicated the floor to move in his direction. The Victoria was quiet at this hour—those who were out on the town were still out, and those who weren't had gone off to bed.

At last, the elevator bell rang quietly, and a bored operator opened the cage with the same mechanical smile he gave every time. Arthur nodded and stepped into the car.

"Fifth floor, please," he said.

"Um, that's the Ladies' Floor, mister," the operator said.

"There's a quarter eagle in it for you." Arthur held out a small gold coin, two and a half dollars. The operator palmed it and shut the cage again.

On the fifth floor, Arthur stepped quickly onto the landing, and the operator just as quickly closed the cage and descended before the man with the gold piece could change his mind.

There was a different but similarly formidable-looking matron sitting in the chair opposite the elevator.

"You're on the Ladies' Floor," she said, none too warmly. "Operator should have known better."

Arthur gave the woman his most charming smile. "Yes, madam—my sister is staying on the floor," he said. "She wasn't feeling well today, and I'd like to check on her."

The matron shook her head. "I can call the house doctor, but you can't go by yourself."

"For heaven's sake, what century is this anyway?" Arthur said. "I'll call the physician myself."

With a fat thumb, the matron mashed the button to summon the elevator. When the car arrived, the woman grunted at the operator, something about how he should know better than to let gentlemen onto the Ladies' Floor. He gave her the same mechanical smile. Arthur took his time about getting on, and then laconically asked the operator to return him to the ground floor. The operator stared straight ahead, hoping that the man wouldn't ask for his $2.50 back.

Back in the lobby, Arthur buttoned up his coat and went out into the cold. He walked south on Broadway, looking for a way up. There was no weakness in the steep brick front of the hotel, five merciless, vertical stories up to the iron balcony encircling the Ladies' Floor. Couldn't have scaled that even in my college days, he thought.

Then an idea struck him. He walked back down Broadway to the corner of the hotel and turned down 27th. Sure enough, at the far corner of the building was the entrance to a narrow service alley running alongside the side of the hotel, to allow for discreet deliveries and garbage collection.

Cold light sifted down from a half-moon hovering above the slates and chimneys as he started down the alley, looking up while dodging ashcans and frozen slops thrown from the kitchens. Still no way up, only the same forbidding wall of sheer brick. At the corner of the building, the alley made a right turn along the rear of the hotel. The light was a little better here, the moon lined up in the slit between the rear of the Victoria and the other surrounding buildings, and he could see that this rear alley ended blindly without connecting to Broadway. Here goes, he thought. Last chance.

Halfway down, he saw what he had been hoping for all along. A fire escape ladder, a rarity in New York and woefully inadequate should it be called upon to save more than a few hotel guests—but an easy way up. As Arthur approached the iron ladder, he noticed a small light flickering along the foundation. It was a skater's lamp, tiny but throwing enough light to illuminate the faces of a ring of men huddled around a dice game, laughing, passing around a bottle, breathing steam.

The scene was familiar—one he'd witnessed a hundred times in The Hooks. Even in Buffalo, the weather never seemed quite bad enough to discourage a few ne'er-do-wells from getting up an impromptu dice game. As best he could tell, there were five, maybe six of them, typical city toughs. He stepped toward them, his heavy shoes crunching across a ribbon of gritty cinders thrown down to give horses purchase on the ice. Five glowing faces looked over at him, and the laughter stopped.

"Christmas greetings, gentlemen," Arthur said.

"Lost your way, pal?" one of the men said, standing up. He was a compact bantamweight, a derby pulled down low over his eyes. He folded his arms over his chest. The other four men rose unsteadily to their feet and stood behind their leader. Five, then. Not six.

What would Harry Price do? Arthur thought. Damned if he wasn't feeling foggy again, though, his thoughts thick and treacly in the cold. I ought to have considered this before I came down here. Harry would say to think ahead and decide what you are willing to do—what you *will* do—before you have to do it. And never let the other fellow get the jump on you.

"Guess I have," Arthur said. "I suppose I thought this connected to Broadway."

The men edged closer. The leader squinted at Arthur's heavy watch chain, glinting in the light of the skater's lamp. "That's a nice chain you've got there," he said, pointing. "I'll bet it's got a nice watch on it, too."

"Gift from my mother. Sentimental value."

"I'm a pretty sentimental guy," the tough said. "I might like a watch and chain like that."

"Sorry to disappoint you," Arthur said. "I don't think a motherless bastard like you is likely to get one."

The whole gang looked nonplussed, even the bantamweight taken a bit aback. "Come again? I don't think I heard you right."

Arthur smoothed his mustache and then put his hands casually into his coat pockets, bobbing up and down on his toes. "Oh, I think you did," he said, smiling. "I called you a motherless bastard. Which you most certainly are."

"I'll show you motherless," the man said, and reached for his boot.

Arthur didn't wait to see the gleam of the knife. He had decided what he would do, and with one long fencer's step, he closed the distance between him and the tough, pulled out the hammerless Smith & Wesson in his coat pocket, and jabbed it into the man's guts, hard. His surprised assailant thought he'd been gut-punched but for a muffled pop, and then another, which took his legs out from under him. He collapsed on the cobblestones, arms flailing but legs strangely still.

It took a second or two to register with the four other toughs that this dandy out-of-towner had gut-shot their leader, but as soon as they did, they all took off running as if the Devil himself was after them. Arthur took a half-step forward and stood over the fallen hoodlum, whose eyes were rolling wildly in the beam of the skater's lamp. He tried to scrabble away from Arthur, oaring himself along on his back by his arms, dragging his dead legs. Looks like one of the lobsters I used to pull out of Casco Bay, he thought.

Arthur knelt next to the man. "At least there's no pain," he said gently. "Your spinal cord is severed, and that's why you don't feel anything. And can't move your legs. You're dying, of course, but you'll go to sleep soon. Freezing isn't a bad way to go. I saw a man freeze in the crow's nest once, rounding Cape Horn in the heaviest weather you ever did see. You know they had to chip him out of it the next day with a hammer and chisel?"

The man whimpered and tried to get away, wheezing and coughing up blood. Arthur picked up the skater's lamp and trained the beam on the man's front. "I'm afraid it's bad," he said. "No coming back from this. But let it be a lesson to you, friend. You never, ever know who you might run into. Now I do need to be going. If we meet again in the next world, no hard feelings, all right?"

He hadn't been angry, not in the least, but suddenly he felt a tidal wave of rage roaring up from someplace deep, clearing out his head. His mind felt sharp, old days sharp, for the first time since his beat-down. Stepping over the fallen tough, he jumped up and grabbed the bottom rung of the fire ladder like a trapeze artist. It came down with a rusty creak, and with the old ease, he chinned himself up, got a foot up, and began to climb. At the fifth level, he swung onto the iron balcony. He looked down into the alley, where his antagonist was sprawled in a pool of lamplight and blood. He may have been dead already, and if not, he would be soon.

Arthur hung over the railing for at least a minute, enjoying the feeling of his heart pumping and his breath coming fast, racing after the confrontation and the climb. He smiled, thinking oddly that this must be what God feels like all the time, looking down on the pathetic beings that he makes to live or die according to his whim. But then he felt a worrisome little wave of vertigo and thought he'd best get inside before it got any worse, and while he still had a raging hard-on that, goddamn it, he was going to bury in Allie, the second he got into her room. The beauty of it was that she'd be ready to fuck, without any of the sentimental preliminaries that most women required to maintain their stupid sense of decorum.

He followed the balcony quietly around to Allie's side of the Victoria, and eased up the sash of a large window left unlocked to provide

access to the fire escape. He peered into the quiet hotel, the sleeping Ladies' Floor, and realized to his delight that it was the window at the end
of the dog-leg corridor. The matron could not see him here. He stepped
over the sill, took three silent strides, and turned the knob of Room 521.
The door was unlocked—good girl!—and the room was dark, but he
could smell her perfume. She was waiting for him.

❦

As dawn came up the following morning, Alicia tiptoed out to the
house phone near the elevator lobby. Smiling at the matron, she rattled
the hook and told the front desk that she was feeling tired today and
would they please not disturb her until midday? Then she padded quietly back to 521 and slid back into bed, next to Arthur.

"Good morning," she said, putting her arm on his shoulder. "I told
the front not to disturb us until noon."

"Perfect," Arthur said. "You kept me up rather late last night, you
know."

"Kept you up?"

He laughed. "How about we order some breakfast?"

"'Hello Operator, I'd like breakfast for one—that is, two omelets,
two rashers of bacon, two fruit tarts, and two cups of coffee.'"

"Tell them you want to share it with the floor matron."

"Good idea. I'll order something in a minute. What else do you
want to do today?"

"I found the reading room very pleasant. They have a string quartet
in the afternoon. And—as much as I hate to bring it up—we do need to
discuss what we're going to do. About Ed and the divorce."

"I know," she said, burying her face into his shoulder. "I don't want
to, though. I want to pretend it's all gone away, and we're married and
here together. Like normal people."

"I do understand that. But I don't see another option."

"How about over breakfast, then? We'll have privacy. In the Reading
Room, there are too many other people around."

"Sounds good to me," he said.

"I'm going to wash up, and then I'll order the breakfast."

Allie slid out of bed and walked into the bathroom, washed and powdered herself, and made something presentable out of her hair. She walked out nude, wondering if Arthur might show some interest before breakfast, but he had fallen fast asleep, still sitting up. She dressed quietly and then walked down the corridor to order breakfast.

When she returned, she found him sitting silently at the desk in the main room, looking out the window over Broadway. He was wearing a ladies-sized robe that didn't fully close in the front and came only to a little above his knees. She laughed. "This sight alone is worth having to bunk on the Ladies' Floor."

"Would you mind if I closed the curtains a bit?" he asked, squinting and shielding his eyes with his hand. "It seems awfully bright in here."

Alicia shrugged, and when the food arrived, they shared breakfast, feeding each other and passing the coffee cup back and forth.

"I wish I had a cigar," Arthur said when they'd finished.

"I'm sure that wouldn't attract any attention here on the Ladies' Floor."

He leaned back on the davenport, the tiny robe giving up any pretense at modesty.

"God almighty," she said. "You're making me horny."

"Allie, I'm bushed. Can we try later?"

"We have until noon. After that, you'll have to hold out until your next appearance as the Human Fly."

"Can we talk about Ed?"

"If you put a pillow over that thing," she said. "I refuse to stare at it the whole time we're talking about my husband."

He reached over and grabbed a brocade pillow from the davenport and put it over his lap. "There. Better?"

"Much. Now then—what's on your mind?"

Arthur fiddled with the tassels on the pillow. "Now that Edward has filed, the worm has turned. We can't prevent a divorce now—our strategy must be to prevent a public one."

"Edward wouldn't want a scandal," she said.

"When a man sends his wife away, in broad daylight, at Christmastime, that isn't a man who cares about appearances anymore. He's bent on revenge now, and nothing less will do. Even if in getting it, he destroys himself and your family, as well as mine."

"Pigheaded little idiot."

"And—since he has my letters—"

"How many times do I have to apologize for that? God's sake, they were in a fucking *bank,* Arthur."

"I'm not looking for an apology. It's simply a fact we must confront. We *must* keep those letters from seeing the light of day. If he'll agree to a quiet, private divorce, we're safe. If not—terrible things will happen."

"What sort of terrible things?"

"What I wrote in those letters about Penrose, the cops—the *system.* I'll go to prison, if I live long enough. Terry Penrose will stop at nothing to keep those letters from coming out."

"He's your best friend. Would he really make a scapegoat of you?"

"Loyalty in politics? That's rich."

She put her hand on his arm. "Then what can we do?"

"One thing and one thing only—get those letters back. No letters, no trial."

"But how? We don't know where they are."

"I assume he has them locked up, and not at his office. The only safe he's got there is open in the day, and besides, Gaines has access to it. He wouldn't keep them in there."

"Then they're in his den," she said. "He's got two locking file drawers in his desk."

"How can we get access to those drawers? Do you still have your key to the house?"

"I do, but I'm sure he's changed the locks when he threw me out. He's a prick, but he's not stupid."

"Then I will have to talk some sense into him, face to face, and persuade him to give them back."

"Good luck," Allie said. "I saw the look on his face when he sent me packing. Maybe we could escape to Maine? No one would find us there."

"I'm sure as hell not going back to Maine with my tail between my legs. I'd rather be dead."

"I can write to him and ask him to see you."

"You'll only be giving him another chance to humiliate you," Arthur said. "No, there has to be another way."

He stood and began pacing back and forth across the room, the ladies' robe flying open in the front. "I have an idea," he said, turning and facing her. "I make my monthly collections on New Year's Eve. If I get started early and hurry, I can finish by midnight. I take a carriage back to Ashwood, as usual, but then I'll go right over to your house. Ed will still be awake, reading or doing whatever he does in that den of his."

"Yes, but he won't let you in, and you can't very well break down the door."

"You see," he said, smiling, "I won't have to—if your mother will agree to leave the door unlatched when everyone goes to bed. I'll walk in quietly and take him by surprise. He can't very well throw me out then, and he's not going to raise a rumpus with everyone asleep upstairs. I'll talk some sense into him, quietly and calmly."

"Barging in on him in the middle of the night? He keeps a revolver these days, you know. I saw it a week or so ago, sitting on his bureau."

Arthur snorted. "I'm not frightened of him. Or his revolver."

Allie shook her head. "Fine. If he doesn't shoot you, your plan might work, but for one little problem."

"Which is?"

"My mother will never agree to it. She doesn't like you."

"She doesn't like Ed, either. If she won't do it for me, she will for you."

Allie smiled her odd, flat smile. "Don't be so sure. She knows he chucked me out with nothing but the clothes on my back, and she hasn't yet flown to my side. For all she knows, I could be sleeping on the street in Niagara Falls."

"A rather unflattering portrait," he said solemnly. "Let's say, then, she won't help any of us. But she will help herself. Tell her to consider the alternative, what she stands to lose. Ed's allowed her to stay only to look after the children, and not tip his hand. He has enough justification—or he thinks he does—to put you out on the street, but people will think him cruel and heartless if he turns out an innocent old woman. But if the divorce evidence is made public, she'll be tossed out as surely as you were. Her day is coming."

"Now *that* may convince her. She'd probably murder him rather than be thrown out of her comfortable situation."

"Then telephone your mother when Ed isn't at the house, and ask her to leave the front door unlatched on New Year's Eve. I'll come in quietly and have a heart-to-heart talk with him. It's our only chance."

"I'll do it," Alicia said. "Nothing ventured, nothing gained."

"We're agreed, then. New Year's Eve, a little after midnight."

"There's something stirring that in the first minutes of 1902, our problem finally goes away."

"Speaking of stirring," he said, "how would you like your Christmas gift a little early?" He let the undersized robe fall to his feet.

"You know how I love presents," she said, lying back. "And I've been a *very* good girl this year, too."

❦

Later that morning, when Arthur stepped off the elevator from the Gentlemen's Floor, freshly shaven and immaculately dressed, the lobby was abuzz with chatter. A few cops were bustling about, looking official.

"What's all the fuss about?" he asked the concierge.

"This morning, the garbage collector found a man lying dead in the alley behind the hotel," the man said. "A local no-good. He'd been shot."

"Probably a disagreement with one of his associates," Arthur said.

"That's what the cops think. They knew the fellow well—always in trouble. No great loss."

"Never is."

The lobby of the Victoria was lavishly hung with evergreens, holly, and a few twinkling strands of electric lights. A large Christmas tree with electric lights and skeins of silver tinsel occupied the corner opposite the bell desk.

Arthur was thinking when he felt a tap on his shoulder. He wheeled around to find Allie standing behind him, smiling up at him.

"I'd like to know what's going on in that amazing brain of yours," she said.

"A headache, mostly."

"Again?"

"Again."

"They'll give you a powder at the desk," she said.

"Let's have a cocktail instead."

"Before lunchtime?"

"Why not? We're on vacation."

"Did you hear about the man they found dead behind the hotel?" she asked as they were drinking their cocktails.

"I did—the concierge mentioned it."

"The body was found near the fire escape. It's a fortunate thing you didn't encounter the culprit."

"It is indeed," he said.

CHAPTER 45

Modern Methods

AFTER A DAY OF TALKING IN THE READING ROOM, ALICIA HAD GONE up to her room directly after supper. Before making his nightly climb, Arthur decided to fortify himself in the Victoria's elegant saloon.

"You strike me as a fellow who's got something weighing on his mind," the bartender said after Arthur spent a few silent minutes nursing his whiskey.

"You couldn't possibly guess," Arthur said. "Pour me another one, and I'll tell you a little."

The bartender raised his eyebrows. "Are you sure?"

"Why not? I've had all of one drink."

"You seemed a little pie-eyed when you came in," the barman said.

"I hadn't had a drop. My head's been off for a few days, that's all. I took a fall."

"Better have that looked after," said another fellow, who was arranging train timetables in a rack at the end of the bar. "That can be dangerous."

Arthur shook his head, stirring his cocktail. "What's wrong with me, no doctor can fix."

"What's ailing you?" the bartender asked.

"Other than a splitting headache?" Arthur said, squeezing his temples with a thumb and forefinger. "Woman problems."

"Everybody's got woman problems," said the man at the timetable rack.

"Not like mine," Arthur said, tilting his glass. "There's a man back at home who got me mixed up with his wife. Intentionally. Ever hear of anything like that?"

"Mixed up?"

"Yes, mixed up. He put us together all the time. Dances, parties, summer outings."

"Why would a man do that?"

Arthur tapped the rim of his glass with a fingernail. "That I will never know. All I know is that I'm in a lot of trouble."

"What sort of trouble?" the timetable man asked.

"Not sure where it ends."

Neither of the other men knew quite how to follow his remark, so they minded their own business.

"My father was a ship's master, you know," Arthur said after a while.

"Did you know that, Hall?" the bartender said, smiling, to the timetable man.

"Can't say as I did, Quinn," Hall replied.

"It wasn't a question," Arthur said. "I was thinking about him just now. He had headaches like mine for a few weeks before he died. Don't you think that's mighty coincidental?"

"Lots of people have headaches," Quinn said.

"Not like his. He didn't last long once they started."

"What kind of ship captain was he?" Hall asked.

"Guano boat."

"Guano?"

"Bird shit," Arthur and Quinn said in unison.

"Is that what gave him the headaches?" Hall asked.

"No," Arthur said, taking a drink. "He was anchored off Callao. On the coast of Peru. There was a terrific earthquake that tossed his ship—a mighty big one, too—around like a cork. He was knocked off his feet and hit his head on the binnacle."

"The what?"

"Binnacle. Like 'pinnacle,' but with a B. It's a big, solid thing—about as tall as this bar—with two iron balls that the ship's compass sits in. Well, he hit his head on it and was out cold for two days. When he came to, he had terrible headaches, day after day, sometimes so bad that his first mate told me that my father begged him to shoot him."

"What happened?"

"He put in to Callao for repairs, then afterward sailed around the

Horn—quite a feat of seamanship in the best of times, but with your head in a whirl?—and up to Rio, where my mother and brother and I were waiting for him.

"We were on board only a few days when he died. Near the end, he commenced wailing like a banshee—holding his head, pounding on it with his fists—for two full days. You could hear it anywhere on the ship. Night and day. You know, I've never prayed so hard for anything as I did for him to die, if only to stop the noise."

"That's horrible," Quinn said.

"Condolences," said Hall.

"Thanks, boys. It was a hell of a thing. I know I don't want to go like that."

"I don't think you have the same thing," Hall said, "unless you hit your head on a pinnacle."

"Binnacle," Arthur said.

"What are you going to do about this man back home?" Quinn asked. "The one who got you mixed up with his wife?"

"I ought to have put him out of the way," Arthur said. "I know people who would do it for me as a favor. Not that I'm scared to do it myself, even if I went to the gallows for it."

"Gallows?" Quinn said. "Your man must live out of state. We have more modern methods in New York."

Arthur shrugged. "There are worse things than a sit in Old Sparky." He raised his glass to the other two men. "Here's to a fellow I knew once who went to the Chair. The final week of his life was his best. Fed well. Shown real compassion. The cops even held his hand when they walked him to the death chamber. Like old friends at the end."

"I've never understood that," Hall said.

"Understood what?"

"The tenderness people show to people they're about to execute."

"Oh, that's an easy one," Arthur said. "They know they've won, but it would be bad form to dance a victory jig. They can rub it in by killing you and still be good chaps about it."

"Man is a strange animal," Hall said.

"You're not serious," Quinn said, "about going to the gallows over this fellow, are you?"

"He's made it an affair of honor," Arthur replied. "Which in itself is droll, because neither of us has a shred of honor left."

The other two men fell silent, Quinn quietly polishing a glass.

"In the meantime," Arthur said, "at this joyous holiday season, I'm passing some of the happiest days of my life."

"If you don't mind my saying," Hall ventured, "you look pretty miserable."

"There was a time when I might have taken that the wrong way."

"He didn't mean anything by it," Quinn said.

"Absolutely not," said Hall.

"But you're right, I expect," Arthur said, waving his hand at them. "I suppose I'm happy because I know when I've been beaten."

"Don't give up the ship," Quinn said. "There's no shame in losing, so long as you fight on until the bitter end."

"*Shame,*" Arthur said carefully, as though he were hearing the word for the first time. "No, I don't think that's the right word. It's *embarrassing* to be beaten. I think shame is different. Something very profound, like reverence. A sign of an active conscience."

"Here's to a clear conscience," said Quinn.

Hall glanced at Arthur's ring finger. "You're a married man," he said.

"Long story," Arthur said.

"Not my business."

"True. Thanks for the talk, boys," Arthur said abruptly and smacked his empty glass down on the bar, along with a $5 gold piece. "I've got to get upstairs and see my lady, while I can."

After he'd left, Quinn and Hall exchanged looks.

"Five dollars in gold for two drinks?" Quinn said. "He must have money to burn."

"Or is running out of time to burn it," Hall replied.

CHAPTER 46

Christmas Day

"YOU SIMPLY CANNOT SPEND CHRISTMAS ALONE," JEANNIE'S VOICE said over the telephone line. "I won't allow it."

"I don't have much choice," Cassie replied. "Arthur is away—handling this awful business with you know who."

"You ought to have gone to stay with your parents, then. Not in that big house all by yourself on Christmas Eve and Christmas Day."

"I don't care to see my parents. They ask so many questions that I don't want to answer. Or can't answer. I'd rather be alone."

"If you don't mind being alone, then—would it matter to you if I told you I don't like being alone?"

"Of course it would matter."

"Well, I don't. And yours is the company I'd like best, if you'll share it with me."

Cassie smiled into the mouthpiece of the telephone. "You know I could never refuse you, Jeannie. When would you like me to come over?"

"An hour ago," Jeannie said.

"All right, I'll get my things together and be there as soon as I can."

"I'll have something nice for us all ready when you get here. Now get a move on."

❧

Jeannie was watching from her front window when Cassie's coach rolled up, and she trotted downstairs to open the door. "It's so good to see you, my dear," she said, giving her a kiss on the cheek. "Thank you for agreeing to spend Christmas with me." Jeannie looked skinnier than before, more gaunt, the skin of her face stretched tight over the cheek-bones, and her large, gentle eyes seeming to protrude.

"I'm glad you coaxed me into it," Cassie said, following her friend up the stairs to the apartment. "Truth be told, I didn't *really* want to be all by myself."

They sat down side by side on a couch overlooking the street. There wasn't much activity on Christmas Eve day, the occasional wagon or solitary pedestrian. A few flurries were drifting past the big window, and the steam radiator near the Christmas tree was creaking cozily.

"In case you're wondering, yes, I made us some cocktails," Jeannie said. "Don't go anywhere."

When she had set down the tray in front of them, Jeannie pulled a big blanket off the back of an overstuffed chair and tossed it to Cassie. "Let's snuggle up underneath that and watch the snow fly," she said. "It's starting to pick up. With any luck, we'll wake up tomorrow to a white Christmas."

"You look like you've lost more weight," Cassie said. "Are you eating enough?"

"I don't cook as much for myself as I might. And you know, the pipe keeps the appetite down."

"Well, let's have a feast tomorrow and put some meat on those bones."

Jeannie laughed. "I hope you won't mind rubbing up against them without more padding on them than they have."

"Never. I can hardly believe we get to sleep together tonight."

"It will be such a nice treat, Cassie."

"Do you ever get used to sleeping alone?" Cassie asked.

"Used to it? I never think about it that way. It's been my lot in life to sleep alone. I suppose I can't miss what I never expected to have."

"It still feels strange to me, but then again, I've not been doing it so long as you have."

"How many years has it been for you, would you say?"

Cassie took a gulp of her cocktail. "Let's see—Arthur and I shared a bed for the first, oh, three years of our marriage, I guess it was. Then each of us started to find excuses—snoring, staying up late, not wanting to disturb each other. 'I'll sleep on my own tonight, dear,' that sort of thing.

And then it became a habit, little by little. Now it's been so long that I think he'd die of apoplexy if I climbed into bed with him."

"It's easier that I've never been married," Jeannie said.

"In some ways, yes. But maybe not in every way."

"That's probably closer to the truth. Now tell me—what exactly is Arthur up to this week?"

"He's in New York with Alicia Miller. Her husband finally got fed up with her carrying on, so he sent her away. Naturally, she had no earthly idea what to do with herself and no one but Arthur to help her sort it out."

"I know I've asked you this before, but don't you mind terribly?"

Cassie shook her head. "Not too much. Any more than he minds what I get up to sometimes. Everyone has his needs."

"Or her needs," Jeannie smiled.

"Or her needs, yes. What does bother me, though—is that he's in no condition to be going anywhere. He came home a few days ago—actually the same day Alicia was put out—beaten nearly to a pulp."

"What in heaven's name?"

"Ed Miller had some hired ruffians give Arthur quite a working-over. He blames Arthur for the failure of his marriage."

"Oh my God. Is he having any lasting ill effects?"

"He's been having headaches and ringing in his ears. I don't know what else. You know Arthur—he's too proud to say much. But I can't help but be worried about him."

"As you should be," Jeannie said. "Sometimes injuries are far worse on the inside of the body than they appear on the outside. It's not a thing to be trifled with."

"Try telling *him* that. He says, 'I'm fine, don't worry about it,' and goes on about his business. But I know him well enough to know he's not the same."

"When he comes back from New York, get him to a doctor, whether he likes it or not."

"I will. Now, what say we change the subject—I'm quite sure Arthur isn't spending his Christmas Eve thinking about me. I don't care to spend mine thinking about him."

"You know, you're right. It was inconsiderate of me to dwell. Let's drink a little, and then maybe we can do something else. I got some more of that strong hop."

"Let's do—but last time you provided the party, and this time I hope to. Hang on."

Cassie got up, rummaged around in her bag, and returned with her little manicure case. She set it on the table and rearranged the blanket over them.

"That's cute," Jeannie said. "What is it?"

Cassie unfastened the clasp and opened the case.

"Is that what I think it is?"

"Morphine," Cassie said.

"Are you a habitué?"

"I started with it, oh, perhaps a year ago. Eating opium nauseated me, smoking was simply not possible in the house, and laudanum tastes terrible no matter what you mix it in. So a doctor friend—actually one of your fellow dentists—showed me how to inject myself." She smiled. "Problem solved."

"Don't you find it frightening?"

"At first, I did, but it's really not difficult. The tiniest nip of this"— she held up the syringe—"does the trick."

"And what is it like?"

"It comes on fast and almost a little rough, but then in a second or two, I feel like I'm floating right out of my body. And my mind still works, but differently—as though I can't think about anything that is, or was, but only what might be."

"That sounds divine."

"All those horribly mangled men in the Civil War didn't call it 'Saint Morphia' for no reason. Later—if you want to—we can sample some together. I can show you how to do it. But only if you want to."

"I'd love to," Jeannie said. "I've wondered about it for years. I rub it on people's gums when I'm extracting a tooth, but I never dared inject it. I was never sure how much to use."

Cassie waved her hand. "I can show you all that in five minutes," she said. "You'll be amazed at how easy it is."

"Wonderful. Would you like a pipe now to tide us over?"

❦

After Jeannie and Cassie had enjoyed a couple of pipes and a long nap, Jeannie set out some supper, and they chatted and laughed in the candlelight until it was getting late. They were washing the dishes at the sink when Cassie poked Jeannie playfully in the arm.

"I'm so happy you forced me to spend Christmas with you," Cassie laughed. "I can be such a fool sometimes."

"You have your pride, my dear, and that's all it is. But I'm happy I forced you, all the same."

"When we're done here, will you be ready for bed?"

Jeannie put her arm around Cassie's waist and drew her close. "I'm ready for bed," she said. "But not for sleep, not right away." She kissed her friend for a long moment.

"You're simply delightful," Cassie said, looking into her friend's eyes. "If I'm not careful, I could fall in love with you."

"Don't be too careful, then. You must know that I'm already head over heels for you. And I have been for quite some time. I wish more than anything I had you with me every day and night."

Cassie turned around and leaned against the countertop. "Would you be surprised if I said I've thought the same thing?"

Jeannie's eyes opened wider. "I suppose I would be."

"I've been afraid to imagine it, until recently," Cassie said. "But it's time for me to change my life."

"Change? What's going on in that pretty head of yours?"

"I've been thinking that perhaps it wouldn't be the worst thing to let Arthur go his way, and I'll go mine."

Jeannie stopped washing one of the dinner plates and looked over at her. "I didn't think you'd ever consider leaving Arthur."

"Nor did I," Cassie said. "But Arthur did something very cruel to me not long ago. After that, I began to wonder why I'm staying around."

"Did he strike you?"

"No, nothing like that. Suffice it to say that I'd never thought him capable of—but let's not spoil our evening with all that. I'll tell you another time."

"I understand, dear," Jeannie said. "Some other time. Do you think you might consider moving in here? There's plenty of room, and I wouldn't be a bother. And I'm making good money."

"A bother? Don't be ridiculous. And I have enough money that if you wanted to keep doing your work, you could. Or you could take time off, and we could sail to Europe or anywhere we'd want."

"We'd tell everyone we're sisters!" Jeannie said. "I love my work, but I wouldn't mind a break from it, all the same."

"Then here's what we do. When Arthur returns, I'm sure he'll have some boo-hoo about how much Alicia needs him, everything I've heard a hundred times. And I know Ed Miller well enough to know that if he's gone to the trouble of throwing his wife out of the house, nothing will change his mind. He and Alicia will divorce, and Arthur will want to go to her. Then he and I will divorce—and frankly, everyone will be much happier."

"You would do that for me?" Jeannie said, her eyes moist. "No one has ever—"

"It's taken me my entire life to stop apologizing for myself," Cassie said. "I only started stopping when I met you."

"Oh, I love you so much!" Jeannie said, throwing her soapy arms around Cassie's back. "I could just eat you up!"

"You have all night," Cassie said.

❦

"Divine Cassandra," Jeannie murmured into Cassie's hair as they lay intertwined on the big bed later that night. "You've made me so very sleepy now. I should put something on so that we can snuggle, but I don't want to get up."

"Don't you dare put anything on," Cassie whispered. "We'll pile on another blanket if we have to. I want to feel your skin against mine all night."

They lay there, propped up on pillows, watching the soft snow fall outside.

"Such big flakes," Cassie said. "Drifting down like feathers."

Jeannie burrowed her head into her friend's shoulder. "Umm. And you feel so soft and warm, too."

"We're going to fatten you up, too. You're too thin. You can't weigh half of what I do."

"I know, I've let myself go a bit these past few months. I haven't felt I had anyone to look good for."

"We're going to fix that."

"Cassie," she said, "before we sleep, do you think we could try some of your morphia? I think it would feel so good to drift off together."

"Why, of course," she said. "I'll get my kit." Cassie retrieved her leather case from the front room and slipped back into bed. She kissed Jeannie on her lips, then her nipples. "Did you miss me?" she said.

"You couldn't possibly know how much."

"All right," Cassie said, opening the little case, "here's how it's done. First, we take the stopper out of the bottle"—she set the little cork aside carefully—"and then we take the needle and draw some of it up."

Jeannie watched intently as Cassie filled the syringe and then recorked the vial of morphine. "So far, so good," Jeannie said. "I'm excited. My first time injecting—and it's with you."

Cassie smiled, examining the syringe carefully. "Now we make ourselves comfortable," she said, "because when this comes on, you won't be doing anything but floating away." She arranged the pillows and tucked Jeannie in. "Leave your arm over the covers so that I can find a vein."

"All right. I'm ready. I'm a little nervous, I will admit."

"You'll be fine. And I'm going to inject myself first," Cassie said, "I'm more used to it and it'll take me longer to fall asleep. And you can see the effect."

She took a rubber tube out of her kit and wrapped it tightly around her upper arm, making the veins stand out. Then Cassie carefully inserted the needle under her skin.

"I pull it out a little and make sure there's blood," she said. "Then I push—like this—and let the hose go." As soon as the tourniquet was released, Cassie's eyes unfocused, and she sat back into the pillows, gasping. "Oh God," she said.

Jeannie looked alarmed. "Is everything all right?" she asked.

"Oh my, yes," Cassie mumbled. "This is good stuff, that's all. Strong." She roused herself with some effort. "Now you. I'm going to have to be quick, because I'm flying right now."

"Wonderful. Do it. I want to feel the way you look right now."

Cassie fumbled in getting the tourniquet situated around Jeannie's arm. After a few failures, she managed to secure the hose tightly. "Now, as soon as I inject you," she said, "you're going to have to release this. I don't think I'll be able to, the way I'm going."

"Understood," Jeannie said. "Come on, give me my dose. I'm ready."

Cassie leaned up on one elbow and groggily examined Jeannie's forearm, but couldn't focus well enough to see a good vein. She felt her friend's arm and found one straining hard against the skin. "Here we go," she said, "a little pinch, that's all." She tried to aim the needle for what felt like the fattest part of the vein, but time was running out as she felt her fingers going numb. At last, she couldn't wait any longer and jabbed the needle into Jeannie's arm.

"Ouch," Jeannie said.

"I'm sorry. That was clumsy. I've got it now."

"It's fine." Jeannie looked tenderly at her friend. "I love you, Cassie," she said.

"I love you, too," Cassie said, depressing the plunger. "Now—"

"I know," Jeannie said and loosened the rubber hose.

Cassie squinted hard, trying to make out the expression on Jeannie's face.

"Oh—*fuck*," Jeannie whispered. "Oh my God, it's heaven."

Cassie couldn't manage to replace her things in her kit, but instead fell backwards onto her pillow. "Now sleep, dear," she said. "It'll be Christmas Day when we wake up."

"Until then, my love," Jeannie said. "How softly the snow falls!"

❧

The first glimmers of dawn were sneaking through Jeannie's bedroom window when Cassie awoke. She looked over at her sleeping friend's hair spilling onto the pillow, her face turned away from her, toward the window. The dear thing had fallen asleep watching the snow, she thought. Cassie leaned over and softly said 'Merry Christmas!' into her ear.

Jeannie didn't awaken, so Cassie propped herself up against the headboard and watched the drifting flakes, still steadily falling. A white Christmas, after all, she thought. She sat there for another twenty minutes and then felt alone without Jeannie, so she reached over and shook her shoulder. "Wake up, sleepy-head. Time to see what Santa Claus brought us."

Jeannie stubbornly refused to stir, and Cassie shook her harder. She leaned all the way over and saw that Jeannie's face was very pale, almost grey. "Jeannie?" she said, with a rising flush of alarm. She jumped up, nude, and ran around to the other side of the bed. She shook Jeannie harder and rolled her over on her back. On the pillow where her head had been was a half-dry mass of vomit. Her alarm turned to cold dread.

"Oh no, no, no, *no*," she whispered, shaking her friend violently. She felt for a pulse in her neck, but the skin was cold and unyielding. Jeannie's eyes were half-open, unblinking, and glassy. How long she had been dead was impossible to know, perhaps even from the moment the morphine had made its first circuit around her frail, underfed body. "God, please don't," Cassie said. "Jeannie, honey, please wake up."

She stood and looked down at her friend, so recently so warm. The syringe was still lying on the bed between them, half full. Cassie grabbed it up and wanted to throw it against the wall, and then thought instead to fill herself with the rest of the poison and join her Jeannie wherever she was now. She gritted her teeth and poised the needle over her arm, then felt a tremendous rage and moved the needle to the side of her neck. She wanted to cut her throat with it, jam it up to the hilt, break it off so that it would hurt before she died and went to Hell, where she belonged. She pushed the sharp tip in until she felt it break the sensitive skin, making her gasp. Cassie centered the pad of her thumb firmly on the plunger.

She looked down at her dead friend, lying still and cold, and her hand started to shake. With one quick push of the thumb, she thought, this torment will be over, this nightmare will end. She uttered a little cry at the thought, pulled the needle free, and threw it on the bed. No, not this way, or not yet. I need to suffer for what I've done.

❦

Cassie sat limply on the edge of the bed, thinking oddly that she might look over and find Jeannie smiling up at her, happy on Christmas morning, and that all of this had been a bad dream. From time to time, she glanced over her shoulder, but there was Jeannie, developing a weird blue-green color, like wet cement, and the vomit stiffening the pillowcase.

She walked numbly to the bathroom, wet a cloth, and carefully cleaned Jeannie's face and the pillowcase as best she could. Then she arranged her neatly on her back and drew the blankets up around her chin to keep her warm. She tried to close the eyes fully, the way she'd heard it was done, but it didn't work, and after multiple tries, Jeannie's left eye remained half-open, looking accusingly at Cassie. She found a soft, cotton towel in the bathroom and gently draped it over the sleeping face. Then she put her kit together, squirted the remaining contents of the syringe into the vial, and carefully closed it up.

She dressed slowly and deliberately, in a kind of daze, packed away the little case in her carpet bag, and was about to go when she turned back to the bed. She lifted the towel from Jeannie's face—her color was going more blotchy and hideous by the minute—and leaned over to kiss her once more on the lips. "I'm sorry," she said. "I'll see you very soon, I promise."

❦

The week at the Victoria passed all too quickly. The raw weather kept them indoors much of the time, and Arthur's dizzy spells made long walks impossible. Every evening, Arthur would climb the fire escape and stay with Allie until nearly noon. Then she would walk to the elevator lobby and converse with the matron while Arthur sneaked out again. Then they would spend the afternoon in the reading room, have dinner, and begin again.

In the mornings, they enjoyed reading to each other by the cozy coal fire in Alicia's room, watching the ebb and flow of the traffic far below. Arthur particularly enjoyed listening to Allie's husky, musical voice, closing his eyes and letting the sound drift through his mind like smoke.

And he could forget that very soon, he'd be on the morning express to Buffalo.

"*The moving finger writes, and having writ, moves on; nor all thy piety nor wit, shall lure it back to cancel half a line, nor all thy tears wash out a word of it,*" she read one morning.

"Omar Khayyam," he murmured, eyes closed. "And very apropos to us, isn't it?"

"Yes, it is," she said, closing the book.

He wiggled his stocking feet in front of the glowing coal. "If you could turn back the hands of time . . . would you do anything differently?"

"How far back do you want me to go?"

"I don't mean your childhood or even when you met Ed. Since you met me."

She considered this question for a moment. "It's not something I would *do* differently," she said. "It's something I would *think* differently."

"That's interesting."

"What I'd think differently is to not give a shit. I wasted precious time I could have spent living because I gave a shit about what people thought. Ed, the neighbors, my mother, the children, on and on. And what does it matter what any of them thinks, anyway?"

"Cultivate a degree of indifference."

"That's a nicer way of saying it. What about you?"

"I would have stopped that woman in the Ferry Street Tunnel, kissed her, and begged her to run away with me."

"Do you she would have gone with you?"

"I do," he said. "What do you think?"

"Without a doubt. Seems like lifetimes ago, doesn't it?"

"I've used up eight of mine already. I hope I still have one left for you when this is all done."

❧

On the 27th, Allie accompanied Arthur to the station and waited with him on the platform, sharing a bench near the stationmaster's office.

"Do you realize that this has been the longest we've been together?" he said.

"I've loved every minute of it."

"A few halcyon days before the end."

"Don't say that, Arthur. We must remain optimistic."

He squeezed her hand. "It's not going to be the same without you. I've gotten too used to it."

She looked up the track, hoping his train would be late. If he missed it, she thought, they could go back to the Victoria for another day.

"Can you stay one more day?"

"I would if I could. Too much at stake, though."

"I know. I wish you could, though."

Allie looked up the tracks again.

"Atlantic City will be lonely," she said.

"I know, but it's better for you to be out of state for a while. You can't even be served with legal papers."

"I feel I ought to be near you—waiting for you after you confront Edward. I don't want you to be alone that night."

"Believe me, I wish I didn't have to do it. But we've agreed that it's best this way. You need to be in Atlantic City."

"I'll take the first train tomorrow," she said. "I'll telegraph you when I arrive."

"Good. I've settled the bill at the Victoria and prepaid the Traymont through the end of the week. There's money in your bag for anything else you might need. And just in case—I signed over one of my life insurance policies to you."

"Why would you do such a thing?"

"So that you'll have some money should anything happen to me."

"Don't say that, Arthur. Remember what we said—if you go, I am going with you."

"I could be flattened by a streetcar," he said, laughing. "Who knows? In any event, my attorney, Maier, has the document. It's for $50,000— enough to live on for a very long time."

"Fifty thousand dollars?" Allie said. "That's an absurd sum, Arthur! My whole house cost five thousand."

A distant whistle came up the tracks. "Allie, listen. If anything should happen—without me around, Ed will leave you high and dry. I cannot allow that."

"All the money in the world couldn't replace you."

"I know," he said, kissing her cheek. "But I want to be practical, for a change. Let me have that satisfaction. But don't worry. I'm not going anywhere."

"Just promise you'll be careful on New Year's Eve."

"I promise. Is everything still in order with your mother?"

"I telephoned her again yesterday. She'll make sure the front door is unlatched."

They stood as Arthur's train rolled up to the platform with a long hiss of steam. Pullman car attendants hopped down from the cars and started collecting baggage.

"Then this is *adieu*," he said, looking down on her upturned face.

"*Au revoir*, you mean, not *adieu*."

"French did always give me fits," he said, smiling. "In English, then. Goodbye, Alicia. I love you."

"I love you too. Be good."

"Too late for that, dear. But I promise to be careful."

He kissed her gently on the lips and hopped onto his carriage moments before the attendant called for all aboard.

CHAPTER 47

Sauve Qui Peut

ARTHUR RETURNED FROM NEW YORK DIZZY AND DRAINED. THE carriage had been stifling hot, compelling the passengers to keep the windows wide open the whole way back from New York. The rush of frigid outdoor air still hadn't cooled down the coach, and his shirt and collar were stained with sweat and cinders. In the foyer, he threw his bag in disgust against the wainscot and hung his coat up crazily on the hook. The gas was turned down to a bare flicker, and there was no sign of Cassie.

"Cassie?" he called up the stairs. "I'm back. Are you up there?"

There wasn't any answer, so he turned up the gas and walked back to the kitchen to get something to eat. The movement of the train and his pounding head had made him half-nauseated the whole trip, and while his head ached still, he had recovered a little appetite. He was rummaging around in the pantry for some cheese and bread when he heard Cassie's slippers on the tile. He turned to see her in a nightshirt, looking drawn and pale, hair disheveled and hanging around her neck.

"What's wrong?" he said. "You look terrible." He stepped over to her and sniffed her hair. "Have you been taking that shit again?"

"You're a fine one to talk. You look worse than I do," she said. She sat down heavily in one of the kitchen chairs. "What day is today?" she said.

"What day is it? It's the evening of the 27th of December. What kind of question is that?"

"I lost track of time."

"You've been intoxicated since I left?"

"I wish I had been. Since Christmas, though, yes."

"What the hell is eating you? Are you trying to get back at me?"

"For once, Arthur, it has nothing to do with you."

"What has happened, then?"

"There's been a terrible accident," she said. "And I truly don't know what to do."

"What kind of accident?"

"I went to Jeannie's house on Christmas Eve," she said. "She asked me to spend the night and have Christmas with her."

"And?"

"She wanted to try my morphia—and something went wrong. I keep racking my brain over it. She was too thin, or not accustomed to it—or I gave her too much—"

"Cassie, do *not* tell me—"

"She fell asleep and didn't wake up. On Christmas morning."

Arthur dropped his head onto his chest. "Oh, for fuck's sake, Cassie."

"You might offer your condolences."

"Good night! That's the least of my worries. Did you call the cops?"

"No. I told you, I haven't known what to do."

"And this was on Christmas Eve?"

"Yes."

"She's still over there?"

"There's been nothing about it in the newspapers," she said. "I've checked. But her offices were to be closed between Christmas and New Year's, and she hasn't any family."

Arthur rubbed his temples. "Jesus," he muttered. "I'll call Terry in the morning. Does she have any narcotics at her house? Other than what you took with you?"

"I injected her with mine, but she has smoking things."

"How did you get over to her house?"

"Hired coach."

"All right," he said. "We can blame her demise on her opium, but Terry will have to get in front of this before the coachman or anyone talks. Do you know who the driver was?"

"I've seen him before, but I don't know his name."

"We'll have to hope no one finds her body before I can talk with Terry," he said. "I'll call him first thing. I can't call him this late at night."

Cassie nodded. "I don't care, Arthur. I should face the music. I murdered her."

"Stop talking like that. It was an accident. And we don't need another scandal. Good God, this on top of everything—"

"I tried to end it, but I wasn't strong enough."

"End it?"

"End *me*. Kill myself."

"Cassie, what good would that have done?"

"I want to die so much," she said, beginning to weep. "But I'm a coward. I wonder if you could do it for me? Take me out somewhere and shoot me, like a dog, or overdose me. Hold my head down in the bathtub. Whatever's easy for you. Anything that will destroy this terrible life inside of me."

"I can't hear this now," Arthur said.

"I'm sorry to spoil your good time," she said. "After Christmas in New York, and with Alicia. And then you have to come home to this."

"Enough, Cassie. It wasn't a vacation."

"I hope at least you fucked her. Did you?"

"I'm not talking about this. I'm going up to bed."

"I told you just now that I *killed* someone, and you can't be honest with me about *that?*"

Arthur sighed. "Yes, then, I did. We did."

"Thank you for that," she said.

❦

It was a thing to discuss in person, not on the telephone. Early the next morning, Arthur hauled his aching body out of bed, dressed, and got to the courthouse before Terry arrived.

When he walked in and saw Arthur, his eyes opened wide.

"What the hell happened to *you?*" he said. "You look like you went over the Falls in a barrel. Without the barrel."

"Slipped on some ice," Arthur said.

"From the top of a building? Come in—I was going to call you myself—I have something I need to go over with you."

Arthur followed Penrose into his office. When he told Terry about One Two Three, the DA rolled his eyes.

"It was inevitable," Terry said, "wouldn't you say?"

"Spying on me was one thing, but beating the shit out of me was unnecessary."

"Miller's got a hard-on for you, boy," Penrose said. "I'm telling you, since you double-crossed him, he's become quite unhinged. Ask around if you don't believe me."

"I don't doubt you."

"Do you want me to do something about him? Is that why you're here?"

"No, I've got Miller under control," Arthur said. "I'm here because I have a problem with Cassie."

"*Another* problem? You're like Hydra when it comes to problems, Arthur. We cut one down and three more sprout."

"Cassie has a little problem. Over Christmas, she and a friend of hers were playing around with morphine."

"Where were you when this was going on?"

"I was in New York. With Alicia."

Terry laughed. "Of course you were. I'll tell you, Arthur, you have to be seen to be believed. The things you get yourself into."

"Go ahead, rub my nose in it," Arthur said. "When you're finished, my problem remains."

"I'm sorry, old man. Sometimes I can't stop myself in time. Tell me the problem."

"Her friend had an overdose."

"Friend? Male or female?"

"Female."

"That's better. Is the lady dead?"

"Quite."

"Where is she?"

"At her house on Pearl Street."

"Her name?"

"Jeannette Sherman. A dentist."

"Dentists are all dope fiends," Penrose said.

"You don't say."

"Not in the mood, I see. I have what I need. I'll get Roscoe to handle it." Terry took off his glasses and tossed them on the blotter. "You know,

Arthur, you are far too respectable a fellow to be mixed up in some of the things you get mixed up in."

"You're not making this any better. It's all I can do lately to get up every morning."

"Brace up, chum. It's not forever."

"I can only hope. Do let me know what you have to give to hush this up. I'll cover any expenses."

Terry waved his hand. "Don't worry about it. Your money's no good here."

"I'm sorry to have to bring this to you."

"It's nothing. The Miller problem is much bigger. Have you given any thought to how you're going to handle it?"

"I plan to talk with him on New Year's Eve. I'll get it all sorted out then."

"He's agreed to meet with you? What changed his mind?"

"Nothing. Alicia's mother is going to leave the house open on New Year's Eve, and after the collections, I'll go over and talk some sense into the man."

"You're going to waltz into his house in the middle of the night?"

"Not to put too fine a point on it."

"I hope you won't be offended if he shoots you."

"He's not going to shoot me," Arthur said.

"Not if you shoot him first. What do you plan to accomplish? He's beyond rational thought."

"I am going to convince him to divorce privately, and get my letters back."

"Both good goals. The second is the more important."

"Believe me, I understand."

"Do you?"

"Yes, I believe I do."

"Maybe not fully. And that's what I was going to call you about today. Yesterday afternoon I had a rather distressing meeting in this very office."

"With whom?"

"My secretary told me I was to have a courtesy visit from some out-of-town law enforcement types working a case. Typical thing, letting me know they were in town. Turned out to be two detectives from Mooney & Boland."

"I see."

"I expect you do. Probably the very fellows who helped you find that slippery patch of ice."

"You're in rare form today."

"I know you don't want to hear it, but it remains beyond me why you had to pick on Ed Miller's wife, when there are dozens of girls in this city who would fuck you blind for a shot of morphine." He cleared his throat. "Oh, I am sorry I said that. That was inapropos."

"It's fine."

"Slipped out. Anyway, these operatives are New York men, and Miller has gotten his money's worth. They have done a lot of digging."

"None of which amounts to anything."

"Maybe not the spicy stuff about you and Mrs. Miller. Unfortunately, in the process of digging dirt about you, they've turned up quite a bit about *me*. The matters we've worked on together. Why, they even followed you on your rounds in The Hooks this past week."

Arthur's eyes widened in disbelief. "I would have known that. I've been at this long enough to know if I'm being tailed."

"And yet you *didn't*. They had a list of names and places."

"I don't know what to say."

"You certainly weren't at a loss for words in your letters to Mrs. Miller. They showed me a half-dozen typescripts, and they said they have at least a hundred more."

"They stole those letters from her," Arthur fumed. "She had them in a safe deposit box—"

Terry held up his hand. "It's of no concern to me *how* they came by them. What is of concern to me is what is *in* them. Not the lovey-dovey stuff. That was entertaining, after a fashion—I didn't know you had it in you! What was distressing was your candor about other things. Do you truly believe that I am 'a third-rate lawyer with a first-rate mouth'?"

Arthur felt sick. "Terry, people say things they don't—"

"Forget it," Penrose said. "I'm well aware that men say all kinds of saucy things to impress their mistresses, and you did it in spades. But in *writing?* I never thought you'd make such a bonehead play. An officer of the court, writing in his own hand, saying that he'd like to see Ed Miller dead? And all the personal stuff. I must hand it to him, Miller is a fellow with inspiring self-control. Most men would have had you castrated for less. You got off easy with a little rough-housing from his detectives."

"Look, I lost my head in those letters. And I'm sorry I did. But I've got it under control. You have nothing to worry about."

"I'm not worried. But you ought to be. You've woefully underestimated Edward Miller."

"I've dealt with far worse than him."

"I'm not so sure," Penrose said. He paused but went on before Arthur had a chance to speak. "Do you know what I like most about being a prosecutor, Arthur?"

He didn't wait for a response. "It's figuring out what makes a man tick. The things that he will let go by and the things that he simply can't control, like a reflex. After a while, you start to see patterns. Types of men.

"Miller, it turns out, is the most dangerous type. The sort that will take all manner of abuse, day after day after day, without so much as a murmur of complaint. Suffer in silence. Blame himself, even. Then, after all that simmering, something sets him off, and boom! He erupts. Like these volcanoes going off in Madagascar or wherever it was this year. And you had better damn well skedaddle when it blows."

"I fail to see—"

"You asked me for a favor today. And I'm now doing you another one, for free. If you'll listen a minute."

"I'm grateful, Terry. I'm listening."

"Where was I?" Penrose said. "Yes. The most dangerous type. I say that because a man like Miller—once he blows his top—will stop at nothing to even the score. And I can tell you, from what his operatives shared with me, he's most definitely blown his stack. Gone entirely off his rocker."

Arthur squirmed in his chair. "What did they say?"

Penrose put his fingertips together in a steeple. "What got Miller riled up was not the dirty letters to his wife. It wasn't the clandestine meetings. It wasn't the drip of insults about his height or his silly little glasses. None of that. What made him boil over was that—he *trusted* you, and her. He *forgave* you. He believed you when you swore it was over, for good, with his wife, and took her back. And what did you do then? You played him for a fool. Made an ass of him."

"He was an ass long before I got to him."

"Keeping your sense of humor, I see. But perhaps you won't find this so funny. After the detectives left, I sat and pondered for a long while. What might be Miller's end game?"

"Embarrass me and leave his wife destitute."

Terry shook his head. "That's only part of it. His strategy is much more complex. The Boland men told me that Miller wants two things from me. First, he requires that we end our business relationship. Naturally, I agreed. Effective today."

"Now, Terry, I need a little time," Arthur said. "Until I get my law practice back up and running."

"I wish I could oblige, but I can't. That leaves one other thing that Miller wanted from me, and I granted him that too. A promise I would not interfere with his divorce suit against his wife or against you as co-respondent. If, in exchange, they agreed to leave me out of it."

Arthur's head was beginning to throb.

"I hope it'll be enough to satisfy him," the DA said. "Though I suspect he'll be back for more, now that he's had a taste of what power feels like. This type of man hasn't known for the longest time—maybe his whole life—what it feels like to be powerful. Quite the contrary. He's felt helpless as he watched you steal his wife, disrupt his peace of mind, and—when nothing else was left—destroy his faith in a man's word of honor. Miller has endured humiliations that would have crushed most other men. But see, this is the interesting thing. They didn't crush him. They made him want to get even.

"And to get even, he'll do whatever it takes and keep on doing it until he has made you feel the way you made him feel. He has come to hate you more than he loves anything else. His wife, his children, his business, his life. He'll give it all up, and gladly, to have his revenge on you."

"He wouldn't dare—"

"There's nothing daring about it. It's all been meticulously plotted as he stewed in his little den, night after night. Surely you can see the exquisite game of chess he's played."

"Frankly, I think you're giving him too much credit."

"I'm not sure you're giving him enough. Listen. His first move—stealing those letters and sending his men to see me—takes me out of play, and cuts off your source of income. His second move is the divorce lawsuit. The odds that he will prevail go way up with me out of the picture. Now for the checkmate. He releases your letters, which he's held in reserve because he has so much other evidence he probably won't need them at trial. And then everyone in Buffalo will know exactly what you are, in your own words. You become a laughingstock, a pariah—drummed out of decent society and probably facing a divorce proceeding of your own. Oh—and any hope you have of resuming your legal career is gone, since you'll certainly be disbarred for the illegal activities detailed in your own hand."

He took a deep breath and gently put both palms flat on the desk. "And after *all that*, if you and your sweetheart do wind up together, you'll be a disgraced former lawyer living with a miserable woman who blames you for ruining her life. Not exactly a happy-ever-after, is it?"

"I won't let him get away with this."

"But don't you see? He *has* gotten away with it. And let's be honest with each other. Look at it dispassionately, from a lawyer's point of view. It's brilliant. Truly. They could have taught this case at New Haven—the man is a prodigy. A second Machiavelli, with ice water in his veins. One has to admire him."

"I won't admire a man like him," Arthur said. "And he's not the only one willing to do what it takes to win."

"That's the spirit! You haven't lost the old spunk, I see. Do you mean it, though, I wonder?"

"You can bet I mean it."

"Then would you entertain a few helpful suggestions from your old friend?"

"Always."

"If you intend to get the divorce action stopped and retrieve those letters, I don't believe that your former methods of persuasion will work. The begging, pleading, and groveling, that is. That worked once, when he was still a sane man. Now he's a rabid dog. And as you know, the only way to deal with a rabid dog is—"

"To put him down."

Terry nodded. "The law of the jungle, I'm afraid, is the only law that applies in a situation like this. So when you ring in the New Year with Ed Miller, you better not leave his house until you've taken care of this. One way or the other. Do we understand each other?"

"Perfectly. I'll handle it."

"That's the old Arthur Pendle I know. And now I'll get busy and take care of your little problem for you."

CHAPTER 48

Last-Ditch Efforts

New Year's Eve, 1901

WHEN ARTHUR GOT HOME FROM TERRY'S OFFICE, CASSIE WAS UP-
stairs taking a nap. He wished he could rest too, but his head was throbbing something fierce, and the ringing was becoming intolerable, like a
mosquito in his ear. The Boland men were no Harry Price, but the big
one with the bad teeth had done a fair job of it. Insomnia was beginning
to make him almost hallucinatory, jostling smells and colors together in
a strange and unsettling way.

He'd witnessed plenty of punishment and knew the routine: the
futile pleading, delinquent promises, pain. However rough, though, it
was justice, and it had never bothered him. In fact, there had been a few
times when some especially detestable reprobate was getting what was
coming to him, good and hard, that he'd felt aroused. Yet it had always
been impersonal, until now. This time, Edward Miller had ordered the
chastisement, and had shown him who was boss.

It was almost finished, though. Tonight, he would get his letters
back, Miller would be vanquished, and his stupid lawsuit would be dead.

❦

"Edward?"

She never called him Edward. "Sarah? What's wrong?" he said into
the telephone.

"May I come over? I need a word with you."

"It's after dinner already. The children are getting ready for bed. Can't it wait until tomorrow?"

"No, it can't."

"Is something wrong?"

"Ed, I need to talk with you."

"Then of course, come over. The girls'll be going to bed around nine. Can you come after that?"

"I'll be there at 9:30," she said and hung up.

At precisely half-past-nine, there was a gentle rap on the front door. Edward opened it to find Sarah there in a dark woolen jacket and dress and a long, black overcoat.

"Working undercover?" he said as he let her in.

"I can be very inconspicuous when I want to be."

He took her coat, and they sat down in the parlor. The fire was guttering, and he put on some more coal.

"What's the matter, dear?" he said. "You seem a bit out of sorts."

"I'm afraid."

"Afraid? You're not afraid of anything."

"I am now."

"Well, what is it?"

"You know I see Cassie at the market most days," she said. "Today, I saw her as usual. Lately she's been so—stupefied that she hardly seems to know who I am or what she's saying. Today she was in a complete daze. As awful as it sounds, I got her to tell me about her husband's comings and goings."

"You needn't have done that. Allie's gone and won't be coming back. They have only a few more days to answer my lawsuit, and then—"

"That's what I'm afraid of."

"That they'll mention you in the response? Raise some suspicion?"

"No, that won't bother me a bit. It's about something that Cassie said today, which struck me as very strange. I've been thinking about it all day."

"What did she say?"

"She said that when you told Allie to go away, that Allie went to Niagara Falls, and Arthur went with her. Then Allie went to New York—"

"Yes, she's still there. She sends letters to the girls and to her mother most days."

"Not now she's not. She's gone off to Atlantic City."

"Atlantic City? At this time of year? I highly doubt it. Cassie was probably mistaken."

"I don't think so. She seemed quite lucid about the detail of Alicia's movements. But you have put your finger on what I find so odd. Atlantic City is a peculiar choice. It's deserted this time of year. With Arthur footing her bills, she could go to Florida. Or out West. Why the Jersey Shore? There's something strange that she's no more than a day's train away, but far enough away to be out of the frame. And across state lines."

"My little detective has been reading too many *Police Gazettes*."

She ignored his joke. "Cassie went on to tell me that Arthur returned from New York yesterday evening."

"Probably to write up their answer to my suit, I'd expect."

Sarah shook her head. "I asked her about that."

"You asked Cassie about my lawsuit?"

"She was in such a state I could have asked her anything and gotten the truth. So yes, I asked her. Her answer was particularly unsettling. She said that Arthur told her that you had refused to consider any possible option other than his complete ruin and public disgrace. She said that you were making a big mistake, underestimating how far Arthur would go to prevent that. She said he'd even—and I quote—'go and take everyone with me rather than let that happen.'"

"You've read his letters. He's made similar threats before. 'I'll kill myself and her,' all that romantic nonsense. Doomed, star-crossed lovers, the two of them."

"And that's why I've warned you before about him. People who say things like that—you don't know what they're capable of. They don't have limits. They aren't to be trifled with."

"I'm not trifling with anyone. It's very straightforward, and he knows it. I am suing for divorce, and he's going to look like the fool he is when I do. That's all."

"Edward."

"What?"

"Arthur Pendle isn't going to let you make a fool of him."

Ed cleared his throat. "I'm sorry, but my mind's made up. He's got to pay for what he's done."

"Don't be such a stubborn ass. You know you're not doing this to teach him anything. You're doing it to salve your wounded pride."

"That is simply not true," he said. "And can you keep your voice down? You'll wake the whole house."

"I ought to wake the whole house, because they'd back me on this," she said. "This is all about your pride. You were perfectly satisfied when you found someone—me—who loved you. And, be honest, you were gratified that Allie was jealous about it. Now you're upset because she's gone and found someone who loves her. However crazy he is, or she is. Who cares? Let them go and be crazy together.

"You and I both know that something is very off about Arthur Pendle. I don't know if he was born that way, or something happened that made him into a monster—but it hardly matters. You think you're going to whack him on the head and teach him a lesson? Think again."

Edward frowned into the fireplace, now leaping with flame.

"I can't back down now."

"Dear Eddie," she said, taking his hand in both of hers. "It's time to let this go and go west."

"I did let it go, once," he said, scowling. "And they threw it back in my face. I won't let myself be humiliated again."

"You made a mistake. You forgave them. Don't make another one because you can't forgive *yourself.*"

"How can I forgive myself if I don't stand up to him? I feel like I'd be letting him get away with murder."

"There is nothing you can do to bring down judgment on Arthur," she said. "Maybe God will do that one day. Maybe not. Maybe he'll keep right on getting away with everything. It's not your job to stop him."

"What do you want me to do, Sarah?"

"First thing tomorrow, withdraw the lawsuit. Let her go, and let the poor fellow who fell in love with her take her off your hands. Call Arthur, and tell him you've dropped it and that you'll be giving his letters back."

"You'd leave me without a shred of dignity."

"Not so. Because tomorrow you and I will leave Buffalo, with our dignity intact, and get on with loving each other. It's long past time. You know it. And I know that if you persist with this crusade of yours, it's not going to end well. For either of us."

"Is this the 'woman's intuition' I hear so much about?"

"Eddie. Sometimes I could just knock you into next week. I'm making two simple, direct requests. Well, three. First, in the morning, withdraw your suit, and settle this privately. Second, give them their damned letters back, which you should never have taken. Third, leave with me for California on the afternoon train. I can't put it more clearly. Now, will you do as I ask?"

"Even if I pulled the suit, I can't bring my children with us if there's a divorce looming."

"We'll send for them as soon as this is cleared up."

"And my business?"

"Howard Gaines is a good man. He will treat you more than fairly. Maybe you can set up a California factory, and Gaines runs the Buffalo operation while you run the West."

Edward sat silently. "Are you honestly so worried about this? And so sure that you're right?"

"Yes, and yes."

"I want to do what pleases you, I do," he said softly. "But I don't know if I can let this go so easily now."

"You can, actually," she said. "The hardest thing is deciding that you will. Everything after that is easy. You can ignore everything I say for the next year, but not this."

"Oh no, you don't. Every time I've ignored you, it's turned out badly for me."

"Shouldn't that tell you something?"

He looked into the fireplace. "I'll do what you ask, Sarah."

"Bless you," she said. "You've made the right decision."

"One of these days, I would like to win an argument with you."

"Why? You're so much happier when you lose."

"Don't rub it in," he said.

"All right. First thing tomorrow, call your attorney. Then call Arthur. Once you've got that sorted out, call me and tell me when Maggie and I should meet you."

"I will follow your instructions to the letter."

She smiled her usual, perfect smile. "See how easy it is to make me a happy woman? And I didn't have to wake up the whole house to get my way, after all. Not that I wouldn't have."

"And I'm a happy man because you didn't. But being with you is what makes me happiest of all."

"Shucks," she said. "You're going to make me blush."

"Before you do, you'd better get on your way. I can walk you to the cab stand."

"No need," she said. "What's the worst that can happen in a fine neighborhood like Ashwood? I'll walk home tonight and take in some cold air. Soon enough, we'll be in California, and I won't be able to do that anymore."

"If you think so."

"Yes, I do. Now before I go—one last request."

"Another one? Haven't you already accomplished enough? What is it this time?"

"Kiss me."

"In my house?' he whispered.

"It's either here or on the front porch."

As usual, Edward couldn't find a good counter-argument.

CHAPTER 49

In Gethsemane

ARTHUR STUMBLED IN THE DOOR A LITTLE PAST MIDNIGHT, AFTER six hours of traipsing around The Hooks in a haze. The cold had made his head pound something fierce, and his forehead felt like a spike was being driven through it. He wanted desperately to sleep, but that would not be possible, not for a while.

Cassie was still awake, staring into the cold fireplace in the front parlor, when he arrived.

"Aren't you tired?" Arthur asked her. "You're usually in bed long before this time of night."

"I can't sleep. I keep thinking about Jeannie."

"You have to sleep."

"I will, sooner or later. How did everything go tonight?"

"Well as can be expected. It's done."

They watched the fire in silence together until the mantel clock struck twelve-thirty. He was starting to get nervous that Ed would turn in before long, and he'd miss his chance to confront him.

"Well, I think I will go up," Cassie said. "Don't stay up too late," she said.

"I won't."

As soon as Cassie had drifted out of the room, Arthur bundled up again and walked out to the small garage behind their house. His little Babcock was dead quiet and would give nothing away to the neighbors, but still, he pushed the machine to the end of the gravel drive. The bitter night air sliced through his long driving coat, whirling snow around in little vortices down the street in front of their house. Snow devils? He wondered. Is there such a thing?

He climbed into the machine and flipped the power switch, but there was no reassuring whirr from the motor. He remembered Mr. Babcock had told him that in very cold weather, the motor's armature could stick and had to be freed with a turn or two with a special tool that fit over the end of its drive shaft.

Cursing softly through chattering teeth, Arthur fumbled around in the toolbox, worried the whole time about all the racket. He found the item he needed, a large, heavy wrench. On one end was a crescent-shaped opening to fit over the armature nut, and on the other tapered to a broad chisel point, used for prying off the rubber tires when they needed changing.

He crawled under the auto, felt for the armature in the darkness, and fitted the tool over it. Sure enough, the shaft was frozen, but with a few good tugs on the big wrench, it creaked and then gave way, spinning freely. He crawled out and leaned into the car to try the switch again. This time the motor hummed into life without any trouble at all. He slipped the wrench into his coat pocket in case he'd need it later. Also, he thought, the flat end would be perfectly suited for prying open Ed's locking file drawers if he needed to.

Arthur climbed quietly onto the driver's bench, arranged a lap robe over his legs, and rolled slowly down the drive.

The trip to the Miller house should have taken five minutes, at most. But Arthur's car was well known in the neighborhood, and while there were precious few people out on a night like this, he couldn't afford to be spotted. He chose to follow a maze of side streets before parking the car in a disused alley two blocks away from the Miller house. He would walk the rest of the distance and stay as much out of sight as he could manage. He was dizzy from the cold wind, and he blinked and squinted, trying to make out the house numbers in the dark.

It was almost 1 o'clock when he ducked into the shadows at the foot of the Millers' porch steps. The house was dark, but a faint golden glow was seeping through the draperies of the room to the left of the front door, Ed's den. Good, he's still awake, Arthur thought.

A fluffy coating of fresh snow deadened his footsteps on the four steps up to the small vestibule. At the top, though, he felt so dizzy that he had to put his arms around one of the porch columns or risk tumbling back down again. He steadied himself after a few seconds and put his hand on the doorknob. If Mrs. Hall did her part, he thought, the door will be unlatched.

Mrs. Hall had indeed done her part and more. The front door was not only unlatched but stood slightly ajar, perhaps an inch. Possibly Mrs. Hall had thought that the latch would make noise. He slipped through the front door and into the foyer.

There was a pair of gas sconces burning in the long hallway that ran from the front door to the kitchen in the back. He stood there in complete silence for a moment or two, breathing hard, suddenly unable to recall what he had rehearsed so many times, his arguments to convince Ed Miller of the error of his ways. He squeezed on his head. Think, come on, think.

The gas jets wobbled in a sharp, cold draft that came down the hall and caused the front door to close with a click, but which seemed to him like the sound of a gunshot. He held his breath, listening for any sign that the sound had aroused anyone. But nothing stirred.

Edward's den was to the left. Arthur had once smoked a cigar with Edward in there soon after he and Cassie had joined the Club, but the few days of their friendship were indistinct now, could have been an age ago. This is it, he thought. The desk is to the right, against the wall. If he's still down here, he's probably working at it. Talk to him, if he is. If he's upstairs, go in, close the door, pry open the desk. Find the letters, and get out. He could feel the weight of the wrench in his coat pocket. Here goes nothing.

He put his ear to the den door. Silence. His heart was pounding out of his chest, every beat a surge of pain in his head. He cautiously turned the knob and ventured the door open a crack. The room was filled with the unsteady, amber glow of gaslight. He pushed the door open wider and peered in. He blinked, trying to focus.

Edward was lying on his side on the long divan in the shadows of the far wall, his face turned away from the door. A newspaper lay on the floor next to the divan. He's fallen asleep reading, Arthur thought. He was struck by a rogue wave of regret that things had come to this hard place. Starting out the New Year like a sneak-thief in another man's house, where once he was welcome, and not sure still—to this very moment—exactly what to do or say.

Arthur felt an urge to run away, as fast as he could down Ashwood Street and to his car, and drive as far as his batteries or pounding head would allow. In the next heartbeat, he flushed with anger at the thought of retreat. He couldn't scurry off, tail between his legs, while the man who was tormenting him slept on, guarding the ill-gotten correspondence that rightly belonged to him and Allie. And what right does he have to a good night's sleep, when I haven't had one since his men put this damned ringing into his ear? Less than ten feet from me is the man who is the author of all this pain.

Arthur stepped across the threshold and into the glowing den. He closed the door silently behind him. He studied the form on the divan, trying to cool his sudden fever of rage. The honorable thing to do, he mused in the flickering gaslight, is to leave him to his dreams.

No, Arthur thought firmly. I haven't come this far to back down now. There's no honor in that. And I could never face Allie again if I did.

The pressure in his head was getting intolerable. He crossed the little room in two strides. At the divan, he reached down and, with unexpected force, shook Edward's shoulder.

❧

When Arthur emerged from Edwards's den only a few minutes later, he almost yelled in surprise. Mrs. Hall was standing at the foot of the stairs, wringing her hands.

"I heard a noise," she whispered. Then she put her hand to her mouth to stifle a cry.

"What—whatever have you done?"

There was blood on the front of Arthur's suit, on his coat, on his hands. He had left a bloody shoeprint in the hall.

"Something very bad has happened," Arthur said flatly.

"Oh my God," Mrs. Hall said.

"Come in here," he whispered. "You'll wake the girls."

They stepped into the den, and Mrs. Hall had to turn away immediately. One of the Oriental carpets had been dragged off the floor and thrown across something lying on the divan. A pool of blood had formed under what must have been the head of the thing.

"What did you do?" Mrs. Hall said, clutching at her chest, still not looking. "In the name of—"

"The door was open. He was sleeping, and I covered him with the rug. That's what I did. Look what he did to me!"

"Is he—"

Arthur didn't reply.

"Oh, God. Dear God. What are we going to do?"

Arthur grabbed her forearm and squeezed it, hard, which lifted the fog in his head. "You're going to shut up," he said. "Or we're both going to be blamed for this. You hear me? Both of us."

Mrs. Hall bent over, her hands on her knees. "What have I done?" she said softly.

"Will you listen? All you need to do is go back upstairs and wait until morning. Then, as usual, you come down. The den will be closed, so naturally, you'll think he's in there. Then you look in, and—you call the police."

"I can't—"

"You don't have a choice. What are you going to say instead? That you left the front door standing open? No. What you tell them is that you went to bed as usual. Edward stayed up to read. In the morning, you noticed his bed was still made. You checked for him in the den. You found him. That's all there is to it. Understand?"

"All right," she said. "The girls . . . what will I tell them?"

"You stay out of that. Let the police handle it. Keep telling yourself to stay calm and stick to the story. Once you've called the police, send a telegram to Alicia. She'll need to come back right away. For the girls."

"Yes." She took a quick glance at the divan, and looked away again.

"It'll all blow over soon enough. Stick to the story. Don't add or subtract anything. If you do, I can't back you up."

They slipped back into the corridor. Arthur eased out the front door and heard it lock behind him. He hung back in the shadows of the front porch to make sure the coast was clear. The street was deserted, except for one light on in Mrs. Stoddard's house, across the street. Arthur thought he saw the curtains part and then drop back into place. As soon as he was satisfied that no one was watching, he trotted down the front steps and walked hastily back toward his machine.

Luckily this time, it started right up without any tinkering, its mechanical heart still warm after only about a half-hour in the damp cold. He took a roundabout way back, trying to clear his head, making a tour of the Ashwood section they'd lived in for years, but which now seemed strange and alien. He passed the houses of many of the members of the Ashwood Social Club, the friends he might have had. That was all in the past, irretrievably. The moving finger writes, and moves on.

At the very periphery of Ashwood, he found himself shivering, not from cold, but with rage and frustration.

❦

After quietly putting the Babcock to bed in the garage, he shed his coat as soon as he was inside and left it lying crumpled in a bloody pile.

He sat down in the parlor for a while. He planned to stay up all night, preparing to face the cops, who were sure to question him as soon as the news was out that Edward Miller was dead. He was the person he'd question first, if he were they. But they would go easy on him and once again he couldn't think clearly, so perhaps it would be better to get some rest. He started up the stairs.

The weak moonlight filtering down the staircase made the wallpaper shimmer with creeping veins of light. Strange, he thought, holding the handrail more tightly as a wave of dizziness passed over him. He heard a voice calling quietly to him from the top of the stairs.

"Cassie?" he said.

"I didn't mean to startle you," came a woman's voice, husky and seductive.

"Alicia?" he whispered, shocked.

"I couldn't stay away, Arthur."

"You're here," he said. "This is a terrible risk."

"We've taken greater ones," she said. "What have we to lose now?"

"Nothing, my love."

"Meet me in your bedroom," she said, and turned away from the staircase.

At the top of the stairs, he went into his bedroom. She was waiting for him, on the bed, in all that glorious nakedness. He stripped off his bloody suit, shirt, trousers, and underwear and stood naked in the darkness.

"You came to me, after all," he said quietly.

"I had to be with you tonight," she said. "Now come and be with me."

Despite the howling in his head, he was harder than he'd ever been before, needing to disappear into this woman who had thrown everything onto the altar of their love. Nothing would stop him, not Edward, not even Cassie in the room next door. Let her listen, he thought. She wanted to hear, once. Let her understand what I've never found words to explain.

His Aphrodite was lying on top of the covers, naked, and opened her legs avidly when he climbed onto her. She raised her hips to meet him, welcome him like a returning warrior, his terrible deeds done but soon to be forgotten in her arms.

"Are you bleeding?" she said as he put his forehead against hers and began to move, forcefully, the way she liked. "You smell like blood."

"Not my blood," he said.

"Good," she said, rising against him. "You're safe, then."

"I'm safe when I'm with you," he said.

"I love you, Arthur."

"I love you, too. And I'm sorry, I don't think I can hold on very long tonight."

"Let it go," she said. "It's all right."

When he rolled off, breathing hard, he stared at the ceiling for a moment, trying to focus his eyes, but without success. He looked over at her. A beam of moonlight had stolen through his bedroom window and was draped across her naked neck. He could see the big vein in it pulsing.

"Say," he said, "where's your torc? The ouroboros?"

"My what?" she said dreamily.

He leaned up on one arm. "The torc."

She lifted her head, questioning, and the moonlight fell across her features. "I don't know what you mean, Arthur," Cassie said.

❦

She was still next to him when he awoke the next morning. His head seemed to have cleared somewhat, and for the first time, he wished it hadn't. If Allie knew that he had—he couldn't even think about it. He lay still, examining the memories of the whole disastrous night, or at least those which had congealed in his sleep and were sharp and hard.

At first, he had only shaken Ed, and that was all. He knew it would startle him, but he fully intended to reassure him that his presence was all in good faith. Then he would instruct him—as calmly as possible—to suspend his pointless vendetta, agree to a private divorce, and return the purloined letters. And he would make it clear that he wasn't leaving until Ed agreed to all his demands.

It hadn't gone as planned, not from the moment Ed's eyes flew open with a dazed and horrified stare, as though awakening from a terrible nightmare. At first, Ed hadn't recognized him at all, that was indisputable. Standing over the divan, collar up and hat pulled down low, and with the Moorish chandelier glowing like the full moon above and behind his shoulder, Arthur may have appeared monstrous, a looming, faceless form, the remnant of a nightmare.

Edward's first reaction—sleepy, unclothed, unarmed, unready—was to open his mouth to scream or summon help—but Arthur clamped his left hand down over it to keep him quiet. His head pinned to the pillow, Ed seized Arthur's wrist with both hands, trying to wriggle free with surprising strength. His larger and stronger opponent also had the advantage of gravity, so Ed did what he could—he bit down hard on Arthur's hand. The pain caused the hand to jerk away, and Ed bobbed up into a sitting position as quickly as a jack-in-the-box.

He was fully aware now of the desperate scope of his problem. Arthur had to admit that he had never seen such eyes, not even in the worst of it in The Hooks—an intolerable, malignant stare, not so much fearful as murderous.

Ed tried to shove Arthur away and scramble to his feet, but Arthur shoved him back onto the divan, and with his injured hand trying to cover Ed's gaping mouth, instinct screaming at him to silence the man before he could raise the alarm. It was then that he felt the weight of the armature wrench in his right-hand coat pocket.

No, it hadn't gone as planned, but then again, it hadn't been all bad. Although his letters were still unaccounted for, there could certainly be no divorce. And other than Mrs. Hall, who had too much to lose to run her mouth about it, he had been able to come and go like a ghost. And how he'd made it to his automobile, dizzy and splattered with blood, without being detected was something of a minor miracle. And then, more good luck—the Babcock had started without wasting time under the machine with the armature wrench.

The wrench, he thought, heat rising into his temples. I put it back into my coat after prying open the drawers. Or did I?

He bolted out of bed and ran down the stairs, stark naked, to the side door, where he'd left his coat in a heap. It was still there, rusty with blood. He picked it up and shoved his hand into the right pocket, where the wrench ought to be. It was empty. He hurriedly spun the coat around and tried the left pocket. Nothing there, either. Nauseated, he wadded up the garment, feeling the fabric for the large piece of steel, but other than buttons, there was nothing rigid anywhere in it. He threw it down on the floor in a blinding temper, stamped on it, then stalked back up the stairs to see if he'd dropped the wrench in his trouser pocket by mistake.

Back in the bedroom, he trod on his heap of clothes, feeling for the wrench. Nothing. He ran his hands through his hair and let his arms drop, noticing some blood that had seeped under his cuffs, making a red bracelet around each wrist. His left palm was sore, and he held it up and flexed it in the improving light. There was a crescent bruise at the base of the thumb—what the palmists called the *mons veneris*—where Ed's teeth had clamped down hard enough to leave a partial bite mark through the leather of Arthur's glove. But all that was minor. All of it could be remedied or would heal. But somewhere between Ed's den on Ashwood Street, and his side door, he had lost the murder weapon. What in the—

"Arthur?" came a groggy voice from the bed. "Won't you come back to bed?"

"No," he said. "You sleep some more. I have to go out this morning."

"So early? Where?"

"Niagara Falls," he said. "Before it gets busy. Can you meet me for lunch at the International?"

She stretched languorously, arms extended over her tousled head.

"I might be able to," she yawned.

"I need you to meet me for lunch."

"On one condition."

"What?" He was starting to get annoyed.

She sat up in bed. "We do it again before you go."

"But Cassie, I need—"

"You won't miss your trolley."

Jesus, he thought. It's one thing if I didn't *know,* but—

She threw back the covers. She was still naked, and he felt himself stirring again.

"See?" she said archly. "Some things don't lie. He doesn't mind a little delay."

"Oh, fine, then," he said.

❦

"Now, that wasn't so bad, now, was it?" she said afterward.

"I'm in a hurry, that's all."

"You can go," she said. "I think I will sleep a little more."

"Bring the morning papers with you when you come."

"Can't you get the Niagara Falls papers?"

"Cassie, if it weren't important, I wouldn't ask. International at noon, bring the Buffalo papers. Understood?"

"Yes, I understand. There's no need to be cross."

"I'm not cross. Go back to sleep, and I'll see you at lunchtime."

"Be safe, Arthur." She pulled the covers over her again and rolled onto her side.

He dressed quickly, stuffed last night's clothes into his valise, and did the same with the crumpled driving coat downstairs. In the garage, he felt around on the floor of his automobile for the armature wrench—his last hope—but it wasn't there, either. Fortunately, the machine started

THE REMNANT OF A NIGHTMARE

up without problem, but there was no time left to put up the convertible canvas rain canopy against the drizzle, so he arrived at the station cold and wet. He gave a dollar coin to the lot attendant and asked the boy to erect the top to keep off the rain. He made it to the platform ten minutes before the first express trolley for Niagara Falls rolled up, and in less than an hour, he was at its Niagara Falls terminus, on Prospect Street, facing the Niagara Reservation.

The Reservation—the enormous park that embraced the Falls like the setting of a massive jewel—was sleeping late on a cold, grey New Year's morning, the few people in town having the good sense to stay under the covers until the skies, or their heads, cleared from the night before. Arthur crossed the street and ducked into the skeleton forest of the Reservation. He walked quickly past Prospect Point, across the bridge to Goat Island, and to the brink of the Horseshoe Falls, which connected the United States and Canada like a huge, curved staple.

After twenty minutes of fast walking, he stood at the jutting corner of the railing that leaned out over the crest of the Falls. He set down his valise and, shaking off the cramps in his hand, watched the relentless, green water sliding by hypnotically. He looked up the path and saw no one. He picked up the valise and set it on the top of the iron railing, and looked over at the cascading ocean of water, battering the rocks far below. How bad could it be, he wondered. A second? Two?

Arthur looked around one last time, opened the valise, fished out his clothes and shoes, sticky with blood that had gone gelatinous overnight. He couldn't abide the warm, dusty smell of the stuff, though, and as quickly as he could manage, he chucked the whole bundle over the edge into the swift stream above the crest. The bundle opened, rippled, blossomed again briefly into human form, and disappeared into the rising mist. He closed the valise with a firm click and headed for the International, where he could wait by the fire for Cassie and think over what they would tell the cops when they did finally show up.

❧

Cassie got there five minutes after the restaurant doors swung open for luncheon, and Arthur was comfortably seated by a radiator. Good girl, she's brought the papers, he noticed. She had an unusual look on her face, which he couldn't quite place.

He had barely finished pushing in her chair when she leaned over the table toward him.

"Arthur, have you heard the news about Ed Miller?" she whispered.

"What news?"

"He was *murdered* last night. At his home. It's terrible."

"Let me see the papers."

Sure enough, front page of the *News*. The *Courier,* too. He scanned the articles quickly. Plenty of lurid details of the murder, nothing about possible suspects. That was good. He folded the papers up again and put them under his chair.

"Arthur, what is the matter with you?" she asked, leaning toward him. "You have nothing to say about Ed Miller?"

"Cassie," he said, extending his hand across the table and placing it on hers, "everything is fine. I assure you. But we do need to talk, and you need to listen to me very carefully. When we get back to Buffalo, we can't talk about this again. That's why I needed you here."

"You're frightening me. Talk about what?"

"About Ed Miller."

"What about him?"

"You know I was at home all last night," he began.

"Yes, of course. How could I forget?"

"And you also know that there's been no love lost between Ed Miller and me recently."

"Certainly not."

"Because of the difficulty between me and Ed—people may think that I had something to do with his death."

She looked at him. "How ridiculous."

"Of course, it's ridiculous. But I want you to be prepared. Whatever anyone may say, remember: Arthur could never do this awful thing."

She nodded quietly and forced herself to study her hands folded in her lap. "I'd so hoped," she said, "after last night and this morning—after everything we've both been through—that today might be the start of a new chapter."

"Don't be so glum," Arthur said. "Everything will be all right in the end. In the meantime, I was at home, and we were together all last night. Right?"

"Yes, I understand."

After breakfast, they took the trolley back to Buffalo, where Arthur found a telegram waiting for him at his office.

❦

Alicia had sent her telegram from the Traymont about 8:30 that morning, soon after she'd received the news from her mother that Edward was dead. It read:

Returning Bflo tomorrow a.m., express. Meet me Terrace Station. Allie.

Not a good plan, he thought. The rumors about them were already too widespread, and meeting his freshly widowed paramour as soon as she stepped off the train would be stupid. A part of him wanted to see her, but it had none of the usual frisson in it. He burned the telegram.

When Alicia alighted from the train at Terrace Station, she fully expected Arthur to be waiting on the platform. But he was nowhere to be seen. She asked the Pullman attendant to pile her things next to a bench in the cold waiting room, and she sat there for an hour. People came and went, giving her strange, unsettling looks. Trains arrived and departed, but no Arthur. At last, she gave up and hailed a porter, who wheeled her things out to the cab stand.

As the carriage neared their house, Alicia could see a small knot of people standing on the sidewalk in front. They were staring at the house, which stared back impassively. Allie got down from the rig and was met by the inescapable Mrs. Stoddard, who looked at her wide-eyed.

"Alicia," she said, "it's so terrible. I'm so very sorry."

"Thank you, Catherine."

"You can take those into the house," she said to the hackman, pointing to her trunk and satchel.

Mrs. Stoddard goggled at her.

"You're going to stay in your house? Tonight?"

"Where else would I stay?"

"Wouldn't you and the children and your mother feel, um, better, safer, in a hotel—until the police locate—" She trailed off, not knowing what words to use. 'The murderer?' 'Culprit?' 'Killer?' Each term was uglier than the one before.

Alicia looked puzzled, as though she'd never considered this question. "Why, thank you, dear. That's kind of you. We'll all be perfectly safe. I'm certain of that."

CHAPTER 50

The Butcher's Bill

EDWARD'S WOUNDS WERE GRUESOME. THE FIRST BLOW SEEMED TO have been struck on his upper forehead, as if he had been sitting upon the divan, looking up at someone standing in front of and over him. Two fingers of his left hand were broken, and badly: defensive wounds. Apparently, he'd had enough time to throw up his arm to fend off the attack. But not for long, because almost any of the other blows—and there were at least 15, the total hard to determine because the skull was so badly crushed—could have killed him outright, or at least rendered him senseless.

At first, the police were certain that the murder weapon was one of the golf clubs standing in a corner of Edward's den. But there was no blood on any of them, and the coffered ceiling was too low to swing a golf club overhead and bring it down on a man's skull. It had to be something shorter, blunt and heavy. They studied a mostly empty bottle of cocktail bitters sitting on the little table in the center of the room but, again, found no signs of blood or hair. And it would have doubtless shattered if it had been employed so savagely.

Edward must have slumped sideways on the divan after the initial attack, and it was after he had fallen over that the real damage had been done. His assailant appeared to have gone into a frenzy at that point, raining down blows on the defenseless and probably already dead man. The side and back of the skull were so pulped that a large piece of the skull, scalp still attached, had come off entirely, exposing the brain tissue beneath. Blood was spattered on the wall and on the ceiling, slung from the weapon as it rose and fell in a deadly arc.

Fury spent, the killer seemed to have examined his handiwork and, for reasons that were unclear, decided to make a few adjustments to the scene. He had pulled the corpse fully onto the divan from its slumped-over, half-sitting position, extended the legs, and pulled the body up toward the head of the couch into a sleeping pose. The battered head had been laid on a tasseled pillow, and a small quilted coverlet wrapped twice around, either to cover the face or to keep more of the brains from oozing out. Then one of the floor rugs had been pulled off the floor and draped over the whole mess.

At the time of his murder, Edward had been wearing an undershirt, dress trousers, and socks; his jacket and dress shirt were found in his bedroom, presumably where he'd taken them off before heading downstairs to relax in his den. Most peculiar of all, after the killing, the culprit had carefully removed Edward's pants and socks, folding them carefully over the back of a chair adjacent to the divan, and leaving the dead man naked from the waist down. If the pants had been on the chair during the murder, they would have been only sprinkled with blood, like the chair itself. But instead, the blood on the pants had run down their front, likely gushing from Edward's head in the few seconds while he was sitting upright, heart pumping hard, eyes fixed on his murderer.

And thus had Edward Miller's life ended: on his favorite divan, in his favorite room, with Sarah's framed photograph watching over him from the desk.

❦

The crime scene added even more mystery. On a small table in the den was a metal tray on which were a few bits of cheese, the remnants of a fruit tart, and some half-eaten crackers. The suspect empty bottle of bitters sat next to the tray. Ed Miller didn't like cheese, rarely ate crackers, didn't drink alcohol, and likely wouldn't know where the maid kept such items in the pantry. Thus, the food must not have been his. It was as though a snack had been prepared for a guest, someone that the victim was expecting. But who? Surely Edward would not have entertained a business contact so late at night and in his private sanctum, which he reserved for his own comfort. A woman, perhaps? Wasn't Ed Miller known to have a fondness for the ladies?

Prior to the fatal attack, Edward had removed his pince-nez glasses and set them on top of the roll-top desk against the adjacent wall. If a guest had sampled the cheese and crackers, it must have happened before Edward had removed the glasses. Would a man with weak eyesight have entertained a visitor without his spectacles? Nor could he have read the newspaper found lying next to the divan without them. But then again, would he have concluded his business with his visitor, gone upstairs to deposit his jacket and shirt, and then returned to the den clad only in trousers and an undershirt? It seemed unlikely. More probably, he had been relaxing in the den, felt sleepy, and decided to save himself a trip up the stairs to bed. But that didn't explain the tray of food.

Teasing out the details wasn't helped by the police, who seemed to make a concerted effort to botch the investigation. Although fingerprinting remained a novel means of identifying criminals, the Buffalo Police Department had been collecting prints for more than a year. Yet instead of carefully dusting the room, the cops pawed over everything with bare hands, to the extent of leaving a very suspicious-looking, bloody handprint on the front door jamb. That provoked a brief flurry of interest in the press, until it turned out that one of the coroner's men had used the jamb to steady himself while maneuvering the blood-soaked corpse out of the house.

Any footprints in the snow on the porch, on the steps, on the sidewalk—all were trampled under by heavy police boots, which then tracked wet into the crime scene itself, hopelessly destroying any shoeprints that may have been left on the rug by the murderer. Within a day, a few items vanished from the den entirely; the bottle of cocktails, a pair of slippers belonging to the dead man, Edward's gold pocket watch, and the photograph of Sarah Payne. Whether they were taken as evidence or merely spirited away, no one knew.

When they arrived that morning, after Mrs. Hall had summoned them, the police found the windows in the Miller house securely latched from the inside, save for one in the kitchen at the rear of the house. That one was found partly open, altogether a strange thing on such a cold night. Could the killer have entered or escaped through this window? Yet no new snow had fallen after 10 p.m., the approximate time when Ed was last seen alive—going into his bedroom, upstairs—or so Mrs. Hall told the detectives.

Furthermore, a crust of older, sooty snow and ice on the outside sill of the open window was entirely undisturbed. Nor were any footprints found under that window or leading to or from it. That theory of an entry through the kitchen window thus seemed untenable.

All that remained, then, was this: Whoever had come and gone from the Miller house that night had done so through the front door. There was no evidence that the door had been forced, and a forcible entry would surely have awakened the sleeping family. It was known that Miller had begun locking his front door when he went to bed—thus, Edward's guest was either known to someone in the household, or had a key. And when that person or persons unknown left the house, he, she, or they had done so calmly and unseen.

❦

The official bungling continued after Ed's mangled remains were removed. The medical examiner, curiously, on first examination of the body, attempted to classify the event as a suicide. It was only after his deputy—caught unawares by a reporter in a local watering hole and a tipsy, sarcastic mood—said on the record that he had never before seen a man commit suicide by bashing in his own head, that the absurd fiction was dropped.

For 48 crucial hours after the murder, the cops called in for questioning people who could never have had the strength required to cave in a man's skull so thoroughly. Sarah Payne was the first one. It was well-known in the neighborhood that Ed Miller had a special fondness for her, which was enough to make Sarah a suspect.

In the collective mind of the cops, the 'woman theory' worked like this: a tray of snacks suitable for a lady, Sarah's blood-spattered photograph on Edward's desk, and a dead man nude from the waist down all pointed to a tryst, late-night carnal conversation gone very wrong. The theory collapsed as soon as Howie Gaines, who had learned of the murder of his friend in the morning news—and immediately rushed to the house on Ashwood Street—arranged for a good attorney to represent Sarah, one with plenty of connections. She was quickly dropped from the suspect list.

Several other Ashwood ladies were then questioned at some length, also until their lawyers arrived. The theory was bogus to begin with, so the swirl of skirts in and out of Police Headquarters was nothing more than a colossal waste of precious time. None of the fine ladies of the Ashwood Set could possibly have the physical power and aggression required to destroy a man—even a smallish one like Edward—so thoroughly and then hoist his dead weight into its final position on the divan.

Casual crime had to be ruled out, too. The pocket watch had vanished after the cops arrived, while Edward's pocketbook with $200 in cash had been left untouched. Nothing else of any value was missing, and in the den were plenty of baubles and decorative items that would have been worth a few dollars to a burglar. And temperamentally, sneak thieves were, as a rule, incapable of the extravagant violence that had been unleashed that night.

That left the most obvious suspect, and the one the cops took particular care to avoid: Arthur Pendle. Plenty of tongues had been wagging about him since the morning the body was discovered. Yet while rumor pointed to the young, handsome lawyer who was somehow mixed up with the now-widowed Alicia Miller, there was a strange unlikelihood about it. Could a man unused to killing—a respected professional man and an Ivy Leaguer at that—pull off such a perfect and hideous crime? To enter a man's locked house, unseen and unheard, in the wee hours, locate and dispatch the victim so decisively, and do so without raising a hue and cry that would awaken anyone in the house, was already a marvel of criminality. But then calmly to stage-manage the battered, seeping corpse to appear that the victim had been caught *in flagrante delicto*? Possibly even have a little bite of cheese and tart, and then again disappear into the night? The whole thing was a masterpiece of cold-bloodedness hardly consistent with a crime of passion, as everyone assumed, and suggested the handiwork of a professional. And 'professional criminal' was an epithet that no respectable person would have associated with Arthur Pendle, Attorney at Law.

Perhaps it was that very incongruity that explained the cops' curious lack of interest in talking with the man who, by right, ought to have been the chief target of any investigation worthy of the name. Or perhaps the cops knew that Pendle was untouchable. As the hours ticked by, and a trickle of ever-more-unlikely 'suspects' were summoned to Police Headquarters, Arthur Pendle, who had been up to his neck in Edward and Alicia Miller's trouble—and who stood most to benefit from Ed's sudden departure from among the living—remained entirely unmolested by the police.

❦

It took the newspapers to catch up to him, on the third day after the murder.

About 6 p.m. and already dark, with snow falling softly outside, Arthur was having a cocktail by a cozy fire in his walnut parlor. He was feeling rather more confident about things. The divorce suit was a moot point now, and the unfound letters—if they still existed at all—were no longer of any serious concern. Except as evidence in a court case, they posed no threat. That morning, two Buffalo detectives, almost apologetically, had at long last come to talk with him and Cassie. Arthur, who knew them both, welcomed them conspicuously on his front porch. He knew they had to visit eventually or be suspected of some conflict of interest. He and Cassie stuck to their story, and the detectives looked relieved to clap their notebooks shut and go off chasing their tails elsewhere.

He was jarred out of his musing by the jangle of the front doorbell. Their maid answered it before Arthur had even had a chance to stop her.

"May I speak with Mr. Pendle?" a man's voice came.

"One moment," she said. She poked her head into the parlor. "Gentleman here to see you, sir."

"Who is it?"

"I don't know, sir."

Arthur sighed. What is it going to take to get this girl to ask people for a calling card? "Very well, send him in."

A young man with sandy hair appeared in the parlor, hat in hand. "Jess Murphy, Buffalo *Courier*," he said, extending his hand.

Arthur shook it rather indifferently and gestured for the reporter to sit. He remained standing by the fire. "What can I do for you, Mr. Murphy?"

"This murder of Edward Miller," the man said, opening a notebook. "I wanted to ask you a few questions if I might."

"An awful business," Arthur said. "Simply horrid. I'm not sure I can shed much light on it."

"I understand you were good friends with Mr. Miller."

"Yes, we were friends. Not close, but friendly."

"And lately, as I understand, you'd had a falling out?"

"Our relations had become somewhat strained." His lawyerly mind screeched at him not to answer anything, but yet another pounding headache and a couple whiskeys dulled his judgment. Now that he was almost in the clear, there couldn't be much harm in adding a little further misdirection.

"If you don't mind . . . why were they strained?"

"I'm sure you already know the answer," Arthur said. "Mr. Miller had filed for a divorce from his wife. She engaged me as her defense counsel, which naturally put me at odds with her husband."

"Yes, I know about that. It's a bit unusual that he would name you as co-respondent, though, isn't it?"

Arthur was growing frustrated. He'd thought his answer very deft.

"Yes, it is, since he had no reason to do so—other than personal animus or a desire to damage my reputation, and his wife's."

"And why would he want to do that, do you think? Mr. Miller seems to have been an unusually even-tempered man, from what I'm told. Not the vindictive sort. Quite an upright fellow, by all accounts."

"Now see here," Arthur blurted, "Edward Miller was no saint. And while I suppose a dead man has a right to defend his reputation—I mean, his friends do—you know what I mean—a living one has as much a right. To do so. As well."

"Naturally," the reporter agreed. "He was no saint, you say? What do you mean by that? Can you give me an example?"

"There are things I could tell you if it comes to it."

"Such as?"

"I'd rather not say anything about that now." Arthur felt a need to redirect but wasn't sure how. Murphy saved him.

"They say that Mr. Miller liked the ladies."

Arthur's eyes narrowed. He finished the last half-inch of liquor in his glass and set it on the mantel. He licked his lips.

"Ed Miller was a ladies' man, yes, I think it's fair to say."

"The cops think a woman did it."

"Women are doing all sorts of novel things these days, aren't they?" His joke didn't get so much as a ghost of a smile from the reporter, who jotted a few words in his little notebook.

"I'm told that the Ashwood Social Club is quite a hive of divorce and intrigue. Would you agree, Mr. Pendle?"

"That's nothing more than idle talk. I don't believe there is any more intrigue, to use your term, which I don't endorse—within the Ashwood Club than in any other similar gathering. That said, my wife and I haven't attended for some time, and thus I cannot say what it is like now."

The reporter scribbled in his notebook again.

"On that note," Murphy said, still looking at his notebook, "I don't mean to pry, and I'm certainly not endorsing any rumors, but can you comment on the claims by some that you and Mr. Miller's wife have a relationship that goes beyond legal advice?"

"That's an outrageous notion, sir. I'll thank you to refrain from that kind of talk, especially here in my home."

"You don't have any such relationship with Mrs. Miller?"

"I most certainly do not. I am her legal representative, as I said, and that is all."

"I see," Murphy said. "Thank you for clearing that up. Mr. Pendle, I've taken up enough of your time for now. Would you mind if I had a follow-up question or two sometime later?"

"I may or may not entertain further questions, Mr. Murphy, but I recognize it's your job to ask them."

"Thank you." The reporter stood. "Oh, you know—I should say that if you need, um, want to tell your side of the story, I'll be willing to give you a sympathetic hearing. I think our readers would very much like to hear what you have to say."

Arthur was a bit taken aback by the sudden wind shift. "Thank you," he said. "I'll keep that in mind."

❦

Jess Murphy aspired, more than anything, to make his bones and get the hell out of Buffalo. The *Courier* was a decent newspaper, but so long as he was at the *Courier,* he'd be a Jess Murphy and never a Julian Hawthorne with the Hearst papers, or even this up-and-comer Mencken, in Baltimore at the *Sun.* If he could get some juice out of this Miller case, it might do the trick. And Murphy was blessed with a poker face. People seemed to tell him things that they shouldn't, forgetting that he was a reporter. It was a very useful gift in his line of work.

Two nights later, Murphy again rang the bell at the Pendle residence. This time Cassie answered the door, and he was squired cordially into the parlor for a second chat.

"Thank you for seeing me again, Mr. Pendle."

After their first conversation, Arthur had read and reread the article that Murphy published, and had been both relieved and impressed. Murphy had done him a very good turn, portraying him as a respectable, educated gentleman, hardly the sort who could commit a brutal murder. And the gossip mill was gathering speed. Arthur had been mulling over whether it might not be wise to get his side of the story on the record. Murphy had beat him to it, but that was fine.

"Glass of Dutch Courage?" Arthur said jovially as the reporter took his seat.

"Don't mind if I do," Murphy said. Arthur poured him a good one from the crystal carafe on the sideboard. Murphy raised his eyebrows appreciatively.

"Much better than the stuff in the bars near the *Courier,*" he said.

"I have it shipped to me from Scotland," Arthur said. "The Canadian whiskey around here tastes like kerosene."

Murphy, who thought Canadian was the good stuff, nodded.

"Where would you like to begin?" Arthur seemed eager to expatiate. "Last we spoke, you'd mentioned your desire to do a sympathetic portrait of me."

"Right," Murphy said. "Before we get to that, though, would you mind if we cleared up a couple things I've heard the past couple days?"

"We can do that."

"After my article," Murphy resumed, "I kept thinking about this beautiful home . . . "

"You're very kind."

"Not at all. It is beautiful. And it seems that you have art from all over the world."

"I did get bitten by the collecting bug a few years ago."

"You have an electric automobile of the latest type. You dress fashionably. And—" he raised his glass "—you drink whiskey all the way from Scotland!"

Arthur was getting a little unsettled by all this unexpected flattery.

"I . . . suppose so," he replied. "In my line of work, it's important to look the part."

"That's exactly what I wanted to ask about."

Arthur looked at the man's protruding Adam's Apple bobbing as he swallowed some of his special Scotch. He felt a sudden urge to punch it, hard.

"Ask what?"

"What exactly is your line of work, Mr. Pendle?"

"What an odd question," Arthur said. "You know already. I'm an attorney. My office is in the Aston Building, downtown."

"Oh, yes, I do know that. New Haven School of Law, 1889. What I mean, though, is this: everyone I talk to says that you haven't had a court case in . . . well, years."

"That's preposterous," Arthur said, clearing his throat. "I'm one of the busiest lawyers in town."

"Not according to the court records I've been going through," Murphy said with a bland smile. "Not a single one since"—he flipped through his notebook—"1898. Robert O'Shea. Death penalty case."

"You must have overlooked quite a few."

Murphy went on. "What I can't understand . . . is how is it that you can afford this beautiful house, these things, the clothes . . . without any clients."

Arthur was now feeling a bit light-headed. "I also have a collection agency, you know," he managed. "That keeps me quite busy."

"In the Ellicott Square Building?"

"That's the one."

"But see, I talked with the landlord, and he said you rented that office for a month, then shut it down. Then opened it up again for another month or so. But without doing any business, either time, so far as he could tell."

Arthur had taken out that lease so that he and Allie could have a place to meet that wasn't as easily watched as their rental houses. And meeting in a first-class office building made whatever happened there automatically above suspicion.

"Still early days," Arthur said, refilling his glass. He didn't offer more to Murphy, who looked wistfully at the bottle.

"I see," said Murphy.

"I thought we were going to take this in a different direction, Mr. Murphy."

"And we will, we will. I have only one more thing to clear up beforehand. I do appreciate your patience."

"All right. One more. But then let's get on with things."

"Of course. It's this. You have an uncle in Maine"—he checked his notebook—"a Cyrus Reid?"

"Yes, I do," Pendle said. "My mother's brother."

"A fellow here told me that you'd been doing some investing for some of your friends and relations back in Maine—and Connecticut, too? Your wife's family?"

"Sometimes they ask me for advice. Real estate, mostly."

"This fellow told me that Cyrus Reid has been making some noise about not getting any dividends from his investment."

Arthur ran his hand through his hair. "My Uncle Cyrus is a crotchety old Yankee. I wouldn't set too much store by what he says."

"Nor would I," Murphy said. "But I did arrange to 'phone him up, and he gave me the names of several other people who have invested with you."

"He did?"

"I talked with a few of them, too. Story's the same. They gave you money to invest in suburban land development. Tonawanda, Kenmore, and so forth. But so far, no dividends."

"Investments take time to pay off. You—and they—know that."

"Without a doubt. But they gave me the property names from some of the deeds that you supplied. I looked them up in the Hall of Records."

Arthur drained his glass. "If you please. What nonsense are we going on about now? Sir, this is an ambush."

"I don't mean it to be at all. I need only to clear up a few things so that the profile will be thorough. I'm sure there's some logical explanation for why I couldn't find a single deed or property record for any of those investment properties. Close to a million dollars' worth of real estate at current prices. You'd think I'd have found something. Anything."

"Take it from a man who knows a thing or two about research," Arthur said. "You need to be more careful in yours. Either they gave you the wrong names, or you looked them up wrong."

"I called them back, and it all checks out. No mistake."

"Then I don't know what to tell you. Other than something is very irregular."

"My point precisely. What exactly became of all that money? You wouldn't have used it for anything other than purchasing real estate, would you?"

"Sir!" Arthur stood, almost knocking the table over. "That is a most serious allegation!"

Murphy stared at Arthur, who began pacing in front of the fireplace.

"It's not an allegation, Mr. Pendle," he said quietly. "It's a natural question. If you were in my shoes, I'm sure you'd ask the same thing. Doesn't it seem curious that you have such a lavish life without a significant income?"

"Mr. Murphy, this is most unwelcome. Not that it's any of your business, but my wife is a woman of some means. And in any event, I refuse to dignify your questions further. I think we have said quite enough for one night. And speaking as an officer of the court, I'd advise you not to publish any of this—gossip, or you might find yourself on the wrong end of a lawsuit."

"If I had a dollar for every time I've heard that one," Murphy said. "Mr. Pendle, I have two corroborating sources for everything we have discussed. I am on very firm ground. I had hoped—sincerely—that you would clear it up. That it'd be an easy matter, easily dismissed. But as that is not to be, I will have to write that you deny any malfeasance and refuse further comment."

"You can write whatever you damn well want and go to Hell, too, so far as I care," Arthur said, raising his voice. "Now, please go. You are no longer welcome here."

"On my way," Murphy said, sliding his infernal little notebook into his jacket pocket. "Thank you for your time, Mr. Pendle. I'm sorry to have discomfited you. Good night."

Arthur slammed the front door as Murphy stepped onto the porch, even though he knew that a tantrum was not going to play well in the papers. But how dare he? Barge in here under false pretenses and—*interrogate* me?

"Arthur?" Cassie called from the top of the staircase. "Is everything all right? It sounded like an argument."

Arthur steadied himself on the newel post. "Everything's fine, dear," he called up with as much cheer as he could muster. "A little misunderstanding. Nothing to worry about."

But Arthur knew that something much more consequential than the death of some stupid, little envelope salesman was swirling down Columbus Avenue. The murder of Ed Miller had pried open his Pandora's Box.

❧

At wits' end, Arthur rang the office of the only person who still could help him: the District Attorney. Penrose's secretary was reluctant to put him through, but Arthur kept at it until he heard Terry in the background, telling her to go ahead.

"Arthur," Penrose said, "Unless you have some news for me, which given the passage of time I very much doubt, I don't need to remind you that we had an understanding."

"I need to see you. I wouldn't ask if I didn't."

Penrose was silent for a few long seconds.

"Please, Terry. Name the time and place," Arthur said.

"Fine," Penrose said at last. "An hour from now. At your house."

"My house?"

"That a problem?"

"No, I'll be here."

❦

"I don't have a lot of time, Roscoe," Terry said. "I've got to go over to see Arthur Pendle. He needs some hand-holding."

"This is timely, then," Roscoe said. "Something you ought to know about at the Miller house. Detective Cusack dropped by to tell me about it."

"What?"

"When he arrived on the scene, Cusack found some sort of heavy tool sitting on Miller's desk. Blood and hair all over it. He told me it's a wrench for a Babcock Electric automobile."

Penrose laughed. "You're telling me that, on top of everything else, the man left behind the murder weapon?"

"Apparently so," Roscoe said. "But Cusack nabbed it."

"Let's make sure we reward him. Who else knows about this?"

"Cusack and the two of us are the only ones."

"Good. Now where is it—the wrench?"

"Cusack tossed it into the Buffalo River."

"Good man."

"He is. That should come as a big relief to Pendle."

"Now, Bill, let's not get ahead of ourselves," Penrose said.

Roscoe looked puzzled.

"*Cui bono,*" Terry said. "Think about it—who benefits? If we tell Arthur his problem is solved?"

"He does, of course. One less thing to worry about."

"And do we? Benefit, I mean."

Roscoe mulled this over. "I suppose I don't know."

"The answer is 'no,' Bill. If Arthur learns that there's only circumstantial evidence against him, he'll fight this thing to the bitter end. I know him—he's not giving up unless the case is hopeless. If he thinks that we have the murder weapon—a wrench from his electric automobile, he'll know he's done for."

"Well, of course. But how does that benefit us?"

"Because Arthur is not the type of man to stick around to endure disgrace and public humiliation, if he knows there's no chance of surviving it."

Roscoe frowned. "Do you mean—"

"Arthur is like Marc Antony. He won't allow himself to be rolled through Rome in a cage. He'll take matters into his own hand first. Falling on his sword, as it were."

"But he's your friend."

"And he always will be. So much more the shame that it's come to this—and with no one to blame but himself for it. Between the stupid letters, the threats he made to a dead man, misappropriation of funds—he's a drowning man, Roscoe. And if you try to rescue a drowning man, he'll pull you under with him. You have to swim away and save yourself, as much as you might like to do otherwise."

❦

"Thank you for coming," Arthur said, letting Terry into his front hallway.

"Sure thing."

They took a seat in the parlor. After a few seconds, Arthur wriggled in his chair and suddenly stood up, leaving Penrose to crane his neck up at him.

"This business about Miller," Arthur stammered out, waving his hands. "Everyone's saying I did him in."

"And that surprises you?" the DA said. "What would you think if you were in their shoes?"

"Maybe so, but that's not the point. I didn't do—anything—to him. He was my friend, for God's sake."

"Methinks thou dost protest too much. Who do you think you're talking to? And before we explore that dimension of the problem, I take it you didn't get those letters back, or you would have handed them over already."

"The damned letters don't matter anymore!" Arthur shouted. "I'm sorry," he said, reacting to Penrose's expression. "No, I didn't find them. Believe me, I looked."

"That's disappointing."

"They're not a problem for anyone now."

"Then why am I here, Arthur? You do realize that in about fifteen minutes, there'll be a half-dozen reporters at your door once they see that I've visited you. Better make it worth your while."

"People are starting to blame me for this thing. And other things too—of a financial nature."

Penrose whistled through his teeth. "You've got a bad case of bedbugs."

"What is that supposed to mean?"

"We're both attorneys, Arthur. You know it doesn't matter to me whether you did something or didn't do something. Your whole life is about to be crawled into. You can't stop it—it's too late for that. All that matters now is how you are going to respond. And respond, you most certainly will have to do. Things have changed in the past couple days."

"That's why I need your help. Only you can make this mess go away, and I'm asking you to defend me for the sake of our friendship." Arthur was beginning to feel beads of sweat breaking out on his forehead, and the ringing in his ear was getting worse by the second, becoming a shrill teakettle whistle.

Penrose went on quite calmly. "Arthur. This was a—*mess*, as you call it—when it was a divorce case. But it was a manageable mess. Then those damned letters popped up in Ed Miller's possession, and all hell broke loose. Still," he said, holding up his index finger, "you had a chance. Retrieve the letters and get Miller to withdraw his suit. But you *failed*, Arthur. *You failed*." He leaned back in his chair, looking up impassively at Arthur. "And now it's a question of *murder*. A prominent, respectable citizen is brained in his own den, in one of the best sections of the city. Oh, and who is this man who was so brutally murdered? The very fellow who was bringing a divorce action that would have ruined you."

"I was only in his house to get those letters for *you!*"

"For the record, I was until this moment unaware that you entered the man's house. And whatever you may have done, you certainly did not do on my order or request."

"You can't mean this."

"Look," Penrose said, rising up slightly in his chair, "the Police Court inquest begins on Monday. You'll be called. It's going to be a circus."

"Won't you help me? I don't have anyone else to turn to. When you've needed something—"

"That was business, Arthur. For which you were generously compensated. Though if there's any mention of our dealings in those letters still floating around, I'll deny that, too, as so much confabulation."

"This is what all of my loyalty comes down to?"

"Loyalty has limits," Penrose said. "Need I remind you how willing you were to dispose of me when I was no longer useful to you?"

"Then set loyalty aside. I'd think you'd want to help to squelch this—if only to keep what only I know from coming out."

"Be careful, now."

"If you won't stop it, then—slow it down. Give me some time to prepare. That's all I ask."

Terry thought about this. "The inquest is a police matter. I can only do so much—a couple additional days to think about your testimony, but that's it. With as much digging as the press and the police are doing right now—"

"What in God's name am I to do about that? I don't even know where they are getting their information, but they have learned some things that have nothing to do—"

"Will you sit *down?*" Penrose said. "You're making me nervous, pacing like a caged animal."

Arthur sat in the chair opposite Penrose, jiggling his foot.

"The Police Court won't end well," Terry said. "It doesn't take much to get an indictment. You'll almost certainly be charged with murder."

Arthur locked eyes with Terry. "It won't stick, and you know it. Circumstantial evidence, at best. No witnesses."

Penrose took off his spectacles and slowly started rubbing them with a handkerchief. "There's one little problem with that," he said.

"It's been days and no progress on either front."

"But there are things that I know that even the newspapers don't," Terry said. "For example, something belonging to you was found in Miller's den."

Arthur went pale, and a sharp, sparkling band of light crept over his field of vision. "That can't be true."

"It is. Cusack found a big wrench. Blood and hair on it, too."

"So what?" Arthur said. "That could belong to anybody."

"It's a wrench from a Babcock automobile, Arthur. What would happen if someone went looking the toolbox in yours, I wonder? If that wrench is missing—"

"Where was it?" Arthur said, his eyes standing out.

"On Miller's desk. Looks to have been used to kill him and open his files."

Arthur put his head in his hands and squeezed hard.

"If I were your attorney," Penrose went on, "I'd tell you that it looks terrible for you. Your relationship with Miller and with his wife. You tried to stop the divorce proceeding, and he refused to listen to reason. You were present in the city the night the man was murdered. Now a wrench belonging to you is found near the body, covered with the dead man's blood. Open and shut case. Why, even Roscoe could prosecute this one."

Arthur stared. "I can't go to prison, Terry."

"Wrong. You can't go to *court*."

"What the hell does that mean?"

"It means that the minute you're indicted, a shitstorm the likes of which you've never seen begins. All your dirty laundry comes out. The notes and reports the Boland men made about you—and me—will be subpoenaed. The letters they have will emerge—as will the others if they are secreted somewhere. All read in open court. Neither of us can let it come to that."

"You mean that you'll stop it? You'll help me?"

"Our former association as law partners will compel me to recuse myself," he said. "That will put Roscoe in charge. Roscoe would love my job—he's ambitious, and he'll smell blood. A case like this, especially if I'm dragged into it, could be his golden opportunity."

"Then I'll win a dismissal. I've won tougher fights," Arthur said.

"Hmm. Maybe, but I rather doubt it. If I were in your shoes—"

"What?"

"I'd walk out that door"—he jerked his thumb in the direction of the front of the house—"get on the next trolley, and go to Canada. I wouldn't take so much as a toothbrush. It can't look like you're leaving town. I'd take as much cash as I could stuff in my overcoat, and that's it."

"Become a fugitive?"

"'Fugitive' sounds so much worse than it is. It is Canada, after all."

"But my life is in Buffalo."

Penrose rubbed his chin. "There's no good way to say this, but here goes nothing. Your life here is over. One way or another. I think the sooner you come to grips with that, the easier it'll be."

This took a moment to settle in.

Arthur smacked his fist down on the table. "And so Miller gets what he wanted all along?" he said, getting red in the face. "My disgrace. My banishment. My ruin. The man's dead, and he still wins."

"Seems so," Penrose said. "I told you he was dangerous. Even dead. He brings to mind certain species of viper, you know, whose venom can still kill you long after they are decapitated."

Arthur fumed silently for a few moments. "How much time do I have?"

"Like I said, a couple days. I can throw a little sand in the gears, buy you another day—but I wouldn't rely on that."

"What about Cassie?"

"What about her?"

"What becomes of her?"

"I suppose you could start over somewhere and forget about her. Or take her with you, if she's willing to go. I don't know how much she knows about everything."

"Now, don't go getting any ideas, Terry. She's not involved in any of this and doesn't even know about the letters. And if she did, she wouldn't say anything."

"Uh-huh. She may well back your play. But you know what a good prosecutor will do to her on the stand. Personally, I wouldn't wish that on my worst enemy, and certainly not on a wife I've been cheating on. We won't even go into what Mrs. Miller might say on the stand. I think it's a good bet that she won't take a fall for you, though. She's not the type."

Arthur put his head into his hands again. "What have I done?" he said quietly. "Cassie's not at fault here. I can't be the man who took her from her parents only to ruin her."

Terence Penrose looked at his friend with a mix of pity and con-tempt. "We all make our own hell, Arthur. You stepped on the wrong toes. You danced on them. And I'm sorry to say, but I've seen this before. All too many times."

Arthur looked at him with empty eyes.

"Maybe I should just end it all. Get it over with."

Terence Penrose considered this as carefully as he did everything he heard.

"That has advantages. It's the easiest way out for you," he said at last. "But, on the other hand, you'd be leaving your poor wife with a moun-tain of trouble."

"Everyone would see me as a moral cripple. A reprobate. I don't de-serve that."

"This is too much morbid talk," Penrose said abruptly, grabbing the arms of his chair. "Doesn't do anyone any good. And I need to be going before our friends from the press arrive. And you need to do something, and do it quickly. It's not too late yet, but it's close. And in the meantime, we don't talk again. And if you *are* charged, Arthur—and you aren't in Canada by the time you are—" He shook his head sadly.

"Go ahead and say it, Terry. I deserve that much."

Penrose looked at his old friend, thought about the days in New Ha-ven, their adjacent desks, and the gulf between them now. "I can't have you come to trial, Arthur," he said softly.

"Thank you for being honest."

"I'm not sorry about much," Penrose said, extending his hand. "But this, I am. For what it's worth."

"It's been quite a ride, hasn't it, Terry?" Arthur said, shaking the DA's hand and then showing him out.

In the carriage back to his office, Penrose allowed himself a moment of regret, a luxury in which he indulged only sparingly. Poor Arthur, he thought. But then again, no. Arthur always knew what he was getting himself into. Edward Miller is the one to be pitied—a babe-in-the-woods who, in sending his men to threaten me, blundered into a tiger trap. Now *that's* sad.

"He's right. You have to go," Cassie said without expression after Terry had departed.

"And leave you here by yourself? To be disgraced? Penniless? Your husband a fugitive and a laughingstock?"

"It's nothing more than we deserve. Both of us. And I'm not letting you go without me. I've got blood on my hands, too."

"The punishment doesn't fit the crime. These were both situations gone wrong."

"Perhaps. But what about Edward Miller? And his three innocent children. Whatever did they do to deserve this? What about poor Jeannie? They met us, and they died because they did. Our punishment is not nearly so great."

"And Alicia—"

Cassie laughed a little drunken laugh. "You'll pardon me if I don't worry too much about Alicia. She'll be pilloried, of course. But she'll survive. You'll see."

"She got me into this."

"Oh, Arthur, let's not play that game anymore. You and she—it was inevitable. From the moment you first danced with her at the Ashwood Club, it was foreordained. But at last, you must let her go. Whether you like it or not."

Arthur nodded. "I'll leave the day after tomorrow."

"I'll come with you," she said.

"I've put you through too much already."

"When I said, 'till death do us part,' I meant it. Even if nothing else turned out the way we'd hoped, I'm not going back on my word now. That much I can control. You can think about it all you like, but I'm with you until the end. Now, if you'll excuse me, dear—I need to go upstairs and put a needle in my arm."

Arthur nodded and, for the first time, didn't try to change her mind.

She got up and glided out of the room and up the stairs. Arthur sat in their parlor, cursing his luck, cursing Alicia and Edward, and finally, cursing himself and this hellish thing called life.

CHAPTER 51

Changes of Heart

ARTHUR SPENT MOST OF THE NEXT DAY IN HIS OFFICE AT HOME, writing a dozen identical letters to friends, protesting his innocence. He sealed them up and put them in the small bag he'd packed for the next day, against Terry's advice. The case sat in the upper hallway all day, out of sight in case anyone might drop by and get ideas. He'd trudged up the stairs a couple of times, looking at the bag, disbelieving. Fleeing to Canada seemed so unworthy. What would his mother and his brother think? Cassie's old New England family? Had his father ever run away from a fight?

The afternoon shadows were starting to lengthen when the telephone rang. Melissa picked it up.

"Mr. Pendle," she called. "It's a Mr. Murphy. Says you know him."

"What does he want now?" Arthur said.

"He said he needs to see you urgently."

Arthur gave a long sigh, knowing that he'd have to leave Buffalo before another interview with pesky Jess Murphy. "Tell him I'm going out," he said. "He may come by at six-thirty o'clock this evening if he likes."

Melissa confirmed it with Murphy, and Arthur walked to the front parlor, where Cassie had been sitting all day long, staring into the fire. She hadn't so much as gone upstairs to her room to soothe herself with her medicines, not since yesterday.

"I need to say goodbye to Alicia," he said.

She turned in her chair and stared at him blankly.

"I have to do that much. Then I'll be back."

Cassie rose slowly, like a wraith, walked to the door with him. They stood facing each other in the hallway.

"If she decides not to go with you," Cassie murmured, "I meant what I said. I'll go with you."

Arthur shook his head. "It's too much, Cassie. Go to your parents for a while. Tell them everything, if you want to. When things settle down, I'll write. You can decide then what you want to do."

She came up close to him and seized his hand. "Listen to me, Arthur. Give me this gift. If she doesn't go with you, take me. Promise me."

He looked down at her upturned face with a mixture of pity and love and self-loathing. He nodded.

"I promise."

❦

The late afternoon sky was thick, the clouds low and dark and bruised. Arthur didn't bother to put the convertible top up so that he could see Alicia's window without having to duck, and she could see him.

A half-block away from the Miller house, he pushed the foot pedal that worked the gong. Two clangs were always enough to alert her and not enough to attract unwanted attention. Today, though, his leg was trembling, and the first push barely made the gong sound weak and tenuous. He steadied his leg with one hand and gave the pedal two more solid pushes. His head was so sore that the bell made it ache.

He drove slowly past the house, wondering if it would look different somehow now that his nemesis was gone. No. Everything was the same as always, and to his relief, there was Alicia standing in her bedroom window, summoned by the gong. She nodded, and he nodded back. He craned his neck around as he went by and saw her turn away from the window. She'd be coming down the stairs. Breathing hard, he put on more speed and almost heeled the machine over as he rounded the corner onto Bryan Street. He pulled up at the end of the alleyway, as usual, and waited. It was as though nothing had changed, even though everything had changed. He shook his head, trying to stop the ringing in his ear, which the clang of the gong had started up again.

❦

Alicia tugged on her raincoat and went out the back door and across the wet, muddy yard. She stepped onto the slushy asphalt of the alleyway and turned back to look at her house. She had promised herself she wouldn't, but she couldn't resist—so much of her life was tied up in this place, the husband who was no more, the mother and children she may never see again.

From the rear, the row of showy homes on Ashwood Street were undistinguished and unembellished, as if the builders had lost interest in beauty by the time they got around to the back. Chimneys artfully concealed from the front street trickled coal smoke, but winter rain and snow had brought it down on their heads all the same, streaking the clapboards beneath the windows with tears of grey grit.

She stepped through the fence door and turned toward Bryan Street, but then felt as though she'd forgotten something in the house. She paused, trying to remember. Allie then thought of Arthur, waiting for her at the end of the alleyway. He had been good to her. Very good. He'd allowed her to escape Edward, to feel again like she was wanted and desired. Arthur had proven that she was still capable of attracting, even bewitching, a man.

Someone had told her once that once you prove something, the better part of valor is to leave it alone. Matthew Webb had shown that a man could swim the English Channel, a thing in all previous human history thought quite impossible. And yet he had done it. With that single achievement, he should have earned a lifetime—many lifetimes—of glory. Yet poor Captain Webb couldn't bring himself to enjoy his fame, always craving to relive the thrill of that great conquest. Only a few years before Alicia and Edward were married, Webb had come to Niagara Falls, bent on swimming the deadly Whirlpool Rapids downstream from the cataract. No one had done that either, but he convinced himself he could, because he'd done the impossible once before. He was wrong, and a half-hour after entering the river, Captain Webb was churned to bits as surely as a man falling into a thresher.

She would always be grateful to Arthur, always love him. He had freed her. Freed her from Edward, certainly—who, unbelievably, was now gone for good—and freed her from her own doubts. He had inoculated her with his confidence, his indifference, his natural brutality, cloaked in worldly sophistication. And now, quite to her surprise, she realized that Edward's murder had been a double miracle, freeing her from both men in one swift stroke.

And only a few days before, the celebrated Erie County District Attorney himself had visited her, in her own home, to offer his condolences. And the great man himself had advised her—warned her—to put some distance between herself and Arthur Pendle. For a while, at least. And if anyone should know how to play a smart hand, it would be the man who had sent the President's assassin to the Chair: Terence Penrose.

She turned around and dodged the dirty puddles on her way back to her house. Arthur waited at the end of the alleyway for a half-hour, the mist seeping through his clothes, and then pointed the Babcock toward home.

❦

Cassie was watching out the front window when Arthur rolled up the drive. He saw the curtains fall. Before he'd even had time to shut off his machine, she was stepping out the side door and onto the garage apron, dressed immaculately in a coffee-and-cream driving coat, dainty dress shoes poking out beneath the hem and a pristine white felt hat with a single short feather.

"It's cold out here," Arthur said. "You'd better go back inside. I'll be in to get my bag in a moment."

"No," she said cheerfully. "We're going for a drive together, aren't we?"

He looked at her intently. "Yes, I suppose we can take a little spin before the rain comes," he said. "Then I'll need to get you back, so I can make the train."

She climbed up onto the bench and arranged the lap robe over their legs.

"Shouldn't I put the top up?" he said. "It looks like it could start pouring any minute."

"Leave it down," Cassie said. "I want to see everything."

They started out down the drive. She snuggled up against him, and he didn't pull away.

"Did you see Alicia?"

He shook his head. "No, she wasn't there."

"I am sorry, Arthur."

"It's just as well."

At the corner of Columbus and Ashwood, he stopped the machine. "Where to?" he said.

"How about out Kensington?"

"A bit dreary out that way, don't you think?"

"Yes, but I thought you liked to run out there when you wanted to think."

"I do. Good pavement."

"I want us to think together for a change," she said. "Let's go."

They went north on Ashwood a little way and, at the edge of their neighborhood, turned east on Delavan. The little automobile scuttled along at a good clip, flat out, the way he never tired of driving it. He settled his hat down on his head to keep it from blowing off as they sped past the rolling snowdrifts of Forest Lawn cemetery, toward Kensington Avenue and the desolate northeastern part of the city.

When they turned up Main, past the cemetery, Cassie squeezed his arm and leaned toward him. "Arthur, you know out on Kensington a little bit, there's that old quarry?"

"Of course," he said, wiping his eyes. The cold wind was making them water, and he hadn't worn his driving goggles. And his head was pounding something fierce as he tried not to think about why Allie had not come.

"That's the old Yammerthal Quarry. German lady owns it."

"That's the one," she said.

"What about it?"

"The way things are, you know—it won't be easy for us from now on."

"No, it most certainly will not. I'm not sure what's next, to be honest. Nothing good. But I can't wait around. I have to go before that damned reporter shows up."

"Who wants to live a life like that?"

He glanced over at her. "What do you mean?"

"I mean that a life without joy isn't a life at all. You've said that yourself. Many times."

"Yes, I have."

"I was wondering—isn't it within our power to choose? Whether to go on if there's nothing but misery ahead?"

"Come out with it, Cassie. What are you driving at?"

"It's a hard thing, I know, but let's say we were driving along past that old quarry, and for a second, you steered the wrong way—and we went over? People know that's a hazardous spot. No fence, nothing, only that pit right off the side of the road."

"God's sake, Cassie." He squinted into the wind, continuing east.

"What? You've said to me many times that suicide isn't always a dishonorable thing."

"It's not that. That quarry is at best 20 feet deep. We could be maimed, crippled for life. That's worse than dying."

They neared the Kensington intersection, slowed, and turned right.

"It's just up here," he said, pointing. "You can see for yourself."

The Yammerthal Quarry was a quarter of a mile or so in front of them, on the right-hand side of Kensington Avenue. They rumbled across the New York Central grade crossing and slowed as he drew alongside the quarry. The old pit was a played-out, jagged thing, its bottom littered with a jumble of forgotten rubble. In its heyday, the limestone it had birthed had built some of the most beautiful buildings in Buffalo. The courthouse, his very own Aston Building. Now it was nothing more than an ugly scar where the Earth had been violated.

"See what I mean?" he said. "It's not that deep. You could fall into it and be mangled. No thank you."

The rain was starting to come down now, light but insistent. "We should probably turn around," he said.

"Can we go just a little farther? I don't mind feeling the rain on my face. It's refreshing."

They continued east, past the bicycle works. There was something liberating about letting the rain come down. You spend your whole life trying to stay out of the rain, he thought. When you stop trying, it's not so bad at all.

"The train," she said.

"I'll be fine," he said. "There's one every hour."

"No, I mean the train tracks we crossed."

He took her meaning. "No one would survive that, that's for sure."

"Stop up here and ask someone what time the trains come through."

He felt her certainty, her steadiness. Something he'd always admired. Tried to emulate, even if without much success. Worse, he'd undermined that special quality of hers, left her no choice but to numb herself until whatever she had been was no more.

"I know this place," he said. "Volkmann is the owner. I've gotten a drink and a cigar from him every now and again."

"Well, go in and get one for me, too. A drink, I mean," she said, laughing. "Not a cigar."

He pulled up in front of Volkmann's place and went in.

"Good afternoon," Arthur said to Volkmann, who was standing behind the bar.

"Mr. Pendle," Volkmann said. "I didn't expect to see you out here on a day like this."

"It's not such a bad day," Arthur said. "How about a couple glasses of Buffalo Club?"

Volkmann put the drinks on the bar, and Arthur downed one of them quickly. "I don't want my wife getting soaked to the skin," he said to the barman. "I'll take this one out and be right back."

"Wouldn't you two be more comfortable inside?"

Arthur glanced up at the clock over the bar and took his watch from his vest pocket.

"When do the trains come through, across Kensington?" he asked, gesturing toward Buffalo.

Volkmann glanced at the clock. "There should be another one coming through in about five minutes. They are about every hour on the half-hour."

"Is that the correct time?"

"Yes, or very close," the saloonkeeper said. "I set it twice a day with the factory whistle. And that's always right on time."

"Must be something wrong with my watch," Arthur said. "I'm six minutes slow. We'd better get a move on." Arthur took the drink out to Cassie.

"Here you go, dear," he said, handing her the glass. "The train will be through in five minutes. We don't want to miss it, now, do we?" He laughed, and she laughed back.

Cassie gulped down as much of the liquor as she could manage. Arthur finished what was left and hustled inside to return the glass to Volkmann.

"Thanks again," he said, setting the glass on the bar. "Oh, one other thing—I'd like a good cigar, if you please. You have one of those Henry Clays?"

"I do indeed," Volkmann said. "Fifteen cents."

Arthur put the coins on the bar, thinking it could use a fresh coat of varnish. He lit his cigar at a gas jet and puffed out a glorious cloud of smoke. "Perfect," he said.

Volkmann scooped the coins off the bar. "Drive carefully," he said. "It's starting to come down hard."

"Oh, that won't bother us," Arthur said and left the bar to rejoin Cassie.

"Five minutes," he said to her, backing up the car and aiming it west on Kensington, toward the tracks. "You sure about this?"

"As sure as I've been about anything. And I'm tired of not being sure. I'm tired of everything."

He nodded. "So am I."

He urged the little car onto Kensington, pushing it to top speed again, the rain pelting hard against their faces, making them squint. His hat blew off, and instinctively his hand shot up to try to grab it, but too late. Again it struck him that the wind and the rain in his hair weren't so awful. Nothing was awful anymore. Every raindrop, every whiff of smoke blowing back from the glowing cigar clenched in his teeth, each tiny bump and roll of the pavement felt good. He had probably never paid so much attention, never felt so alive. He wanted to shout, cry out, like a Viking hurling himself into battle, with no further use for life but to do the work of slaughter.

At the tracks, he slowed, stopped, and looked one way and then the other. The New York Central Express, right on time, was steaming toward them.

"Do it," Cassie said. "Come on."

"I won't let you down."

"You never have, Arthur."

He pulled up onto the tracks, glanced at her, and felt the long-avoided shame. He shut off the motor. She gave him a little playful wink, the way she used to do when they'd first met. He tried to wink back, but his eyes were too full, and he wanted to be brave. Then they both simply looked straight ahead, up the road back to the city, toward home, silent except for the rain weeping down and a horn blaring in the distance.

CHAPTER 52

The Inquest

HOWEVER HAM-HANDED THE INITIAL INVESTIGATION OF ED'S murder may have been, the inquest set a new standard for self-parody. Over three long days in court, Alicia tirelessly bore up on the witness stand as, one by one, the handful of Arthur's love-struck *billets-doux* that had been transcribed were read aloud to her, line by awful line. Deprived of any living context, they now seemed risibly maudlin, sometimes even provoking titters from the local folk lucky enough to get one of the fifty seats available each day. Newspapermen breathlessly transmitted every detail of Alicia's ritual humiliation, and each had a favorite theory on what had become of poor Mr. Miller.

The inquest lurched between murder investigation and morality play. The unfortunate Edward Miller was all but canonized: the epitome of the long-suffering husband, sacrificing his all to provide a good life for his thankless, unfaithful wife. Alicia, naturally, played the Whore of Babylon to Arthur's turn as fool-in-love. Cassie was forgotten, as overlooked in death as she had been in life. And no one seemed the least interested in poor old Mrs. Hall, who uttered not a word about what she had seen that night, let alone what role she had played in the drama. No one alive could challenge or corroborate her actions. Why bother?

In truth, the Pendles' sensational dual demise let more than a little air out of the balloon. Not only that, but it also left plenty of room for Alicia to embellish a little without Arthur or Cassie having to hear a word of it. What was the point of defending a dead lover at the expense of the living? Notwithstanding, and much to her credit, she did precisely the opposite—freely admitting to having been madly in love with

Arthur and utterly out of love with Edward. She could have chosen to sweep those little facts under the rug, but didn't.

In fact, Alicia was a good sport. She dutifully wore deep mourning, then shocked people with an exuberant sprig of snowbells on her lapel. She let the dour legal men traduce her and make fun of what they obviously took as the silly, spooney feelings she and Arthur had for each other. She let them paint their passion as nothing short of a grifter's game. She knew it wouldn't last forever, so she bore it patiently, answering their horrid little questions in a dry monotone and with a thin, Mona Lisa smile. Letting the time go by.

And so it was that after an ocean of newspaper ink spilt and tireless speculation in every corner of the city about fresh leads or new suspects that never came, to no one's surprise, the verdict came back: *Willful murder by person or persons unknown.* There would be no indictments. Alicia had been in Atlantic City, as airtight an alibi as could be imagined. Mrs. Hall was nothing more sinister than a doddering, old woman. No credible burglar or other local ne'er-do-well had turned up. That left only Arthur Pendle, and a dead man is an easy one to blame.

❦

As soon as the inquest was done and the bodies had been released from the morgue, Arthur's brother John hastily arranged for a memorial service to be held in the Pendles' parlor on Columbus Avenue. Two identical caskets, draped with garlands of white roses, were laid side by side. Perhaps forty friends and associates came to pay their respects, crowding into the front parlor. With no fire in the hearth, the room didn't feel like the cozy nook it had been so recently. It smelled instead of damp, huddled humanity and dirty snow.

Alicia Miller was not in attendance, although some of the guests discreetly stole glances at the cards on the funeral wreaths to see if any had come from the new widow. No one from the Miller faction of the Ashwood Social Club was there, either, but there was near-perfect attendance by the Pendle clique.

After the minister had finished his eulogy, the gathering shuffled after the pallbearers out of the vacant residence to the waiting mortuary wagon standing curbside. Penrose and some of his and Arthur's fellow members of the Buffalo Bar Association did the honors.

The cold, damp air kept the outdoor formalities short. As soon as the mortuary wagon had pulled away, bearing Arthur and Cassie away to the New York Central station for their return to Maine, peremptory handshakes and condolences were exchanged. The mourners then hustled away to their trolleys and carriages and important commitments. Roscoe and Penrose were left standing off by themselves, smoking, waiting for their carriage to be brought around.

"Hell of a thing, isn't it?" Roscoe said. "I suppose we'll never know the whole story."

The whole story? Whatever that is, Penrose thought wryly. Only Edward Miller and Arthur Pendle knew the *whole* story. Even in death, they would share a secret, forever.

And without them to reveal that secret, there was only gossip. Penrose had been at this game long enough to know that people would eventually tire of gossip, no matter how lurid. The details of whatever happened in Miller's den late on New Year's Eve would never be known. The witnesses were dead, the only clue buried in the poisonous muck at the bottom of the Buffalo River.

"Not a chance," said Penrose. "But does it matter? After things cool down, drop it. Oh, and all the private testimony and the detective reports—put it all under seal. It's a personal matter now, and revealing it would only cause more pain for the families."

"Will do. I am curious, though, if you don't mind, Mr. Penrose—what's your take? On all of this."

Penrose puffed on his cigar and exhaled, stepping onto the cobblestones to wave at his carriage. He shrugged. "That Brutus was an honorable man, after all."

CHAPTER 53

Benediction

WITH THE INQUEST CONCLUDED, THE VERDICT RENDERED, AND the bodies buried, the papers soon lost interest. Alicia was back home. With some help from sympathetic lenders, Howie Gaines purchased Ed's interest in the Miller Envelope Company.

Terry Penrose himself took charge of settling Arthur's estate. In addition to the Pendles' house, furnishings, and art, there was the matter of Arthur's $100,000 in insurance—made $200,000, double indemnity—due to the accidental nature of his death. As expected, the insurance companies balked at making good on a bet they had never imagined they'd lose. They tried everything to find reasons not to pay, or at least to have Arthur's death ruled a suicide so that the double-indemnity clause wouldn't apply. Terry was at his bulldog best with them, though, and pay up they did, every red cent. With the house and chattels, and after any small debts settled, Arthur and Cassie were no longer bankrupt, but instead worth almost $250,000, a princely sum indeed when $10 a week for six, 12-hour days was a living wage. Arthur's brother tried manfully to prevent Alicia from getting the $50,000 that Arthur had settled on her, but Terry was far too wily than to let the camel's nose under the tent.

The rest of the estate had been stipulated as security against the investments that their family members had made with them. The insurance payout meant that Arthur and Cassie's investors nearly doubled their money in less than a year, the best investment any of them had ever made. Arthur had kept in his desk drawer a long letter, addressed to his brother, detailing the investment they had made in Montana Copper, and the tremendous losses that wiped them out. In the event of his untimely death, he wanted John to know that their investors were to be paid first and fully. His brother was tempted to burn the document—$200,000 would have set him up for life—but loyalty to his brother stayed his hand, as well as a healthy dread of Terry Penrose. If he'd destroyed the letter, then Arthur's malfeasances would have been impossible to conceal. Terry, always one to repay a debt, made sure that brother John got the Pendles' house.

As for Sarah, her world had been swept away in a single night. The brutal, cold-blooded murder of her beloved Eddie was unfathomable, unspeakable. She went to the morgue in full view of a throng of rubber-neckers, only to be turned away, denied permission by Alicia Miller to view Ed's battered body. Worst of all, though, were the ghoulish news-papermen, virtuously envious as always, gleefully reporting the travails of the stylish, beautiful woman who must somehow have brought down all this suffering on herself.

She stood the storm alone. There was no one to talk with, no one she could confide in. Not Seth, and certainly not the ladies of Ashwood.

The day after the inquest closed, a small parcel arrived addressed to Sarah from the Millers' address on Ashwood. In it was the photograph she'd given Ed, spattered with his blood. She didn't know who sent it, or whether it was intended as a kindness or another cut. She cried over it for a long time, and then something else rose up in her.

As soon as they could pack their things, Sarah and Maggie escaped to Batavia. The little town was too far from Buffalo for the gossip columnists and curiosity seekers, and soon enough, they would find another scandal to gorge on. To supplement the dwindling income from Seth's moribund dental practice, Sarah took a job as a stenographer for a local attorney. She and Maggie again settled two blocks away from Seth, where Sarah could keep an eye on him without exposing her daughter to her father's dissolution.

Seth died on a perfect spring day, only a few months after Ed's murder. Her husband's long, slow suicide hadn't prepared her for his death as well as she'd imagined. For the first time in her life, she was alone, except, of course, for Maggie. As difficult as that adjustment was, being alone and ignored nourished a part of her that she hadn't known existed. One bright summer morning, after only three months of wearing mourning dress, Sarah decided she'd had quite enough moping. She packed away the black weeds, and later that day, she and plucky little Maggie shocked the good citizens of Batavia by strolling the sidewalk in matching gowns of rustling, pale green taffeta.

One final move was in store. With the money she'd saved up from stenography and Seth's small residual estate, she left Batavia for good and reopened their house in Ashwood. She secured a modest office for herself downtown, adjacent to the courthouse. On the window of her office door, she had a sign-painter letter in gold:

Avenging Angel Detective Agency, Inc.
Sarah M. Payne, Principal.

—with a little halo and set of wings painted above. From her office window, she had a perfect line of sight to the office of the District Attorney.

With everything neatly settled and life going on again, the one loose end that Terry had never been able to tie up was those letters, those damned letters that ought to have been burned, or never written. During the inquest and afterward, he had used every one of the legal tools at his disposal to search Ed's office and den, turn Arthur's home and office upside-down, rifle through post office and safe deposit boxes. After all that, he had only located three more lousy typescripts of what must have been a hundred letters. It irritated him that he didn't know what they had contained. But if they hadn't turned up by now, he reasoned, they were probably gone for good.

And yet every so often, Terence Penrose would be standing at his office window, looking down over his city, mulling over some poor fool's fate, and see Sarah Payne cheerfully waving at him from her office across the street.

THE END

Coming Soon: "A Murder in Ashwood," a new Avenging Angel Detective Agency™ Mystery. Find out more at RobertBrightonAuthor.com.

Acknowledgments

DESPITE DECADES OF SUSTAINED EFFORT TO REDUCE IT TO RUB-ble, the City of Buffalo is one of the few remaining places in the United States where history still feels within reach. Some of the places in this tale still exist, although most are long gone.

Yet the incomparable Ted's Hot Dogs on Sheridan Drive remains, and heavenly Paula's Donuts right across the street. Don't be shocked if you bump into me at one of them.

Heartfelt thanks are due to my sister, Sis, for her abiding enthusiasm and support throughout this project.

My deepest gratitude belongs forever to my wife, Laura.

Robert Brighton
October 2022

About the Author

A NATIVE OF BUFFALO, NEW YORK, ROBERT BRIGHTON IS AN authority on the Gilded Age, and a great believer that the Victorian era was anything but stuffy. On the contrary, in his books Brighton takes special care to expose the turbulent passions of the era, often kept carefully under wraps but always bubbling just below the surface—against a backdrop of careful research on the places, sights, sounds, and smells of the time.

When he is not walking the streets of Buffalo, sniffing out unsolved mysteries, Brighton is a wanderer. He has traveled in more than 50 countries around the world, personally throwing himself into every situation his characters will face—from underground ruins to opium dens—and (so far) living to tell about it.

A graduate of the Sorbonne, Paris, Brighton is an avid student of early 20th Century history and literature, an ardent and relentless investigator, and an admirer of Emily Dickinson and Jim Morrison. Currently he lives in Virginia with his wife and their two cats.